ALFRED

HITCHCOCK

PRESENTS:

STORIES

THAT

SCARED

EVEN

ME

RANDOM HOUSE  NEW YORK

ALFRED HITCHCOCK PRESENTS: STORIES THAT

SCARED EVEN ME

First Printing

© Copyright, 1967, by Random House, Inc.

All rights reserved under International and Pan-American Copyright
Conventions.
Published in New York by Random House, Inc., and simultaneously
in Toronto, Canada, by Random House of Canada Limited.

Library of Congress Catalog Card Number: 67–22678

Manufactured in the United States of America
by The Book Press Incorporated, Brattleboro, Vermont
Designed by Carl Weiss

ACKNOWLEDGMENTS

CASABLANCA, by Thomas M. Disch. Printed by permission of the author and the author's agent, Robert P. Mills. © Copyright 1967, by Thomas M. Disch.

FISHHEAD, by Irvin S. Cobb. Reprinted by permission of Doubleday & Company, Inc. From *The Escape of Mr. Trimm*, by Irvin S. Cobb. Copyright, 1913, by Frank A. Munsey Company.

CAMERA OBSCURA, by Basil Copper. Reprinted by permission of the author. © Copyright 1965, by Basil Copper.

A DEATH IN THE FAMILY, by Miriam Allen deFord. Reprinted by permission of the author. Originally appeared in *The Dude*, November, 1961. © Copyright 1961, by Miriam Allen deFord.

MEN WITHOUT BONES, by Gerald Kersh. Reprinted by permission of Joan Daves. Originally appeared in *Esquire*. Copyright, 1954, by Gerald Kersh.

NOT WITH A BANG, by Damon Knight. Reprinted by permission of the author. From *Far Out*, by Damon Knight. Originally appeared in *Magazine of Fantasy and Science Fiction*. Copyright, 1949, by Mercury Press, Inc.

PARTY GAMES, by John Burke. Reprinted by permission of the author and London Authors. © Copyright 1965, by John Burke.

X MARKS THE PEDWALK, by Fritz Leiber. Reprinted by permission of the author and the author's agent, Robert P. Mills. © Copyright 1963, by The Barmaray Co., Inc.

CURIOUS ADVENTURE OF MR. BOND, by Nugent Barker. Reprinted from *Best Tales of Terror* (No. 2), Faber and Faber.

TWO SPINSTERS, by E. Phillips Oppenheim. Reprinted by permission of Peter Janson-Smith Ltd., London. Copyright, 1926, by the Executors of E. Phillips Oppenheim deceased.

THE KNIFE, by Robert Arthur. Reprinted by permission of the author. Copyright, 1951, by Grace Publishing Co., Inc.

THE CAGE, by Ray Russell. Reprinted by permission of the author and his agents, Scott Meredith Literary Agency, Inc. © Copyright 1959, by Ray Russell.

IT, by Theodore Sturgeon. Reprinted by permission of the author. Copyright, 1940, by Street & Smith, Inc. Copyright, 1951, by Theodore Sturgeon.

THE ROAD TO MICTLANTECUTLI, by Adobe James. Reprinted by permission of the author and London Authors. Originally appeared in *Adam Reader* #20. © Copyright 1965, by the Knight Pub. Corp., Los Angeles, California.

GUIDE TO DOOM, by Ellis Peters. Reprinted by permission of Joyce Weiner Associates, London. Reprinted from *This Week Magazine*. © Copyright 1963, by the United Newspapers Magazine Corporation.

THE ESTUARY, by Margaret St. Clair. Reprinted by permission of McIntosh and Otis, Inc. Originally appeared in *Weird Tales*. Copyright, 1950, by *Weird Tales*.

TOUGH TOWN, by William Sambrot. Reprinted by permission of Curtis Brown, Ltd. Originally appeared as "Stranger in Town." © Copyright 1957, by Official Magazine Corporation.

THE TROLL, by T. H. White. Reprinted by permission of David Higham Associates, Ltd., London. Copyright by the Estate of T. H. White. All rights reserved.

EVENING AT THE BLACK HOUSE, by Robert Somerlott. Reprinted by permission of McIntosh and Otis, Inc. Originally appeared in *Cosmopolitan*. © Copyright 1964, by Hearst Magazines, Inc.

ONE OF THE DEAD, by William Wood. Reprinted by permission of the author and his agent, James Brown Associates, Inc. © Copyright 1966, by William Wood.

THE REAL THING, by Robert Specht. Reprinted by permission of the author. Originally appeared in *Alfred Hitchcock's Mystery Magazine.* © Copyright 1966, by Robert Specht.

JOURNEY TO DEATH, by Donald E. Westlake. Reprinted by permission of the author and his agent, Henry Morrison, Inc. © Copyright 1959, by Shelton Publishing Corp.

MASTER OF THE HOUNDS, by Algis Budrys. Reprinted by permission of the author and his agent, Russell & Volkening, Inc. © Copyright 1966, by A. J. Budrys.

THE CANDIDATE, by Henry Slesar. Reprinted by permission of the author's agent, Theron Raines. Originally appeared in *Rogue Magazine.* © Copyright 1961, by Greenleaf Publishing Company.

OUT OF THE DEEPS, by John Wyndham. Reprinted by permission of the author and the author's agents, Scott Meredith Literary Agency, Inc., and Michael Joseph, Ltd., London. Published in England as *The Kraken Wakes.* Copyright, 1953, by John Wyndham.

*The editor gratefully acknowledges
the invaluable assistance of Robert Arthur
in the preparation of this volume*

AHEM!

IF

I

MAY

HAVE

A

MOMENT—

I hope no one will construe the title of this tome as a challenge. It is—in case you were so eager to get to the stories that you didn't notice—*Stories That Scared Even Me*. This is meant as a simple statement of fact, not as a summons for you to cry in ringing tones that some of the stories didn't scare *you*. Why the word *Even* is in there I don't know. I proposed to call the book, in a simple and dignified manner, *Stories That Scared Me*. I was overruled. It seems that *Stories That Scared Even Me* has more swing to it. And this is, obviously, the day of the swinger.

For myself, I do no more than affirm that the stories in this book all gave me one or more of the pleasurable sensations associated with fear. Some quite terrified me. Some profoundly disturbed me and left me with a sense of deep uneasiness. Others prickled my nerve ends pleasurably, touched my spine with chills, or made me swallow hard as I registered their impact. Some did several of these things at once.

On that basis I offer them to you, trusting you will share with me these emotions, so enjoyable when they can be experienced in the snug embrace of an easy chair in the comfort of one's home.

And now I relinquish the screen to the main feature.

Alfred Hitchcock

CONTENTS

Novelette:

Stories:

Novel:

ALFRED

HITCHCOCK

PRESENTS:

STORIES

THAT

SCARED

EVEN

ME

FISHHEAD

It goes past the powers of my pen to try to describe Reelfoot Lake for you so that you, reading this, will get the picture of it in your mind as I have it in mine. For Reelfoot Lake is like no other lake that I know anything about. It is an afterthought of Creation.

The rest of this continent was made and had dried in the sun for thousands of years—for millions of years for all I know—before Reelfoot came to be. It's the newest big thing in nature on this hemisphere probably, for it was formed by the great earthquake of 1811, just a little more than a hundred years ago. That earthquake of 1811 surely altered the face of the earth on the then far frontier of this country. It changed the course of rivers, it converted hills into what are now the sunk lands of three states, and it turned the solid ground to jelly and made it roll in waves like the sea. And in the midst of the retching of the land and the vomiting of the waters it depressed to varying depths a section of the earth crust sixty miles long, taking it down—trees, hills, hollows and all; and a crack broke

3

through the Mississippi River so that for three days the river ran up stream, filling the hole.

The result was the largest lake south of the Ohio, lying mostly in Tennessee, but extending up across what is now the Kentucky line, and taking its name from a fancied resemblance in its outline to the splay, reeled foot of a cornfield Negro. Niggerwool Swamp, not so far away, may have got its name from the same man who christened Reelfoot; at least so it sounds.

Reelfoot is, and has always been, a lake of mystery. In places it is bottomless. Other places the skeletons of the cypress trees that went down when the earth sank still stand upright, so that if the sun shines from the right quarter and the water is less muddy than common, a man peering face downward into its depths sees, or thinks he sees, down below him the bare top-limbs upstretching like drowned men's fingers, all coated with the mud of years and bandaged with pennons of the green lake slime. In still other places the lake is shallow for long stretches, no deeper than breast-deep to a man, but dangerous because of the weed growths and the sunken drifts which entangle a swimmer's limbs. Its banks are mainly mud, its waters are muddied too, being a rich coffee color in the spring and a copperish yellow in the summer, and the trees along its shore are mud-colored clear up to their lower limbs after the spring floods, when the dried sediment covers their trunks with a thick, scrofulous-looking coat.

There are stretches of unbroken woodland around it and slashes where the cypress trees rise countlessly like headstones and footstones for the dead snags that rot in the soft ooze. There are deadenings with the lowland corn growing high and rank below and the bleached, fire-blackened girdled trees rising above, barren of leaf and limb. There are long, dismal flats where in the spring the clotted frog-spawn clings like patches of white mucus among the weed stalks and at night the turtles crawl out to lay clutches of perfectly round, white eggs with tough, rubbery shells in the sand. There are bayous leading off to nowhere and sloughs that wind aimlessly, like great, blind worms, to finally join the big river that rolls its semi-liquid torrents a few miles to the westward.

So Reelfoot lies there, flat in the bottoms, freezing lightly in the winter, steaming torridly in the summer, swollen in the spring when the woods have turned a vivid green and the buffalo gnats by the million and the billion fill the flooded hollows with their pestilential buzzing, and in the fall ringed about gloriously with all the colors which the first frost brings—gold of hickory, yellow-russet of sycamore, red of dogwood and ash and purple-black of sweet-gum.

But the Reelfoot country has its uses. It is the best game and fish country, natural or artificial, that is left in the South to-day. In their appointed seasons the duck and the geese flock in, and even semitropical birds, like the brown pelican and the Florida snake-bird, having been known to come there to nest. Pigs, gone back to wildness, range the ridges, each razor-backed drove captained by a gaunt, savage, slab-sided old boar. By night the bull frogs, inconceivably big and tremendously vocal, bellow under the banks.

It is a wonderful place for fish—bass and crappie and perch and the snouted buffalo fish. How these edible sorts live to spawn and how their spawn in turn live to spawn again is a marvel, seeing how many of the big fish-eating cannibal fish there are in Reelfoot. Here, bigger than anywhere else, you find the garfish, all bones and appetite and horny plates, with a snout like an alligator, the nearest link, naturalists say, between the animal life of to-day and the animal life of the Reptilian Period. The shovel-nose cat, really a deformed kind of freshwater sturgeon, with a great fan-shaped membranous plate jutting out from his nose like a bowsprit, jumps all day in the quiet places with mighty splashing sounds, as though a horse had fallen into the water. On every stranded log the huge snapping turtles lie on sunny days in groups of four and six, baking their shells black in the sun, with their little snaky heads raised watchfully, ready to slip noiselessly off at the first sound of oars grating in the row-locks.

But the biggest of them all are the catfish. These are monstrous creatures, these catfish of Reelfoot—scaleless, slick things, with corpsy dead eyes and poisonous fins like javelins and long whiskers dangling from the sides of their cavernous heads. Six and seven feet long they grow to be and to weigh two hundred pounds or more, and they have mouths wide enough to take a man's foot or a man's fist and strong enough to break any hook save the strongest and greedy enough to eat anything, living or dead or putrid, that the horny jaws can master. Oh, but they are wicked things, and they tell wicked tales of them down there. They call them man-eaters and compare them, in certain of their habits, to sharks.

Fishhead was of a piece with this setting. He fitted into it as an acorn fits its cup. All his life he had lived on Reelfoot, always in the one place, at the mouth of a certain slough. He had been born there, of a Negro father and a half-breed Indian mother, both of them now dead, and the story was that before his birth his mother was frightened by one of the big fish, so that the child came into the world most hideously marked. Anyhow, Fishhead was a human monstrosity, the veritable embodiment of nightmare. He had the body of a man—a short, stocky, sinewy body—but his face was as near to being the face of a great fish as any face could be and yet retain some trace of human aspect. His skull sloped back so abruptly that he could hardly be said to have a forehead at all; his chin slanted off right into nothing. His eyes were small and round with shallow, glazed, pale-yellow pupils, and they were set wide apart in his head and they were unwinking and staring, like a fish's eyes. His nose was no more than a pair of tiny slits in the middle of the yellow mask. His mouth was the worst of all. It was the awful mouth of a catfish, lipless and almost inconceivably wide, stretching from side to side. Also when Fishhead became a grown man his likeness to a fish increased, for the hair upon his face grew out into two tightly kinked, slender pendants that drooped down either side of the mouth like the beards of a fish.

If he had any other name than Fishhead, none excepting he knew it. As Fishhead he was known and as Fishhead he answered. Because he knew the waters and the woods of Reelfoot better than any other man there, he was valued as a guide by the city men who came every year to hunt or fish; but there were few such jobs that Fishhead would take. Mainly he kept to himself, tending his corn patch, netting the lake, trapping a little and in season pot hunting for the city markets. His neighbors, ague-bitten whites and malaria-proof Negroes alike, left him to himself. Indeed, for the most part they had a superstitious fear of him. So he lived alone, with no kith nor kin, nor even a friend, shunning his kind and shunned by them.

His cabin stood just below the state line, where Mud Slough runs into the lake. It was a shack of logs, the only human habitation for four miles up or down. Behind it the thick timber came shouldering right up to the edge of Fishhead's small truck patch, enclosing it in thick shade except when the sun stood just overhead. He cooked his food in a primitive fashion, outdoors, over a hole in the soggy earth or upon the rusted red ruin of an old cook stove, and he drank the saffron water of the lake out of a dipper made of a gourd, faring and fending for himself, a master hand at skiff and net, competent with duck gun and fish spear, yet a creature of affliction and loneliness, part savage, almost amphibious, set apart from his fellows, silent and suspicious.

In front of his cabin jutted out a long fallen cottonwood trunk, lying half in and half out of the water, its top side burnt by the sun and worn by the friction of Fishhead's bare feet until it showed countless patterns of tiny scrolled lines, its under side black and rotted and lapped at unceasingly by little waves like tiny licking tongues. Its farther end reached deep water. And it was a part of Fishhead, for no matter how far his fishing and trapping might take him in the daytime, sunset would find him back there, his boat drawn up on the bank and he on the outer end of this log. From a distance men had seen him there many times, sometimes squatted, motionless as the big turtles that would crawl upon its dipping tip in his absence, sometimes erect and vigilant like a creek crane, his misshapen yellow form outlined against the yellow sun, the yellow water, the yellow banks—all of them yellow together.

If the Reelfooters shunned Fishhead by day they feared him by night and avoided him as a plague, dreading even the chance of a casual meeting. For there were ugly stories about Fishhead—stories which all the Negroes and some of the whites believed. They said that a cry which had been heard just before dusk and just after, skittering across the darkened waters, was his calling cry to the big cats, and at his bidding they came trooping in, and that in their company he swam in the lake on moonlight nights, sporting with them, diving with them, even feeding with them on what manner of unclean things they fed. The cry had been heard many times, that much was certain, and it was certain also that the big fish were noticeably thick at the mouth of Fishhead's slough. No native Reelfooter, white or black, would willingly wet a leg or an arm there.

Here Fishhead had lived and here he was going to die. The Baxters were going to kill him, and this day in midsummer was to be the time of the killing. The two Baxters—Jake and Joel—were coming in their dugout to do it. This murder had been a long time in the making. The Baxters had to brew their hate over a slow fire for months before it reached the pitch of action. They were poor whites, poor in everything—repute and worldly goods and standing—a pair of fever-ridden squatters who lived on whisky and tobacco when they could get it, and on fish and cornbread when they couldn't.

The feud itself was of months' standing. Meeting Fishhead one day in the spring on the spindly scaffolding of the skiff landing at Walnut Log, and being themselves far overtaken in liquor and vainglorious with a bogus alcoholic substitute for courage, the brothers had accused him, wantonly and without proof, of running their trotline and stripping it of the hooked catch—an unforgivable sin among the water dwellers and the shanty boaters of the South. Seeing that he bore this accusation in silence, only eyeing them steadfastly, they had been emboldened then to slap his face, whereupon he turned and gave them both the beating of their lives—bloodying their noses and bruising their lips with hard blows against their front teeth, and finally leaving them, mauled and prone, in the dirt. Moreover, in the onlookers a sense of the everlasting fitness of things had triumphed over race prejudice and allowed them—two freeborn, sovereign whites—to be licked by a nigger.

Therefore, they were going to get the nigger. The whole thing had been planned out amply. They were going to kill him on his log at sundown. There would be no witnesses to see it, no retribution to follow after it. The very ease of the undertaking made them forget even their inborn fear of the place of Fishhead's habitation.

For more than an hour now they had been coming from their shack across a deeply indented arm of the lake. Their dugout, fashioned by fire and adz and draw-knife from the bole of a gum tree, moved through the water as noiselessly as a swimming mallard, leaving behind it a long, wavy trail on the stilled waters. Jake, the better oarsman, sat flat in the stern of the round-bottomed craft, paddling with quick, splashless strokes. Joel, the better shot, was squatted forward. There was a heavy, rusted duck gun between his knees.

Though their spying upon the victim had made them certain sure he would not be about the shore for hours, a doubled sense of caution led them to hug closely the weedy banks. They slid along the shore like shadows, moving so swiftly and in such silence that the watchful mud turtles barely turned their snaky heads as they passed. So, a full hour before the time, they came slipping around the mouth of the slough and made for a natural ambuscade which the mixed breed had left within a stone's jerk of his cabin to his own undoing.

Where the slough's flow joined deeper water a partly uprooted tree was stretched, prone from shore, at the top still thick and green with leaves that drew nourishment from the earth in which the half-uncovered roots yet held, and twined about with an exuberance of trumpet vines and wild fox-grapes. All about was a huddle of drift— last year's cornstalks, sheddy strips of bark, chunks of rotted weed, all the riffle and dunnage of a quiet eddy. Straight into this green clump glided the dugout and swung, broadside on, against the protecting trunk of the tree, hidden from the inner side by the intervening curtains of rank growth, just as the Baxters had intended it should be hidden, when days before in their scouting they marked this masked place of waiting and included it, then and there, in the scope of their plans.

There had been no hitch or mishap. No one had been abroad in the late afternoon to mark their movements—and in a little while Fishhead ought to be due. Jake's woodman's eye followed the downward swing of the sun speculatively. The shadows, thrown shoreward, lengthened and slithered on the small ripples. The small noises of the day died out; the small noises of the coming night began to multiply. The green-bodied flies went away and big mosquitoes, with speckled gray legs, came to take the places of the flies. The sleepy lake sucked at the mud banks with small mouthing sounds as though it found the taste of the raw mud agreeable. A monster crawfish, big as a chicken lobster, crawled out on the top of his dried mud chimney and perched himself there, an armored sentinel on the watchtower. Bull bats began to flitter back and forth above the tops of the trees. A pudgy muskrat, swimming with head up, was moved to sidle off briskly as he met a cottonmouth moccasin snake, so fat and swollen with summer poison that it looked almost like a legless lizard as it moved along the surface of the water in a series of slow torpid s's. Directly above the head of either of the waiting assassins a compact little swarm of midges hung, holding to a sort of kite-shaped formation.

A little more time passed and Fishhead came out of the woods at the back, walking swiftly, with a sack over his shoulder. For a few seconds his deformities showed in the clearing, then the black inside of the cabin swallowed him up. By now the sun was almost down. Only the red nub of it showed above the timber line across the lake, and the shadows lay inland a long way. Out beyond, the big cats were stirring, and the great smacking sounds as their twisting bodies leaped clear and fell back in the water came shoreward in a chorus.

But the two brothers in their green covert gave heed to nothing except the one thing upon which their hearts were set and their nerves tensed. Joel gently shoved his gun-barrels across the log, cuddling the stock to his shoulder and slipping two fingers caressingly back and forth upon the triggers. Jake held the narrow dugout steady by a grip upon a fox-grape tendril.

A little wait and then the finish came. Fishhead emerged from the cabin door and came down the narrow footpath to the water and out upon the water on his log. He was barefooted and bareheaded, his cotton shirt open down the front to show his yellow neck and breast, his dungaree trousers held about his waist by a twisted tow string. His broad splay feet, with the prehensile toes outspread, gripped the polished curve of the log as he moved along its swaying, dipping surface until he came to its outer end and stood there erect, his chest filling, his chinless face lifted up and something of mastership and dominion in his poise. And then—his eye caught what another's eyes might have missed—the round, twin ends of the gun barrels, the fixed gleams of Joel's eyes, aimed at him through the green tracery.

In that swift passage of time, too swift almost to be measured by seconds, realization flashed all through him, and he threw his head still higher and opened wide his shapeless trap of a mouth, and out across the lake he sent skittering and rolling his cry. And in his cry was the laugh of a loon, and the croaking bellow of a frog, and the bay of a hound, all the compounded night noises of the lake. And in it, too, was a farewell and a defiance and an appeal. The heavy roar of the duck gun came.

At twenty yards the double charge tore the throat out of him. He came down, face forward, upon the log and clung there, his trunk twisting distortedly, his legs twitching and kicking like the legs of a speared frog, his shoulders hunching and lifting spasmodically as the life ran out of him all in one swift coursing flow. His head canted up between the heaving shoulders, his eyes looked full on the staring face of his murderer, and then the blood came out of his mouth and Fishhead, in death still as much fish as man, slid flopping, head first, off the end of the log and sank, face downward, slowly, his limbs all extended out. One after another a string of big bubbles came up to burst in the middle of a widening reddish stain on the coffee-colored water.

The brothers watched this, held by the horror of the thing they had done, and the cranky dugout, tipped far over by the recoil of the gun, took water steadily across its gunwale; and now there was a sudden stroke from below upon its careening bottom and it went over and they were in the lake. But shore was only twenty feet away, the trunk of the uprooted tree only five. Joel, still holding fast to his hot gun, made for the log, gaining it with one stroke. He threw his free arm over it and clung there, treading water, as he shook his eyes free. Something gripped him—some great, sinewy, unseen thing gripped him fast by the thigh, crushing down on his flesh.

He uttered no cry, but his eyes popped out and his mouth set in a square shape of agony, and his fingers gripped into the bark of the tree like grapples. He was pulled down and down, by steady jerks, not rapidly but steadily, so steadily, and as he went his fingernails tore four little white strips in the tree bark. His mouth went under, next his popping eyes, then his erect hair, and finally his clawing, clutching hand, and that was the end of him.

Jake's fate was harder still, for he lived longer—long enough to see Joel's finish. He saw it through the water that ran down his face, and with a great surge of his whole body he literally flung himself across the log and jerked his legs up high into the air to save them. He flung himself too far, though, for his face and chest hit the water on the far side. And out of this water rose the head of a great fish, with the lake slime of years on its flat, black head, its whiskers bristling, its corpsy eyes alight. Its horny jaws closed and clamped in the front of Jake's flannel shirt. His hand struck out wildly and was speared on a poisoned fin, and unlike Joel, he went from sight with a great yell and a whirling and a churning of the water that made the cornstalks circle on the edges of a small whirlpool.

But the whirlpool soon thinned away into widening rings of ripples and the cornstalks quit circling and became still again, and only the multiplying night noises sounded about the mouth of the slough.

The bodies of all three came ashore on the same day near the same place. Except for the gaping gunshot wound where the neck met the chest, Fishhead's body was unmarked. But the bodies of the two Baxters were so marred and mauled that the Reelfooters buried them together on the bank without ever knowing which might be Jake's and which might be Joel's.

CAMERA

OBSCURA

As Mr. Sharsted pushed his way up the narrow, fussily conceived lanes that led to the older part of the town, he was increasingly aware that there was something about Mr. Gingold he didn't like. It was not only the old-fashioned, outdated air of courtesy that irritated the moneylender but the gentle, absent-minded way in which he continually put off settlement. Almost as if money were of no importance.

The moneylender hesitated even to say this to himself; the thought was a blasphemy that rocked the very foundations of his world. He pursed his lips grimly and set himself to mount the ill-paved and flinty roadway that bisected the hilly terrain of this remote part of the town.

The moneylender's narrow, lopsided face was perspiring under his hard hat; lank hair started from beneath the brim, which lent him a

13

curious aspect. This, combined with the green-tinted spectacles he wore, gave him a sinister, decayed look, like someone long dead. The thought may have occurred to the few, scattered passers-by he met in the course of his ascent, for almost to a person they gave one cautious glance and then hurried on as though eager to be rid of his presence.

He turned in at a small courtyard and stood in the shelter of a great old ruined church to catch his breath; his heart was thumping uncomfortably in the confines of his narrow chest and his breath rasped in his throat. Assuredly, he was out of condition, he told himself. Long hours of sedentary work huddled over his accounts were taking their toll; he really must get out more and take some exercise.

The moneylender's sallow face brightened momentarily as he thought of his increasing prosperity, but then he frowned again as he remembered the purpose of his errand. Gingold must be made to toe the line, he told himself, as he set out over the last half-mile of his journey.

If he couldn't raise the necessary cash, there must be many valuables in that rambling old house of his which he could sell and realize on. As Mr. Sharsted forged his way deeper into this forgotten corner of the town, the sun, which was already low in the sky, seemed to have already set, the light was so constricted by the maze of small courts and alleys into which he had plunged. He was panting again when he came at last, abruptly, to a large green door, set crookedly at the top of a flight of time-worn steps.

He stood arrested for a moment or two, one hand grasping the old balustrade, even his mean soul uplifted momentarily by the sight of the smoky haze of the town below, tilted beneath the yellow sky. Everything seemed to be set awry upon this hill, so that the very horizon rushed slanting across the far distance, giving the spectator a feeling of vertigo. A bell pealed faintly as he seized an iron scrollwork pull set into a metal rose alongside the front door. The moneylender's thoughts were turned to irritation again; everything about Mr. Gingold was peculiar, he felt. Even the fittings of his household were things one never saw elsewhere.

Though this might be an advantage if he ever gained control of Mr. Gingold's assets and had need to sell the property; there must be a lot of valuable stuff in this old house he had never seen, he mused. Which was another reason he felt it strange that the old man was unable to pay his dues; he must have a great deal of money, if not in cash, in property, one way or another.

He found it difficult to realize why Mr. Gingold kept hedging over a matter of three hundred pounds; he could easily sell the old place and go to live in a more attractive part of town in a modern, well-appointed villa and still keep his antiquarian interests. Mr. Sharsted sighed. Still, it was none of his business. All he was concerned with was the matter of the money; he had been kept waiting long enough, and he wouldn't be fobbed off any longer. Gingold had got to settle by Monday, or he'd make things unpleasant for him.

Mr. Sharsted's thin lips tightened in an ugly manner as he mused on, oblivious of the sunset staining the upper storeys of the old houses and dyeing the mean streets below the hill a rich carmine. He pulled the bell again impatiently, and this time the door was opened almost immediately.

Mr. Gingold was a very tall, white-haired man with a gentle, almost apologetic manner. He stood slightly stooping in the doorway, blinking as though astonished at the sunlight, half afraid it would fade him if he allowed too much of it to absorb him.

His clothes, which were of good quality and cut, were untidy and sagged loosely on his big frame; they seemed washed-out in the bright light of the sun and appeared to Mr. Sharsted to be all of a part with the man himself; indeed, Mr. Gingold was rinsed to a pale, insipid shade by the sunshine, so that his white hair and face and clothing ran into one another and, somehow, the different aspects of the picture became blurred and indeterminate.

To Mr. Sharsted he bore the aspect of an old photograph which had never been properly fixed and had turned brown and faded with time. Mr. Sharsted thought he might blow away with the breeze that had started up, but Mr. Gingold merely smiled shyly and said, "Oh, there you are, Sharsted. Come on in," as though he had been expecting him all the time.

Surprisingly, Mr. Gingold's eyes were of a marvellous shade of blue and they made his whole face come vividly alive, fighting and challenging the overall neutral tints of his clothing and features. He led the way into a cavernous hall. Mr. Sharsted followed cautiously, his eyes adjusting with difficulty to the cool gloom of the interior. With courteous, old-world motions Mr. Gingold beckoned him forward.

The two men ascended a finely carved staircase, whose balustrades, convoluted and serpentine, seemed to writhe sinuously upwards into the darkness.

"My business will only take a moment," protested Sharsted, anxious to present his ultimatum and depart. But Mr. Gingold merely continued to ascend the staircase.

"Come along, come along," he said gently, as though he hadn't heard Mr. Sharsted's expostulation. "You must take a glass of wine with me. I have so few visitors . . ."

Mr. Sharsted looked about him curiously; he had never been in this part of the house. Usually, Mr. Gingold received occasional callers in a big, cluttered room on the ground floor. This afternoon, for some reason known only to himself, he had chosen to show Mr. Sharsted another part of his domain. Mr. Sharsted thought that perhaps Mr. Gingold intended to settle the matter of his repayments. This might be where he transacted business, perhaps kept his money. His thin fingers twitched with nervous excitement.

They continued to ascend what seemed to the moneylender to be enormous distances. The staircase still unwound in front of their measured progress. From the little light which filtered in through rounded windows, Sharsted caught occasional glimpses of objects that aroused his professional curiosity and acquisitive sense. Here a large oil painting swung into view round the bend of the stair; in the necessarily brief glance that Mr. Sharsted caught, he could have sworn it was a Poussin.

A moment later, a large sideboard laden with porcelain slid by the corner of his eye. He stumbled on the stair as he glanced back over his shoulder and in so doing, almost missed a rare suit of Genoese armour which stood concealed in a niche set back from the staircase. The moneylender had reached a state of confused bewilderment when at length Mr. Gingold flung aside a large mahogany door, and motioned him forward.

Mr. Gingold must be a wealthy man and could easily realize enormous amounts on any one of the *objets d'art* Sharsted had seen; why then, thought the latter, did he find it necessary to borrow so frequently, and why was it so difficult to obtain repayment? With interest, the sum owed Sharsted had now risen to a considerable figure; Mr. Gingold must be a compulsive buyer of rare items. Allied to the general shabbiness of the house as seen by the casual visitor, it must mean that his collector's instinct would refuse to allow him to part with anything once bought, which had made him run himself into debt. The moneylender's lips tightened again; well, he must be made to settle his debts, like anyone else.

If not, perhaps Sharsted could force him to part with something—porcelain, a picture—that could be made to realize a handsome profit on the deal. Business was business, and Gingold could not expect him to wait for ever. His musings were interrupted by a query from his host and Sharsted muttered an apology as he saw that Mr. Gingold was waiting, one hand on the neck of a heavy silver and crystal decanter.

"Yes, yes, a sherry, thank you," he murmured in confusion, moving awkwardly. The light was so bad in this place that he felt it difficult to focus his eyes, and objects had a habit of shifting and billowing as though seen under water. Mr. Sharsted was forced to wear tinted spectacles, as his eyes had been weak from childhood. They made these apartments seem twice as dark as they might be. But though Mr. Sharsted squinted over the top of his lenses as Mr. Gingold poured the sherry, he still could not make out objects clearly. He really would have to consult his oculist soon, if this trouble continued.

His voice sounded hollow to his own ears as he ventured a commonplace when Mr. Gingold handed him the glass. He sat down gingerly on a ladderback chair indicated to him by Mr. Gingold, and sipped at the amber liquid in a hesitant fashion. It tasted uncommonly good, but this unexpected hospitality was putting him on a wrong footing with Gingold. He must assert himself and broach the subject of his business. But he felt a curious reluctance and merely sat on in embarrassed silence, one hand round the stem of his goblet, listening to the soothing tick of an old clock, which was the only thing which broke the silence.

He saw now that he was in a large apartment, expensively furnished, which must be high up in the house, under the eaves. Hardly a sound from outside penetrated the windows, which were hung with thick blue-velvet curtains; the parquet floor was covered with exquisitely worked Chinese rugs and the room was apparently divided in half by heavy velvet curtaining to match those which masked the windows.

Mr. Gingold said little, but sat at a large mahogany table, tapping his sherry glass with his long fingers; his bright blue eyes looked with mild interest at Mr. Sharsted as they spoke of everyday matters. At last Mr. Sharsted was moved to broach the object of his visit. He spoke of the long-outstanding sum which he had advanced to Mr. Gingold, of the continued applications for settlement and of the necessity of securing early payment. Strangely, as Mr. Sharsted progressed, his voice began to stammer and eventually he was at a loss for words; normally, as working-class people in the town had reason to know, he was brusque, businesslike, and ruthless. He never hesitated to distrain on debtor's goods, or to evict if necessary and that he was the object of universal hatred in the outside world, bothered him not in the slightest.

In fact, he felt it to be an asset; his reputation in business affairs preceded him, as it were, and acted as an incentive to prompt repayment. If people were fool enough to be poor or to run into debt and couldn't meet their dues, well then, let them; it was all grist to his mill and he could not be expected to run his business on a lot of sentimental nonsense. He felt more irritated with Mr. Gingold than he need have been, for his money was obviously safe; but what continued to baffle him was the man's gentle docility, his obvious wealth, and his reluctance to settle his debts.

Something of this must have eventually permeated his conversation, for Mr. Gingold shifted in his seat, made no comment whatever on Mr. Sharsted's pressing demands and only said, in another of his softly spoken sentences, "Do have another sherry, Mr. Sharsted."

The moneylender felt all the strength going out of him as he weakly assented. He leaned back on his comfortable chair with a swimming head and allowed the second glass to be pressed into his hand, the thread of his discourse completely lost. He mentally cursed himself for a dithering fool and tried to concentrate, but Mr. Gingold's benevolent smile, the curious way the objects in the room shifted and wavered in the heat haze; the general gloom and the discreet curtaining, came more and more to weigh on and oppress his spirits.

So it was with something like relief that Sharsted saw his host rise from the table. He had not changed the topic, but continued to speak as though Mr. Sharsted had never mentioned money to him at all; he merely ignored the whole situation and with an enthusiasm Sharsted found difficult to share, murmured soothingly on about Chinese wall paintings, a subject of which Mr. Sharsted knew nothing.

He found his eyes closing and with an effort opened them again. Mr. Gingold was saying, "I think this will interest you, Mr. Sharsted. Come along . . ."

His host had moved forward and the moneylender, following him down the room, saw that the large expanse of velvet curtaining was in motion. The two men walked through the parted curtains, which closed behind them, and Mr. Sharsted then saw that they were in a semicircular chamber.

This room was, if anything, even dimmer than the one they had just left. But the moneylender's interest began to revive; his head felt clearer and he took in a large circular table, some brass wheels and levers which winked in the gloom, and a long shaft which went up to the ceiling.

"This has almost become an obsession with me," murmured Mr. Gingold, as though apologizing to his guest. "You are aware of the principles of the camera obscura, Mr. Sharsted?"

The moneylender pondered slowly, reaching back into memory. "Some sort of Victorian toy, isn't it?" he said at length. Mr. Gingold looked pained, but the expression of his voice did not change.

"Hardly that, Mr. Sharsted," he rejoined. "A most fascinating pursuit. Few people of my acquaintance have been here and seen what you are going to see."

He motioned to the shafting, which passed up through a louvre in the ceiling.

"These controls are coupled to the system of lenses and prisms on the roof. As you will see, the hidden camera, as the Victorian scientists came to call it, gathers a panorama of the town below and transmits it here on to the viewing table. An absorbing study, one's fellow man, don't you think? I spend many hours up here."

Mr. Sharsted had never heard Mr. Gingold in such a talkative mood and now that the wretchedness which had assailed him earlier had disappeared, he felt more suited to tackle him about his debts. First, he would humour him by feigning interest in his stupid toy. But Mr. Sharsted had to admit, almost with a gasp of surprise, that Mr. Gingold's obsession had a valid cause.

For suddenly, as Mr. Gingold moved his hand upon the lever, the room was flooded with light of a blinding clarity and the money-lender saw why gloom was a necessity in this chamber. Presumably, a shutter over the camera obscura slid away upon the rooftop and almost at the same moment, a panel in the ceiling opened to admit a shaft of light directed upon the table before them.

In a second of God-like vision, Mr. Sharsted saw a panorama of part of the old town spread out before him in superbly natural colour. Here were the quaint, cobbled streets dropping to the valley, with the blue hills beyond; factory chimneys smoked in the early evening air; people went about their business in half a hundred roads; distant traffic went noiselessly on its way; once, even, a great white bird soared across the field of vision, so apparently close that Mr. Sharsted started back from the table.

Mr. Gingold gave a dry chuckle and moved a brass wheel at his elbow. The viewpoint abruptly shifted and Mr. Sharsted saw with another gasp, a sparkling vista of the estuary with a big coaling ship moving slowly out to sea. Gulls soared in the foreground and the sullen wash of the tide ringed the shore. Mr. Sharsted, his errand quite forgotten, was fascinated. Half an hour must have passed, each view more enchanting than the last; from this height, the squalor of the town was quite transformed.

He was abruptly recalled to the present, however, by the latest of the views; Mr. Gingold spun the control for the last time and a huddle of crumbling tenements wheeled into view. "The former home of Mrs. Thwaites, I believe," said Mr. Gingold mildly.

Mr. Sharsted flushed and bit his lip in anger. The Thwaites business had aroused more notoriety than he had intended; the woman had borrowed a greater sum than she could afford, the interest mounted, she borrowed again; could he help it if she had a tubercular husband and three children? He had to make an example of her in order to keep his other clients in line; now there was a distraint on the furniture and the Thwaiteses were being turned on to the street. Could he help this? If only people would repay their debts all would be well; he wasn't a philanthropic institution, he told himself angrily.

And at this reference to what was rapidly becoming a scandal in the town, all his smouldering resentment against Mr. Gingold broke out afresh; enough of all these views and childish playthings. Camera obscura, indeed; if Mr. Gingold did not meet his obligations like a gentleman he could sell this pretty toy to meet his debt.

He controlled himself with an effort as he turned to meet Mr. Gingold's gently ironic gaze.

"Ah, yes," said Mr. Sharsted. "The Thwaites business is my affair, Mr. Gingold. Will you please confine yourself to the matter in hand. I have had to come here again at great inconvenience; I must tell you that if the £300, representing the current installment on our loan is not forthcoming by Monday, I shall be obliged to take legal action."

Mr. Sharsted's cheeks were burning and his voice trembled as he pronounced these words; if he expected a violent reaction from Mr. Gingold, he was disappointed. The latter merely gazed at him in mute reproach.

"This is your last word?" he said regretfully. "You will not reconsider?"

"Certainly not," snapped Mr. Sharsted. "I must have the money by Monday."

"You misunderstand me, Mr. Sharsted," said Mr. Gingold, still in that irritatingly mild voice. "I was referring to Mrs. Thwaites. Must you carry on with this unnecessary and somewhat inhuman action? I would . . ."

"Please mind your own business!" retorted Mr. Sharsted, exasperated beyond measure. "Mind what I say . . ."

He looked wildly round for the door through which he had entered.

"That is your last word?" said Mr. Gingold again. One look at the moneylender's set, white face was his mute answer.

"Very well, then," said Mr. Gingold, with a heavy sigh. "So be it. I will see you on your way."

He moved forward again, pulling a heavy velvet cloth over the table of the camera obscura. The louvre in the ceiling closed with a barely audible rumble. To Mr. Sharsted's surprise, he found himself following his host up yet another flight of stairs; these were of stone, fringed with an iron balustrade which was cold to the touch.

His anger was now subsiding as quickly as it had come; he was already regretting losing his temper over the Thwaites business and he hadn't intended to sound so crude and cold-blooded. What must Mr. Gingold think of him? Strange how the story could have got to his ears; surprising how much information about the outside world a recluse could obtain just by sitting still.

Though, on this hill, he supposed Mr. Gingold could be said to be at the centre of things. He shuddered suddenly, for the air seemed to have grown cold. Through a slit in the stone wall he could see the evening sky was already darkening. He really must be on his way; how did the old fool expect him to find his way out when they were still mounting to the very top of the house?

Mr. Sharsted regretted, too, that in antagonizing Mr. Gingold, he might have made it even more difficult to obtain his money; it was almost as though, in mentioning Mrs. Thwaites and trying to take her part, he had been trying a form of subtle blackmail.

He would not have expected it of Gingold; it was not like him to meddle in other people's affairs. If he was so fond of the poor and needy he could well afford to advance the family some money themselves to tide them over their difficulties.

His brain seething with these confused and angry thoughts, Mr. Sharsted, panting and dishevelled, now found himself on a worn stone platform where Mr. Gingold was putting the key into an ancient wooden lock.

"My workshop," he explained, with a shy smile to Mr. Sharsted, who felt his tension eased away by this drop in the emotional atmosphere. Looking through an old, nearly triangular window in front of him, Mr. Sharsted could see that they were in a small, turreted superstructure which towered a good twenty feet over the main roof of the house. There was a sprawl of unfamiliar alleys at the foot of the steep overhang of the building, as far as he could make out through the grimy panes.

"There is a staircase down the outside," explained Mr. Gingold, opening the door. "It will lead you down the other side of the hill and cut over half a mile off your journey."

The moneylender felt a sudden rush of relief at this. He had come almost to fear this deceptively mild and quiet old man who, though he said little and threatened not at all, had begun to exude a faint air of menace to Mr. Sharsted's now over-heated imagination.

"But first," said Mr. Gingold, taking the other man's arm in a surprisingly powerful grip, "I want to show you something else—and this really has been seen by very few people indeed."

Mr. Sharsted looked at the other quickly, but could read nothing in Mr. Gingold's enigmatic blue eyes.

He was surprised to find a similar, though smaller, chamber to the one they had just left. There was another table, another shaft ascending to a domed cupola in the ceiling, and a further arrangement of wheels and tubes.

"This camera obscura," said Mr. Gingold, "is a very rare model, to be sure. In fact, I believe there are only three in existence today, and one of those is in Northern Italy."

Mr. Sharsted cleared his throat and made a non-committal reply.

"I felt sure you would like to see this before you leave," said Mr. Gingold softly. "You are quite sure you won't change your mind?" he added, almost inaudibly, as he bent ot the levers. "About Mrs. Thwaites, I mean.'

Sharsted felt another sudden spirt of anger, but kept his feelings under control.

"I'm sorry . . ." he began.

"No matter," said Mr. Gingold, regretfully. "I only wanted to make sure, before we had a look at this."

He laid his hand with infinite tenderness on Mr. Sharsted's shoulder as he drew him forward.

He pressed the lever and Mr. Sharsted almost cried out with the suddenness of the vision. He was God; the world was spread out before him in a crazy pattern, or at least the segment of it representing the part of the town surrounding the house in which he stood.

He viewed it from a great height, as a man might from an aeroplane; though nothing was quite in perspective.

The picture was of enormous clarity; it was like looking into an old cheval glass which had a faint distorting quality. There was something oblique and elliptical about the sprawl of alleys and roads that spread about the foot of the hill.

The shadows were mauve and violet, and the extremes of the picture were still tinged with the blood red of the dying sun.

It was an appalling, cataclysmic vision, and Mr. Sharsted was shattered; he felt suspended in space, and almost cried out at the dizziness of the height.

When Mr. Gingold twirled the wheel and the picture slowly began to revolve, Mr. Sharsted did cry out and had to clutch at the back of a chair to prevent himself from falling.

He was perturbed, too, as he caught a glimpse of a big, white building in the foreground of the picture.

"I thought that was the old Corn Exchange," he said in bewilderment. "Surely that burned down before the last war?"

"Eigh," said Mr. Gingold, as though he hadn't heard.

"It doesn't matter," said Mr. Sharsted, who now felt quite confused and ill. It must be the combination of the sherry and the enormous height at which he was viewing the vision in the camera obscura.

It was a demoniacal toy and he shrank away from the figure of Mr. Gingold, which looked somewhat sinister in the blood-red and mauve light reflected from the image in the polished table surface.

"I thought you'd like to see this one," said Mr. Gingold, in that same maddening, insipid voice. "It's really special, isn't it? Quite the best of the two . . . you can see all sorts of things that are normally hidden."

As he spoke there appeared on the screen two old buildings which Mr. Sharsted was sure had been destroyed during the war; in fact, he was certain that a public garden and car park had now been erected on the site. His mouth suddenly became dry; he was not sure whether he had drunk too much sherry or the heat of the day had been too much for him.

He had been about to make a sharp remark that the sale of the camera obscura would liquidate Mr. Gingold's current debt, but he felt this would not be a wise comment to make at this juncture. He felt faint, his brow went hot and cold and Mr. Gingold was at his side in an instant.

Mr. Sharsted became aware that the picture had faded from the table and that the day was rapidly turning to dusk outside the dusty windows.

"I really must be going," he said with feeble desperation, trying to free himself from Mr. Gingold's quietly persistent grip.

"Certainly, Mr. Sharsted," said his host. "This way." He led him without ceremony over to a small oval doorway in a corner of the far wall.

"Just go down the stairs. It will bring you on to the street. Please slam the bottom door—it will lock itself." As he spoke, he opened the door and Mr. Sharsted saw a flight of clean, dry stone steps leading downwards. Light still flooded in from windows set in the circular walls.

Mr. Gingold did not offer his hand and Mr. Sharsted stood rather awkwardly, holding the door ajar.

"Until Monday, then," he said.

Mr. Gingold flatly ignored this.

"Goodnight, Mr. Gingold," said the moneylender with nervous haste, anxious to be gone.

"Goodbye, Mr. Sharsted," said Mr. Gingold with kind finality.

Mr. Sharsted almost thrust himself through the door and nervously fled down the staircase, mentally cursing himself for all sorts of a fool. His feet beat a rapid tattoo that echoed eerily up and down the old tower. Fortunately, there was still plenty of light; this would be a nasty place in the dark. He slowed his pace after a few moments and thought bitterly of the way he had allowed old Gingold to gain the ascendancy over him; and what an impertinence of the man to interfere in the matter of the Thwaites woman.

He would see what sort of man Mr. Sharsted was when Monday came and the eviction went according to plan. Monday would also be a day of reckoning for Mr. Gingold—it was a day they would both remember and Mr. Sharsted felt himself quite looking forward to it.

He quickened his pace again, and presently found himself confronted by a thick oak door.

It gave beneath his hand as he lifted the big, well-oiled catch and
the next moment he was in a high-walled alley leading to the street.
The door slammed hollowly behind him and he breathed in the cool
evening air with a sigh of relief. He jammed his hard hat back onto
his head and strode out over the cobbles, as though to affirm the
solidity of the outside world.

Once in the street, which seemed somewhat unfamiliar to him,
he hesitated which way to go and then set off to the right. He remembered that Mr. Gingold had told him that this way took him over
the other side of the hill; he had never been in this part of the town
and the walk would do him good.

The sun had quite gone and a thin sliver of moon was showing
in the early evening sky. There seemed few people about and when,
ten minutes later, Mr. Sharsted came out into a large square which
had five or six roads leading off it, he determined to ask the correct
way back down to his part of the town. With luck he could catch a
tram, for he had now had enough of walking for one day.

There was a large, smoke-grimed chapel on a corner of this
square and as Mr. Sharsted passed it, he caught a glimpse of a board
with gold-painted letters.

NINIAN'S REVIVALIST BROTHERHOOD, it said. The date, in flaked
gold paint, was 1925.

Mr. Sharsted walked on and selected the most important of the
roads which faced him. It was getting quite dark and the lamps had
not yet been lit on this part of the hill. As he went farther down, the
buildings closed in about his head, and the lights of the town below
disappeared. Mr. Sharsted felt lost and a little forlorn. Due, no doubt,
to the faintly incredible atmosphere of Mr. Gingold's big house.

He determined to ask the next passer-by for the right direction,
but for the moment he couldn't see anyone about; the absence of
street lights also bothered him. The municipal authorities must have
overlooked this section when they switched on at dusk, unless it came
under the jurisdiction of another body.

Mr. Sharsted was musing in this manner when he turned the corner
of a narrow street and came out opposite a large, white building that

looked familiar. For years Mr. Sharsted had a picture of it on the yearly calendar sent by a local tradesman, which used to hang in his office. He gazed at its façade with mounting bewilderment as he approached. The title, CORN EXCHANGE, winked back dully in the moonlight as he got near enough to make out the lettering.

Mr. Sharsted's bewilderment changed to distinct unease as he thought frantically that he had already seen this building once before this evening, in the image captured by the lens of Mr. Gingold's second camera obscura. And he knew with numbing certainty that the old Corn Exchange had burned down in the late thirties.

He swallowed heavily, and hurried on; there was something devilishly wrong, unless he were the victim of an optical illusion engendered by the violence of his thoughts, the unaccustomed walking he had done that day, and the two glasses of sherry.

He had the uncomfortable feeling that Mr. Gingold might be watching him at that very moment, on the table of his camera obscura, and at the thought a cold sweat burst out on his forehead.

He sent himself forward at a smart trot and had soon left the Corn Exchange far behind. In the distance he heard the sharp clopping and the grating rattle of a horse and cart, but as he gained the entrance of an alley he was disappointed to see its shadow disappear round the corner into the next road. He still could not see any people about and again had difficulty in fixing his position in relation to the town.

He set off once more, with a show of determination he was far from feeling, and five minutes later arrived in the middle of a square which was already familiar to him.

There was a chapel on the corner and Mr. Sharsted read for the second time that evening the legend: NINIAN'S REVIVALIST BROTHERHOOD.

He stamped his foot in anger. He had walked quite three miles and had been fool enough to describe a complete circle; here he was, not five minutes from Gingold's house, where he had set out, nearly an hour before.

He pulled out his watch at this and was surprised to find it was only a quarter past six, though he could have sworn this was the time he had left Gingold.

Though it could have been a quarter past five; he hardly knew what he was doing this afternoon. He shook it to make sure it was still going and then replaced it in his pocket.

His feet beat the pavement in his fury as he ran down the length of the square. This time he wouldn't make the same silly mistake. He unhesitatingly chose a large, well-kept metalled road that ran fair and square in the direction he knew must take him back to the centre of the town. He found himself humming a little tune under his breath. As he turned the next corner, his confidence increased.

Lights burned brightly on every hand; the authorities must have realized their mistake and finally switched on. But again he was mistaken; there was a little cart parked at the side of the road, with a horse in the shafts. An old man mounted a ladder set against a lamp-post and Mr. Sharsted saw the thin blue flame in the gloom and then the mellow blossoming of the gas lamp.

Now he felt irritated again; what an incredibly archaic part of the town old Gingold lived in. It would just suit him. Gas lamps! And what a system for lighting them; Sharsted thought this method had gone out with the Ark.

Nevertheless, he was most polite.

"Good evening," he said, and the figure at the top of the lamp-post stirred uneasily. The face was in deep shadow.

"Good evening, sir," the lamplighter said in a muffled voice. He started climbing down.

"Could you direct me to the town center?" said Mr. Sharsted with simulated confidence. He took a couple of paces forward and was then arrested with a shock.

There was a strange, sickly stench which reminded him of something he was unable to place. Really, the drains in this place were terrible; he certainly would have to write to the town hall about this backward part of the locality.

The lamplighter had descended to the ground now and he put something down in the back of his cart; the horse shifted uneasily and again Mr. Sharsted caught the charnel stench, sickly sweet on the summer air.

"This is the town center as far as I know, sir," said the lamplighter.

As he spoke he stepped forward and the pale lamplight fell on to his face, which had been in shadow before.

Mr. Sharsted no longer waited to ask for any more directions but set off down the road at breakneck speed, not sure whether the green pallor of the man's face was due to a terrible suspicion or the green-tinted glasses he wore.

What he was certain of was that something like a mass of writhing worms projected below the man's cap, where his hair would normally have been. Mr. Sharsted hadn't waited to find out if this Medusa-like supposition were correct; beneath his hideous fear burned a savage anger at Gingold, whom somehow he suspected to be at the back of all these troubles.

Mr. Sharsted fervently hoped that he might soon wake to find himself at home in bed, ready to begin the day that had ended so ignominiously at Gingold's, but even as he formulated the thought, he knew this was reality. This cold moonlight, the hard pavement, his frantic flight, and the breath rasping and sobbing in his throat.

As the mist cleared from in front of his eyes, he slowed to a walk and then found himself in the middle of a square; he knew where he was and he had to force his nerves into a terrible, unnatural calm, just this side of despair. He walked with controlled casualness past the legend, NINIAN'S REVIVALIST BROTHERHOOD, and this time chose the most unlikely road of all, little more than a narrow alley that appeared to lead in the wrong direction.

Mr. Sharsted was willing to try anything which would lead him off this terrifying, accursed hill. There were no lights here and his feet stumbled on the rough stones and flints of the unmade roadway, but at least he was going downhill and the track gradually spiralled until he was in the right direction.

For some little while Mr. Sharsted had heard faint, elusive stirrings in the darkness about him and once he was startled to hear, some way ahead of him, a muffled cough. At least there were other people about, at last, he thought and he was comforted, too, to see, far ahead of him, the dim lights of the town.

As he grew nearer, Mr. Sharsted recovered his spirits and was relieved to see that they did not recede from him, as he had half suspected they might. The shapes about him, too, were solid enough.

Their feet rang hollow on the roadway; evidently they were on their way to a meeting.

As Mr. Sharsted came under the light of the first lamp, his earlier panic fear had abated. He still couldn't recognize exactly where he was, but the trim villas they were passing were more reminiscent of the town proper.

Mr. Sharsted stepped up onto the pavement when they reached the well-lit area and in so doing, cannoned into a large, well-built man who had just emerged from a gateway to join the throng in the roadway.

Mr. Sharsted staggered under the impact and once again his nostrils caught the sickly sweet perfume of decay. The man caught him by the front of the coat to prevent him from falling.

"Evening, Mordecai," he said in a thick voice. "I thought you'd be coming, sooner or later."

Mr. Sharsted could not resist a cry of bubbling terror. It was not just the greenish pallor of the man's face or the rotted, leathery lips drawn back from the decayed teeth. He fell back against the fence as Abel Joyce passed on—Abel Joyce, a fellow moneylender and usurer who had died in the nineteen-twenties and whose funeral Mr. Sharsted had attended.

Blackness was about him as he rushed away, a sobbing whistle in his throat. He was beginning to understand Mr. Gingold and that devilish camera obscura; the lost and the damned. He began to babble to himself under his breath.

Now and again he cast a sidelong glimpse at his companions as he ran; there was old Mrs. Sanderson who used to lay out corpses and rob her charges; there Grayson, the estate agent and undertaker; Amos, the war profiteer; Drucker, a swindler, all green of pallor and bearing with them the charnel stench.

All people Mr. Sharsted had business with at one time or another and all of whom had one thing in common. Without exception all had been dead for quite a number of years. Mr. Sharsted stuffed his handkerchief over his mouth to blot out that unbearable odour and heard the mocking laughter as his racing feet carried him past.

"Evening, Mordecai," they said. "We thought you'd be joining us." Mr. Gingold equated him with these ghouls, he sobbed, as he ran on at headlong speed; if only he could make him understand. Sharsted didn't deserve such treatment. He was a businessman, not like these bloodsuckers on society; the lost and the damned. Now he knew why the Corn Exchange still stood and why the town was unfamiliar. It existed only in the eye of the camera obscura. Now he knew that Mr. Gingold had been trying to give him a last chance and why he had said goodbye, instead of goodnight.

There was just one hope; if he could find the door back to Mr. Gingold's perhaps he could make him change his mind. Mr. Sharsted's feet flew over the cobbles as he thought this, his hat fell down and he scraped his hands against the wall. He left the walking corpses far behind, but though he was now looking for the familiar square he seemed to be finding his way back to the Corn Exchange.

He stopped for a moment to regain his breath. He must work this out logically. How had it happened before? Why, of course, by walking away from the desired destination. Mr. Sharsted turned back and set himself to walk steadily towards the lights. Though terrified, he did not despair, now that he knew what he was up against. He felt himself a match for Mr. Gingold. If only he could find the door!

As he reached the warm circle cast by the glow of the street lamps, Mr. Sharsted breathed a sigh of relief. For as he turned a corner there was the big square, with the soot-grimed chapel on the corner. He hurried on. He must remember exactly the turnings he had taken; he couldn't afford to make a mistake.

So much depended on it. If only he could have another chance— he would let the Thwaites family keep their house, he would even be willing to forget Gingold's debt. He couldn't face the possibility of walking these endless streets—for how long? And with the creatures he had seen . . .

Mr. Sharsted groaned as he remembered the face of one old woman he had seen earlier that evening—or what was left of that face, after years of wind and weather. He suddenly recalled that she had died before the 1914 war. The sweat burst out on his forehead and he tried not to think of it.

Once off the square, he plunged into the alley he remembered. Ah! there it was. Now all he had to do was to go to the left and there was the door. His heart beat higher and he began to hope, with a sick longing, for the security of his well-appointed house and his rows of friendly ledgers. Only one more corner. He ran on and turned up the road towards Mr. Gingold's door. Another thirty yards to the peace of the ordinary world.

The moolight winked on a wide, well-paved square. Shone, too, on a legend painted in gold leaf on a large board: NINIAN'S RE-VIVALIST BROTHERHOOD. The date was 1925.

Mr. Sharsted gave a hideous yell of fear and despair and fell to the pavement.

Mr. Gingold sighed heavily and yawned. He glanced at the clock. It was time for bed. He went over once again and stared into the camera obscura. It had been a not altogether unsuccessful day. He put a black velvet cloth over the image in the lens and went off slowly to bed.

Under the cloth, in pitiless detail, was reflected the narrow tangle of streets round Mr. Gingold's house, seen as through the eye of God; there went Mr. Sharsted and his colleagues, the lost and the damned, trapped for eternity, stumbling, weeping, swearing, as they slipped and scrabbled along the alleys and squares of their own private hell, under the pale light of the stars.

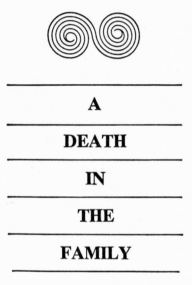

A

DEATH

IN

THE

FAMILY

At fifty-eight, Jared Sloane had the settled habits of a lifelong bachelor. At seven o'clock in summer and six in winter, he put out the lights, locked up and went back to his living quarters. He showered and shaved and put on clothes less formal than his profession demanded, then cooked his supper and cleared it away.

Then he laid the phone extension on the bedroom floor where he would be sure to hear it if it rang, unlocked the tight-fitting door leading from the kitchen, and went downstairs for the evening with his family.

Old Mr. Shallcross, from whom he had bought the building twenty years before, had used the cellar only for storage. But every man who was young and on his own in the big Depression acquired a smattering of many skills, and Jared was no exception; he had sawed and hammered and painted, and what had once been a cellar was now a big, comfortable sitting room, its two small high-up windows always covered with heavy curtains. He was not competent to install electric lights, but he had run a pipe from the kitchen range to the old gas chandelier which, like most of the furniture he had repainted and re-upholstered, had come from a glorified junk shop he patronized in McMinnville, the county seat. The room was always cool, and in winter it was so chilly that he had to wear his overcoat, but that was necessary and he no longer noticed it.

They were always there, waiting for him. Dad was in the big easy chair, reading the Middleton *Gazette*. Mother was knitting a sock. Grandma was dozing on the couch—she dozed all the time; she was nearly ninety. Brother Ben and sister Emma were playing whist, sitting in straight chairs at the little table, the cards held cannily against Ben's white shirt and Emma's ruffled foulard print. Gussie, Jared's wife, sat at the piano, her fingers arrested on the keys, her head turned to smile at him as he entered. Luke, his ten-year-old son, sat on the floor, a half-built model ship before him.

Jared would sit down in the one vacant place, a big comfortable club chair upholstered in plum-colored plush, and would chat with them until bedtime. He told them all the day's doings upstairs, commented on news of the town and of the people they knew, repeated stories and jokes (carefully expurgated) he had heard from salesmen, expressed his views and opinions on any subject that came into his mind. They never argued or contradicted him. They never answered.

Their clothes changed with the seasons and the styles; otherwise the scene never altered. When bedtime came, Jared yawned, stretched, said, "Well, goodnight all—pleasant dreams," turned out the overhead light, climbed the stairs, locked the door behind him and went to bed. For a while he had always kissed his wife on the forehead for goodnight, but he felt that the others might be jealous, and now he showed no favoritism.

The family had not always played their present roles. Once they had all had different names. They had been other people's grandmother and father and mother and sister and brother and wife and son. Now they were his.

He had waited a long time for some of them—for relatives of just the right age, with the right family resemblance. Gussie he had loved, quietly and patiently, for years before she became his wife; she had been Mrs. Ralph Stiegeler then, the wife of the Middleton Drugstore owner, and she had never guessed that Jared Sloane was in love with her. Her name really was Gussie; Ben and Emma and Luke just had names he liked. She was the nucleus of the family; all the others had been added later, one by one. Grandma, strange to say, had been with them the shortest time—little more than a year. All the family needed now to be complete was a daughter, and Jared had already picked her name—she would be called Martha. He liked old-fashioned names; they belonged to the past, to his lonely boyhood in the orphan asylum where he had lived all his life until he was sixteen.

He still remembered bitterly how the others had jeered at him, a foundling whose very name had been given at the whim of the superintendent after he had been found, wrapped in a torn sheet, on the asylum steps. The others were orphans, but they knew who they were; they had aunts and uncles and cousins who wrote them letters and came to see them and sent them presents at Christmas and birthdays, whom they visited sometimes and who often paid for all or part of their keep. Jared Sloane had nobody.

That was why he had wanted so large a family. Every evening now he was a man with parents, a brother, a sister, a wife and child. (Grandma was a lucky fluke; he had kept an eye on old Mrs. Atkinson and it had paid off.) There was no more room for another adult member of the family, but Martha, when he found her, could sit on a cushion on the floor beside her brother, and play with a doll he would buy for her or do something else domestic and childish and feminine. He decided that she should be younger than Luke—say seven or eight, old enough to enjoy her father's conversation, not so young as to need the care called for by a small child.

Every night, in bed, before he set the alarm and put his teeth in the tumbler, Jared Sloane uttered a grateful little unvoiced prayer to someone or something—perhaps to himself—a prayer of thanks for the wonderful, unheard-of idea that had come to him ten years ago when, in the middle of a sleepless, mourning night, he had suddenly realized how he could make Gussie his wife and keep her with him as long as he himself lived. Ralph Stiegeler had called him only that afternoon. Out of nowhere there had come to him the daring, frightening scheme, full-fledged as Pallas Athene from the head of Zeus.

He had gambled on discovery, ruin, imprisonment, disgrace, against the fulfillment of his dearest and most secret dream—to have a family of his own. And he had won. After Gussie, the rest had been easy. He could not foresee, but he could choose. He blessed Middleton for being a small town where there was need for only one man of his profession, and he could get all the business there was. He had hesitated when first he came here, fresh from college, fearing there would not be a livelihood for him in the town and the farms around it. But he was frugal, he loved quiet, and he dreaded the scramble and competition of a big city firm; here he would be on his own from the beginning. When he had learned through a notice in a trade paper that old Mr. Shallcross wanted to sell his establishment and good will and retire, Jared had answered him.

To his happiness he found that the little nest egg he had accumulated by hard labor all through his younger years—he had been too young for one war and too old for the other—which had enabled him to be trained in the one profession that had always attracted him, would stretch to cover Mr. Shallcross's modest demands. Within a week the business had changed hands. Now he had long been a settled feature of Middleton; and if he had never been a mixer or made any close friends, he was well-known, respected—and, beyond all, above suspicion.

Everything was always done just as the mourners wished. The funeral was held from the home of the deceased or from his own beautifully redecorated chapel, as they preferred. (That had been his chief terror about Gussie, but everything went his way—Ralph immediately asked for the chapel. He remembered with chagrin how, later on, he had lost a splendid former candidate for brother Ben, because Charles Holden's mother insisted on having the services at the farmhouse.) The deceased, a work of art by a fine embalmer worthy of any big city funeral parlor, lay dressed in his best in the casket, surrounded by flowers and wreaths and set pieces. When the minister had finished, Miss Hattie Blackstock played the organ softly, and then at Jared Sloane's signal the company passed in single file for the last look. The immediate relatives came last. Then they all filed out to enter the waiting cars for the trip to the cemetery. (No one who was to be cremated instead of buried could ever become a member of Jared's family, of course.)

Then came the crucial moment. Most vividly Jared remembered that first time, when it was Gussie, when everything depended on timing and resolution and luck.

The pallbearers waited for him to close the casket, so that they could carry it out to the hearse. In a city funeral, the assistants would have been taking the flowers out, but Jared had no assistant. In that small town, where he knew everybody and everybody knew him, it was natural to say: "Look, fellows, I don't want to hold things up too long; it's hard enough on her folks as it is. I've taken the cards off all the floral offerings; would you mind carrying them to the hearse, all of you, and putting them around the bier? Then by the time you get back I'll have the casket closed and ready for you."

If just one person had said: "I can't get near the roses—they make me sneeze," or "You don't need us all; I'll wait here and rest my bad knee," or "That's not a good idea, Jared—the casket will crush them if we put them in first,"—if that had happened, then the whole desperate gamble would have been lost. Gussie would never have been his wife; the rest of his family would never have come to read and knit and play cards and build model ships in the big sitting room. But from Gussie to Grandma, it had worked.

The instant the last back was turned, bending under its load of flowers, Jared moved like lightning. Quick—lift the body out of the casket. Quick—lay it on the couch concealed behind the heavy velvet curtains. Quick—bring out the life size, carefully weighted dummy prepared and ready, and put it in place. Quick—close the lid and fasten it. It all took between two and three minutes. When the first pallbearer returned, everything was set. Nobody ever knew what rode out to the cemetery, what was lowered into the grave.

He himself drove the hearse, of course. The funeral parlor was safely locked until he returned. Then, with the last sober, sympathetic handshake, he was left alone.

Once inside, he did nothing until closing time. Then, with the office and display room and slumber room and chapel dark, he went behind the velvet curtain and lifted the new member of his family respectfully and tenderly from the couch and took him or her back to the preparation room. Nobody could ever have claimed that the embalming job already done was not as good as anyone could wish for. But now came the last extra refinements of his art—the special preservative he had perfected, the cosmetic changes which increased the resemblances of kindred, the new clothes he had bought in a fast trip to McMinnville. The clothing provided by the "former family" —that was how he always thought of them—he put thriftily away to help stuff the next dummy: if Jared Sloane had been given to frivolity, which he was not, he might have found amusement in the thought that, for instance, the "former" sister Emma's last garments now occupied the coffin of the "former" dad. Last of all, he arranged the new member in the pose which he had decided on for his or her future in the family gathering in the sitting room. Then he carried his newly acquired relative downstairs. No introductions were necessary; it was to be assumed that the Sloane family knew one another. Jared got to bed late on those seven red-letter evenings; it was hard to tear himself away from the companionship of his augmented family circle and go to his lonely room.

As the years went by, he ceased to fret and worry and fear for weeks or months afterward, as he had done at first. After all, he averaged about fifty funerals a year, counting the country around Middleton and occasional Middleton-born people who had left town but were brought home for burial. In ten years that meant some five hundred and out of all these he had taken the big gamble only seven times.

Some day, of course, he himself would die, and then inevitably the discovery would be made. But by that time he would be past caring, and the scandal and excitement and newspaper headlines would be of no concern to him. He was only fifty-eight, and he had never been ill a day in his life; he would count on twenty or twenty-five years more—the only man in Middleton who would never have to dread a lonely old age. He remembered his terribly lonely childhood and youth, and to his grateful little silent prayer he added thanks that by his own efforts he had compensated for it. He was grateful for another thing, too—that the fate that had deprived him of mother-love as a helpless infant had seemed to paralyze his emotional nature; never in his life had he felt or understood what seemed to him the disgusting sexual impulses of other men. Even his long love of Gussie Stiegeler had been made up—as it was now that she was Gussie Sloane—wholly of tenderness and protectiveness and dependency.

Once in a book on psychology he had read about a horrible perversion called necrophilia, and had shuddered. He tried, with an attempt at understanding, to imagine himself taking Gussie—his lovely, precious Gussie, whom he dressed in silk and pearls, for whom he had bought the piano that the "former" Gussie had played so well—away from her piano and into his narrow bed, kissing her embracing her . . . He felt sick. For days thereafter it embarrassed him even to look at Gussie; he blushed at the thought that she might have guessed what foul fancies he had permitted to enter his mind.

He loved his family because they *were* his family, because they were his and no one else's, because with them he could expand and be himself and know that they would always belong to him. He was doing their former selves and their former dear ones no injury. He loved dad and mother and grandma filially, he loved sister Emma and brother Ben as an older brother should, he adored Gussie and little Luke. All he needed now for perfect happiness was a sweet little daughter; it wasn't good for a boy like Luke to be the only child.

Naturally he couldn't look around and pick and choose or even speculate—good heavens, only a ghoul would do that! He must wait, as with all the others, until just the right opportunity came—a seven- or eight-year-old girl, with dark hair (both he and Gussie were dark), a pretty little girl because her mother was pretty, provided for him by good fortune and the kindness of heaven, as all the rest of the family had been. There was no hurry; Luke would always stay ten years old, just as Grandma would always be eighty-nine. Jared would have shrunk from feeling interest or curiosity if he had been told of the illness of somebody's little daughter. He could wait. But his heart gave a little excited jump every time he got a call from a household where there were children, until he learned—as he always did—that it was grandfather or uncle William or old cousin Sarah in whose behalf his services were required. Twice he handled the funerals of little girls, but one was a scrawny, homely blonde brat, and the other had been killed in an auto accident and was dreadfully mangled.

In the early hours of March 31st Jared Sloane was wakened from a sound sleep by a loud knock at the front door. That happened sometimes—people came instead of phoning; like a doctor he was inured to night calls, and he shrugged drowsily into bathrobe and slippers. As he switched on the lights in the front he heard a car driving away; when he opened the door, the street—the main business street of Middleton was part of a state highway—was dark and deserted.

Then his eyes fell to a little bundle, wrapped in a blanket, lying on the porch at his feet. He stooped and picked it up, knowing at once what it must be. Inside, he drew the blanket away from the little corpse.

Even with the head hanging limp on the broken neck, he recognized her at once—the papers had been full of her photographs. It was the Manning child. Manning had disobeyed orders and notified the police, and the kidnappers had brutally made good their threat.

Why they had deposited their victim on the doorstep of a country undertaker two hundred miles away, in another state from the city where the millionaire's child had been snatched, Jared Sloane could not imagine. Probably, making good their escape with the ransom money, they had chanced on the sign as they drove through Middleton, and as a bit of macabre humor had presented him with the body. Much as he disliked the idea of being brought to public notice and having FBI men and police officers and reporters invading his privacy, Jared knew his duty; he must telephone at once to the sheriff's office in McMinnville.

Then he looked down at the blanket and what it held. Diana Manning had been nine, but she was small for her age. She had been a pretty, delicately cared for child. Her hair was long and soft and dark, the blank eyes staring up at him were brown.

He stood for a long time, pondering. Then quietly he lifted Diana and carried her back to the preparation room. Before he returned to bed, he took all her clothing and the thin old blanket out to the incinerator in the back yard, near the garage; he could not arouse suspicion by lighting a fire at three o'clock in the morning, but he burned trash every few days.

The next evening, for the first time since Grandma, Jared dropped in on the family only long enough to tell them the good news. He was moved; he whispered it to Gussie first. After all, Martha was going to be her daughter. He worked till late, then hid Martha carefully away. He had no funeral scheduled for the rest of the week, and there was nobody in the slumber room whom relatives and friends would be coming to visit; he could leave a sign in the door around noon and drive to McMinnville for a wardrobe and a big doll for his little girl. He always did the shopping for the family in McMinnville, which was large enough for him to be a stranger.

There was nothing new in the paper or on the radio about the Manning case. Perhaps the father, poor fool, was still dreaming he could get his daughter back by paying the ransom, and had asked too late for silence and secrecy.

That night Jared Sloane sat in his plum-colored chair and beamed at little Martha, perched on a cushion near her brother, smiling up at her mother at the piano. The family was complete. He was the happiest man on earth.

Three days later, as he worked in his office on accounts, the front door opened and a tall young man entered, carrying a brief case. Jared adjusted his expression to greet a salesman instead of a client.

"Mr. Sloane?" the young man asked amiably. Jared nodded, "Can you spare me a moment?"

"I don't know that there's anything I need right now, thanks."

"Need? Oh," he laughed. "I'm not a salesman."

He opened his wallet and showed a badge and a card. Investigator. His name was Ennis.

Jared slumped in his chair, gripping the arms to hide the sudden shaking of his hands. Ennis seated himself opposite without an invitation.

"About the Manning child's body," he said easily.

Jared had control of himself by now. He stared at Ennis with a puzzled frown.

"The Manning child? The one that was kidnapped? Have they found her?"

"Now, Mr. Sloane—" The man glanced around him at the small, tidy office, at the respectable elderly undertaker in his neat black suit. He seemed disconcerted. Then he leaned forward confidentially.

"Perhaps there's been some mistake," he said. "This isn't for publication yet, but we have a man in custody—a man who's a very hot suspect."

"Good. I hope you nail him. Anybody who would kidnap a child, let alone murder her, killing's too good for him."

"Did I say she was murdered?"

"You said 'the Manning child's body.' "

"So I did. Well, I'll level with you, Mr. Sloane. This man—we've had him for two days now, and he's begun to talk. In fact, to be frank, we have a full confession. And he says that on March 30th he drove through Middleton with the body in his car, and left it on the porch in front of a funeral parlor just off the highway. He told us the name on the sign was Sloane."

"Nobody left any remains or anything else on my porch on the night of March 30th," Jared said steadily. It was perfectly true; it had been quarter to three on the morning of March 31st.

"Now look, Mr. Sloane, please understand we're not accusing you of anything. Of course concealment of a dead body is a criminal offense, but we're not disposed to be tough about it. I can understand very well what a shock it must have been, and that you might want a little while to make up your mind what to do about it—after all, it isn't pleasant to have a lot of that kind of publicity turned on you through no fault of your own. I'll give you my word—you let us take the child away quietly and we may never have to make public at all where we found the body."

If you had come that very day, Jared thought, I might have done it. Then he had a vision of Martha, in her short pink dress, her dark hair tied with a big pink ribbon, fondling her doll and smiling at her mother. He shook his head stubbornly.

"The man is lying to you," he said. "He must have noticed my sign as he passed through here and sent you on a wild goose chase. I've been in business in Middleton for twenty years, everybody knows me. Do you think I'd be likely to help a kidnapper by hiding the evidence against him? Besides—"

It had been on the tip of his tongue to add that he had a little girl of his own: he stopped himself just in time.

"Besides," he went on, "nobody would know better than a man in my profession that it's a crime to dispose of remains illegally. It's the last thing I'd do."

"Well, you may be right, Mr. Sloane. We'll go over it with him again. So, just for the record, let me have a look around your place so I can report that the body's not here, and we may never have to bother you again. You surely have no objection to that."

Jared felt himself turning pale. He had a sudden swift picture of Ennis, finding the display room and the slumber room and the preparation room and the chapel all empty, asking next to go through his living quarters—and in the kitchen saying: "Where does that door lead to?"

"What are you aiming to do?" he asked sarcastically. "Dig up my back yard to see if I've buried Diana Manning in it for no reason under the sun? Yes, I do object. This is my home as well as my place of business. I know my rights as a citizen. I'm not going to have anybody snooping through my private property without a search warrant—and I take it you haven't got that."

"No, I haven't, Mr. Sloane." The young man's friendly eyes had turned cold, and his voice was hard. "If that's the way you feel about it, I can go to McMinnville and get one, and be back here with it and the sheriff within an hour. I don't know why a respectable business man like you should want to obstruct justice and help a dirty rat like the man we've got in custody, but that's what it amounts to.

"Very well. I'll see you an hour from now. And if you've got that body here and make any attempt to hide it or take it away somewhere in your hearse, we'll find that out, too." He paused. His voice grew more conciliatory. "If you want to change your mind—" he said. Jared shook his head again. Ennis picked up his brief case and marched out of the building. Jared watched him climb into the car parked in front and make a U-turn back toward McMinnville.

He stood still for a long minute. Then he picked up the sign which said: "Closed—Be Back Soon," and stuck it in the front door and locked up. He went back to the kitchen and unlocked the door to the sitting room, and this time he took out the key and relocked it on the inside. Then slowly, he walked downstairs to the family.

He reached up and pulled the curtain open on the two windows— the first time they had ever been opened since the room had been furnished for Gussie. It was a risk, though a small one, but it had to be taken for a few moments.

In the white light of day there was something bleak and forlorn about the cozy scene. Dad was reading the paper, Mother knitting, Ben and Emma playing cards, Luke working on his model ship, Gussie at the piano, just as always. Somehow they seemed a little withered, less like living people than like mummies—even darling Gussie, in her new blue dress. Only Martha, the newcomer, looked as fresh and blooming as they all had been in the warm gaslight of his happy evenings.

He sighed deeply. He reached up to the chandelier, and turned on all the jets. Then he sat down in his chair.

He loved them so much. They were his, they belonged to him and he belonged to them. An orphan and a foundling, but he had a family, he had not gone lonely through all his life. A man not made like other men, yet he had loved a woman, and for ten years now she had been his dearly beloved wife.

On an impulse, still half-embarrassed by the eyes of the others on him, he went to the piano bench, put his arms around Gussie, and for the first time kissed her on the lips. Her mouth was cold and dry, but he had never known it warm and moist. Then he went back to sit in his chair.

After a while he began to smell the gas—it was natural gas, but they put something in it to warn people if it was turned on by accident. When waves of giddiness began to flow over him, he knew the room was full. He must not delay until he was too sick and dizzy.

He reached into his coat pocket, took out a kitchen match and struck it on the sole of his shoe.

© By Gerald Kersh

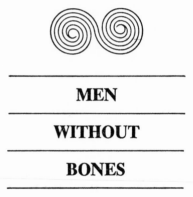

MEN

WITHOUT

BONES

We were loading bananas into the *Claire Dodge* at Puerto Pobre, when a feverish little fellow came aboard. Everyone stepped aside to let him pass—even the soldiers who guard the port with nickel-plated Remington rifles, and who go barefoot but wear polished leather leggings. They stood back from him because they believed that he was afflicted-of-God, mad; harmless but dangerous; best left alone.

All the time the naphtha flares were hissing, and from the hold came the reverberation of the roaring voice of the foreman of the gang down below crying: "Fruta! Fruta! *FRUTA!*" The leader of the dock gang bellowed the same cry, throwing down stem after stem of brilliant green bananas. The occasion would be memorable for this, if for nothing else—the magnificence of the night, the bronze of

46

the Negro foreman shining under the flares, the jade green of that fruit, and the mixed odors of the waterfront. Out of one stem of bananas ran a hairy grey spider, which frightened the crew and broke the banana-chain, until a Nicaraguan boy, with a laugh, killed it with his foot. It was harmless, he said.

It was about then that the madman came aboard, unhindered, and asked me: "Bound for where?"

He spoke quietly and in a carefully modulated voice; but there was a certain blank, lost look in his eyes that suggested to me that I keep within ducking distance of his restless hands which, now that I think of them, put me in mind of the gray, hairy, bird-eating spider.

"Mobile, Alabama," I said.

"Take me along?" he asked.

"None of my affair. Sorry. Passenger myself," I said. "The skipper's ashore. Better wait for him on the wharf. He's the boss."

"Would you happen, by any chance, to have a drink about you?"

Giving him some rum, I asked: "How come they let you aboard?"

"I'm not crazy," he said. "Not actually . . . a little fever, nothing more. Malaria, dengue fever, jungle fever, rat-bite fever. Feverish country, this, and others of the same nature. Allow me to introduce myself. My name is Goodbody, Doctor of Science of Osbaldeston University. Does it convey nothing to you? No? Well then; I was assistant to Professor Yeoward. Does *that* convey anything to you?"

I said: "Yeoward, Professor Yeoward? Oh yes. He was lost, wasn't he, somewhere in the upland jungle beyond the source of the Amer River?"

"Correct!" cried the little man who called himself Goodbody. "I saw him get lost."

Fruta!—Fruta!—Fruta!—Fruta! came the voices of the men in the hold. There was rivalry between their leader and the big black stevedore ashore. The flares spluttered. The green bananas came down. And a kind of sickly sigh came out of the jungle, off the rotting river—not a wind, not a breeze—something like the foul breath of high fever.

Trembling with eagerness and, at the same time, shaking with fever chills, so that he had to use two hands to raise his glass to his lips—even so, he spilled most of the rum—Doctor Goodbody said:

"For God's sake, get me out of this country—take me to Mobile—hide me in your cabin!"

"I have no authority," I said, "but you are an American citizen; you can identify yourself; the Consul will send you home."

"No doubt. But that would take time. The Consul thinks I am crazy too. And if I don't get away, I fear that I really will go out of my mind. Can't you help me? I'm afraid."

"Come on, now," I said. "No one shall hurt you while I'm around. What are you afraid of?"

"Men without bones," he said, and there was something in his voice that stirred the hairs on the back of my neck. "Little fat men without bones!"

I wrapped him in a blanket, gave him some quinine, and let him sweat and shiver for a while, before I asked, humoring him: "What men without bones?"

He talked in fits and starts in his fever, his reason staggering just this side of delirium:

". . . What men without bones? . . . They are nothing to be afraid of, actually. It is they who are afraid of you. You can kill them with your boot, or with a stick. . . . They are something like jelly. No, it is not really fear—it is the nausea, the disgust they inspire. It overwhelms. It paralyses! I have seen a jaguar, I tell you—a full-grown jaguar—stand frozen, while they clung to him, in hundreds, and ate him up alive! Believe me, I saw it. Perhaps it is some oil they secrete, some odor they give out . . . I don't know . . ."

Then, weeping, Doctor Goodbody said: "Oh, nightmare—nightmare—nightmare! To think of the depths to which a noble creature can be degraded by hunger! Horrible, horrible!"

"Some debased form of life that you found in the jungle above the source of the Amer?" I suggested. "Some degenerate kind of anthropoid?"

"No, no, no. *Men!* Now surely you remember Professor Yeoward's ethnological expedition?"

"It was lost," I said.

"All but me," he said. ". . . We had bad luck. At the Anaña Rapids we lost two canoes, half our supplies and most of our instruments.

And also Doctor Terry, and Jack Lambert, and eight of our carriers . . .

"Then we were in Ahu territory where the Indians use poison darts, but we made friends with them and bribed them to carry our stuff westward through the jungle . . . because, you see, all science starts with a guess, a rumor, an old wives' tale; and the object of Professor Yeoward's expedition was to investigate a series of Indian folk tales that tallied. Legends of a race of gods that came down from the sky in a great flame when the world was very young. . . .

"Line by criss-cross line, and circle by concentric circle, Yeoward localized the place in which these tales had their root—an unexplored place that has no name because the Indians refuse to give it a name, it being what they call a 'bad place'."

His chills subsiding and his fever abating, Doctor Goodbody spoke calmly and rationally now. He said, with a short laugh: "I don't know why, whenever I get a touch of fever, the memory of those boneless men comes back in a nightmare to give me the horrors. . . .

"So, we went to look for the place where the gods came down in flame out of the night. The little tattooed Indians took us to the edge of the Ahu territory and then put down their packs and asked for their pay, and no consideration would induce them to go further. We were going, they said, to a very bad place. Their chief, who had been a great man in his day, sign-writing with a twig, told us that he had strayed there once, and drew a picture of something with an oval body and four limbs, at which he spat before rubbing it out with his foot in the dirt. Spiders? we asked. Crabs? What?

"So we were forced to leave what we could not carry with the old chief against our return, and go on unaccompanied, Yeoward and I, through thirty miles of the rottenest jungle in the world. We made about a quarter of a mile in a day . . . a pestilential place! When that stinking wind blows out of the jungle, I smell nothing but death, and panic. . . .

"But, at last, we cut our way to the plateau and climbed the slope, and there we saw something marvelous. It was something that had been a gigantic machine. Originally it must have been a pear-shaped thing, at least a thousand feet long and, in its widest part, six hundred feet in diameter. I don't know of what metal it had been made, because there was only a dusty outline of a hull and certain ghostly remains of unbelievably intricate mechanisms to prove that it had ever been. We could not guess from where it had come; but the impact of its landing had made a great valley in the middle of the plateau.

"It was the discovery of the age! It proved that countless ages ago, this planet had been visited by people from the stars! Wild with excitement, Yeoward and I plunged into this fabulous ruin. But whatever we touched fell away to fine powder.

"At last, on the third day, Yeoward found a semicircular plate of some extraordinarily hard metal, which was covered with the most maddeningly familiar diagrams. We cleaned it, and for twenty-four hours, scarcely pausing to eat and drink, Yeoward studied it. And, then, before the dawn of the fifth day he awoke me, with a great cry, and said: 'It's a map, a map of the heavens, and a chart of a course from Mars to Earth!'

"And he showed me how those ancient explorers of space had proceeded from Mars to Earth, via the Moon. . . . 'To crash on this naked plateau in this green hell of a jungle?' I wondered. 'Ah, but was it a jungle then?' said Yeoward. 'This may have happened five million years ago!'

"I said: 'Oh, but surely! it took only a few hundred years to bury Rome. How could this thing have stayed above ground for five thousand years, let alone five million?' Yeoward said: 'It didn't. The earth swallows things and regurgitates them. This is a volcanic region. One little upheaval can swallow a city, and one tiny peristalsis in the bowels of the earth can bring its remains to light again a million years later. So it must have been with the machine from Mars . . .'

" 'I wonder who was inside it,' I said. Yeoward replied: 'Very likely some utterly alien creatures that couldn't tolerate the Earth, and died, or else were killed in the crash. No skeleton could survive such a space of time.'

"So, we built up the fire, and Yeoward went to sleep. Having slept, I watched. Watched for what? I didn't know. Jaguars, peccaries, snakes? None of these beasts climbed up to the plateau; there was nothing for them up there. Still, unaccountably, I was afraid.

"There was the weight of ages on the place. *Respect old age,* one is told. . . . The greater the age, the deeper the respect, you might say. But it is not respect; it is dread, it is fear of time and death, sir! . . . I must have dozed, because the fire was burning low—I had been most careful to keep it alive and bright—when I caught my first glimpse of the boneless men.

"Starting up, I saw, at the rim of the plateau, a pair of eyes that picked up luminosity from the fading light of the fire. *A jaguar,* I thought, and took up my rifle. But it could not have been a jaguar because, when I looked left and right I saw that the plateau was ringed with pairs of shining eyes . . . as it might be, a collar of opals; and there came to my nostrils an odor of God knows what.

"Fear has its smell as an animal-trainer will tell you. Sickness has its smell—ask any nurse. These smells compel healthy animals to fight or to run away. This was a combination of the two, plus a stink of vegetation gone bad. I fired at the pair of eyes I had first seen. Then, all the eyes disappeared while, from the jungle, there came a chattering and a twittering of monkeys and birds, as the echoes of the shot went flapping away.

"And then, thank God, the dawn came. I should not have liked to see by articial light the thing I had shot between the eyes.

"It was grey and, in texture, tough and gelatinous. Yet in form, externally, it was not unlike a human being. It had eyes, and there were either vestiges—or rudiments—of head, and neck, and a kind of limbs.

"Yeoward told me that I must pull myself together; overcome my 'childish revulsion,' he called it; and look into the nature of the beast. I may say that he kept a long way away from it when I opened it. It was my job as zoologist of the expedition, and I had to do it. Microscopes and other delicate instruments had been lost with the canoes. I worked with a knife and forceps. And found? Nothing: a kind of digestive system enclosed in very tough jelly, a rudimentary nervous system, and a brain about the size of a walnut. The entire creature, stretched out, measured four feet.

"In a laboratory I could tell you, perhaps, something about it . . . with an assistant or two, to keep me company. As it was, I did what I could with a hunting-knife and forceps, without dyes or microscope, swallowing my nausea—it was a nauseating thing!—memorizing what I found. But, as the sun rose higher, the thing liquefied, melted, until by nine o'clock there was nothing but a glutinous gray puddle, with two green eyes swimming in it. . . . And these eyes—I can see them now—burst with a thick *pop,* making a detestable sticky ripple in that puddle of corruption. . . .

"After that, I went away for a while. When I came back, the sun had burned it all away, and there was nothing but something like what you see after a dead jellyfish has evaporated on a hot beach. Slime. Yeoward had a white face when he asked me: 'What the devil is it?' I told him that I didn't know, that it was something outside my experience, and that although I pretended to be a man of science with a detached mind, nothing would induce me ever to touch one of the things again.

"Yeoward said: 'You're getting hysterical, Goodbody. Adopt the proper attitude. God knows, we are not here for the good of our health. Science, man, science! Not a day passes but some doctor pokes his fingers into fouler things than that!' I said: 'Don't you believe it. Professor Yeoward, I have handled and dissected some pretty queer things in my time, but this is something repulsive. I have nerves, I dare say. Maybe we should have brought a psychiatrist. . . . I notice, by the way, that you aren't too anxious to come close to me after I've tampered with that thing. I'll shoot one with pleasure, but if you want to investigate it, try it yourself and see!'

"Yeoward said that he was deeply occupied with his metal plate. There was no doubt, he told me, that this machine that had been had come from Mars. But, evidently, he preferred to keep the fire between himself and me, after I had touched that abomination of hard jelly.

"Yeoward kept himself to himself, rummaging in the ruin. I went about my business, which was to investigate forms of animal life. I do not know what I might have found, if I had had—I don't say the courage, because I didn't lack that—if I had had some company. Alone, my nerve broke.

"It happened one morning. I went into the jungle that surrounded us, trying to swallow the fear that choked me, and drive away the sense of revulsion that not only made me want to turn and run, but made me afraid to turn my back even to get away. You may or may not know that, of all the beasts that live in that jungle, the most impregnable is the sloth. He finds a stout limb, climbs out on it, and hangs from it by his twelve steely claws; a tardigrade that lives on leaves. Your tardigrade is so tenacious that even in death, shot through the heart, it will hang on to its branch. It has an immensely tough hide covered by an impenetrable coat of coarse, matted hair. A panther or a jaguar is helpless against the passive resistance of such a creature. It finds itself a tree, which it does not leave until it has eaten every leaf, and chooses for a sleeping place a branch exactly strong enough to bear its weight.

"In this detestable jungle, on one of my brief expeditions—brief, because I was alone and afraid—I stopped to watch a giant sloth hanging motionless from the largest bough of a half-denuded tree, asleep, impervious, indifferent. Then, out of that stinking green twilight came a horde of those jellyfish things. They *poured up* the tree, and writhed along the branch.

"Even the sloth, which generally knows no fear, was afraid. It tried to run away, hooked itself on to a thinner part of the branch, which broke. It fell, and at once was covered with a shuddering mass of jelly. Those boneless men do not bite: they suck. And, as they suck, their color changes from gray to pink and then to brown.

"But they are afraid of us. There is race-memory involved here. We repel them, and they repel us. When they became aware of my presence, they—I was going to say, ran away—they slid away, dissolved into the shadows that kept dancing and dancing and dancing under the trees. And the horror came upon me, so that I ran away, and arrived back at our camp, bloody about the face with thorns, and utterly exhausted.

"Yeoward was lancing a place in his ankle. A tourniquet was tied under his knee. Near-by lay a dead snake. He had broken its back with that same metal plate, but it had bitten him first. He said: 'What kind of a snake do you call this? I'm afraid it is venomous. I feel a numbness in my cheeks and around my heart, and I cannot feel my hands.'

"I said: 'Oh my God! You've been bitten by a jarajaca!'

" 'And we have lost our medical supplies,' he said, with regret.

'And there is so much work left to do. Oh, dear me, dear me! . . . Whatever happens, my dear fellow, take *this* and get back.'

"And he gave me that semi-circle of unknown metal as a sacred trust. Two hours later, he died. That night the circle of glowing eyes grew narrower. I emptied my rifle at it, time and again. At dawn, the boneless men disappeared.

"I heaped rocks on the body of Yeoward. I made a pylon, so that the men without bones could not get at him. Then—oh, so dreadfully lonely and afraid!—I shouldered my pack and took my rifle and my machete, and ran away, down the trail we had covered. But I lost my way.

"Can by can of food, I shed weight. Then my rifle went, and my ammunition. After that, I threw away even my machete. A long time later, that semi-circular plate became too heavy for me, so I tied it to a tree with liana-vine, and went on.

"So I reached the Ahu territory, where the tattooed men nursed me and were kind to me. The women chewed my food for me, before they fed me, until I was strong again. Of the stores we had left there, I took only as much as I might need, leaving the rest as payment for guides and men to man the canoe down the river. And so I got back out of the jungle. . . .

"Please give me a little more rum." His hand was steady, now, as he drank, and his eyes were clear.

I said to him: "Assuming that what you say is true: these 'boneless men'—they were, I presume, the Martians? Yet it sounds unlikely, surely? Do invertebrates smelt hard metals and——"

"Who said anything about Martians?" cried Doctor Goodbody. "No, no, no! The Martians came here, adapted themselves to new conditions of life. Poor fellows, they changed, sank low; went through a whole new process— a painful process of evolution. What I'm trying to tell you, you fool, is that Yeoward and I did *not* discover Martians. Idiot, don't you see? *Those boneless things are men. We are Martians!*"

◎ By Damon Knight

NOT

WITH

A

BANG

Ten months after the last plane passed over, Rolf Smith knew beyond doubt that only one other human being had survived. Her name was Louise Oliver, and he was sitting opposite her in a department-store café in Salt Lake City. They were eating canned Vienna sausages and drinking coffee.

Sunlight struck through a broken pane like a judgment. Inside and outside, there was no sound; only a stifling rumor of absence. The clatter of dishware in the kitchen, the heavy rumble of streetcars:

never again. There was sunlight; and silence; and the watery, astonished eyes of Louise Oliver.

He leaned forward, trying to capture the attention of those fishlike eyes for a second. "Darling," he said, "I respect your views, naturally. But I've got to make you see that they're impractical."

She looked at him with faint surprise, then away again. Her head shook slightly. *No. No, Rolf, I will not live with you in sin.*

Smith thought of the women of France, of Russia, of Mexico, of the South Seas. He had spent three months in the ruined studios of a radio station in Rochester, listening to the voices until they stopped. There had been a large colony in Sweden, including an English cabinet minister. They reported that Europe was gone. Simply gone; there was not an acre that had not been swept clean by radioactive dust. They had two planes and enough fuel to take them anywhere on the Continent; but there was nowhere to go. Three of them had the plague; then eleven; then all.

There was a bomber pilot who had fallen near a government radio station in Palestine. He did not last long, because he had broken some bones in the crash; but he had seen the vacant waters where the Pacific Islands should have been. It was his guess that the Arctic ice fields had been bombed.

There were no reports from Washington, from New York, from London, Paris, Moscow, Chungking, Sydney. You could not tell who had been destroyed by disease, who by the dust, who by bombs.

Smith himself had been a laboratory assistant in a team that was trying to find an antibiotic for the plague. His superiors had found one that worked sometimes, but it was a little too late. When he left, Smith took along with him all there was of it—forty ampoules, enough to last him for years.

Louise had been a nurse in a genteel hospital near Denver. According to her, something rather odd had happened to the hospital as she was approaching it the morning of the attack. She was quite calm when she said this, but a vague look came into her eyes and her shattered expression seemed to slip a little more. Smith did not press her for an explanation.

Like himself, she had found a radio station which still functioned, and when Smith discovered that she had not contracted the plague, he agreed to meet her. She was, apparently, naturally immune. There must have been others, a few at least; but the bombs and the dust had not spared them.

It seemed very awkward to Louise that not one Protestant minister was left alive.

The trouble was, she really meant it. It had taken Smith a long time to believe it, but it was true. She would not sleep in the same hotel with him, either; she expected and received, the utmost courtesy and decorum. Smith had learned his lesson. He walked on the outside of the rubble-heaped sidewalks; he opened doors for her, when there were still doors; he held her chair; he refrained from swearing. He courted her.

Louise was forty or thereabout, at least five years older than Smith. He often wondered how old she thought she was. The shock of seeing whatever it was that had happened to the hospital, the patients she had cared for, had sent her mind scuttling back to her childhood. She tacitly admitted that everyone else in the world was dead, but she seemed to regard it as something one did not mention.

A hundred times in the last three weeks, Smith had felt an almost irresistible impulse to break her thin neck and go his own way. But there was no help for it; she was the only woman in the world, and he needed her. If she died, or left him, he died. Old bitch! he thought to himself furiously, and carefully kept the thought from showing on his face.

"Louise, honey," he told her gently, "I want to spare your feelings as much as I can. You know that."

"Yes, Rolf," she said, staring at him with the face of a hypnotized chicken.

Smith forced himself to go on. "We've got to face the facts, unpleasant as they may be. Honey, we're the only man and the only woman there are. We're like Adam and Eve in the Garden of Eden."

Louise's face took on a slightly disgusted expression. She was obviously thinking of fig leaves.

"Think of the generations unborn," Smith told her, with a tremor in his voice. Think about me for once. Maybe you're good for another ten years, maybe not. Shuddering, he thought of the second stage of the disease—the helpless rigidity, striking without warning.

He'd had one such attack already, and Louise had helped him out of it. Without her, he would have stayed like that till he died, the hypodermic that would save him within inches of his rigid hand. He thought desperately, If I'm lucky, I'll get at least two kids out of you before you croak. Then I'll be safe.

He went on, "God didn't mean for the human race to end like this. He spared us, you and me, to—" he paused; how could he say it without offending her? "parents" wouldn't do—too suggestive "—to carry on the torch of life," he ended. There. That was sticky enough.

Louise was staring vaguely over his shoulder. Her eyelids blinked regularly, and her mouth made little rabbitlike motions in the same rhythm.

Smith looked down at his wasted thighs under the table-top. I'm not strong enough to force her, he thought. Christ, if I were strong enough!

He felt the futile rage again, and stifled it. He had to keep his head, because this might be his last chance. Louise had been talking lately, in the cloudy language she used about everything, of going up in the mountains to pray for guidance. She had not said "alone," but it was easy enough to see that she pictured it that way. He had to argue her around before her resolve stiffened. He concentrated furiously and tried once more.

The pattern of words went by like a distant rumbling. Louise heard a phrase here and there; each of them fathered chains of thought, binding her reverie tighter. "Our duty to humanity . . ." Mama had often said—that was in the old house on Waterbury Street, of course, before Mama had taken sick—she had said, "Child, your duty is to be clean, polite, and God-fearing. Pretty doesn't matter. There's plenty of plain women that have got themselves good, Christian husbands."

Husbands . . . To have and to hold . . . Orange blossoms, and the bridesmaids; the organ music. Through the haze, she saw Rolf's lean, wolfish face. Of course, he was the only one she'd ever get; *she* knew that well enough. Gracious, when a girl was past twenty-five, she had to take what she could get.

But I sometimes wonder if he's really a nice man, she thought.

". . . in the eyes of God . . ." She remembered the stained-glass windows in the old First Episcopalian Church, and how she always thought God was looking down at her through the brilliant transparency. Perhaps He was still looking at her, though it seemed sometimes that He had forgotten. Well, of course she realized that marriage customs changed, and if you couldn't have a regular minister . . . But it was really a shame, an outrage almost, that if she were actually going to marry this man, she couldn't have all those nice things. . . . There wouldn't even be any wedding presents. Not even that. But of course Rolf would give her anything she wanted. She saw his face again, noticed the narrow black eyes staring at her with ferocious purpose, the thin mouth that jerked in a slow, regular tic, the hairy lobes of the ears below the tangle of black hair.

He oughtn't to let his hair grow so long, she thought. It isn't quite decent. Well, she could change all that. If she did marry him, she'd certainly make him change his ways. It was no more than her duty.

He was talking now about a farm he'd seen outside town—a good big house and a barn. There was no stock, he said, but they could get some later. And they'd plant things, and have their own food to eat, not go to restaurants all the time.

She felt a touch on her hand, lying pale before her on the table. Rolf's brown, stubby fingers, black-haired above and below the knuckles, were touching hers. He had stopped talking for a moment, but now he was speaking again, still more urgently. She drew her hand away.

He was saying, ". . . and you'll have the finest wedding dress you ever saw, with a bouquet. Everything you want, Louise, everything . . ."

A wedding dress! And flowers, even if there couldn't be any minister! Well, why hadn't the fool said so before?

Rolf stopped halfway through a sentence, aware that Louise had said quite clearly. "Yes, Rolf, I will marry you if you wish."

Stunned, he wanted her to repeat it but dared not ask, "What did you say?" for fear of getting some fantastic answer, or none at all. He breathed deeply. He said, "Today, Louise?"

She said, "Well, *today* . . . I don't know quite . . . Of course if you think you can make all the arrangements in time, but it does seem . . ."

Triumph surged through Smith's body. He had the advantage now, and he'd ride it. "Say you will, dear," he urged her. "Say yes, and make me the happiest man . . ."

Even then, his tongue balked at the rest of it; but it didn't matter. She nodded submissively. "Whatever you think best, Rolf."

He rose, and she allowed him to kiss her pale, sapless cheek. "We'll leave right away," he said. "If you'll excuse me for just a minute, dear?"

He waited for her "Of course" and then left, making footprints in the furred carpet of dust down toward the end of the room. Just a few more hours he'd have to speak to her like that, and then, in her eyes, she'd be committed to him forever. Afterward, he could do with her as he liked—beat her when he pleased, submit her to any proof of his scorn and revulsion, use her. Then it would not be too bad, being the last man on earth—not bad at all. She might even have a daughter. . . .

He found the washroom door and entered. He took a step inside, and froze, balanced by a trick of motion, upright but helpless. Panic struck at his throat as he tried to turn his head and failed; tried to scream, and failed. Behind him, he was aware of a tiny click as the door, cushioned by the hydraulic check, shut forever. It was not locked; but its other side bore the warning MEN.

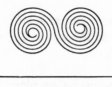

PARTY

GAMES

The moment Alice Jarman opened the front door and saw Simon Potter on the step she knew that there would be trouble.

Behind her the party was growing noisy. Already a fight had broken out. Two boys were shouting at each other and there was an occasional thump as one or other of them was thrown heavily against the wall. But it was the usual sort of fight. A party at which small boys didn't fight wasn't much of a party.

Simon Potter said: "Good afternoon, Mrs. Jarman."

He was eight years of age and he was not the kind of boy who would become involved in a fight. He was polite, neat, quiet, and clever; and he was unpopular. His unpopularity was such as to keep him out of a scuffle rather than bring one down upon him. He was a cold little boy. Even as he stood there with his deferential smile he gave Alice the shivers.

He wore a new raincoat, his shoes were highly polished—probably by himself, she thought—and his pallid brown hair was sleeked back. He carried a neatly wrapped present.

Alice stepped back. Simon came on into the hall.

At the same moment the door of the sitting-room was flung back and Ronnie came pounding out. He stopped when he saw Simon. He said what Alice had been sure he would say.

"I didn't invite *him*."

"Now, Ronnie—"

"Many happy returns, Ronnie," said Simon, holding out the package.

Ronnie could not help looking at it. He could not help the instinctive movement of his hand towards it. Then he shook his head and looked up at Alice.

"But, mum . . ."

She smoothed it over—or, rather, blurred it over. The noise and exuberance from the sitting-room helped. Ronnie was unable to concentrate. He wanted to stay and argue, wanted to accept the present, and wanted to get back into the uproar. The three things bubbled up and blended in his mind. Alice took Simon's coat and steered him toward the gaiety. He didn't need to be told to wipe his feet; he added nothing to the muddy treads which some of them had left. Ronnie tried to say something, but somehow he was holding the package and then he began to unwrap it as he followed Simon into the room.

Alice stood by the door for a minute or two and looked in.

"Hey . . . look . . . super!"

Ronnie tossed shreds of paper aside and opened the box within. He took out a model crane and held it up.

"It's battery operated," said Simon quietly.

It was a simple statement, but it wiped the pleasure off Ronnie's face. The others, who had crowded closer, edged back and turned to stare at Simon. His present was more expensive than any which they had brought. He had done the wrong thing. He was always doing the wrong thing. The fact that he did a thing made it wrong.

A large boy with carroty hair pushed Ronnie. Ronnie put the crane on a chair and pushed him back. A girl with a blue hair-ribbon said, "Oh, don't start that again," and stepped to one side. She found herself close to Simon. He smiled. He looked at her and then at another girl a few feet away as though to draw them both nearer to him. "Always talking to girls," Ronnie had once said of Simon to his mother. Alice watched. Yes, she could see that he was a boy who would talk to girls because he had nothing to say to boys. But the girls were not flattered. Instead of listening to him they giggled and made eyes at each other and then scurried away, looking back and still giggling.

Alice went towards the kitchen and drew the curtains. It would soon be quite dark outside. In summer they could have had the party in the garden; but Ronnie had elected to be born in the winter, so most of his celebrations had been accompanied by a trampling of wet feet into the house and a great fussing over scarves and gloves and rain hoods and mackintoshes when the guests left.

Tom would be home in another twenty minutes or so. She would be glad to see him. Even though the din would not diminish, it would somehow be more tolerable when shared. Tom would organize games, jolly them all along, and make the little girls in particular shriek with laughter. Until he came she couldn't concentrate on the food or on anything else. She had to keep dashing back to the sitting-room to make sure that nobody was really getting hurt and nobody was being neglected. She had started them off on a game of musical chairs, but her piano playing was pretty terrible, and while she was at the keyboard there had been chaos behind her. Then she had suggested a treasure hunt, only to realize that she had done nothing about hiding the treasure before the party started.

She was not very good at organizing parties. The sheer pressure of the children's excitement overpowered her. No matter how much trouble she took in the days beforehand, when the birthday itself came she was never ready for it.

Not that it mattered, Tom assured her. Just open the door, let 'em in, and leave 'em to it. When there were signs of the furniture cracking up under the strain, bring on the sandwiches and jelly and cake and ice cream.

It was all very well for Tom. He did not get home until after she had taken the first shock of the impact. Twenty children together were not just twenty separate children added together, one plus one and so on: they combined into something larger and more terrifying. There was no telling what they might do if the circumstances were right . . . or wrong, depending on the way you looked at it.

There was a howl of derision from the sitting-room. Alice nerved herself to go and make another inspection.

By the time she got there it was impossible to tell what the cause of the howl had been. Simon Potter was backed against a wall, while Ronnie and his best friend grinned and bobbed their heads with a lunatic merriment, exaggerating the movement, slapping their sides like bad actors in a school play.

Ronnie saw his mother watching him. His grin became genuine and affectionate. Then, before she could frown or ask him a silent question, he swung round and gathered up an armful of his presents.

"Come and look! Look what my Dad gave me!"

Somebody groaned theatrically; a boy with pimples blew a loud raspberry. But they all gathered obediently round. It was the accepted thing to do. This was Ronnie's party and Ronnie's birthday, and at some stage it was only fair that he should insist on their inspecting his trophies.

"My Dad gave me this." Alice felt soft inside at the sound of adoration in his voice. "And this. My Dad gave me this as well." It would have been just the same if Tom had given him a cheap scribbling pad or a box of crayons: the devotion would have been there, unwavering. She loved him for loving so intensely.

Simon was watching gravely. He showed neither excitement nor boredom. He did not make approving noises; and he did not exchange glances of sly boredom with anyone. He was remote, dispassionate, unmoved.

Yet somewhere behind that bleak little face there must be envy or, at the very least, sadness. Simon's father had died years ago. His mother had brought him up with a single-minded fervour that allowed him no relaxation and little contact with other children, even though he spent so many hours and days and weeks at school with them. She worked hard in a solicitor's office and managed to run the home as well, determined that the boy should not feel the loss of his father too deeply. Each afternoon he stayed on at school for an hour in a class set aside for children with difficult journeys, difficult home backgrounds, or with working parents who could not leave their jobs in time to meet their children. By the time he did get home Mrs. Potter was in the house waiting for him, ready to devote herself to him. She was proud of the life they made together, proud of their home, and proud of Simon's unfailing neatness and politeness and cleverness.

Alice saw him clear his throat. She saw it rather than heard it—the way he ducked his chin and gulped. He edged forward. She thought for a moment that he was going to ask if he could have a closer look at one of Ronnie's presents. Then he said:

"What about a game?"

The heads turned. They stared at him. It was a little girl who broke the sudden silence. She seemed glad of the diversion.

"Yes. Let's do something. What shall we play?"

"If we could get some pieces of paper"—Simon glanced swiftly at Alice and she realized that all along he must have been aware of her scrutiny—"we could put someone's name on it and—"

"Oh, *paper* games," groaned someone.

"Choose a name," Simon persisted, "and write it down one side of the paper. Then divide the paper up into squares, and have, say, flowers and trees and the names of—well, footballers if you like—and they have to begin with the letters of the name."

The boy who specialized in blowing raspberries blew another. "What's he talking about?" said the girl with the blue hair-ribbon.

"It's easy." Simon's voice rose pleadingly. "You write the name down one side of the paper. Then you write the things you're going to have across the top—that is, I mean, the categories you've chosen. And—"

"Oh, *paper* games."

Alice intervened. It was time for an adult to take control and tell them what to do. She walked into the room and tried desperately to recall the games they had played when she was a child. Her mind refused to render up its memories. All she could remember was a girl going through the seat of a chair and screaming, and a squat little boy who had gathered an audience around him while he practised spitting into the fire.

She said: "Now, everybody." They turned thankfully towards her. "What about Postman's Knock?" she ventured.

There were shrugs and hisses and moans; but the girls squealed hopefully and nudged one another, and in no time at all they were playing Postman's Knock. Alice retreated again, leaving them to it. From the kitchen door she glanced occasionally across the hall and then felt absurdly like a voyeur. Some of the boys behaved with a flamboyant confidence that indicated a prolonged study of films which they ought never to have been allowed to see. Some of the girls wriggled, others relaxed and enjoyed themselves. It was frightening to see in these children of eight and nine years of age the pattern of what they would be as adults—patterns already forming, some already established.

And there was Simon outside the door, waiting. He knocked. The girl who came looked at him warily, prepared to be haughty or coquettish. After they had kissed she wiped her lips with the back of her hand. Simon went back into the room. The girl looked up at the ceiling, and said, loudly enough for him and the others inside to hear: "Ugh!"

They soon tired—the boys sooner than the girls.

"Murder. Let's play murder!"

As the door opened and Ronnie came racing out, Alice tried to assemble good reasons why they should not play murder. She was not quick enough. Already they were racing upstairs. Two boys came into the kitchen, making for the back door, and stopped when they saw her.

"Not outside," said Alice quickly. This, at any rate, she could prevent. "It's too muddy in the back garden. You've got to stay indoors."

They turned and dashed away. She heard footsteps pounding overhead. There was a distant slamming of doors. Lights were switched off. Ronnie appeared suddenly in the splash of brightness thrown out from the kitchen. He and the pimply boy were grinning and whispering. Simon Potter passed them on his way towards the stairs. As he went they clutched each other conspiratorially.

Before Alice could make a move, Ronnie swung towards her.

"Don't mind if we close the door, Mum?" He did not wait for an answer, but closed it quietly and made her a prisoner. She knew there would be yells of protest if she opened it again.

There was a full minute of uneasy silence. In her head it was incongruously noisier than the last hour had been. In the hush a tension was building up. Something was going to snap.

A muffled thump came from upstairs. It was repeated. It might have been somebody banging insistently on the floor or somebody hammering to be let out. If, she thought apprehensively, they had locked somebody into one of the rooms or one of the old cupboards at the far end of the landing . . . the creaky, cold end of this old, cold house . . . Somebody. Simon.

Then there was a convincingly blood-curdling scream.

Alice jerked the door open.

"Put that light out!"

"No, it's all right"—Ronnie's voice came from the landing—"it's over."

Feet pounded downstairs again. Lights were snapped on everywhere. Everyone was shouting at everyone else. Who had been murdered? Who was it?

To Alice's relief the victim was Marion Pickering, a fluffy little blonde with eyes too knowing for her years. There was indeed quite a possibility, thought Alice uncharitably, that Marion would finish up on the front page of certain Sunday newspapers.

Boys and girls swarmed out of every cranny. The hall seemed to boil with activity, then they were all jostling into the sitting-room. There seemed to be twice as many people here as when the party began.

She could hear the shouting. Ronnie was trying to establish some kind of order.

"Who was on the stairs . . . shut up, will you . . . we've got to find who was upstairs and who was downstairs. Now sit down . . . oh, shut up a minute, will you . . ."

The inquiry was going to be a disorderly one. It needed a strong hand to control it. Instead, there was a shouting and shrieking, a carry-over from the tenseness in the dark.

It was really dark now. Alice had not realized how swiftly the evening had taken over. Twenty minutes earlier it would still have been too hazy to play murder; now there was blackness outside the windows.

Through the hubbub of voices she heard a faint but unmistakable sound. It was Tom's key in the front door.

She was halfway across the hall as he came in.

"Darling!"

He had to lean precariously forward to kiss her. He was laden with an armful of garden tools—a trowel sticking out of some torn brown paper, a pair of secateurs, and a short-handled axe.

"Going well?" He nodded towards the sitting-room door.

"I'm so glad you're back."

"Ah. That means it's getting out of hand, mm?"

"Any minute now."

It was so wonderful to see him. His lean, furrowed face was so reassuring. The smell of pipe smoke in his hair, the quiet confidence in his eyes, the sight of his competent, capable hands: everything about him strengthened her and at the same time soothed her.

Yet there was something wrong. Something nagged at her and demanded her attention.

As he turned to lay the garden tools across the umbrella stand she realized that the sound was still going on upstairs—the intermittent thumping she had heard earlier.

"I'll just dump these," Tom was saying, "and then plunge into the fray."

She was jolted into awareness of what he had done with the tools.

"Don't leave them there! For goodness' sake! With all these little monsters in and out . . ."

"All right, all right. I'll take them out to the shed right away."

"It's filthy out there. You'll get mud all over your shoes if . . ." She broke off and laughed, and Tom laughed. "I do sound a nagger, don't I?" she said.

He tucked the implements under his arm and headed for the stairs. "I'll leave them in our room," he said firmly.

Ronnie emerged abruptly and ecstatically from the sitting-room.

"Dad!" He threw himself at his father and butted him, tried to get one arm round him, smiled up at him. "Come on in here—come and see—I've got lots more things. But nothing like you gave me."

"In a minute or two, son. I've just got to go upstairs with some things. I'll be right down."

Alice looked past them into the sitting-room. She moved closer to the door. Then she said:

"Ronnie, where's Simon?"

"Mm?"

"Simon. Where is he?"

Ronnie shrugged and pummelled his father again. "Dunno. Probably gone up to the lavatory."

"Ronnie, if you've done anything . . . locked him in anywhere . . ."

"Don't be long, Dad."

Ronnie twisted away and slid cunningly past his mother. She could not bring herself to pursue him into that whirlpool of arms and legs and boisterous faces.

Tom said: "Anything wrong?"

"I don't know. I just wonder if they've played some horrid joke on Simon Potter."

"Didn't think he'd been invited."

"He wasn't. But he came, poor kid. They've kept him on the edge of things. And now I think they've done something." The din from the sitting-room was so overpowering that she could not swear to hearing the spasmodic thudding from above. "If they've locked him in one of the cupboards, or one of the rooms at the far end of the landing . . ."

"I'll see," said Tom reassuringly.

She was glad to turn away towards the kitchen and leave it all to him. Now everything was going to be all right.

Two boys scuttled out of the sitting-room.

"Mrs. Jarman—where is it, please?"

"First door on the left at the top of the stairs."

They went up two stairs at a time behind Tom. Alice felt comfortable and safe when she returned to the kitchen, instead of being a frightened outcast. She began to put the cups of jelly on a large tray. In another fifteen minutes they could start eating. After that, Tom would organize them while she cleared the food away and did the washing-up.

Ronnie came in. "Mum, where's the stuff for the game? You know, the corpse stuff."

The thudding upstairs had stopped. But there was a louder thump, as though someone had fallen or banged something heavy against the floor. Perhaps it was Tom wrenching open one of the cupboard doors: they were old, stiff, and misshapen.

"Ronnie," she began, "*did* you—"

He did not wait for her to finish. He scooped up the small tray that he had so carefully prepared earlier today, covered with a sheet of thin brown paper, and was gone again.

She heard him yelling at the top of his voice.

"All right, everyone. Come on, sit down. Now, I'm going to put the lights out . . ."

"Hey, wait for us!"

Footsteps hastened down the stairs and two or three boys dashed into the sitting-room. They must have been queueing up for the lavatory. Once one wanted to go, they all wanted to go. Soon, thought Alice, the girls would begin: they would all be smitten at the same time by the idea rather than by the necessity.

"Now," Ronnie was shouting, his voice so hoarse with continuous exertion that it cracked on every third or fourth word, "there's just been a murder. We worked out who did it, but we never got round to dealing with the corpse, did we?"

"That was me," piped up Marion.

"Yes, we know, but . . . hey, shut that door!"

There was the slam of the door and the voice was muffled. After a few minutes there was a loud squeal and a burst of laughter, then another squeal. Alice arranged triangular sandwiches on a plate. She could almost follow the progress of the game by the pitch of the shrieks. "Here's the corpse's hand," Ronnie would be saying—and then he would pass a rubber glove stuffed with rags along the line in the darkness. "Here's some of its hair"—and along would go some of the coarse strands from the old sofa which was rotting away in the garden shed. "And here are its eyeballs." Two peeled grapes would pass from flinching hand to flinching hand.

Everything was ready for the party tea. She went to the door. It was time Tom came down. She could hear no sound from him.

She went to the foot of the stairs and looked up.

"Tom—are you nearly ready?"

There was no reply. Perhaps he had had to join the end of the queue for the lavatory, having more self-control than the over-excited little boys.

Alice decided to put an end to games for the time being. She went to the sitting-room door and opened it.

"Ah, Mum, close the door."

"Time for tea." She switched on the light.

There was a squeal. Then another. And all at once it was hysteria, no longer a joke. One little girl sat staring at what was in her hand and began to scream and scream.

Alice took a step into the room, not believing.

One boy held a severed human hand from which blood dripped over his knees. The girl who could not stop screaming was holding a human eye in her right hand. The girl next to her also held a human eye, squashed and torn. On her left the pimply boy went pale and let a tuft of hair fall between his fingers to the floor.

Alice said: "No." Somehow she kept herself upright. "No. Simon —where's Simon?"

"I'm here, Mrs. Jarman."

The voice was quite calm. She turned to find him standing at one side of the room. She tried to find words. Still cool and detached, he said:

"They locked me in. Ronnie and that one over there locked me in. But I'm all right now. I was let out, and everything's all right now."

She stared at that hideous hand, chopped bloodily off at the wrist. And she recognized it and also the colour of the hair that lay on the floor.

Simon Potter stood quite still as Alice Jarman ran from the room and up the stairs.

She found her husband lying in front of the bedroom cupboard from which he had released the boy. The garden tools lay beside him, splashed with red—the axe that had first smashed in his head and then chopped off a hand, the secateurs that had snipped off a tuft of his hair, and the trowel that had clumsily gouged out his eyes.

Simon, pale but content, was now not the only boy in that room downstairs without a father.

© By Fritz Leiber

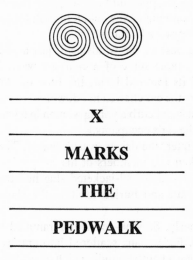

X

MARKS

THE

PEDWALK

Based on material in Ch. 7—"First Clashes of the Wheeled and Footed Sects"—of Vol. 3 of Burger's monumental *History of Traffic*, published by the Foundation for Twenty-Second Century Studies.

The raggedy little old lady with the big shopping bag was in the exact center of the crosswalk when she became aware of the big black car bearing down on her.

Behind the thick bullet-proof glass its seven occupants had a misty look, like men in a diving bell.

She saw there was no longer time to beat the car to either curb. Veering remorselessly, it would catch her in the gutter.

Useless to attempt a feint and double-back, such as any venturesome child executed a dozen times a day. Her reflexes were too slow.

Polite vacuous laughter came from the car's loudspeaker over the engine's mounting roar.

From her fellow pedestrians lining the curbs came a sigh of horror.

The little old lady dipped into her shopping bag and came up with a big blue-black automatic. She held it in both fists, riding the recoils like a rodeo cowboy on a bucking bronco.

Aiming at the base of the windshield, just as a big-game hunter aims at the vulnerable spine of a charging water buffalo over the horny armor of its lowered head, the little old lady squeezed off three shots before the car chewed her down.

From the right-hand curb a young woman in a wheelchair shrieked an obscenity at the car's occupants.

Smythe-de Winter, the driver, wasn't happy. The little old lady's last shot had taken two members of his car pool. Bursting through the laminated glass, the steel-jacketed slug had traversed the neck of Phipps-McHeath and buried itself in the skull of Horvendile-Harker.

Braking viciously, Smythe-de Winter rammed the car over the right-hand curb. Pedestrians scattered into entries and narrow arcades, among them a youth bounding high on crutches.

But Smythe-de Winter got the girl in the wheelchair.

Then he drove rapidly out of the Slum Ring into the Suburbs, a shred of rattan swinging from the flange of his right fore mudguard for a trophy. Despite the two-for-two casualty list, he felt angry and depressed. The secure, predictable world around him seemed to be crumbling.

While his companions softly keened a dirge to Horvy and Phipps and quietly mopped up their blood, he frowned and shook his head.

"They oughtn't to let old ladies carry magnums," he murmured.

Witherspoon-Hobbs nodded agreement across the front-seat corpse. "They oughtn't let 'em carry anything. God, how I hate

Feet," he muttered, looking down at his shrunken legs. "Wheels forever!" he softly cheered.

The incident had immediate repercussions throughout the city. At the combined wake of the little old lady and the girl in the wheelchair, a fiery-tongued speaker inveighed against the White-Walled Fascists of Suburbia, telling to his hearers, the fabled wonders of old Los Angeles, where pedestrians were sacrosanct, even outside crosswalks. He called for a hobnail march across the nearest lawn-bowling alleys and perambulator-traversed golf courses of the motorists.

At the Sunnyside Crematorium, to which the bodies of Phipps and Horvy had been conveyed, an equally impassioned and rather more grammatical orator reminded his listeners of the legendary justice of old Chicago, where pedestrians were forbidden to carry small arms and anyone with one foot off the sidewalk was fair prey. He broadly hinted that a holocaust, primed if necessary with a few tankfuls of gasoline, was the only cure for the Slums.

Bands of skinny youths came loping at dusk out of the Slum Ring into the innermost sections of the larger doughnut of the Suburbs, slashing defenseless tires, shooting expensive watchdogs and scrawling filthy words on the pristine panels of matrons' runabouts which never ventured more than six blocks from home.

Simultaneously, squadrons of young suburban motorcyclists and scooterites roared through the outermost precincts of the Slum Ring, harrying children off sidewalks, tossing stink-bombs through second-story tenement windows and defacing hovel-fronts with paint.

Incident—a thrown brick, a cut corner, monster tracks in the portico of the Auto Club—were even reported from the center of the city, traditionally neutral territory.

The Government hurriedly acted, suspending all traffic between the Center and the Suburbs and establishing a 24-hour curfew in the Slum Ring. Government agents moved only by centipede-car and pogo-hopper to underline the point that they favored neither contending side.

The day of enforced non-movement for Feet and Wheels was spent in furtive vengeful preparations. Behind locked garage doors, machine-guns that fired through the nose ornament were mounted under hoods, illegal scythe blades were welded to oversize hubcaps and the stainless-steel edges of flange fenders were honed to razor sharpness.

While nervous National Guardsmen hopped about the deserted sidewalks of the Slum Ring, grim-faced men and women wearing black arm-bands moved through the webwork of secret tunnels and hidden doors, distributing heavy-caliber small arms and spike-studded paving blocks, piling cobblestones on strategic rooftops and sapping upward from the secret tunnels to create car-traps. Children got ready to soap intersections after dark. The Committee of Pedestrian Safety, sometimes known as Robespierre's Rats, prepared to release its two carefully hoarded anti-tank guns.

At nightfall, under the tireless urging of the Government, representatives of the Pedestrians and the Motorists met on a huge safety island at the boundary of the Slum Ring and the Suburbs.

Underlings began a noisy dispute as to whether Smythe-de Winter had failed to give a courtesy honk before charging, whether the little old lady had opened fire before the car had come within honking distance, how many wheels of Smythe-de's car had been on the sidewalk when he hit the girl in the wheelchair and so on. After a little while the High Pedestrian and the Chief Motorist exchanged cautious winks and drew aside.

The red writhing of a hundred kerosene flares and the mystic yellow pulsing of a thousand firefly lamps mounted on yellow sawhorses ranged around the safety island illumined two tragic, strained faces.

"A word before we get down to business," the Chief Motorist whispered. "What's the current S.Q. of your adults?"

"Forty-one and dropping," the High Pedestrian replied, his eyes fearfully searching from side to side for eavesdroppers. "I can hardly get aides who are halfway *compos mentis*."

"Our own Sanity Quotient is thirty-seven," the Chief Motorist revealed. He shrugged helplessly. "The wheels inside my people's heads are slowing down. I do not think they will be speeded up in my lifetime."

"They say Government's only fifty-two," the other said with a matching shrug.

"Well, I suppose we must scrape out one more compromise," the one suggested hollowly, "though I must confess there are times when I think we're all the figments of a paranoid's dream."

Two hours of concentrated deliberations produced the new Wheel-Foot Articles of Agreement. Among other points, pedestrian handguns were limited to a slightly lower muzzle velocity and to .38 caliber and under, while motorists were required to give three honks at one-block distance before charging a pedestrian in a crosswalk. Two wheels over the curb changed a traffic kill from third-degree manslaughter to petty homicide. Blind pedestrians were permitted to carry hand grenades.

Immediately the Government went to work. The new Wheel-Foot Articles were loudspeakered and posted. Detachments of police and psychiatric social hoppers centipedaled and pogoed through the Slum Ring, seizing outsize weapons and giving tranquilizing jet-injections to the unruly. Teams of hypnotherapists and mechanics scuttled from home to home in the Suburbs and from garage to garage, in-chanting a conformist serenity and stripping illegal armament from cars. On the advice of a rogue psychiatrist, who said it would channel off aggressions, a display of bull-fighting was announced, but this had to be cancelled when a strong protest was lodged by the Decency League, which had a large mixed Wheel-Foot membership.

At dawn, curfew was lifted in the Slum Ring and traffic reopened between the Suburbs and the Center.

After a few uneasy moments it became apparent that the *status quo* had been restored.

Smythe-de Winter tooled his gleaming black machine along the Ring. A thick steel bolt with a large steel washer on either side neatly filled the hole the little old lady's slug had made in the windshield.

A brick bounced off the roof. Bullets pattered against the side windows.

Smythe-de Winter ran a handkerchief around his neck under his collar and smiled.

A block ahead children were darting into the street, cat-calling and thumbing their noses. Behind one of them limped a fat dog with a spiked collar.

Smythe-de suddenly gunned his motor. He didn't hit any of the children, but he got the dog.

A flashing light on the dash showed him the right front tire was losing pressure. Must have hit the collar as well. He thumbed the matching emergency-air button and the flashing stopped.

He turned toward Witherspoon-Hobbs and said with thoughtful satisfaction, "I like a normal orderly world, where you always have a little success, but not champagne-heady; a little failure, but just enough to brace you."

Witherspoon-Hobbs was squinting at the next crosswalk. Its center was discolored by a brownish stain ribbon-tracked by tires.

"That's where you bagged the little old lady, Smythe-de," he remarked. "I'll say this for her now: she had spirit."

"Yes, that's where I bagged her," Smythe-de agreed flatly. He remembered wistfully the witchlike face growing rapidly larger, the jerking shoulders in black bombazine, the wild white-circled eyes. He suddenly found himself feeling that this was a very dull day.

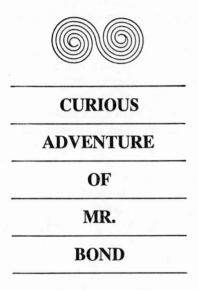

CURIOUS

ADVENTURE

OF

MR.

BOND

Mr. Bond climbed from the wooded slopes of the valley into broad daylight. His Inverness cape, throwing his portly figure into still greater prominence against the floor of tree-tops at his back, was torn and soiled by twigs and thorns and leaves, and he stooped with prim concern to brush off the bits and pieces. After this, he eased his knapsack on his shoulder; and now he blinked his eyes upon the country stretching out before him.

Far away, across the tufted surface of the tableland, there stood a house, with its column of smoke, lighted and still, on the verge of a forest.

A house—an *inn*—he felt it in his very bones! His hunger returned, and became a source of gratification to him. Toiling on, and pulling the brim of his hat over his eyes, he watched the ruby gleam grow bigger and brighter, and when at last he stood beneath the sign, he cried aloud, scarcely able to believe in his good fortune.

"The Rest of the Traveller," he read; and there, too, ran the name of the landlord: "Crispin Sasserach."

The stillness of the night discouraged him, and he was afraid to tap at the curtained window. And now, for the first time, the full weight of his weariness fell upon the traveler. Staring into the black mouth of the porch, he imagined himself to be at rest, in bed, sprawled out, abundantly sleeping, drugged into forgetfulness by a full stomach. He shut his eyes, and drooped a little under his Inverness cape; but when he looked again into the entrance, there stood Crispin Sasserach, holding a lamp between their faces. Mr. Bond's was plump and heavy-jawed, with sagging cheeks, and eyes that scarcely reflected the lamplight; the other face was smooth and large and oval, with small lips pressed into a smile.

"Come in, come in," the landlord whispered, "*do* come in. She is cooking a *lovely* broth to-night!"

He turned and chuckled, holding the lamp above his head.

Through the doorway of this lost, upland inn, Mr. Bond followed the monstrous back of his host. The passage widened and became a hall; and here, amongst the shadows that were gliding from their lurking-places as the lamp advanced, the landlord stopped, and tilted the flat of his hand in the air, as though enjoining his guest to listen. Then Mr. Bond disturbed the silence of the house with a sniff and a sigh. Not only could he smell the "lovely broth"— already, in this outer hall, he tasted it . . . a complex and subtle flavour, pungent, heavy as honey, light as a web in the air, nipping him in the stomach, bringing tears into his eyes.

Mr. Bond stared at Crispin Sasserach, at the shadows beyond, and back again to Crispin Sasserach. The man was standing there, with his huge, oval, hairless face upturned in the light of the lamp he carried; then, impulsively, as though reluctant to cut short such sweet anticipation, he plucked the traveller by the cape and led him to the cheerful living-room, and introduced him, with a flourish of the hand, to Myrtle Sasserach, the landlord's young and small and busy wife, who at that very moment was standing at a round table of great size, beneath the massive centre-beam of the ceiling, her black hair gleaming in the light of many candles, her plump hand dipping a ladle soundlessly into a bowl of steam.

On seeing the woman, whose long lashes were once more directed towards the bowl, Mr. Bond drew his chin primly into his neckcloth, and glanced from her to Crispin Sasserach, and finally he fixed his eyes on the revolutions of the ladle. In a moment, purpose fell upon the living-room, and with swift and nervous gestures the landlord seated his guest at the table, seized the ladle from his wife, plunged it into the bowl, and thrust the brimming plate into the hands of Myrtle, who began at once to walk towards the traveller, the steam of the broth rising into her grave eyes.

After a muttered grace, Mr. Bond pushed out his lips as though he were whispering "spoon."

"Oh, what a lovely broth!" he murmured, catching a drip in his handkerchief.

Crispin Sasserach grinned with delight. "I always say it's the best in the world." Whereupon, with a rush, he broke into peals of falsetto laughter, and blew a kiss towards his wife. A moment later, the two Sasserachs were leaving their guest to himself, bending over their own platefuls of broth, and discussing domestic affairs, as though they had no other person sitting at their table. For some time their voices were scarcely louder than the sound of the broth-eating; but when the traveller's plate was empty, then, in a flash, Crispin Sasserach became again a loud and attentive host. "Now then, sir—another helping?" he suggested, picking up the ladle, and beaming down into the bowl, while Myrtle left her chair and walked a second time towards the guest.

Mr. Bond said that he would, and pulled his chair a little closer to the table. Into his blood and bones, life had returned with twice its accustomed vigour; his very feet were as light as though he had soaked them in a bath of pine needles.

"There you are, sir! Myrtle's coming! Lord a'mighty, how I wish I was tasting it for the first time!" Then, spreading his elbows, the landlord crouched over his own steaming plateful, and chuckled again. "This broth is a wine in itself! It's a wine in itself, b'God! It staggers a man!" Flushed with excitement, his oval face looked larger than ever, and his auburn hair, whirled into bellicose corkscrews, seemed to burn brighter, as though someone had brought the bellows to it.

Stirred by the broth, Mr. Bond began to describe minutely his journey out of the valley. His voice grew as prosy, his words as involved, as though he were talking at home amongst his own people. "Now, let me see—where was I?" he buzzed again and again. And later: "I was very glad to see your light, I can tell you!" he chuckled. Then Crispin jumped up from the table, his small mouth pouting with laughter.

The evening shifted to the fireside. Fresh logs cracked like pistol shots as Crispin Sasserach dropped them into the flames. The traveller could wish for nothing better than to sit here by the hearth, talking plangently to Crispin, and slyly watching Myrtle as she cleared away the supper things; though, indeed, among his own people, Mr. Bond was thought to hold women in low esteem. He found her downcast eyes modest and even pretty. One by one she blew the candles out; with each extinguishment she grew more ethereal, while reaping a fuller share of the pagan firelight. "Come and sit beside us now, and talk," thought Mr. Bond, and presently she came.

They made him very comfortable. He found a log fire burning in his bedroom, and a bowl of broth on the bedside table. "Oh, but they're overdoing it!" he cried aloud, petulantly; "they're crude, crude! They're nothing but school-children!"—and seizing the bowl, he emptied it onto the shaggy patch of garden beneath his window. The black wall of the forest seemed to stand within a few feet of his eyes. The room was filled with the mingled light of moon, fire, and candle.

Mr. Bond, eager at last for the dreamless rest, the abandoned sleep, of the traveller, turned and surveyed the room in which he was to spend the night. He saw with pleasure the four-poster bed, itself as large as a tiny room; the heavy oaken chairs and cupboards; the tall, twisting candlesticks, their candles burnt half-way, no doubt, by a previous guest; the ceiling, that he could touch with the flat of his hand. He touched it.

In the misty morning he could see no hint of the forest, and down the shallow staircase he found the hall thick with the odour of broth. The Sasserachs were seated already at the breakfast-table, like two children, eager to begin the day with their favourite food. Crispin Sasserach was lifting his spoon and pouting his lips, while Myrtle was stirring her ladle round the tureen, her eyes downcast; and Mr. Bond sighed inaudibly as he saw again the woman's dark and lustrous hair. He noticed also the flawless condition of the Sasserach skin. There was not a blemish to be seen on their two faces, on their four hands. He attributed this perfection to the beneficial qualities of the broth, no less than to the upland air; and he began to discuss, in his plangent voice, the subject of health in general. In the middle of this discourse Crispin Sasserach remarked, excitedly, that he had a brother who kept an inn a day's journey along the edge of the forest.

"Oh," said Mr. Bond, pricking up his ears, "so you have a brother, have you?"

"Certainly," whispered the innkeeper. "It is most convenient."

"Most convenient for what?"

"Why, for the inns. His name's Martin. We share our guests. We help each other. The proper brotherly spirit, b'God!"

Mr. Bond stared angrily into his broth. "They share their guests. . . . But what," he thought, "has that to do with me?" He said aloud: "Perhaps I'll meet him one day, Mr. Sasserach."

"To-day!" cried Crispin, whacking his spoon onto the table. "I'm taking you there to-day! But don't you worry," he added, seeing the look on the other's face, and flattering himself that he had read it aright; "you'll be coming back to us. Don't you worry! Day after to-morrow—day after that—one of these days! Ain't that right, Myr? Ain't that right?" he repeated, bouncing up and down in his chair like a big child.

"Quite right," answered Myrtle Sasserach to Mr. Bond, whose eyes were fixed upon her with heavy attention.

A moment later the innkeeper was out of his chair, making for the hall, calling back to Myrtle to have his boots ready. In the midst of this bustle, Mr. Bond bowed stiffly to Myrtle Sasserach, and found his way with dignity to the back garden, that now appeared wilder than he had supposed—a fenced-in plot of grass reaching above his knees and scattered with burdock, whose prickly heads clung to his clothes as he made for the gate in the fence at the foot of this wilderness. He blinked his eyes, and walked on the rough turf that lay between him and the forest. By this time the sun was shining in an unclouded sky; a fine day was at hand; and Mr. Bond was sweeping his eye along the endless wall of the forest when he heard the innkeeper's voice calling to him in the stillness. "Mr. Bond! Mr. Bond!" Turning reluctantly, and stepping carefully through the garden in order to avoid the burrs of the burdock, the traveller found Crispin Sasserach on the point of departure, in a great bustle, with a strong horse harnessed to a two-wheeled cart, and his wife putting up her face to be kissed.

"Yes, I'll go with you," cried Mr. Bond, but the Sasserachs did not appear to hear him. He lingered for a moment in the porch, scowling at Myrtle's back, scowling at the large young horse that seemed to toss its head at him with almost human insolence, then he sighed, and, slinging his knapsack over his shoulder, sat himself beside the driver; the horse was uncommonly large, restless between the shafts, and in perfect fettle, and without a word from Crispin the animal began to plunge forward rapidly over the worn track.

For some time the two men drove in silence, on the second stage of Mr. Bond's adventure above the valley. The traveller sat up stiffly, inflating his lungs methodically, glaring through his small eyes, and forcing back his shoulders. Presently he began to talk about the mountain air, and received no answer. On his right hand the wall of the forest extended as far as his eyes could see, while on his left hand ran the brink of the valley, a mile away, broken here and there by rowan trees.

The monotony of the landscape, and the continued silence of the innkeeper, soon began to pall on Mr. Bond, who liked talking and was seldom at ease unless his eyes were busy picking out new things. Even the horse behaved with the soundless regularity of a machine;

so that, besides the traveller, only the sky showed a struggle to make progress.

Clouds came from nowhere, shaped and broke, and at midday the sun in full swing was riding between white puffs of cloud, glistening by fits and starts on the moist coat of the horse. The forest beneath, and the stretch of coarse grass running to the valley, were constantly shining and darkening, yet Crispin Sasserach never opened his mouth, even to whisper, though sometimes, between his teeth, he spat soundlessly over the edge of the cart. The landlord had brought with him a casserole of the broth; and during one of these sunny breaks he pulled up the horse, without a word, and poured the liquor into two pannikins, which he proceeded to heat patiently over a spirit stove.

In the failing light of the afternoon, when the horse was still making his top speed, when Crispin Sasserach was buzzing fitfully between his teeth, and sleep was flirting with the traveller, a shape appeared obscurely on the track ahead, and with it came the growing jingle of bells. Mr. Bond sat up and stared. He had not expected to meet, in such a God-forsaken spot, another cart, or carriage. He saw at length, approaching him, a four-wheeled buggy, drawn by two sprightly horses in tandem. A thin-faced man in breeches and a bowler hat was driving it. The two drivers greeted each other solemnly, raised their whips, but never slackened speed.

"Well—who was that?" asked Mr. Bond, after a pause.

"My brother Martin's manservant."

"Where is he going?" asked Mr. Bond.

"To 'The Rest of The Traveller.' With news."

"Indeed? What news?" persisted Mr. Bond.

The landlord turned his head.

"News for my Myrtle," he whispered, winking at the traveller.

Mr. Bond shrugged his shoulders. "What is the use of talking to such a boor?" he thought, and fell once more into his doze; the harvest-moon climbed up again, whitening the earth; while now and then the landlord spat towards the forest, and never spoke another word until he came to Martin Sasserach's.

Then Crispin leapt to life.

"Out with you!" he cried. "Pst! Mr. Bond! Wake up! Get out at once! We've reached 'The Headless Man,' sir!"

Mr. Bond, staggered by so much energy, flopped to the ground. His head felt as large as the moon. He heard the horse panting softly, and saw the breath from its nostrils flickering upwards in the cold air; while the white-faced Crispin Sasserach was leaping about under the moon, whistling between his teeth, and calling out enthusiastically: "Mar-tin! Mar-tin! Here he is!"

The sheer wall of forest echoed back the name. Indeed, the whole of the moonlight seemed to be filled with the name "Martin"; and Mr. Bond had a fierce desire to see this Martin Sasserach whose sign was hanging high above the traveller's head. After repeated calls from Crispin, the landlord of "The Headless Man" appeared, and Mr. Bond, expecting a very giant in physical stature, was shocked to see the small and bespectacled figure that had emerged from the house. Crispin Sasserach grew quick and calm in a moment. "Meet again," he whispered to Mr. Bond, shutting his eyes, and stretching his small mouth as though in ecstasy; then he gave the traveller a push towards the approaching Martin, and a moment later he was in his cart, and the horse was springing its way back to "The Rest of the Traveler."

Mr. Bond stood where he was, listening to the dying sound of the horse, and watching the landlord of "The Headless Man"; and presently he was staring at two grey flickering eyes behind the landlord's glasses.

"Anyone arriving at my inn from my brother's is trebly welcome. He is welcome not only for Crispin's own sake and mine, but also for the sake of our brother Stephen." The voice was as quiet and as clear as the moonlight, and the speaker began to return to his inn with scarcely a pause between speech and movement. Mr. Bond examined curiously the strongly-lighted hall that in shape and size was the very double of Crispin's. Oil-lamps, gracefully columned, gleamed almost as brightly from their fluted silver surfaces as from their opal-lighted heads; and there was Martin stooping up the very stairs, it seemed, that Mr. Bond had walked at Crispin Sasserach's—a scanty man, this brother, throwing out monstrous shadows, turning once to peer back at his guest, and standing at last in a bright and airy bedroom, where, with courteous words from which his eyes, lost in thought and gently flickering, seemed to be far distant, he invited his guest to wash before dining.

Martin Sasserach fed Mr. Bond delicately on that evening of his arrival, presenting him with small, cold dishes of various kinds and always exquisitely cooked and garnished; and these, together with the almost crystalline cleanliness of the room and of the table, seemed appropriate to the chemist-like appearance of the host. A bottle of wine was opened for Mr. Bond, who, amongst his own people, was known to drink nothing headier than bottled cider. During dinner, the wine warmed up a brief moment of attention in Martin Sasserach. He peered with sudden interest at his guest. " 'The Headless Man?' There is, in fact, a story connected with that name. If you can call it a story." He smiled briefly, tapping his finger, and a moment later was examining an ivory piece, elaborately carved, that held the bill of fare. "Lovely! Lovely! Isn't it? . . . In fact, there are many stories," he ended, as though the number of stories excused him from wasting his thought over the recital of merely one. Soon after dinner he retired, alluding distantly to work from which he never liked to be away long.

Mr. Bond went to bed early that night, suffering from dyspepsia, and glowering at the absence of home comforts in his bright and efficient bedroom.

The birds awakened him to a brisk, autumnal morning. Breathing heavily, he told himself that he was always very fond of birds and trees and flowers; and soon he was walking sleepily in Martin Sasserach's garden. The trimness of the beds began to please him. He followed the right-angled paths with dignified obesity, his very bones were proud to be alive.

A green gate at the garden-foot attracted Mr. Bond's attention; but, knowing that it would lead him on to the wild grass beyond, and thence to the forest, whose motionless crest could be seen all this while over the privet hedge, he chose to linger where he was, sniffing the clear scent of the flowers, and losing, with every breath and step, another whiff of Crispin's broth, to his intense delight.

Hunger drew him back into the house at last, and he began to pace the twilit rooms. Martin Sasserach, he saw, was very fond of ivory. He stooped and peered at the delicate things. Ivory objects of every description, perfectly carved: paper-knives, chess-men, salad-spoons; tiny busts and faces, often of grotesque appearance; and even delicate boxes, fretted from ivory.

The echo of his feet on the polished floors intensified the silence of "The Headless Man"; yet even this indoor hush was full of sound, when compared with the stillness of the scene beyond the uncurtained windows. The tufted grass was not yet lighted by the direct rays of the sun. The traveller stared towards the rowan trees that stood on the brink of the valley. Beyond them stretched a carpet of mist, raising the rest of the world to the height of the plateau; and Mr. Bond, recalling the house and town that he had left behind him, began to wonder whether he was glad or sorry that his adventures had brought him to this lost region. "Cold enough for my cape," he shivered, fetching it from the hall, and hurrying out of the inn; the desire had seized him to walk on the tufted grass, to foot it as far as the trees; and he had indeed gone some distance on his journey, wrapped in his thoughts and antique Inverness cape, when the note of a gong came up behind him, like a thread waving on the air.

"Hark at that," he whispered, staring hard at the ragged line of rowan trees on which his heart was set; then he shrugged his shoulders, and turned back to "The Headless Man," where his host was standing lost in thought at the breakfast-table that still held the crumbs of the night before.

"Ah, yes. Yes. It's you . . . You slept well?"

"Tolerably well," said Mr. Bond.

"We breakfast rather early here. It makes a longer day. Stennet will be back later. He's gone to my brother Crispin's."

"With news?" said Mr. Bond.

Martin Sasserach bowed courteously, though a trifle stiffly. He motioned his guest towards a chair at the table. Breakfast was cold and short and silent. Words were delicate things to rear in this crystalline atmosphere. Martin's skin sagged and was the colour of old ivory. Now and then he looked up at his guest, his grey eyes focused beyond mere externals; and it seemed as though they lodged themselves in Mr. Bond's very bones. On one of these occasions the traveller made great play with his appetite. "It's all this upland air," he asserted, thumping his chest.

The sun began to rise above the plateau. Again the landlord vanished, murmuring his excuses; silence flooded "The Headless Man," the garden purred in full blaze of the sun that now stood higher than the forest, and the gravelled paths crunched slowly beneath Mr. Bond's feet. "News for Myrtle," he pondered, letting his thoughts stray back over his journey; and frequently he drifted through the house where all was still and spacious: dusty, museum-like rooms brimming with sunlight, while everywhere those ivory carvings caught his eye, possessing his sight as completely as the taste of Crispin's broth had lodged in his very lungs.

Lunch was yet another meal of cold food and silence, broken only by coffee that the landlord heated on a spirit stove at the end of the table, and by a question from the traveller, to which this thin-haired Martin, delicately flicking certain greyish dust off the front of his coat and sleeve, replied that he had been a collector of carvings for years past, and was continually adding to his collection. His voice drew out in length and seemed, in fact, to trail him from the sunlit dining-room, back to his ever-lasting work . . . and now the afternoon itself began to drag and presently to settle down in the sun as though the whole of time were dozing.

"Here's my indigestion back again," sighed Mr. Bond, mooning about. At home he would have rested in his bedroom, with its pink curtains and flowered wallpaper.

He crept into the garden and eyed the back of the house. Which of those windows in the trimly-creepered stone lit up the landlord and his work? He listened for the whirring of a lathe, the scraping of a knife . . . and wondered, startled, why he had expected to hear such things. He felt the forest behind his back, and turned, and saw it looming above the privet hedge. Impulsively, he started to cross the sun-swept grass beyond the gate; but within a few yards of the forest his courage failed him again: he could not face the wall of trees: and with a cry he fled into the house, and seized his Inverness.

His eyes looked far beyond the rowans on the skyline as he plodded over the tufted grass. Already he could see himself down there below, counties and counties away, on the valley level, in the house of his neighbours the Allcards, drinking their coffee or tea and telling them of his adventures and especially of *this* adventure. It was not often that a man of his age and secure position in the world went off alone, in search of joy or trouble. He scanned the distant line of rowan trees, and nodded, harking back: "As far as it has gone. I'll tell them this adventure, as far as it ever went." And he would say to them: "The things I might have seen, if I had stayed! Yes, Allcard, I was very glad to climb down into the valley that day, I can tell you! I don't mind admitting I was a bit frightened!"

The tippet of his cape caressed his shoulders, like the hand of a friend.

Mr. Bond was not yet half-way to the rowan trees when, looking back, he saw, against the darkness of the forest wall, a carriage rapidly approaching "The Headless Man." At once there flashed into his memory the eyes of the manservant Stennet who went between the Sasserach inns.

He knew that Stennet's eyes were on him now. The sound of the horses' feet was coming up to him like a soft ball bouncing over the grass. Mr. Bond shrugged his shoulders, and stroked his pendulous cheeks. Already he was on his way back to "The Headless Man," conscious that two flying horses could have overtaken him long before he had reached the rowans. "But why," he thought, holding himself with dignity, "should I imagine that these people are expecting me to run away? And why that sudden panic in the garden? It's all that deathly quietness of the morning getting on my nerves."

The carriage had disappeared some time before he reached the inn, over whose tiled and weather-stained roof the redness of the evening was beginning to settle. And now the traveller was conscious of a welcome that seemed to run out and meet him at the very door. He found a log fire crackling in the dining-room, and Mr. Bond, holding his hands to the blaze, felt suddenly at ease, and weary. He had intended to assert himself—to shout for Martin Sasserach—to demand that he be escorted down at once from the plateau . . . but now he wished for nothing better than to stand in front of the fire, waiting for Stennet to bring him tea.

A man began to sing in the heart of the house. Stennet? The fellow's eyes and hawk-like nose were suddenly visible in the fire. The singing voice grew louder . . . died at length discreetly into silence and the tread of footsteps in the hall . . . and again the traveller was listening to the flames as they roared in the chimney.

"Let me take your coat, sir," Stennet said.

Then Mr. Bond whipped round, his cheeks shaking with anger.

Why did they want to force this hospitality upon him, making him feel like a prisoner? He glared at the large-checked riding-breeches, at the muscular shoulders, at the face that seemed to have grown the sharper through swift driving. He almost shouted: "Where's that bowler hat?"

Fear? . . . Perhaps . . . But if fear had clutched him for a moment, it had left him now. He knew that the voice had pleased him, a voice of deference breaking into the cold and irreverent silence of "The Headless Man." The cape was already off his shoulders, hanging on Stennet's bent and respectful arm. And—God be praised!—the voice was announcing that tea would be ready soon. Mr. Bond's spirits leapt with the word. He and Stennet stood there, confidentially plotting. "China? Yes, sir. We have China," Stennet said.

"And buttered toast," said Mr. Bond, softly rubbing his chin. Some time after tea he was awakened from his doze by the hand of the manservant, who told him that a can of boiling water was waiting in his room.

Mr. Bond felt that dinner would be a rich meal that night, and it was. He blushed as the dishes were put before him. Hare soup! How did they know his favourite soup? Through entrée, remove, and roast, his hands, soft and pink from washing, were busier than they had been for days. The chicken was braised to a turn. Oh, what mushrooms *au gratin!* The partridge brought tears to his eyes. The Saxony pudding caused him to turn again to Martin, in Stennet's praise.

The landlord bowed with distant courtesy. "A game of chess?" he suggested, when dinner was over. "My last opponent was a man like yourself, a traveller making a tour of the inns. We started a game. He is gone from us now. Perhaps you will take his place?" smiled Martin Sasserach, his precise voice dropping and seeming to transmit its flow of action to the thin hand poised above the board. "My move," he whispered, playing at once; he had thought it out for a week. But although Mr. Bond tried to sink his thoughts into the problem so suddenly placed before him, he could not take them off his after-dinner dyspepsia, and with apologies and groans he scraped back his chair. "I'm sorry for that," smiled Martin, and his eyes flickered over the board. "I'm very sorry. Another night . . . undoubtedly . . . with your kind help . . . another night . . ."

The prospect of another day at "The Headless Man" was at once disturbing and pleasant to Mr. Bond as he went wheezing up to bed.

"Ah, Stennet! Do *you* ever suffer from dyspepsia?" he asked mournfully, seeing the man at the head of the staircase. Stennet snapped his fingers, and was off downstairs in a moment; and a minute later he was standing at the traveller's door, with a bowl of Crispin's famous broth. "Oh, that!" cried Mr. Bond, staring down at the bowl. Then he remembered its fine effect on his indigestion at Crispin's; and when at last he pulled the sheets over his head, he fell asleep in comfort and did not wake until the morning.

At breakfast Martin Sasserach looked up from his plate.

"This afternoon," he murmured, "Stennet will be driving you to my brother Stephen's."

Mr. Bond opened his eyes. "Another inn? Another of you Sasserachs?"

"Crispin—Martin—Stephen. Just the three of us. A perfect number . . . if you come to think of it."

The traveller strode into the garden. Asters glowed in the lustreless light of the morning. By ten o'clock the sun was shining again, and by midday a summer heat lay on the plateau, penetrating even into Mr. Bond's room. The silence of the forest pulled him to the window, made him lift up his head and shut his eyes upon that monstrous mass of trees. Fear was trying to overpower him. He did not want to go to Stephen Sasserach's; but the hours were running past him quickly now, the stillness was gone from the inn.

At lunch, to which his host contributed a flow of gentle talk, the traveller felt rising within him an impatience to be off on the third stage of his journey, if such a stage must be. He jumped up from his chair without apology, and strode into the garden. The asters were now shining dimly in the strong sunlight. He opened the gate in the privet hedge, and walked onto the tufted grass that lay between it and the forest. As he did so, he heard the flap of a wing behind him and saw a pigeon flying from a window in the roof. The bird flew over his head and over the forest and out of sight; and for the first time he remembered seeing a pigeon taking a similar course when he was standing in the garden at Crispin's inn.

His thoughts were still following the pigeon over the boundless floor of tree-tops when he heard a voice calling to him in the silence. "Mr. Bond! Mr. Bond!" He walked at once to the gate and down the garden and into the house, put on his Inverness, and hitched his knapsack onto his shoulder; and in a short while he was perched beside Stennet in the flying buggy, staring at the ears of the two horses, and remembering that Martin, at the last moment, instead of bidding his guest good-bye, had gone back to his work.

Though he never lost his fear of Stennet, Mr. Bond found Martin's man a good companion on a journey, always ready to speak when spoken to, and even able to arouse the traveller's curiosity, at times, in the monotonous landscape.

"See those rowans over there?" said Stennet, nodding to the left. "Those rowans belong to Mr. Martin. He owns them half-way to Mr. Crispin's place, and half-way on to Mr. Stephen's. And so it is with Mr. Crispin and Mr. Stephen in their turn."

"And what about the forest?"

"Same again," said Stennet, waving his hand towards the right. "It's round, you know. And they each own a third, like a huge slice of cake."

He clicked his tongue, and the horses pricked up their ears, though on either side of the dashboard the performance was no more than a formality, so swiftly was the buggy moving. "Very much quicker than Crispin's cart!" gasped the passenger, feeling the wind against his face; yet, when the evening of the autumn day was closing in, he looked about him with surprise.

He saw the moon rise up above the valley.

Later still, he asked for information regarding the names of the three inns, and Stennet laughed.

"The gentlemen are mighty proud of them, I can tell you! Romantic and a bit fearsome, that's what I call them. Poetical, too.

They don't say 'The Traveller's Rest,' but 'The Rest of the Traveller,' mind you. That's poetical. I don't think it was Mr. Crispin's idea. I think it was Mr. Martin's—or Mrs. Crispin's. They're the clever ones. 'The Headless Man' is merely grim—a grim turn of mind Mr. Martin has—and it means, of course, no more than it says—a man without a head. And then again," continued Stennet, whistling to his horses, whose backs were gleaming in the moonlight, "the inn you're going to now—'The Traveller's Head'—well, inns are called 'The King's Head' sometimes, aren't they, in the King's honour? Mr. Stephen goes one better than that. He dedicates his inn to the traveller himself." By this time a spark of light had become visible in the distance, and Mr. Bond fixed his eyes upon it. Once, for a moment, the spark went out, and he imagined that Stephen's head had passed in front of the living-room lamp. At this picture, anger seized him, and he wondered, amazed, why he was submitting so tamely to the commands—he could call them no less—of these oddly hospitable brothers. Fanned by his rage, the spark grew steadily bigger and brighter, until at last it had achieved the shape and size of a glowing window through which a man's face was grinning into the moonshine.

"Look here, what's all this?" cried Mr. Bond, sliding to his feet.

" 'The Traveller's Head,' sir," answered Stennet, pointing aloft.

They both stared up at the sign above their heads, then Mr. Bond scanned the sprawling mass of the inn, and scowled at its surroundings. The night was still and vibrant, without sound; the endless forest stood like a wall of blue-white dust; and the traveller was about to raise his voice in wrath against the brothers Sasserach, when a commotion burst from the porch of the inn, and onto the moon-drenched grass there strode a tall and ungainly figure, swinging its arms, with a pack of creatures flopping and stumbling at its heels. "Here *is* Mr. Stephen," Stennet whispered, watching the approach; the landlord of "The Traveller's Head" was smiling pleasantly, baring his intensely white teeth, and when he had reached the traveller he touched his forehead with a gesture that was at once respectful and overbearing.

"Mr. Bond, sir?" Mr. Bond muttered and bowed, and stared down at the landlord's children—large-headed, large-bellied, primitive creatures flopping round their father and pulling the skirts of the Inverness cape.

Father and children gathered round the traveller, who, lost within this little crowd, soon found himself at the entrance of "The Traveller's Head," through which his new host urged him by the arm while two of the children pushed between them and ran ahead clumsily into the depths of the hall. The place was ill-lighted and ill-ventilated; and although Mr. Bond knew from experience exactly where the living-room would be situated, yet, after he had passed through its doorway, he found no further resemblance to those rooms in which he had spent two stages of a curious adventure. The oil-lamp, standing in the middle of the round centre table, was without a shade; a moth was plunging audibly at the blackened chimney, hurling swift shadows everywhere over the ceiling and figured wall-paper; while, with the return of the children, a harmonium had started fitfully to grunt and blow.

"Let me take your cloak, your cape, Mr. Bond, sir," the landlord said, and spread it with surprising care on one of the vast sofas that looked the larger because of their broken springs and the stuffing that protruded through their soiled covers: but at once the children seized upon the cape and would have torn it to pieces had not Mr. Bond snatched it from them—at this, they cowered away from the stranger, fixing him with their eyes.

Amidst this congestion of people and furniture, Stephen Sasserach smiled and moved continuously, a stooping giant whom none but Mr. Bond obeyed. Here was the type of man whose appearance the traveller likened to that of the old-time executioner, the axe-man of the Middle Ages—harsh, loyal, simple, excessively domesticated, with a bulging forehead and untidy eyebrows and arms muscled and ready for deeds. Stephen kept no order in his house. Noise was everywhere, yet little seemed to be done. The children called their father Steve, and put out their tongues at him. They themselves were unlovely things, and their inner natures seemed to ooze through their skins and form a surface from which the traveller recoiled. Three of their names were familiar to Mr. Bond. Here were Crispin and Martin and Stephen over again, while Dorcas and Lydia were sisters whose only virtue was their mutual devotion.

The food at "The Traveller's Head" was homely and palatable, and Stephen the father cooked it and served it liberally on chipped plates. He sat in his soiled blue shirt, his knotted arms looking richly sunburnt against the blue. He was never inarticulate, and this surprised Mr. Bond. On the contrary, he spoke rapidly and almost as if to himself, in a low rugged voice that was always a pleasure to hear. At moments he dropped into silence, his eyes shut, his eyebrows lowered, and his bulging forehead grew still more shiny with thought; on such occasions, Dorcas and Lydia would steal to the harmonium, while, backed by a wail from the instrument, Crispin the Younger and Martin the Younger would jump from the sofas onto the floor.

Rousing himself at last, Stephen the Elder thumped his fist on the table, and turned in his chair to shout at the children: "Get along with you, devils! Get out your board, and *practise,* you little devils!" Whereupon the children erected a huge board, punctured with holes; and each child began to hurl wooden balls through the holes and into the pockets behind them with astonishing accuracy, except for Dorcas and Lydia. And presently their father reminded them: "The moon is shining!" At once the children scuttled out of the room, and Mr. Bond never saw them again.

The noise and the figured wall-paper, and the fat moth beating itself against the only source of light, had caused the traveller's head to grow heavy with sleep; and now it grew heavier still as he sat by the fire with Stephen after supper was over, listening to the talk of that strangely attractive man in the soiled blue shirt. "You fond of children, Mr. Bond, sir?" Mr. Bond nodded.

"Children and animals . . ." he murmured drowsily.

"One has to let them have their way," sighed Stephen Sasserach. The rugged voice came clearly and soothingly into Mr. Bond's ears, until at last it shot up, vigorously, and ordered the guest to bed. Mr. Bond pulled himself out of his chair, and smiled, and said good night, and the moth flew into his face. Where were the children, he wondered. Their voices could not be heard. Perhaps they had fallen asleep, suddenly, like animals. But Mr. Bond found it difficult to imagine those eyes in bed, asleep.

Lying, some minutes later, in his own massive bed in this third of the Sasserach inns, with an extinguished candle on his bedside table, and gazing towards the open window from which he had drawn apart one of the heavy embroidered curtains, Mr. Bond fancied that he could hear faint cries of triumph, and sounds of knocking coming from the direction of the forest. Starting up into complete wakefulness, he went to the window, and stared at the forest beyond the tufted grass. The sounds, he fancied, putting his hand to his ear, were as those given forth by the children during their game—but louder, as though the game were bigger. Perhaps strange animals were uttering them. Whatever their origin, they were coming from that depth of trees whose stillness was deepened by the light of the moon.

"Oh, God!" thought Mr. Bond, "I'm sick to death of the moonlight!"—and with a sweep of the arm he closed the curtains, yet could not shut out the sounds of the forest, nor the sight of the frosted grass beneath the moon. Together, sound and sight filled him with foreboding, and his cheeks shook as he groped for the unlighted candle. He must fetch his Inverness from below, fetch it at once, and get away while there was time. He found his host still sitting by the lamp in the living-room. Stephen's fist, lying on the table, was closed; he opened it, and out flew the moth.

"He thinks he has got away," cried Stephen, looking up, and baring his teeth in a smile: "but he hasn't! He never will!"

"I've come for my Inverness," said Mr. Bond.

It was lying on one of the massive sofas. The fire was out, and the air chilly, and the depth of the room lay in darkness. An idea crossed the mind of Mr. Bond. He said, lifting up the cape: "I thought I'd like it on my bed." And he shivered to show how cold he was. From one of the folds the moth flew out, and whirled round the room like a mad thing.

"That's all right, Mr. Bond, sir. That's all right." The man had fallen into a mood of abstraction; his forehead shone in the rays of the lamp; and the traveller left the room, holding himself with dignity in his gay dressing-gown, the Inverness hanging on his arm.

He was about to climb the staircase when a voice spoke softly in his ear, and wished him good night.

Stennet! What was the man doing here? Mr. Bond lifted his candle and gazed in astonishment at the back of Martin's manservant. The figure passed into the shadows, and the soft and deliberate ticking of the grandfather clock in the hall deepened the silence and fear of the moments that followed.

Mr. Bond ran to his room, locked himself in, and began to dress. His dyspepsia had seized him again. If only he were back at Crispin's! He parted the curtains, and peeped at the night. The shadow of the inn lay on the yard and the tufted grass beyond, and one of the chimneys, immensely distorted, extended as far as the forest. The forest-wall itself was solid with moonlight; from behind it there came no longer the sounds of the knocking, and the silence set Mr. Bond trembling again.

"I shall escape at dawn," he whispered, "when the moon's gone down."

Feeling no longer sleepy, he took from his knapsack a volume of *Mungo Park,* and, fully dressed, settled himself in an easy chair, with the curtains drawn again across the window, and the candle burning close beside him. At intervals he looked up from his book, frowning, running his eye over the group of three pagodas, in pale red, endlessly repeated on the wallpaper. The restful picture made him drowsy, and presently he slept and snored and the candle burned on.

At midnight he was awakened by crashing blows on his door; the very candle seemed to be jumping with fear, and Mr. Bond sprang up in alarm.

"Yes? Who's that?" he called out feebly.

"What in the name of God is *that?*" he whispered, as the blows grew louder.

"What are they up to now?" he asked aloud, with rising terror.

A splinter flew into the room, and he knew in a flash that the end of his journey had come. Was it Stephen or Stennet, Stephen or Stennet behind the door? The candle flickered as he blundered to and fro. He had no time to think, no time to act. He stood and watched the corner of the axe-blade working in the crack in the panel. "Save me, save me," he whispered, wringing his hands. They fluttered towards his Inverness, and struggled to push themselves into the obstinate sleeves. "Oh, come on, come on," he whimpered, jerking his arms about, anger rising with terror. The whole room shuddered beneath the axe. He plunged at the candle and blew it out. In the darkness a ray of light shot through a crack in the door, and fell on the window curtain.

Mr. Bond remembered the creeper clinging beneath his window and as soon as possible he was floundering, scrambling, slipping down to the house-shadowed garden below. Puffing out his cheeks, he hurried onward, while the thuds of the axe grew fainter in his ears. Brickbats lay in his path, a zinc tub wrenched at his cape and ripped it loudly, an iron hoop caught in his foot and he tottered forward with outstretched hands. And now, still running in the far-flung shadow of the house, he was on the tufted grass, whimpering a little, struggling against desire to look back over his shoulder, making for the forest that lay in the full beams of the moonlight. He tried to think, and could think of nothing but the size and safety of the shadow on which he was running. He reached the roof of the inn at last: plunged aside from his course of flight: and now he was running up the monstrous shadow of the chimney, thinking of nothing at all because the forest stood so near. Blindingly, a moon-filled avenue stretched before him: the chimney entered the chasm, and stopped: and it was as though Mr. Bond were a puff of smoke blowing into the forest depths. His shadow, swinging its monstrously distorted garments, led him to an open space at the end of the avenue. The thick-set trees encircled it with silence deeper than any Mr. Bond had known. Here, in this glade, hung silence within a silence. Yet, halting abruptly, and pressing the flat of his hands to his ribs in the pain of his sudden burst of breathing, Mr. Bond had no ears for the silence, nor eyes for anything beyond the scene that faced him in the centre of the forest glade: a group of upright posts, or stakes, set in a concave semicircle, throwing long shadows, and bearing on each summit a human skull. " 'The Traveller's Head,' 'The Headless Man,' " he whispered, stricken with terror, whipping his back on the skulls; and there was Stephen Sasserach in silhouette, leaping up the avenue, brandishing his axe as though he were a demented wood-cutter coming to cut down trees.

The traveller's mind continued to run swiftly through the names of the three inns. " 'The Traveller's Head,' " he thought, 'The Head-less Man,' 'The Rest of the Traveller.' " He remembered the carrier pigeons that had flown ahead of him from inn to inn; he remembered the dust on the front of Martin's coat. . . .

He was staring at the figure in the soiled blue shirt. It had halted now, as still as a tree, on the verge of the moon-filled glade: but the whirling thoughts of Mr. Bond were on the verge of light more blinding than this; they stopped, appalled: and the traveller fled beyond the skulls, fruitlessly searching for covert in the farthest wall of trees.

Then Stephen sprang in his wake, flinging up a cry that went knocking against the tree-trunks.

The echoes were echoed by Mr. Bond, who, whipping round to face his enemy, was wriggling and jerking in his Inverness cape, slipping it off at last, and swinging it in his hand, for his blood was up. And now he was deep in mortal combat, wielding his Inverness as the gladiators used to wield their nets in the old arenas. Time and again the axe and the cape engaged each other; the one warding and hindering; the other catching and ripping, clumsily enough, as though in sport. Around the skulls the two men fought and panted, now in darkness, now in the full light pouring down the avenue. Their moon-cast shadows fought another fight together, wilder still than theirs. Then Stephen cried: "Enough of this!" and bared his teeth for the first time since the strife had started.

"B-but you're my friend!" bleated Mr. Bond; and he stared at the shining thread of the axe.

"The best you ever had, sir, Mr. Bond, sir!" answered Stephen Sasserach; and, stepping back, the landlord of "The Traveller's Head" cut off the traveller's head.

The thump of the head on the sticks and leaves and grass of the forest glade was the first sound in the new and peaceful life of Mr. Bond, and he did not hear it; but to the brothers Sasserach it was a promise of life itself, a signal that all was ready now for them to apply their respective talents busily and happily in the immediate future.

Stephen took the head of Mr. Bond, and with gentle though rather clumsy fingers pared it to a skull, grinning back at it with simple satisfaction when the deed was over, and after that he set it up as a fine mark for his brood of primitives, the game's endeavour being to see who could throw the ball into the eyesockets; and to his brother

Martin, landlord of "The Headless Man," he sent the headless man, under the care of Stennet: and Martin, on a soft, autumnal day, reduced the headless body to a skeleton, with all its troubles gone, and through the days and nights he sat at work, with swift precision in his fingers, carving and turning, powdering his coat with dust, creating his figures and trinkets, his paper-knives and salad-spoons and fretted boxes and rare chess-men; and to his brother Crispin, landlord of "The Rest of the Traveller," Martin sent the rest of the traveller, the soft and yielding parts, the scraps, the odds and ends, the miscellaneous pieces, all the internal lumber that had gone to fill the skin of the man from the Midlands and to help to render him in middle years a prey to dyspepsia. Crispin received the parcel with a pursing of his small mouth, and a call to Myrtle in his clear falsetto: "Stennet's here!"

She answered from the kitchen. "Thank you, Cris!" Her hands were soft and swollen as she scoured the tureen. The back of the inn was full of reflected sunlight, and her dark hair shone.

"It's too late in the season now," she said, when tea-time came. "I don't suppose we'll have another one before the spring."

Yet she was wrong. That very evening, when the moon had risen from beyond the valley, Myrtle murmured: "There he comes," and continued to stir her ladle in the bowl.

Her husband strolled into the hall and wound the clock.

He took the lamp from its bracket on the wall.

He went to the door, and flung it open to the moonlight; holding the lamp above his head.

"Come in, come in," he said, to the stranger standing there. "She is cooking a *lovely* broth to-night!"

BY E. PHILLIPS OPPENHEIM

TWO

SPINSTERS

Erneston Grant was without doubt a very first-class detective, but as a wayfarer across Devonshire byroads with only a map and a compass to help him he was simply a washout. Even his fat little white dog, Flip, sheltered under a couple of rugs, after two hours of cold, wet, and purposeless journeying, looked at him reproachfully. With an exclamation of something like despair, Grant brought his sobbing automobile to a standstill at the top of one of the wickedest hills a Ford had ever been asked to face even on first speed, and sat looking around him.

In every direction the outlook was the same. There were rolling stretches of common divided by wooded valleys of incredible depth. There was no sign of agricultural land, no sign of the working of any human being upon the endless acres, and not a single vehicle had he passed upon the way. There were no sign-posts, no villages, no

102

shelter of any sort. The one thing that abounded was rain—rain and mist. Gray wreaths of it hung over the commons, making them seem like falling fragments of cloud, blotted out the horizon, hung over every hopeful break in the distance—an encircling, enveloping obscurity. Then, vying with the mists in wetness, came the level rain —rain which had seemed beautiful early in the afternoon, slanting from the heavens onto the mountainside, but which had long ago lost all pretense to being anything but damnably offensive, chilling, miserably wet. Flip, whose nose only now appeared uncovered, sniffed disgustedly, and Grant, as he lit a pipe, cursed slowly but fluently under his breath. What a country! Miles of byways without a single direction post, endless stretches without a glimpse of a farm-house or village. And the map! Grant solemnly cursed the man who had ordained it, the printer who had bound it, and the shop where he had bought it. When he had finished Flip ventured upon a gentle bark of approval.

"Somewhere or other," Grant muttered to himself, "should lie the village of Nidd. The last sign-post in this blasted region indicated six miles to Nidd. Since then we have traveled at least twelve, there has been no turning to the left or to the right, and the village of Nidd is as though it had never been."

His eyes pierced the gathering darkness ahead. Through a slight uplifting in the clouds it seemed to him that he could see for miles, and nowhere was there any sign of village or of human habitation. He thought of the road along which they had come, and the idea of retracing it made him shiver. It was at that moment, when bending forward to watch the steam from his boiling radiator, that he saw away on the left a feebly flickering light. Instantly he was out of the car. He scrambled onto the stone wall and looked eagerly in the direction from which he had seen it. There was without doubt a light; around that light must be a house. His eyes could even trace the rough track that led to it. He climbed back to his place, thrust in his clutch, drove for about forty yards, and then paused at a gate. The track on the other side was terrible, but then so was the road. He opened it and drove through, bending over his task now with every sense absorbed.

Apparently traffic here, if traffic existed at all, consisted only of an occasional farm wagon of the kind he was beginning to know all about—springless, with holes in the boarded floor and with great, slowly turning wheels. Nevertheless he made progress, skirted the edge of a tremendous combe, passed, to his joy, a semi-cultivated field, through another gate, up it seemed suddenly into the clouds, and down a fantastic corkscrew way until at last the light faced him directly ahead. He passed a deserted garden and pulled up before a broken-down iron gate which he had to get out of the car to open. He punctiliously closed it after him, traversed a few yards of grass-grown, soggy avenue, and finally reached the door of what might once have been a very tolerable farmhouse, but which appeared now, notwithstanding the flickering light burning upstairs, to be one of the most melancholy edifices the mind of man could conceive.

With scant anticipations in the way of a welcome, but with immense relief at the thought of a roof, Grant descended and knocked upon the oak door. Inside he could hear almost at once the sound of a match being struck; the light of a candle shone through the blindless windows of a room on his left. There were footsteps in the hall, and the door was opened. Grant found himself confronted by a woman who held the candle so high that it half illumined, half shadowed her features. There was a certain stateliness, however, about her figure which he realized even in those first few seconds at the door.

"What do you want?" she asked.

Grant, as he removed his hat, fancied that the answer was sufficiently obvious. Rain streamed from every angle of his be-mackintoshed body. His face was pinched with the cold.

"I am a traveler who has lost his way," he explained. "For hours I have been trying to find a village and inn. Yours is the first human habitation I have seen. Can you give me a night's shelter?"

"Is there any one with you?" the woman inquired.

"I am alone," he replied. "Except for my little dog," he added, as he heard Flip's hopeful yap.

The woman considered.

"You had better drive your car into the shed on the left-hand side of the house," she said. "Afterwards you can come in. We will do what we can for you. It is not much."

"I am very grateful, madam," Grant declared in all sincerity.

He found the shed, which was occupied only by two farm carts in an incredible state of decay. Afterwards he released Flip and returned to the front door which had been left open. Guided by the sound of crackling logs, he found his way to a huge stone kitchen. In a high-backed chair in front of the fire, seated with her hands upon her knees but gazing eagerly towards the door as though watching for his coming, was another woman, also tall, approaching middle age, perhaps, but still of striking presence and fine features. The woman who had admitted him was bending over the fire. He looked from one to the other in amazement. They were fearfully and wonderfully alike.

"It is very kind of you, ladies, to give us shelter," he began. "Flip! Behave yourself, Flip!"

A huge sheep dog had occupied the space in front of the fire. Flip without a moment's hesitation had run towards him, yapping fiercely. The dog, with an air of mild surprise, rose to his feet, and looked inquiringly downwards. Flip insinuated herself into the vacant place, stretched herself out with an air of content, and closed her eyes.

"I must apologize for my little dog," Grant continued. "She is very cold."

The sheep dog retreated a few yards and sat on his haunches considering the matter. Meanwhile the woman who had opened the door produced a cup and saucer from a cupboard, a loaf of bread, and a small side of bacon, from which she cut some slices.

"Draw your chair to the fire," she invited. "We have very little to offer you, but I will prepare something to eat."

"You are good Samaritans indeed," Grant declared fervently.

He seated himself opposite the woman who as yet had scarcely spoken or removed her eyes from his. The likeness between the two was an amazing thing, as was also their silence. They wore similar clothes—heavy, voluminous clothes they seemed to him—and their hair, brown and slightly besprinkled with gray, was arranged in precisely the same fashion. Their clothes belonged to another world, as did also their speech and manners, yet there was a curious but unmistakable distinction about them both.

"As a matter of curiosity," Grant asked, "how far am I from the village of Nidd?"

"Not far," the woman who was sitting motionless opposite to him answered. "To any one knowing the way, near enough. Strangers are foolish to trust themselves to these roads. Many people are lost who try."

"Yours is a lonely homestead," he ventured.

"We were born here," the woman answered. "Neither my sister nor I have felt the desire for travel."

The bacon began to sizzle. Flip opened one eye, licked her mouth and sat up. In a few minutes the meal was prepared. A high-backed oak chair was placed at the end of the table. There was tea, a dish of bacon and eggs, a great loaf of bread and a small pat of butter. Grant took his place.

"You have had your supper?" he asked.

"Long ago," the woman who had prepared his meal replied. "Please to serve yourself."

She sank into the other oak chair exactly opposite her sister. Grant, with Flip by his side, commenced his meal. Neither had tasted food for many hours and for a time both were happily oblivious to anything save the immediate surroundings. Presently, however, as he poured out his second cup of tea, Grant glanced towards his hostesses. They had moved their chairs slightly away from the fire and were both watching him—watching him without curiosity, yet with a certain puzzling intentness. It occurred to him then for the first time that although both had in turn addressed him, neither had addressed the other.

"I can't tell you how good this tastes," Grant said presently. "I am afraid I must seem awfully greedy."

"You have been for some time without food, perhaps," one of them said.

"Since half past twelve."

"Are you traveling for pleasure?"

"I thought so before to-day," he answered, with a smile to which there was no response.

The woman who had admitted him moved her chair an inch or

two nearer to his. He noticed with some curiosity that immediately she had done so her sister did the same thing.

"What is your name?"

"Erneston Grant," he replied. "May I know whom I have to thank for this hospitality?"

"My name is Mathilda Craske," the first one announced.

"And mine is Annabelle Craske," the other echoed.

"You live here alone?" he ventured.

"We live here entirely alone," Mathilda acquiesced. "It is our pleasure."

Grant was more than ever puzzled. Their speech was subject to the usual Devonshire intonation and soft slurring of the vowels, but otherwise it was almost curiously correct. The idea of their living alone in such a desolate part, however, seemed incredible.

"You farm here, perhaps?" he persisted. "You have laborers' cottages, or some one close at hand?"

Mathilda shook her head.

"The nearest hovel," she confided, "is three miles distant. We have ceased to occupy ourselves with the land. We have five cows—they give us no trouble—and some fowls."

"It is a lonely life," he murmured.

"We do not find it so," Annabelle said stiffly.

He turned his chair towards them. Flip, with a little gurgle of satisfaction, sprang onto his knees.

"Where do you do your marketing?" he asked.

"A carrier from Exford," Mathilda told him, "calls every Saturday. Our wants are simple."

The large room, singularly empty of furniture as he noticed looking round, was full of shadowy places, unilluminated by the single oil lamp. The two women themselves were only dimly visible. Yet every now and then in the flickering firelight he caught a clearer glimpse of them. They were so uncannily alike that they might well be twins. He found himself speculating as to their history. They must once have been very beautiful.

"I wonder whether it will be possible," he asked, after a somewhat prolonged pause, "to encroach further upon your hospitality and beg for a sofa or a bed for the night? Any place will do," he added hastily.

Mathilda rose at once to her feet. She took another candle from the mantelpiece and lit it.

"I will show you," she said, "where you may sleep."

For a moment Grant was startled. He had happened to glance towards Annabelle and was amazed at a sudden curious expression —an expression almost of malice in her face. He stooped to bring her into the little halo of lamplight more completely, and stared at her incredulously. The expression, if ever it had been there, had vanished. She was simply looking at him patiently with something in her face which he failed utterly to understand.

"If you will follow me," Mathilda invited.

Grant rose to his feet. Flip turned round with a final challenging bark to the huge sheep dog who had accepted a position remote from the fire, and failing to elicit any satisfactory response trotted after her master. They passed into a well-shaped but almost empty hall, up a broad flight of oak stairs to the first landing. Outside the room from which Grant had seen the candlelight she paused for a moment and listened.

"You have another guest?" he inquired.

"Annabelle has a guest," she replied. "You are mine. Follow me, please."

She led the way to a bedchamber in which was a huge four-poster and little else. She set the candle upon a table and turned down a sort of crazy quilt which covered the bed-clothes. She felt the sheets and nodded approvingly. Grant found himself unconsciously following her example. To his surprise they were warm. She pointed to a great brass bed-warmer with a long handle at the further end of the room, from which a little smoke was still curling upwards.

"You were expecting someone to-night?" he asked curiously.

"We are always prepared," she answered.

She left the room, apparently forgetting to wish him good-night. He called out pleasantly after her, but she made no response. He heard her level footsteps as she descended the stairs. Then again there was silence—silence down below, silence in the part of the house where he was. Flip, who was sniffing round the room, at times showed signs of excitement, at times growled. Grant, opening the window, ventured upon a cigaret.

"Don't know that I blame you, old girl," he said. "It's a queer place."

Outside there was nothing to be seen and little to be heard save the roaring of a water torrent close at hand and the patter of rain. He suddenly remembered his bag, and, leaving the door of his room open, descended the stairs. In the great stone kitchen the two women were seated exactly as they had been before his coming, and during his meal. They both looked at him but neither spoke.

"If you don't mind," he explained, "I want to fetch my bag from the car."

Mathilda, the woman who had admitted him, nodded acquiescence. He passed out into the darkness, stumbled his way to the shed, and unstrapped his bag. Just as he was turning away he thrust his hand into the tool chest and drew out an electric torch which he slipped into his pocket. When he reëntered the house the two women were still seated in their chairs and still silent.

"A terrible night," he remarked. "I can't tell you how thankful I am to you for so hospitably giving me shelter."

They both looked at him but neither made any reply. This time when he reached his room he closed the door firmly, and noticed with a frown of disappointment that except for the latch there was no means of fastening it. Then he laughed to himself softly. He, the famous captor of Ned Bullivant, the victor in a score of scraps with desperate men, suddenly nervous in this lonely farmhouse inhabited by a couple of strange women.

"Time I took a holiday," he muttered to himself. "We don't understand nerves, do we, Flip?" he added.

Flip opened one eye and growled. Grant was puzzled.

"Something about she doesn't like," he ruminated. "I wonder who's in the room with the lighted candles?"

He opened his own door once more softly and listened. The silence was almost unbroken. From downstairs in the great kitchen he could hear the ticking of a clock, and he could see the thin streak of yellow light underneath the door. He crossed the landing and

listened for a moment outside the room with the candles. The silence
within was absolute and complete—not even the sound of the ordinary breathing of a sleeping person. He retraced his steps, closed his
own door, and began to undress. At the bottom of his bag was a
small automatic. His fingers played with it for a moment. Then he
threw it back. The electric torch, however, he placed by the side of
his bed. Before he turned in he leaned once more out of the window.
The roar of the falling water seemed more insistent than ever. Otherwise there was no sound. The rain had ceased but the sky was black
and starless. With a little shiver he turned away and climbed into
bed.

He had no idea of the time but the blackness outside was just as
intense when he was suddenly awakened by Flip's low growling.
She had shaken herself free from the coverlet at the foot of the bed
and he could see her eyes, wicked little spots of light, gleaming
through the darkness. He lay quite still for a moment, listening.
From the first he knew that there was someone in the room. His
own quick intuition had told him that, although he was still unable
to detect a sound. Slowly his hand traveled out to the side of the bed.
He took up the electric torch and turned it on. Then with an in-
voluntary cry he shrank back. Standing within a few feet of him was
Mathilda, still fully dressed, and in her hand, stretched out towards
him, was the cruelest-looking knife he had ever seen. He slipped out
of bed, and, honestly and self-confessedly afraid, kept the light
fixed upon her.

"What do you want?" he demanded, amazed at the unsteadiness
of his own voice. "What the mischief are you doing with that knife?"

"I want you, William," she answered, a note of disappointment in
her tone. "Why do you keep so far away?"

He lit the candle. The finger which on the trigger of his automatic
had kept Bullivant with his hands up for a life-long two minutes,
was trembling. With the light in the room now established, however,
he felt more himself.

"Throw that knife on the bed," he ordered, "and tell me what you
were going to do with it?"

She obeyed at once and leaned a little towards him.

"I was going to kill you, William," she confessed.

"And why?" he demanded.

She shook her head sorrowfully.

"Because it is the only way," she replied.

"My name isn't William, for one thing," he objected, "and what do you mean by saying it is the only way?"

She smiled, sadly and disbelievingly.

"You should not deny your name," she said. "You are William Foulsham. I knew you at once, though you had been away so long. When *he* came," she added, pointing towards the other room, "Annabelle believed that he was William. I let her keep him. I knew. I knew if I waited you would come."

"Waiving the question of my identity," he struggled on, "why do you want to kill me? What do you mean by saying it is the only way?"

"It is the only way to keep a man," she answered. "Annabelle and I found that out when you left us. You knew each of us loved you, William; you promised each of us never to leave—do you remember? So we sat here and waited for you to come back. We said nothing, but we both knew."

"You mean that you were going to kill me to keep me here?" he persisted.

She looked towards the knife lovingly.

"That isn't killing," she said. "Don't you see—you could never go away. You would be here always."

He began to understand, and a horrible idea stole into his brain.

"What about the man she thought was William?" he asked.

"You shall see him if you like," she answered eagerly. "You shall see how peaceful and happy he is. Perhaps you will be sorry then that you woke up. Come with me."

He possessed himself of the knife and followed her out of the room and across the landing. Underneath the door he could see the little chink of light—the light which had been his beacon from the road. She opened the door softly and held the candle over her head. Stretched upon another huge four-poster bed was the figure of a man with a ragged, untidy beard. His face was as pale as the sheet and Grant knew from the first glance that he was dead. By his side, seated stiffly in a high-backed chair, was Annabelle. She raised her finger and frowned as they entered. She looked across at Grant.

"Step quietly," she whispered. "William is asleep."

Just as the first gleam of dawn was forcing a finger of light through the sullen bank of clouds, a distraught and disheveled-looking man, followed by a small, fat, white dog stumbled into the village of Nidd, gasped with relief at the sight of the brass plate upon a door, and pulled the bell for all he was worth. Presently a window was opened and a man's shaggy head thrust out.

"Steady there!" he expostulated. "What's the trouble with you, anyway?"

Grant looked up.

"I've spent a part of the night in a farmhouse a few miles from here," he shouted. "There's a dead man there and two mad women and my car's broken down."

"A dead man?" the doctor repeated.

"I've seen him. My car's broken down in the road or I should have been here before."

"I'll be with you in five minutes," the doctor promised.

Presently the two men were seated in the doctor's car on their way back to the farm. It was light now, with signs of clearing, and in a short time they drew up in front of the farmhouse. There was no answer to their knock. The doctor turned the handle of the door and opened it. They entered the kitchen. The fire was out, but each in her high-backed chair, Mathilda and Annabelle were seated, facing one another, speechless, yet with wide-open eyes. They both turned their heads as the two men entered. Annabelle nodded with satisfaction.

"It is the doctor," she said. "Doctor, I am glad that you have come. You know, of course, that William is back. He came for me. He is lying upstairs but I cannot wake him. I sit with him and hold his hand and I speak to him, but he says nothing. He sleeps so soundly. Will you wake him for me, please. I will show you where he lies."

She led the way from the room, and the doctor followed her.

Mathilda listened to their footsteps. Then she turned to Grant with that strange smile once more upon her lips.

"Annabelle and I do not speak," she explained. "We quarreled just after you went away. We have not spoken for so many years that I forget how long it is. I should like someone to tell her, though, that the man who lies upstairs is not William. I should like someone to make her realize that you are William, and that you have come back for *me*. Sit down, William. Presently, when the doctor has gone, I will build the fire and make you some tea."

Grant sat down and again he felt his hands trembling. The woman looked at him kindly.

"You have been gone a long time," she continued. "I should have known you anywhere, though. It is strange that Annabelle does not recognize you. Sometimes I think we have lived together so long here that she may have lost her memory. I am glad you fetched the doctor, William. Now Annabelle will know her mistake."

There was the sound of footsteps descending the stairs. The doctor entered. He took Grant by the arm and led him to one side.

"You were quite right," he said gravely. "The man upstairs is a poor traveling tinker who has been missing for over a week. I should think that he has been dead at least four days. One of us must stay here while the other goes to the police station."

Grant caught feverishly at his hat.

"I will go for the police," he said.

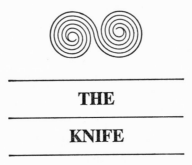

THE

KNIFE

Edward Dawes stifled his curiosity as long as he could, then he sidled over and lowered his large bulk carefully onto the chair opposite Herbert Smithers. Leaning on the table, he watched the other man clean away rusty mud from the object in his hands. It was a knife, that much was apparent. What was not apparent was why Smithers was so intent upon it, in its present condition. Edward Dawes nursed his glass of half-and-half and waited for Smithers to speak.

When Smithers continued to ignore him, Dawes drained his glass and banged it down with a gesture.

"Doesn't look like much, that there knife doesn't," he remarked disdainfully. " 'Ardly worth cleanin' it, I say."

"Ho!" Herbert Smithers retorted, and continued to work delicately with the point of a fingernail file at the caked dirt on his find.

"What is it?" Gladys, the Three Oaks' buxom barmaid, asked with open curiosity as she collected the empty glasses in front of them.

"It's a knife," Smithers vouchsafed. "A rare antique knife wot belongs to me because I found it."

It was now Mr. Dawes' turn to say, "Ho!"

"Thinks it's valuable, 'e does," he stated to the room at large, though it was empty save for the three of them.

"It don't look valuable to me," Gladys said frankly. "It looks like a nasty rusty old thing that ought to be put back on the rubbish heap it came from."

Smithers' silence was more eloquent than words. Discarding the file, he now moistened the corner of a grimy handkerchief with saliva, and rubbed at a small scarlet spot in the end of the still-obscured hilt. The spot enlarged and emerged from the grime as a faceted stone which glowed redly.

"Why, it's a jool!" Gladys exclaimed with quickened interest. "Look at it shine. Maybe it's real."

"Another half-and-half, if you please!" Smithers said pointedly, and Gladys flounced off. The swing of her well-curved hips disclaimed all interest, but her backward glance revealed what the swinging hips tried to deny.

"A jewel!" There was a hollow quality in Dawes' disdain now, and he leaned forward to stare as Smithers rubbed. "Not likely!"

"And 'ow," Smithers asked, with composed logic, "do you know?"

He breathed upon the red stone, polished it with his sleeve, and held it to admire it. Like a red eye it winked and glittered, seeming to gather into itself every crimson gleam from the tiny grate fire in the corner behind their table.

"Prob'ly," he remarked, with the quiet dignity befitting one who has just come into wealth, "it's a ruby."

"A ruby!" The larger Mr. Dawes seemed to choke on the word. "And wot would a knife with a real ruby in its 'ilt be doin' out in plain sight on the street for you to find?"

"Wasn't," Smithers said succinctly. He picked up the file again and began digging the dirt out of the crevices of the intricately worked handle. "It was in a pile of muck where they're fixin' th' drains, down Dorset street. Prob'ly been in th' drains no tellin' how many years."

His small figure straightened inside its shabby covering of clothes; his thin lips tightened.

"Look at th' rust an' muck on it!" he challenged. "That proves 'ow long it's been lyin' there. Nobody can't claim they lost it in th' blitz."

Reluctantly Mr. Dawes conceded the point.

"It's good steel, though," he added. "Still got a point to it, rust or no rust."

"Only a minute ago," Smithers pointed out, "you said as 'ow it wasn't worth while cleanin'."

Having removed enough of the encrusting dirt to show a slender, ornate hilt and a long tapering blade, he let his fingers close about the weapon. The hilt slipped naturally into the curve of his palm. He swung it a little, made a practice thrust-and-cut.

"It 'andles like it was part of me," he remarked dreamily. "Sends a kind of warm feelin' all up me arm, just to 'old it. Tingles it does, like electricity."

"Let me try," Mr. Dawes suggested, all disdain forgotten. Smithers scowled and drew his hand back.

"It's mine!" he said, a new truculent note in his voice. "Nobody else is touchin' it but me."

He thrust-and-cut again, and the red stone in the hilt flashed fire.

Smithers' thin, pinched face was flushed, as if reflecting the firelight, and he swayed, as though suddenly a little drunk.

"It's worth a 'eap," he said huskily. "This 'ere is a foreign knife, a old one, and it 'as a real ruby in the 'andle. I've made a find, I 'ave."

Gladys set down two glasses and forgot to complete her mechanical wiping of the table top. Smithers held the knife steady, to find the brightest possible glow of the stone in the hilt, and Gladys stared at it with covetous eyes.

"Maybe it is a real ruby at that," she said. "Let me have a look, ducky."

Her moist, outstretched fingers touched Smithers' hand, and the little man whirled, was on his feet.

"No!" he shouted. "It's mine, d'you hear?"

"Just a look," Gladys said eagerly. "I'll give it right back, promise."

She followed him a step, coaxingly, and the flush on Smithers' pinched features deepened.

"I tell you it's mine!" he cried shrilly. "An' no pretty face is gettin' it away from me. D'you hear! D'you hear!"

And then all three of them, even Gladys, were deathly silent, staring transfixed at the winking red eye which now of a sudden stood out some five inches from Gladys' heart, Smithers' fingers still gripped about the hilt.

Gladys' eyes grew wide and wider.

"You stabbed me," she said slowly and distinctly. "You stabbed me!" And then with no other sound but a queer rattling noise in her throat, she crumpled. Her body struck the floor with a crash that seemed to shake the room, and sprawled there emptily. A little red tongue licked across her breast and spread hungrily.

But even that, for a moment, did not change the position of the two men—Smithers standing, the knife left in his hand by Gladys' fall, and Dawes half risen, his hands on the table, his jaw slack.

The power of speech returned first to the little scavenger.

"I didn't do it!" he cried hoarsely. "I never did it! The knife stabbed her! 's truth, it did! And I couldn't stop it."

Then recovering a semblance of self-possession, he flung the knife down. Turning, he stumbled sobbingly toward the door and was gone.

Edward Dawes moved at last. Breathing hard, as if after a long run, he stood up. The knife lay at his feet. He listened. There was no sound, no outcry. He stooped. When he straightened, he held the knife gingerly in his hand. Mechanically, his gaze darting to the door and back, he wiped the blade on half his evening paper. Then he wrapped it in the other half. A moment later he was moving at a shambling run for the door.

His plan, formulated quite without conscious thought, was simple.

The lodging house run by his wife was directly across the street. From there he would phone the police. He was taking the knife to protect it as evidence. When the police arrived, he would turn it over to them minus the stone in the hilt. If Smithers, on being caught, mentioned it, he would swear that it must have been knocked out and lost when the knife was thrown to the floor.

Who was to prove different? . . .

Still breathing hard, Edward Dawes pried at the glittering red stone with the blade of a penknife. He was in the kitchen, just outside which was the phone. He had perhaps three minutes before the police got there in response to his call. He worked with the sweat pouring from his brow and his heart thudding as if he was exerting himself to the utmost.

Two minutes more. The prongs that held the stone were stout. His penknife slipped and cut him. He cursed under his breath, and went on working. The blood from his cut made his fingers slippery, and a moment later the knife shot from between them and clattered to the floor, the steel blade giving out a ringing note.

Dawes stooped, his bulk making the movement difficult, and snatched at the knife. It eluded him and skidded a foot away. A minute left. He followed it, not even taking time to curse now, and had it in his hand when his wife entered and stopped just inside the doorway.

"Edward," she began shrilly, "I heard you at the phone just now. What nonsense were you talking about a murder at the Three Oaks?"

Then she took in the whole scene as he straightened up—his flushed and furious face, the knife in his hand, the blood staining his fingers.

"Edward!" she shrieked. "You've killed somebody! You've killed somebody!"

He took a step toward her. There was a singing in his ears, and a strange warmth shooting up his arm. A reddish mist floated up before his eyes, hiding his wife from him.

"Shut up, you bloody fool!" he shouted.

His stout wife became silent at that, except for a blubbery gasping through which words seemed to be trying to come.

Then the reddish mist cleared, and Edward Dawes saw that she was lying on the floor, the hilt of the knife standing out from her plump white throat just beneath her chin, the red eye in the end of it winking and blinking up at him, holding him transfixed so that he did not hear the pounding on the outer door. Nor, a moment later, the sound of it opening. Nor the tramp of heavy official feet coming down the hallway . . .

"That's it, sir." Sergeant Tobins' tone was respectful, to a full inspector. "Killed two women inside ten minutes, it did. Two different men used it. Both of them claim they don't know why they did it."

He smiled, as if to say that he for one would never be taken in by such a claim.

"Hmm." The tall, gaunt man turned the knife delicately between his fingers. "Indian workmanship, I see. Sixteenth or seventeenth century."

"Get that, Miss Mapes?"

The plain, middle-aged woman standing at the inspector's elbow nodded. "Yes, sergeant," She made a few squiggles in her notebook.

"It's been cleaned up some, Inspector Frayne," Sergeant Tobins ventured. "No prints on it. Anyway, they both confessed."

"The stone?" The tall man tapped the hilt. "Is it real?"

"It's a ruby, right enough," the thickset sergeant agreed. "Badly flawed, though. Has an air bubble right in the middle of it, shaped like a drop of blood—" he coughed delicately—"like a teardrop, I mean."

Inspector Frayne continued turning the thing. Pencil ready, Miss Mapes waited.

"It's a genuine rarity, all the same." Frayne said. "Glad you asked me to look at it. Probably brought to this country by one of our Tommies after the Sepoy rebellion. Bit of looting done after it was put down, you know."

Miss Mapes' pencil scribbled busily.

"Found in a drain, wasn't it?" the inspector asked. "Been there a long time, that's plain. Which of them found it—Smithers or Dawes?"

"Smithers, sir. Funny thing, that. He was cleaning it, hadn't 'ad . . . had it more than an hour, when he used it on a barmaid. Then Dawes cops it and ten minutes later sticks it in his wife's throat.

And both of them said the same thing, when we questioned them."

"They did, eh? Just what did they say?"

"Well, sir, they said they got a warm, tingly feeling just from holding the knife. It came on all of a sudden like when they got angry at the women. They didn't know why they got so angry, they just did . . . and just like that the women were dead! They said—" Sergeant Tobins allowed himself to smile—"that they didn't have anything to do with it. That the knife just sort of moved by itself, with them holding it."

"They said that, eh? . . . Good Lord!" The tall man stared at the knife with a new interest. "Sergeant, just where was the drain in which this thing was found?"

"Dorset street, sir," Sergeant Tobins stated. "Near the corner of Commercial street."

"Dorset street, did you say?" Inspector Frayne's voice was sharp, his eyes alight. "By George, I wonder—"

Neither Tobins nor Miss Mapes interrupted. After a moment, Frayne put the knife back in its box on Sergeant Tobins' desk.

"I was having a brainstorm," he said, smiling. "This knife—well, do you know what happened on Dorset street a good while ago?"

Sergeant Tobins shook his head.

"I seem to remember of reading about it," he said. "But I can't just put my mind on where."

"It's mentioned in one of the largest files in our record department. It happens that in November of 1888 a woman was brutally murdered—with a knife—in Millers Court, off Dorset street. Her name was Marie Kelley."

Sergeant Tobins stared.

"I remember now," he blurted out. "Jack the Ripper!"

"Exactly. His last murder, we believe. The last of twelve. All women. He seemed to have a special, venomous hatred for women. And I was toying with the thought of a murderer hurrying from that spot in the dead of night, with a bloodstained knife in his hand. I could see him dropping it into a drain opening as he fled, to lie there until now . . . Well, as I say, a brainstorm."

Sergeant Tobins watched the door close, then turned.

"The inspector would do great writing thrillers," he said with ponderous humor. A regular information for it, he has!"

He picked up the knife, gripped it firmly, and struck a pose, winking broadly.

"Be careful, Miss Mapes!" he said. "Jack the Ripper!"

Miss Mapes giggled.

"Well now," she breathed. "Let me look at it, may I Sergeant Tobins, if you don't mind?"

Her fingers touched his, and Sergeant Tobins drew his hand back abruptly. His face flushed, and a fierce anger unaccountably flared up in him at the touch of Miss Mapes' hand. But as he stared into her plain, bewildered face, the anger was soothed by the pleasurable tingling warmth in his right wrist and arm. And as he took a swift step toward her, there was a strange, sweet singing in his ears, high and shrill and faraway.

Or was it the sound of a woman screaming?

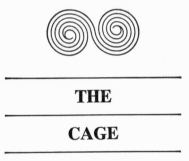

THE

CAGE

"They say," said the Countess, absently fondling the brooch at her young throat, "that he's the devil."

Her husband snorted, "Who says that? Fools and gossips. That boy is a good overseer. He manages my lands well. He may be a little—ruthless? cold?—but I doubt very much that he is the Enemy Incarnate."

"Ruthless, yes," said the Countess, gazing at the departing black-cowled, black-hosed, black-gloved figure. "But cold? He seems to be a favorite with the women. His conquests, they say, are legion."

" 'They' say. Gossips again. But there you are—would the angel Lucifer bed women?" The Count snorted again, pleased at his logical triumph.

"He might," replied his wife. "To walk the earth, he must take

122

the shape of a man. Might not the appetites of a man go with it?"

"I am sure I do not know. These are delicate points of theology. I suggest you discuss them with a Holy Father."

The Countess smiled. "What did he want?"

"Nothing. Business. Shall we go in to dinner?"

"Yes." The Count proffered his arm and they walked slowly through the tapestried halls of the castle. "He seemed most insistent about something," the Countess said after a moment.

"Who did?"

"Your efficient overseer."

"He was urging more stringent measures with the serfs. He said his authority had no teeth if he could not back it up with the threat of severe punishment. In my father's day, he said, the thought of the castle's torture chamber kept them in line."

"Your father's day? But does he know of your father?"

"My father's harshness, my dear, has ever been a blight on our family's escutcheon. It has created enemies on many sides. That is why I am especially careful to be lenient. History shall not call us tyrants if I can help it."

"I still believe he is the devil."

"You are a goose," said the Count, chuckling. "A beautiful goose."

"That makes you a gander, my lord."

"An old gander."

They sat at table. "My lord—" said the Countess.

"Yes?"

"That old torture chamber. How strange I've never seen it."

"In a mere three months," said the Count, "you could not possibly have seen the entire castle. Besides, it can be reached only by descending a hidden stairwell with a disguised door. We'll go down after dinner, if you like, although there's really nothing there to interest a sweet young goose."

"Three months . . ." said the Countess, almost inaudibly, fingering the brooch again.

"Does it seem longer since our marriage?" asked the Count.

"Longer?" She smiled, too brightly. "My lord, it seems like yesterday."

* * *

"They say," said the Countess, brushing her hair, "that you're the devil."

"Do you mind?"

"Should I mind? Will you drag me down to the Pit?"

"In one way or another."

"You speak in metaphor?"

"Perhaps."

"You are equivocal."

"Like the devil."

"And, like him, very naughty."

"Why? Because I am here in your boudoir and you are dressed in hardly anything at all?"

"Because of that, yes; and because you counsel my dear husband to be a tyrant, like his father."

"Did he tell you that?"

"Yes. And he showed me the torture chamber you advised him to reopen. How wicked of you! It is a terrible place. So dark and damp, and so deep underground—why, a poor wretch could split his lungs screaming and never be heard in the castle proper."

"Your eyes are shining. I assume you found it fascinating."

"Fascinating! Of course not! It was disgusting. That horrible rack . . . ugh! to think of the limbs stretching, the tendons tearing! . . . "

"You shudder deliciously. It becomes you."

"And that dreadful wheel, aud the iron boot . . . I have a pretty foot, don't you think?"

"Perfect."

"Such a high arch; and the toes so short and even. I hate long toes. You don't have long toes, do you?"

"You forget—I have no toes at all. Only hooves."

"Careful. I may believe you. And where are you horns?"

"They are invisible. Like those your husband will be wearing very soon."

"Indeed. You think highly of your charms."

"As do you. Of yours."

"Do you know what struck me as the most horrible?"

"Eh? Horrible about what?"

"The torture chamber, of course."

"Oh, of course. What struck you as most horrible?"

"There was a cage. A little cage. It looked like something you might keep a monkey in. It was too small for anything larger. And do you know what my husband said they kept in it?"

"What?"

"People!"

"No!"

"They kept people in it," he said. "They could not stand up straight, or lie down; they could not even sit, for there were only spikes to sit on. And they kept them crouching there for days. Sometimes weeks. Until they screamed to be let out. Until they went mad. I would rather be torn apart on the rack . . ."

"Or have this pretty foot crushed in the boot?"

"Don't. That tickles . . ."

"It was meant to."

"You must leave. The Count might walk in at any moment."

"Until tomorrow then, my lady . . ."

Alone, smiling to herself, the Countess absractedly rubbed the tops of her toes where he had kissed them. She had heard of burning kisses, they were a commonplace of bad troubadours, but until this evening she had thought the term a poetic extravagance. He wanted her—oh, how he wanted her! And he would have her. But not right away. Let him wait. Let him smoulder. Let him gaze at her in her diaphanous nightdress; let him, as she lifted her arms to brush her hair, admire the high beauty of her breasts. Allow him a kiss now and then. Oh, not on the mouth, not yet—on the feet, the fingertips, the forehead. Those burning kisses of his. Let him plead and groan. Let him suffer. She sighed happily as she turned down her bed. It was fine to be a woman and to be beautiful to dole out little favors like little crumbs and to watch men lick them up and pant and beg for more and then to laugh in their faces and let them starve. This one was already panting. Soon he would beg. And he would starve for a long, long time. Then, some night when she thought he had suffered long enough, she would allow him to feast. What a glutton he would make of himself! He would try to make up for lost time, for all the weeks of starvation, and he would feast too rapidly and it would all be over too soon and she would have to make him hungry again very quickly so he could gorge himself again. It would all be very amusing . . .

*   *   *

"If I *am* the devil, as you say they say, then why do I not overwhelm you with my infernal magic? Why do I grovel here at your feet, sick and stiff with love?"

"Perhaps it entertains you, my Dark Prince. Here: Kiss."

"No. I want your lips."

"Oh? You grow presumptuous. Perhaps you would rather leave."

"No . . . no . . ."

"That's better. I may yet grant you a promotion."

"Ah! my love! Then—"

"Oh, sit down. Not what you call my 'favor.' Just a *little* promotion. Though I don't know if you deserve even that. You want everything but you give nothing."

"Anything. Anything."

"What a large word! But perhaps *you* could indeed give me anything . . ."

"Anything."

"But they say you demand fearful things in return. I would suffer torment without end, through eternity . . . Ah, I see you do not deny this. I do believe you *are* the devil."

"I'll give you anything you desire. You have but to ask."

"I am young. Men tell me—and so does my mirror—that I am beautiful, a delight from head to toe. Do you want all this?"

"Yes! Yes!"

"Then make this beauty never fade. Make it withstand the onslaught of time and violence. Make me—no matter what may befall —live forever."

"Forever . . ."

"Haha! I've got you, haven't I? If I never die, then what of that eternal torment? Do you grant me this boon, Evil One?"

"I cannot."

"Wonderful! Oh, what an actor you are! I begin to admire you! Other men, impersonating the Adversary, would have said Yes. But you . . . how clever you are."

"I cannot grant that."

"Stop—I'm weak with laughing! This game amuses me *so* much! It lends such spice to this dalliance! I would play it to the end. Satan, look here: you really cannot grant my wish, even if I give you in return—all this?"

"Tormentress!"

"All this, my demon? In return for that one thing I desire? All this?"

"The Powers of Night will swirl and seethe, but—yes, yes, anything!"

"Ah! You disarming rogue, come take these lips, come take it all!"

* * *

"You said he was the devil and now I am inclined to believe you. The treacherous whelp! To bed my own wife in my own castle!"

"My lord, how can you think that *I*—"

"Silence! Stupid goose, do you still dissemble? He left without a word, under cover of night. Why? And your brooch—the brooch of my mother!—was found in his empty room; in your bedchamber, one of his black gloves. Wretched woman!"

"Indeed, indeed I am wretched . . ."

"Tears will avail you nothing. You must be humbled and you will be humbled. Give thanks that I am not my father. *He* would have left you crammed naked in this little cage until your mind rotted and your body after it. But I am no tyrant. All night long, without your supper, you will shiver and squirm down here in repentance, but in the morning I will release you. I hope with sincerity you will have learned your lesson by then. Now I am going. In a few hours, you will probably start screaming to be let out. Save your breath. I will not be able to hear you. Think of your sins! Repent!"

* * *

"They said he was the devil, but I place no stock in such talk. All I know is that he came to me directly from the old Count's castle where he had been overseer or something, and gave me complete plans for the storming of the battlements: information about the placement of the cannon, the least securely barricaded doors, the weakest walls, measurements, location of rooms, the exact strength of the castle guard and a schedule of its watch . . . everything I needed. My forces had been on a one-hour alert for months. I attacked that very night. Thanks to my informant, the battle was over before dawn."

"You are to be congratulated, Duke. And where is he now?"

"Gone. Vanished. I paid him handsomely, and just between the two of us, Baron, I was beginning to make plans for his disposal. A dangerous man to have near one. But the rascal was smart. He disappeared soon after my victory."

"And that head on the pike up there, with the gray beard fluttering in the wind—it belonged to the late Count?"

"Yes. To this end may *all* enemies of my family come."

"I'll drink to that. And what disposition was made of the old fool's wife?"

"The Countess? Ah. That is the only sourness in my triumph. I'd have enjoyed invading that pretty body before severing it from its pretty head. But she must have been warned. We searched and searched the castle that night. She was nowhere to be seen. She had escaped. Well . . . wherever she may be, I hope she gets wind of what I'm doing to her husband's castle."

"Razing it, aren't you?"

"Down to its foundation blocks—leaving only enough to identify it—and building on that foundation an edifice of solid stone that will be a monument to its downfall and to my victory. Forever."

"Where do you suppose the Countess is now?"

"The devil only knows. May the wench scream in torment for eternity."

◎ By Theodore Sturgeon

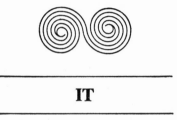

IT

It walked in the woods.

It was never born. It existed. Under the pine needles the fires burn, deep and smokeless in the mold. In heat and in darkness and decay there is growth. There is life and there is growth. It grew, but it was not alive. It walked unbreathing through the woods, and thought and saw and was hideous and strong, and it was not born and it did not live. It grew and moved about without living.

It crawled out of the darkness and hot damp mold into the cool of a morning. It was huge. It was lumped and crusted with its own hateful substances, and pieces of it dropped off as it went its way, dropped off and lay writhing, and stilled, and sank putrescent into the forest loam.

It had no mercy, no laughter, no beauty. It had strength and great intelligence. And—perhaps it could not be destroyed. It crawled out of its mound in the wood and lay pulsing in the sunlight for a long moment. Patches of it shone wetly in the golden glow, parts of it were nubbled and flaked. And whose dead bones had given it the form of a man?

It scrabbled painfully with its half-formed hands, beating the ground and the bole of a tree. It rolled and lifted itself up on its crumbling elbows, and it tore up a great handful of herbs and shredded them against its chest, and it paused and gazed at the gray-green juices with intelligent calm. It wavered to its feet, and seized a young sapling and destroyed it, folding the slender trunk back on itself again and again, watching attentively the useless, fibered splinters. And it snatched up a fear-frozen field-creature, crushing it slowly, letting blood and pulpy flesh and fur ooze from between its fingers, run down and rot on the forearms.

It began searching.

Kimbo drifted through the tall grasses like a puff of dust, his bushy tail curled tightly over his back and his long jaws agape. He ran with an easy lope, loving his freedom and the power of his flanks and furry shoulders. His tongue lolled listlessly over his lips. His lips were black and serrated, and each tiny pointed liplet swayed with his doggy gallop. Kimbo was all dog, all healthy animal.

He leaped high over a boulder and landed with a startled yelp as a long-eared cony shot from its hiding place under the rock. Kimbo hurtled after it, grunting with each great thrust of his legs. The rabbit bounced just ahead of him, keeping its distance, its ears flattened on its curving back and its little legs nibbling away at distance hungrily. It stopped, and Kimbo pounced, and the rabbit shot away at a tangent and popped into a hollow log. Kimbo yelped again and rushed snuffling at the log, and knowing his failure, curvetted but once around the stump and ran on into the forest. The thing that watched from the wood raised its crusted arms and waited for Kimbo.

Kimbo sensed it there, standing dead-still by the path. To him it was a bulk which smelled of carrion not fit to roll in, and he snuffled distastefully and ran to pass it.

The thing let him come abreast and dropped a heavy twisted fist on him. Kimbo saw it coming and curled up tight as he ran, and the hand clipped stunningly on his rump, sending him rolling and yipping down the slope. Kimbo straddled to his feet, shook his head, shook his body with a deep growl, came back to the silent thing with green murder in his eyes. He walked stiffly, straight-legged, his tail as low as his lowered head and a ruff of fury round his neck. The thing raised its arm again, waited.

Kimbo slowed, then flipped himself through the air at the monster's throat. His jaws closed on it; his teeth clicked together through a mass of filth, and he fell choking and snarling at its feet. The thing leaned down and struck twice, and after the dog's back was broken, it sat beside him and began to tear him apart.

"Be back in an hour or so," said Alton Drew, picking up his rifle from the corner behind the wood box. His brother laughed.

"Old Kimbo 'bout runs your life, Alton," he said.

"Ah, I know the ol' devil," said Alton. "When I whistle for him for half an hour and he don't show up, he's in a jam or he's treed something wuth shootin' at. The ol' son of a gun calls me by not answerin'."

Cory Drew shoved a full glass of milk over to his nine-year-old daughter and smiled. "You think as much o' that houn' dog o' yours as I do of Babe here."

Babe slid off her chair and ran to her uncle. "Gonna catch me the bad fella, Uncle Alton?" she shrilled. The "bad fella" was Cory's invention—the one who lurked in corners ready to pounce on little girls who chased the chickens and played around mowing machines and hurled green apples with powerful young arms at the sides of the hogs, to hear the synchronized thud and grunt; little girls who swore with an Austrian accent like an ex-hired man they had had; who dug caves in haystacks till they tipped over, and kept pet crawfish in tomorrow's milk cans, and rode work horses to a lather in the night pasture.

"Get back here and keep away from Uncle Alton's gun!" said Cory. "If you see the bad fella, Alton, chase him back here. He has a date with Babe here for that stunt of hers last night." The preceding evening, Babe had kind-heartedly poured pepper on the cows' salt block.

"Don't worry, kiddo," grinned her uncle, "I'll bring you the bad fella's hide if he don't get me first."

Alton Drew walked up the path toward the wood, thinking about Babe. She was a phenomenon—a pampered farm child. Ah well— she had to be. They'd both loved Clissa Drew, and she'd married Cory, and they had to love Clissa's child. Funny thing, love. Alton was a man's man, and thought things out that way; and his reaction to love was a strong and frightened one. He knew what love was because he felt it still for his brother's wife and would feel it as long as he lived for Babe. It led him through his life, and yet he embarrassed himself by thinking of it. Loving a dog was an easy thing, because you and the old devil could love one another completely without talking about it. The smell of gun smoke and wet fur in the rain were perfume enough for Alton Drew, a grunt of satisfaction and the scream of something hunted and hit were poetry enough. They weren't like love for a human, that choked his throat so he could not say words he could not have thought of anyway. So Alton loved his dog Kimbo and his Winchester for all to see, and let his love for his brother's women, Clissa and Babe, eat at him quietly and unmentioned.

His quick eyes saw the fresh indentations in the soft earth behind the boulder, which showed where Kimbo had turned and leaped with a single surge, chasing the rabbit. Ignoring the tracks, he looked for the nearest place where a rabbit might hide, and strolled over to the stump. Kimbo had been there, he saw, and had been there too late. "You're an ol' fool," muttered Alton. "Y' can't catch a cony by chasin' it. You want to cross him up some way." He gave a peculiar trilling whistle, sure that Kimbo was digging frantically under some nearby stump for a rabbit that was three counties away by now. No answer. A little puzzled, Alton went back to the path. "He never done this before," he said softly.

He cocked his .32-40 and cradled it. At the county fair someone had once said of Alton Drew that he could shoot at a handful of corn and peas thrown in the air and hit only the corn. Once he split a bullet on the blade of a knife and put two candles out. He had no need to fear anything that could be shot at. That's what he believed.

The thing in the woods looked curiously down at what it had done to Kimbo, and tried to moan the way Kimbo had before he died. It stood a minute storing away facts in its foul, unemotional mind. Blood was warm. The sunlight was warm. Things that moved and bore fur had a muscle to force the thick liquid through tiny tubes in their bodies. The liquid coagulated after a time. The liquid on rooted green things was thinner and the loss of a limb did not mean loss of life. It was very interesting, but the thing, the mold with a mind, was not pleased. Neither was it displeased. Its accidental urge was a thirst for knowledge, and it was only—interested.

It was growing late, and the sun reddened and rested awhile on the hilly horizon, teaching the clouds to be inverted flames. The thing threw up its head suddenly, noticing the dusk. Night was ever a strange thing, even for those of us who have known it in life. It would have been frightening for the monster had it been capable of fright, but it could only be curious; it could only reason from what it had observed.

What was happening? It was getting harder to see. Why? It threw its shapeless head from side to side. It was true—things were dim, and growing dimmer. Things were changing shape, taking on a new and darker color. What did the creatures it had crushed and torn apart see? How did they see? The larger one, the one that had attacked, had used two organs in its head. That must have been it, because after the thing had torn off two of the dog's legs it had struck at the hairy muzzle; and the dog, seeing the blow coming, had dropped folds of skin over the organs—closed its eyes. Ergo, the dog saw with its eyes. But then after the dog was dead, and its body still, repeated blows had had no effect on the eyes. They remained open and staring. The logical conclusion was, then, that a being that had ceased to live and breathe and move about lost the use of its eyes. It must be that to lose sight was, conversely, to die. Dead things did not walk about. They lay down and did not move. Therefore the thing in the wood concluded that it must be dead, and so it lay down by the path, not far away from Kimbo's scattered body, lay down and believed itself dead.

Alton Drew came up through the dusk to the wood. He was frankly worried. He whistled again, and then called, and there was still no response, and he said again, "The ol' flea-bus never done this before," and shook his heavy head. It was past milking time, and Cory would need him. "Kimbo!" he roared. The cry echoed through the shadows, and Alton flipped on the safety catch of his rifle and put the butt on the ground beside the path. Leaning on it, he took off his cap and scratched the back of his head, wondering. The rifle butt sank into what he thought was soft earth; he staggered and stepped into the chest of the thing that lay beside the path. His foot went up to the ankle in its yielding rottenness, and he swore and jumped back.

"*Whew!* Somp'n sure dead as hell there! Ugh!" He swabbed at his boot with a handful of leaves while the monster lay in the growing blackness with the edges of the deep footprint in its chest sliding into it, filling it up. It lay there regarding him dimly out of its muddy eyes, thinking it was dead because of the darkness, watching the articulation of Alton Drew's joints, wondering at this new uncautious creature.

Alton cleaned the butt of his gun with more leaves and went on up the path, whistling anxiously for Kimbo.

Clissa Drew stood in the door of the milk shed, very lovely in red-checked gingham and a blue apron. Her hair was clean yellow, parted in the middle and stretched tautly back to a heavy braided knot. "Cory! Alton!" she called a little sharply.

"Well?" Cory responded gruffly from the barn, where he was stripping off the Ayrshire. The dwindling streams of milk plopped pleasantly into the froth of a full pail.

"I've called and called," said Clissa. "Supper's cold, and Babe won't eat until you come. Why—where's Alton?"

Cory grunted, heaved the stool out of the way, threw over the stanchion lock and slapped the Ayrshire on the rump. The cow backed and filled like a towboat, clattered down the line and out into the barn-yard. "Ain't back yet."

"Not back?" Clissa came in and stood beside him as he sat by the next cow, put his forehead against the warm flank. "But, Cory, he said he'd—"

"Yeh, yeh, I know. He said he'd be back fer the milkin'. I heard him. Well, he ain't."

"And you have to—Oh, Cory, I'll help you finish up. Alton would be back if he could. Maybe he's—"

"Maybe he's treed a blue jay," snapped her husband. "Him an' that damn dog." He gestured hugely with one hand while the other went on milking. "I got twenty-six head o' cows to milk. I got pigs to feed an' chickens to put to bed. I got to toss hay for the mare and turn the team out. I got harness to mend and a wire down in the night pasture. I got wood to split an' carry." He milked for a moment in silence, chewing on his lip. Clissa stood twisting her hands together, trying to think of something to stem the tide. It wasn't the first time Alton's hunting had interfered with the chores. "So I got to go ahead with it. I can't interfere with Alton's spoorin'. Every damn time that hound o' his smells out a squirrel I go without my supper. I'm gettin' sick and—"

"Oh, I'll help you!" said Clissa. She was thinking of the spring, when Kimbo had held four hundred pounds of raging black bear at bay until Alton could put a bullet in its brain, the time Babe had found a bear cub and started to carry it home, and had fallen into a freshet, cutting her head. You can't hate a dog that has saved your child for you, she thought.

"You'll do nothin' of the kind!" Cory growled. "Get back to the house. You'll find work enough there. I'll be along when I can. Dammit, Clissa, don't cry! I didn't mean to—Oh, shucks!" He got up and put his arms around her. "I'm wrought up," he said. "Go on now. I'd no call to speak that way to you. I'm sorry. Go back to Babe. I'll put a stop to this for good tonight. I've had enough. There's work here for four farmers an' all we've got is me an' that . . . that huntsman.

"Go on now, Clissa."

"All right," she said into his shoulder. "But, Cory, hear him out first when he comes back. He might be unable to come back. He might be unable to come back this time. Maybe he . . . he—"

"Ain't nothin' kin hurt my brother that a bullet will hit. He can take care of himself. He's got no excuse good enough this time. Go on, now. Make the kid eat."

Clissa went back to the house, her young face furrowed. If Cory quarreled with Alton now and drove him away, what with the drought and the creamery about to close and all, they just couldn't manage. Hiring a man was out of the question. Cory'd have to work himself to death, and he just wouldn't be able to make it. No one man could. She sighed and went into the house. It was seven o'clock, and the milking not done yet. Oh, why did Alton have to—

Babe was in bed at nine when Clissa heard Cory in the shed, slinging the wire cutters into a corner. "Alton back yet?" they both said at once as Cory stepped into the kitchen; and as she shook her head he clumped over to the stove, and lifting a lid, spat into the coals. "Come to bed," he said.

She laid down her stitching and looked at his broad back. He was twenty-eight, and he walked and acted like a man ten years older, and looked like a man five years younger. "I'll be up in a while," Clissa said.

Cory glanced at the corner behind the wood box where Alton's rifle usually stood, then made an unspellable, disgusted sound and sat down to take off his heavy muddy shoes.

"It's after nine," Clissa volunteered timidly. Cory said nothing, reaching for house slippers.

"Cory, you're not going to—"

"Not going to what?"

"Oh, nothing. I just thought that maybe Alton—"

"Alton," Cory flared. "The dog goes hunting field mice. Alton goes hunting the dog. Now you want me to go hunting Alton. That's what you want?"

"I just—He was never this late before."

"I won't do it! Go out lookin' for him at nine o'clock in the night? I'll be damned! He has no call to use us so, Clissa."

Clissa said nothing. She went to the stove, peered into the wash boiler set aside at the back of the range. When she turned around, Cory had his shoes and coat on again.

"I knew you'd go," she said. Her voice smiled though she did not.

"I'll be back durned soon," said Cory. "I don't reckon he's strayed far. It is late. I ain't feared for him, but—" He broke his 12-gauge shotgun, looked through the barrels, slipped two shells in the breech and a box of them into his pocket. "Don't wait up," he said over his shoulder as he went out.

"I won't," Clissa replied to the closed door, and went back to her stitching by the lamp.

The path up the slope to the wood was very dark when Cory went up it, peering and calling. The air was chill and quiet, and a fetid odor of mold hung in it. Cory blew the taste of it out through impatient nostrils, drew it in again with the next breath, and swore. "Nonsense," he muttered. "Houn' dawg. Huntin', at ten in th' night, too. Alton!" he bellowed. "Alton Drew!" Echoes answered him, and he entered the wood. The huddled thing he passed in the dark heard him and felt the vibrations of his footsteps and did not move because it thought it was dead.

Cory strode on, looking around and ahead and not down since his feet knew the path.

"Alton!"

"That you, Cory?"

Cory Drew froze. That corner of the wood was thickly set and as dark as a burial vault. The voice he heard was choked, quiet, penetrating.

"Alton?"

"I found Kimbo, Cory."

"Where the hell have you been?" shouted Cory furiously. He disliked this pitch-darkness; he was afraid at the tense hopelessness of Alton's voice, and he mistrusted his ability to stay angry at his brother.

"I called him, Cory. I whistled at him, an' the ol' devil didn't answer."

"I can say the same for you, you . . . you louse. Why weren't you to milkin'? Where are you? You caught in a trap?"

"The houn' never missed answerin' me before, you know," said the tight, monotonous voice from the darkness.

"Alton! What the devil's the matter with you? What do I care if your mutt didn't answer? Where—"

"I guess because he ain't never died before," said Alton, refusing to be interrupted.

"You *what?*" Cory clicked his lips together twice and then said, "Alton, you turned crazy? What's that you say?"

"Kimbo's dead."

"Kim . . . oh! Oh!" Cory was seeing that picture again in his mind—Babe sprawled unconscious in the freshet, and Kimbo raging and snapping against a monster bear, holding her back until Alton could get there. "What happened, Alton?" he asked more quietly.

"I aim to find out. Someone tore him up."

"*Tore him up?*"

"There ain't a bit of him left tacked together, Cory. Every damn joint in his body tore apart. Guts out of him."

"Good God! Bear, you reckon?"

"No bear, nor nothin' on four legs. He's all here. None of him's been et. Whoever done it just killed him an'—tore him up."

"Good God!" Cory said again. "Who could've—" There was a long silence, then. "Come 'long home," he said almost gently. "There's no call for you to set up by him all night."

"I'll set. I aim to be here at sunup, an' I'm going to start trackin', an' I'm goin' to keep trackin' till I find the one done this job on Kimbo."

"You're drunk or crazy, Alton."

"I ain't drunk. You can think what you like about the rest of it. I'm stickin' here."

"We got a farm back yonder. Remember? I ain't going to milk twenty-six head o' cows again in the mornin' like I did jest now, Alton."

"Somebody's got to. I can't be there. I guess you'll just have to, Cory."

"You dirty scum!" Cory screamed. "You'll come back with me now or I'll know why!"

Alton's voice was still tight, half-sleepy. "Don't you come no nearer, bud."

Cory kept moving toward Alton's voice.

"I said"—the voice was very quiet now—"*stop where you are.*" Cory kept coming. A sharp click told of the release of the .32-40's safety. Cory stopped.

"You got your gun on me, Alton?" Cory whispered.

"Thass right, bud. You ain't a-trompin' up these tracks for me. I need 'em at sunup."

A full minute passed, and the only sound in the blackness was that of Cory's pained breathing. Finally:

"I got my gun, too, Alton. Come home."

"You can't see to shoot me."

"We're even on that."

"We ain't. I know just where you stand, Cory. I been here four hours."

"My gun scatters."

"My gun kills."

Without another word Cory Drew turned on his heel and stamped back to the farm.

Black and liquidescent it lay in the blackness, not alive, not understanding death, believing itself dead. Things that were alive saw and moved about. Things that were not alive could do neither. It rested its muddy gaze on the line of trees at the crest of the rise, and deep within it thoughts trickled wetly. It lay huddled, dividing its new-found facts, dissecting them as it had dissected live things when there was light; comparing, concluding, pigeonholing.

The trees at the top of the slope could just be seen, as their trunks were a fraction of a shade lighter than the dark sky behind them. At length they, too, disappeared, and for a moment sky and trees were a monotone. The thing knew it was dead now, and like many a being before it, it wondered how long it must stay like this. And then the sky beyond the trees grew a little lighter. That was a manifestly impossible occurrence, thought the thing, but it could see it and it must be so. Did dead things live again? That was curious. What about dismembered dead things? It would wait and see.

The sun came hand over hand up a beam of light. A bird somewhere made a high yawning peep, and as an owl killed a shrew, a skunk pounced on another, so that the night-shift deaths and those of the day could go on without cessation. Two flowers nodded archly to each other, comparing their pretty clothes. A dragonfly nymph decided it was tired of looking serious and cracked its back open, to crawl out and dry gauzily. The first golden ray sheared down between the trees, through the grasses, passed over the mass in the shadowed bushes. "I am alive again," thought the thing that could not possibly live. "I am alive, for I see clearly." It stood up on its thick legs, up into the golden glow. In a little while the wet flakes that had grown during the night dried in the sun, and when it took its first steps, they cracked off and a small shower of them fell away. It walked up the slope to find Kimbo, to see if he, too, were alive again.

Babe let the sun come into her room by opening her eyes. Uncle Alton was gone—that was the first thing that ran through her head. Dad had come home last night and had shouted at mother for an hour. Alton was plumb crazy. He'd turned a gun on his own brother. If Alton ever came ten feet into Cory's land, Cory would fill him so full of holes, he'd look like a tumbleweed. Alton was lazy, shiftless, selfish, and one or two other things of questionable taste but undoubted vividness. Babe knew her father. Uncle Alton would never be safe in this county.

She bounced out of bed in the enviable way of the very young, and ran to the window. Cory was trudging down to the night pasture with two bridles over his arm, to get the team. There were kitchen noises from downstairs.

Babe ducked her head in the washbowl and shook off the water like a terrier before she toweled. Trailing clean shirt and dungarees, she went to the head of the stairs, slid into the shirt, and began her morning ritual with the trousers. One step down was a step through the right leg. One more, and she was into the left. Then, bouncing step by step on both feet, buttoning one button per step, she reached the bottom fully dressed and ran into the kitchen.

"Didn't Uncle Alton come back a-tall, Mum?"

"Morning, Babe. No, dear." Clissa was too quiet, smiling too much, Babe thought shrewdly. Wasn't happy.

"Where'd he go, Mum?"

"We don't know, Babe. Sit down and eat your breakfast."

"What's a misbegotten, Mum?" the Babe asked suddenly. Her mother nearly dropped the dish she was drying. "Babe! You must never say that again!"

"Oh. Well, why is Uncle Alton, then?"

"Why is he what?"

Babe's mouth muscled around an outsize spoonful of oatmeal. "A misbe—"

"Babe!"

"All right, Mum," said Babe with her mouth full. "Well, why?"

"I told Cory not to shout last night," Clissa said half to herself.

"Well, whatever it means, he isn't," said Babe with finality. "Did he go hunting again?"

"He went to look for Kimbo, darling."

"Kimbo? Oh Mummy, is Kimbo gone, too? Didn't he come back either?"

"No dear. Oh, please, Babe, stop asking questions!"

"All right. Where do you think they went?"

"Into the north woods. Be quiet."

Babe gulped away at her breakfast. An idea struck her; and as she thought of it she ate slower and slower, and cast more and more glances at her mother from under the lashes of her tilted eyes. It would be awful if daddy did anything to Uncle Alton. Someone ought to warn him.

Babe was halfway to the woods when Alton's .32-40 sent echoes giggling up and down the valley.

Cory was in the south thirty, riding a cultivator and cussing at the team of grays when he heard the gun. "Hoa," he called to the horses, and sat a moment to listen to the sound. "One-two-three. Four," he counted. "Saw someone, blasted away at him. Had a chance to take aim and give him another, careful. My God!" He threw up the cultivator points and steered the team into the shade of three oaks. He hobbled the gelding with swift tosses of a spare strap, and headed for the woods. "Alton a killer," he murmured, and doubled back to the house for his gun. Clissa was standing just outside the door.

"Get shells!" he snapped and flung into the house. Clissa followed him. He was strapping his hunting knife on before she could get a box off the shelf. "Cory—"

"Hear that gun, did you? Alton's off his nut. He don't waste lead. He shot at someone just then, and he wasn't fixin' to shoot pa'tridges when I saw him last. He was out to get a man. Gimme my gun."

"Cory, Babe—"

"You keep her here. Oh, God, this is a helluva mess. I can't stand much more." Cory ran out the door.

Clissa caught his arm: "Cory I'm trying to tell you. Babe isn't here. I've called, and she isn't here."

Cory's heavy, young-old face tautened. "Babe—Where did you last see her?"

"Breakfast." Clissa was crying now.

"She say where she was going?"

"No. She asked a lot of questions about Alton and where he'd gone."

"Did you say?"

Clissa's eyes widened, and she nodded, biting the back of her hand.

"You shouldn't ha' done that, Clissa," he gritted, and ran toward the woods, Clissa looking after him, and in that moment she could have killed herself.

Cory ran with his head up, straining with his legs and lungs and eyes at the long path. He puffed up the slope to the woods, agonized for breath after the forty-five minutes' heavy going. He couldn't even notice the damp smell of mold in the air.

He caught a movement in a thicket to his right, and dropped. Struggling to keep his breath, he crept forward until he could see clearly. There was something in there, all right. Something black, keeping still. Cory relaxed his legs and torso completely to make it easier for his heart to pump some strength back into them, and slowly raised the 12-gauge until it bore on the thing hidden in the thicket.

"Come out!" Cory said when he could speak.

Nothing happened.

"Come out or by God I'll shoot!" rasped Cory.

There was a long moment of silence, and his finger tightened on the trigger.

"You asked for it," he said, and as he fired, the thing leaped sideways into the open, screaming.

It was a thin little man dressed in sepulchral black, and bearing the rosiest baby-face Cory had ever seen. The face was twisted with fright and pain. The man scrambled to his feet and hopped up and down saying over and over, "Oh, my hand. Don't shoot again! Oh, my hand. Don't shoot again!" He stopped after a bit, when Cory had climbed to his feet, and he regarded the farmer out of sad china-blue eyes. "You shot me," he said reproachfully, holding up a little bloody hand. "Oh, my goodness."

Cory said, "Now, who the hell are you?"

The man immediately became hysterical, mouthing such a flood of broken sentences that Cory stepped back a pace and half-raised his gun in self-defense. It seemed to consist mostly of "I lost my papers," and "I didn't do it," and "It was horrible. Horrible. Horrible," and "The dead man," and "Oh, don't shoot again."

Cory tried twice to ask him a question, and then he stepped over and knocked the man down. He lay on the ground writhing and moaning and blubbering and putting his bloody hand to his mouth where Cory had hit him.

"Now what's going on around here?"

The man rolled over and sat up. "I didn't do it!" he sobbed. "I didn't. I was walking along and I heard the gun and I heard some swearing and an awful scream and I went over there and peeped and I saw the dead man and I ran away and you came and I hid and you shot me and—"

"*Shut up!*" The man did, as if a switch had been thrown. "Now," said Cory, pointing along the path, "you say there's a dead man up there?"

The man nodded and began crying in earnest. Cory helped him up. "Follow this path back to my farmhouse," he said. "Tell my wife to fix up your hand. *Don't* tell her anything else. And wait there until I come. Hear?"

"Yes. Thank you. Oh, thank you. *Snff.*"

"Go on now." Cory gave him a gentle shove in the right direction and went alone, in cold fear, up the path to the spot where he had found Alton the night before.

He found him here now, too, and Kimbo. Kimbo and Alton had spent several years together in the deepest friendship; they had hunted and fought and slept together, and the lives they owed each other were finished now. They were dead together.

It was terrible that they died the same way. Cory Drew was a strong man, but he gasped and fainted dead away when he saw what the thing of the mold had done to his brother and his brother's dog.

The little man in black hurried down the path, whimpering and holding his injured hand as if he rather wished he could limp with it. After a while the whimper faded away, and the hurried stride changed to a walk as the gibbering terror of the last hour receded. He drew two deep breaths, said: "My goodness!" and felt almost normal. He bound a linen handkerchief around his wrist, but the hand kept bleeding. He tried the elbow, and that made it hurt. So he stuffed the handkerchief back in his pocket and simply waved the hand stupidly in the air until the blood clotted. He did not see the great moist horror that clumped along behind him, although his nostrils crinkled with its foulness.

The monster had three holes close together on its chest, and one hole in the middle of its slimy forehead. It had three close-set pits in its back and one on the back of its head. These marks were where Alton Drew's bullets had struck and passed through. Half of the monster's shapeless face was sloughed away, and there was a deep indentation on its shoulder. This was what Alton Drew's gun butt had done after he clubbed it and struck at the thing that would not lie down after he put his four bullets through it. When these things happened the monster was not hurt or angry. It only wondered why Alton Drew acted that way. Now it followed the little man without hurrying at all, matching his stride step by step and dropping little particles of muck behind it.

The little man went on out of the wood and stood with his back against a big tree at the forest's edge, and he thought. Enough had happened to him here. What good would it do to stay and face a horrible murder inquest, just to continue this silly, vague search? There was supposed to be the ruin of an old, old hunting lodge deep in this wood somewhere, and perhaps it would hold the evidence he wanted. But it was a vague report—vague enough to be forgotten without regret. It would be the height of foolishness to stay for all the hick-town red tape that would follow that ghastly affair back in the wood. Ergo, it would be ridiculous to follow that farmer's advice, to go to his house and wait for him. He would go back to town.

The monster was leaning against the other side of the big tree.

The little man snuffled disgustedly at a sudden overpowering odor of rot. He reached for his handkerchief, fumbled and dropped it. As he bent to pick it up, the monster's arm *whuffed* heavily in the air where his head had been—a blow that would certainly have removed that baby-face protuberance. The man stood up and would have put the handkerchief to his nose had it not been so bloody. The creature behind the tree lifted its arm again just as the little man tossed the handkerchief away and stepped out into the field, heading across country to the distant highway that would take him back to town. The monster pounced on the handkerchief, picked it up, studied it, tore it across several times and inspected the tattered edges. Then it gazed vacantly at the disappearing figure of the little man, and finding him no longer interesting, turned back into the woods.

Babe broke into a trot at the sound of the shots. It was important to warn Uncle Alton about what her father had said, but it was more interesting to find out what he had bagged. Oh, he'd bagged it, all right. Uncle Alton never fired without killing. This was about the first time she had ever heard him blast away like that. Must be a bear, she thought excitedly, tripping over a root, sprawling, rolling to her feet again, without noticing the tumble. She'd love to have another bearskin in her room. Where would she put it? Maybe they could line it and she could have it for a blanket. Uncle Alton could sit on it and read to her in the evening—Oh, no. No. Not with this trouble between him and dad. Oh, if she could only do something! She tried to run faster, worried and anticipating, but she was out of breath and went more slowly instead.

At the top of the rise by the edge of the woods she stopped and looked back. Far down in the valley lay the south thirty. She scanned it carefully, looking for her father. The new furrows and the old were sharply defined, and her keen eyes saw immediately that Cory had left the line with the cultivator and had angled the team over to the shade trees without finishing his row. That wasn't like him. She could see the team now, and Cory's pale-blue denim was nowhere in sight. She giggled lightly to herself as she thought of the way she would fool her father. And the little sound of laughter drowned out, for her, the sound of Alton's hoarse dying scream.

She reached and crossed the path and slid through the brush beside it. The shots came from up around here somewhere. She stopped and listened several times, and then suddenly heard something coming toward her, fast. She ducked under cover, terrified, and a little baby-faced man in black, his blue eyes wide with horror, crashed blindly past her, the leather case he carried catching on the branches. It spun a moment and then fell right in front of her. The man never missed it.

Babe lay there for a long moment and then picked up the case and faded into the woods. Things were happening too fast for her. She wanted Uncle Alton, but she dared not call. She stopped again and strained her ears. Back toward the edge of the wood she heard her father's voice, and another's—probably the man who had dropped the brief case. She dared not go over there. Filled with enjoyable terror, she thought hard, then snapped her fingers in triumph. She and Alton had played Injun many times up here; they had a whole repertoire of secret signals. She had practiced birdcalls until she knew them better than the birds themselves. What would it be? Ah —bluejay. She threw back her head and by some youthful alchemy produced a nerve-shattering screech that would have done justice to any jay that ever flew. She repeated it, and then twice more.

The response was immediate—the call of a bluejay, four times, spaced two and two. Babe nodded to herself happily. That was the signal that they were to meet immediately at The Place. The Place was a hide-out that he had discovered and shared with her, and not another soul knew of it; an angle of rock beside a stream not far away. It wasn't exactly a cave, but almost. Enough so to be entrancing. Babe trotted happily away toward the brook. She had just known that Uncle Alton would remember the call of the bluejay, and what it meant.

In the tree that arched over Alton's scattered body perched a large jay bird, preening itself and shining in the sun. Quite unconscious of the presence of death, hardly noticing the Babe's realistic cry, it screamed again four times, two and two.

It took Cory more than a moment to recover himself from what he had seen. He turned away from it and leaned weakly against a pine, panting. Alton. That was Alton lying there, in—parts.

"God! God, God, God—"

Gradually his strength returned, and he forced himself to turn again. Stepping carefully, he bent and picked up the .32–40. Its barrel was bright and clean, but the butt and stock were smeared with some kind of stinking rottenness. Where had he seen the stuff before? Somewhere—no matter. He cleaned it off absently, throwing the befouled bandanna away afterward. Through his mind ran Alton's words—was that only last night?—*"I'm goin' to start trackin'. An' I'm goin' to keep trackin' till I find the one done this job on Kimbo."*

Cory searched shrinkingly until he found Alton's box of shells. The box was wet and sticky. That made it—better, somehow. A bullet wet with Alton's blood was the right thing to use. He went away a short distance, circled around till he found heavy footprints, then came back.

"I'm a-trackin' for you, bud," he whispered thickly, and began. Through the brush he followed its wavering spoor, amazed at the amount of filthy mold about, gradually associating it with the thing that had killed his brother. There was nothing in the world for him any more but hate and doggedness. Cursing himself for not getting Alton home last night, he followed the tracks to the edge of the woods. They led him to a big tree there, and there he saw something else—the footprints of the little city man. Nearby lay some tattered scraps of linen, and—what was that?

Another set of prints—small ones. Small, stub-toed ones.

"Babe!"

No answer. The wind sighed. Somewhere a bluejay called.

Babe stopped and turned when she heard her father's voice, faint with distance, piercing.

"Listen at him holler," she crooned delightedly. "Gee, he sounds mad." She sent a jay bird's call disrespectfully back to him and hurried to The Place.

It consisted of a mammoth boulder beside the brook. Some upheaval in the glacial age had cleft it, cutting out a huge V-shaped chunk. The widest part of the cleft was at the water's edge, and the narrowest was hidden by bushes. It made a little ceilingless room, rough and uneven and full of pot-holes and cavelets inside, and yet with quite a level floor. The open end was at the water's edge.

Babe parted the bushes and peered down the cleft.

"Uncle Alton!" she called softly. There was no answer. Oh, well, he'd be along. She scrambled in and slid down to the floor.

She loved it here. It was shaded and cool, and the chattering stream filled it with shifting golden lights and laughing gurgles. She called again, on principle, and then perched on an outcropping to wait. It was only then she realized that she still carried the little man's brief case.

She turned it over a couple of times and then opened it. It was divided in the middle by a leather wall. On one side were a few papers in a large yellow envelope, and on the other some sandwiches, a candy bar, and an apple. With a youngster's complacent acceptance of manna from heaven, Babe fell to. She saved one sandwich for Alton, mainly because she didn't like its highly spiced bologna. The rest made quite a feast.

She was a little worried when Alton hadn't arrived, even after she had consumed the apple core. She got up and tried to skim some flat pebbles across the roiling brook, and she stood on her hands, and she tried to think of a story to tell herself, and she tried just waiting. Finally, in desperation, she turned again to the brief case, took out the papers, curled up by the rocky wall and began to read them. It was something to do, anyway.

There was an old newspaper clipping that told about strange wills that people had left. An old lady had once left a lot of money to whoever would make the trip from the Earth to the Moon and back.

Another had financed a home for cats whose masters and mistresses had died. A man left thousands of dollars to the first person who could solve a certain mathematical problem and prove his solution. But one item was blue-penciled. It was:

> One of the strangest of wills still in force is that of Thaddeus M. Kirk, who died in 1920. It appears that he built an elaborate mausoleum with burial vaults for all the remains of his family. He collected and removed caskets from all over the country to fill the designated niches. Kirk was the last of his line; there were no relatives when he died. His will stated that the mausoleum was to be kept in repair permanently, and that a certain sum was to be set aside as a reward for whoever could produce the body of his grandfather, Roger Kirk, whose niche is still empty. Anyone finding this body is eligible to receive a substantial fortune.

Babe yawned vaguely over this, but kept on reading because there was nothing else to do. Next was a thick sheet of business correspondence, bearing the letterhead of a firm of lawyers. The body of it ran:

> In regard to your query regarding the will of Thaddeus Kirk, we are authorized to state that his grandfather was a man about five feet, five inches, whose left arm had been broken and who had a triangular silver plate set into his skull. There is no information as to the whereabouts of his death. He disappeared and was declared legally dead after the lapse of fourteen years.
>
> The amount of the reward as stated in the will, plus accrued interest, now amounts to a fraction over sixty-two thousand dollars. This will be paid to anyone who produces the remains, providing that said remains answer descriptions kept in our private files.

There was more, but Babe was bored. She went on to the little black notebook. There was nothing in it but penciled and highly abbreviated records of visits to libraries; quotations from books with titles like "History of Angelina and Tyler Counties" and "Kirk Family History." Babe threw that aside, too. Where could Uncle Alton be?

She began to sing tunelessly, "Tumalumalum tum, ta ta ta," pretending to dance a minuet with flowing skirts like a girl she had seen in the movies. A rustle of the bushes at the entrance to The Place stopped her. She peeped upward, saw them being thrust aside. Quickly she ran to a tiny cul-de-sac in the rock wall, just big enough for her to hide in. She giggled at the thought of how surprised Uncle Alton would be when she jumped out at him.

She heard the newcomer come shuffling down the steep slope of the crevice and land heavily on the floor. There was something about the sound—What was it? It occurred to her that though it was a hard job for a big man like Uncle Alton to get through the little opening in the bushes, she could hear no heavy breathing. She heard no breathing at all!

Babe peeped out into the main cave and squealed in utmost horror. Standing there was, not Uncle Alton, but a massive caricature of a man: a huge thing like an irregular mud doll, clumsily made. It quivered and parts of it glistened and parts of it were dried and crumbly. Half of the lower left part of its face was gone, giving it a lopsided look. It had no perceptible mouth or nose, and its eyes were crooked, one higher than the other, both a dingy brown with no whites at all. It stood quite still looking at her, its only movement a steady unalive quivering.

It wondered about the queer little noise Babe had made.

Babe crept far back against a little pocket of stone, her brain running round and round in tiny circles of agony. She opened her mouth to cry out, and could not. Her eyes bulged and her face flamed with the strangling effort, and the two golden ropes of her braided hair twitched and twitched as she hunted hopelessly for a way out. If only she were out in the open—or in the wedge-shaped half-cave where the thing was—or home in bed!

The thing clumped toward her, expressionless, moving with a slow inevitability that was the sheer crux of horror. Babe lay wide-eyed and frozen, mounting pressure of terror stilling her lungs, making her heart shake the whole world. The monster came to the mouth of the little pocket, tried to walk to her and was stopped by the sides. It was such a narrow little fissure, and it was all Babe could do to get in. The thing from the wood stood straining against the rock at its shoulders, pressing harder and harder to get to Babe. She sat up slowly, so near to the thing that its odor was almost thick enough to see, and a wild hope burst through her voiceless fear. It couldn't get in! It couldn't get in because it was too big! The substance of its feet spread slowly under the tremendous strain and at its shoulder appeared a slight crack. It widened as the monster unfeelingly crushed itself against the rock, and suddenly a large piece of the shoulder came away and the being twisted slushily three feet farther in. It lay quietly with its muddy eyes fixed on her, and then brought one thick arm up over its head and reached.

Babe scrambled in the inch farther she had believed impossible, and the filthy clubbed hand stroked down her back, leaving a trail of muck on the blue denim of the shirt she wore. The monster surged suddenly and, lying full length now, gained that last precious inch. A black hand seized one of her braids, and for Babe the lights went out.

When she came to, she was dangling by her hair from that same crusted paw. The thing held her high, so that her face and its feature-less head were not more than a foot apart. It gazed at her with a mild curiosity in its eyes, and it swung her slowly back and forth. The agony of her pulled hair did what fear could not do—gave her a voice. She screamed. She opened her mouth and puffed up her powerful young lungs, and she sounded off. She held her throat in the position of the first scream, and her chest labored and pumped more air through the frozen throat. Shrill and monotonous and in-finitely piercing, her screams.

The thing did not mind. It held her as she was, and watched. When it had learned all it could from this phenomenon, it dropped her jarringly, and looked around the half-cave, ignoring the stunned and huddled Babe. It reached over and picked up the leather brief case and tore it twice across as if it were tissue. It saw the sandwich Babe had left, picked it up, crushed it, dropped it.

Babe opened her eyes, saw that she was free, and just as the thing turned back to her she dove between its legs and out into the shallow pool in front of the rock, paddled across and hit the other bank screaming. A vicious little light of fury burned in her; she picked up a grapefruit-sized stone and hurled it with all her frenzied might. It flew low and fast, and struck squashily on the monster's ankle. The thing was just taking a step toward the water; the stone caught it off balance, and its unpracticed equilibrium could not save it. It tottered for a long, silent moment at the edge and then splashed into the stream. Without a second look Babe ran shrieking away.

Cory Drew was following the little gobs of mold that somehow indicated the path of the murderer, and he was nearby when he first heard her scream. He broke into a run, dropping his shotgun and holding the .32–40 ready to fire. He ran with such deadly panic in his heart that he ran right past the huge cleft rock and was a hundred yards past it before she burst out through the pool and ran up the bank. He had to run hard and fast to catch her, because anything behind her was that faceless horror in the cave, and she was living for the one idea of getting away from there. He caught her in his arms and swung her to him, and she screamed on and on and on.

Babe didn't see Cory at all, even when he held her and quieted her.

The monster lay in the water. It neither liked nor disliked this new element. It rested on the bottom, its massive head a foot beneath the surface, and it curiously considered the facts that it had garnered. There was the little humming noise of Babe's voice that sent the monster questing into the cave. There was the black material of the brief case that resisted so much more than green things when he tore it. There was the little two-legged one who sang and brought him near, and who screamed when he came. There was this new cold moving thing he had fallen into. It was washing his body away. That had never happened before. That was interesting. The monster decided to stay and observe this new thing. It felt no urge to save itself; it could only be curious.

The brook came laughing down out of its spring, ran down from its source beckoning to the sunbeams and embracing freshets and helpful brooklets. It shouted and played with streaming little roots, and nudged the minnows and pollywogs about in its tiny backwaters. It was a happy brook. When it came to the pool by the cloven rock it found the monster there, and plucked at it. It soaked the foul substances and smoothed and melted the molds, and the waters below the thing eddied darkly with its diluted matter. It was a thorough brook. It washed all it touched, persistently. Where it found filth, it removed filth; and if there were layer on layer of foulness, then layer by foul layer it was removed. It was a good brook. It did not mind the poison of the monster, but took it up and thinned it and spread it in little rings round rocks downstream, and let it drift to the rootlets of water plants, that they might grow greener and lovelier. And the monster melted.

"I am smaller," the thing thought. "That is interesting. I could not move now. And now this part of me which thinks is going, too. It will stop in just a moment, and drift away with the rest of the body. It will stop thinking and I will stop being, and that, too, is a very interesting thing."

So the monster melted and dirtied the water, and the water was clean again, washing and washing the skeleton that the monster had left. It was not very big, and there was a badly-healed knot on the left arm. The sunlight flickered on the triangular silver plate set into the pale skull, and the skeleton was very clean now. The brook laughed about it for an age.

They found the skeleton, six grimlipped men who came to find a killer. No one had believed Babe, when she told her story days later. It had to be days later because Babe had screamed for seven hours without stopping, and had lain like a dead child for a day. No one believed her at all, because her story was all about the bad fella, and they knew that the bad fella was simply a thing that her father had made up to frighten her with. But it was through her that the skeleton was found, and so the men at the bank sent a check to the Drews for more money than they had ever dreamed about. It was old Roger Kirk, sure enough, that skeleton, though it was found five miles from where he had died and sank into the forest floor where the hot molds builded around his skeleton and emerged—a monster.

So the Drews had a new barn and fine new livestock and they hired four men. But they didn't have Alton. And they didn't have Kimbo. And Babe screams at night and has grown very thin.

CASABLANCA

In the morning the man with the red fez always brought them coffee and toast on a tray. He would ask them how it goes, and Mrs. Richmond, who had some French, would say it goes well. The hotel always served the same kind of jam, plum jam. That eventually became so tiresome that Mrs. Richmond went out and bought their own jar of strawberry jam, but in a little while that was just as tiresome as the plum jam. Then they alternated, having plum jam one day, and strawberry jam the next. They wouldn't have taken their breakfasts in the hotel at all, except for the money it saved.

When, on the morning of their second Wednesday at the Belmonte, they came down to the lobby, there was no mail for them at the desk. "You can't really expect them to think of us here," Mrs. Richmond said in a piqued tone, for it had been her expectation.

"I suppose not," Fred agreed.

"I think I'm sick again. It was that funny stew we had last night. Didn't I tell you? Why don't *you* go out and get the newspaper this morning?"

154

So Fred went, by himself, to the newsstand on the corner. It had neither the *Times* nor the *Tribune*. There weren't even the usual papers from London. Fred went to the magazine store nearby the Marhaba, the big luxury hotel. On the way someone tried to sell him a gold watch. It seemed to Fred that everyone in Morocco was trying to sell gold watches.

The magazine store still had copies of the *Times* from last week. Fred had read those papers already. "Where is today's *Times*?" he asked loudly, in English.

The middle-aged man behind the counter shook his head sadly, either because he didn't understand Fred's question or because he didn't know the answer. He asked Fred how it goes

"Byen," said Fred, without conviction, "byen."

The local French newspaper, *La Vigie Marocaine,* had black, portentous headlines, which Fred could not decipher. Fred spoke "four languages: English, Irish, Scottish, and American." With only those languages, he insisted, one could be understood anywhere in the free world.

At ten o'clock, Bulova-watch time, Fred found himself, as though by chance, outside his favorite ice cream parlor. Usually, when he was with his wife, he wasn't able to indulge his sweet tooth, because Mrs. Richmond, who had a delicate stomach, distrusted Moroccan dairy products, unless boiled.

The waiter smiled and said, "Good morning, Mr. Richmon." Foreigners were never able to pronounce his name right for some reason.

Fred said, "Good morning."

"How are you?"

"I'm just fine, thank you."

"Good, good," the waiter said. Nevertheless, he looked saddened. He seemed to want to say something to Fred, but his English was very limited.

It was amazing, to Fred, that he had had to come halfway around the world to discover the best damned ice cream sundaes he'd ever tasted. Instead of going to bars, the young men of the town went to ice cream parlors, like this, just as they had in Fred's youth, in Iowa, during Prohibition. It had something to do, here in Casablanca, with the Moslem religion.

A ragged shoeshine boy came in and asked to shine Fred's shoes, which were very well shined already. Fred looked out the plate-glass window to the travel agency across the street. The boy hissed *monsieur, monsieur,* until Fred would have been happy to kick him. The wisest policy was to ignore the beggars. They went away quicker if you didn't look at them. The travel agency displayed a poster showing a pretty young blonde, rather like Doris Day, in a cowboy costume. It was a poster for Pan-American airlines.

At last the shoeshine boy went away. Fred's face was flushed with stifled anger. His sparse white hair made the redness of the flesh seem all the brighter, like a winter sunset.

A grown man came into the ice cream parlor with a bundle of newspapers, French newspapers. Despite his lack of French, Fred could understand the headlines. He bought a copy for twenty francs and went back to the hotel, leaving half the sundae uneaten.

The minute he was in the door, Mrs. Richmond cried out, "Isn't it terrible?" She had a copy of the paper already spread out on her bed. "It doesn't say *anything* about Cleveland."

Cleveland was where Nan, the Richmonds' married daughter, lived. There was no point in wondering about their own home. It was in Florida, within fifty miles of the Cape, and they'd always known that if there were a war it would be one of the first places to go.

"The dirty reds!" Fred said, flushing. His wife began to cry. "God damn them to hell. What did the newspaper say? How did it start?"

"Do you suppose," Mrs. Richmond asked, "That Billy and Midge could be at Grandma Holt's farm?"

Fred paged through *La Vigie Marocaine* helplessly, looking for pictures. Except for the big cutout of a mushroom cloud on the front page and a stock picture on the second of the president in a cowboy hat, there were no photos. He tried to read the lead story but it made no sense.

Mrs. Richmond rushed out of the room, crying aloud.

Fred wanted to tear the paper into ribbons. To calm himself he poured a shot from the pint of bourbon he kept in the dresser. Then he went out into the hall and called through the locked door to the W.C.: "Well, I'll bet we knocked hell out of *them* at least."

This was of no comfort to Mrs. Richmond.

Only the day before Mrs. Richmond had written two letters—one to her granddaughter Midge, the other to Midge's mother, Nan. The letter to Midge read:

December 2

Dear Mademoiselle Holt,

Well, here we are in romantic Casablanca, where the old and the new come together. There are palm trees growing on the boulevard outside our hotel window, and sometimes it seems that we never left Florida at all. In Marrakesh we bought presents for you and Billy, which you should get in time for Christmas if the mails are good. Wouldn't you like to know what's in those packages! But you'll just have to wait till Christmas!

You should thank God every day, darling, that you live in America. If you could only see the poor Moroccan children, begging on the streets. They aren't able to go to school, and many of them don't even have shoes or warm clothes. And don't think it doesn't get cold here, even if it is Africa! You and Billy don't know how lucky you are!

On the train ride to Marrakesh we saw the farmers plowing their fields in *December*. Each plow has one donkey and one camel. That would probably be an interesting fact for you to tell your geography teacher in school.

Casablanca is wonderfully exciting, and I often wish that you and Billy were here to enjoy it with us. Someday, perhaps! Be good—remember it will be Christmas soon.

Your loving Grandmother,
"Grams"

The second letter, to Midge's mother, read as follows:

Dec. 2, Monday afternoon

Dear Nan,

There's no use my pretending any more with *you!* You saw it in my first letter—before I even knew my own feelings. Yes, Morocco has been a terrible disappointment. You wouldn't believe some of the things that have happened. For instance, it is almost impossible to mail a package out of this country! I will have to wait till we get to

Spain, therefore, to send Billy and Midge their Xmas presents. Better not tell B & M that however!

Marrakesh was terrible. Fred and I got *lost* in the native quarter, and we thought we'd never escape! The filth is unbelievable, but if I talk about that it will only make me ill. After our experience on "the wrong side of the tracks" I wouldn't leave our hotel. Fred got very angry, and we took the train back to Casablanca the same night. At least there are decent restaurants in Casablanca. You can get a very satisfactory French-type dinner for about $1.00.

After all this you won't believe me when I tell you that we're going to stay here two more weeks. That's when the next boat leaves for Spain. Two more weeks!!! Fred says, take an airplane, but you know me. And I'll be d——d if I'll take a trip on the local railroad with all our luggage, which is the only other way.

I've finished the one book I brought along, and now I have nothing to read but newspapers. They are printed up in Paris and have mostly the news from India and Angola, which I find too depressing, and the political news from Europe, which I can't ever keep up with. Who is Chancellor Zucker and what does he have to do with the war in India? I say, if people would just sit down and try to *understand* each other, most of the world's so-called problems would disappear. Well, that's my opinion, but I have to keep it to myself, or Fred gets an apoplexy. You know Fred! He says, drop a bomb on Red China and to H—— with it! Good old Fred!

I hope you and Dan are both fine and *dan*-dy, and I hope B & M are coming along in school. We were both excited to hear about Billy's A in geography. Fred says it's due to all the stories he's told Billy about our travels. Maybe he's right for once!

Love & kisses,
"Grams"

Fred had forgotten to mail these two letters yesterday afternoon, and now, after the news in the paper, it didn't seem worthwhile. The Holts, Nan and Dan and Billy and Midge, were all very probably dead.

"It's so strange," Mrs. Richmond observed at lunch at their restaurant. "I can't believe it really happened. Nothing has changed here. You'd think it would make more of a difference."

"God-damned reds."

"Will you drink the rest of my wine? I'm too upset."

"What do you suppose we should do? Should we try and telephone to Nan?"

"Trans-*Atlantic*? Wouldn't a telegram do just as well?"

So, after lunch, they went to the telegraph office, which was in the main post office, and filled out a form. The message they finally agreed on was: IS EVERYONE WELL QUESTION WAS CLEVELAND HIT QUESTION RETURN REPLY REQUESTED. It cost eleven dollars to send off, one dollar a word. The post office wouldn't accept a travellers' check, so while Mrs. Richmond waited at the desk, Fred went across the street to the Bank of Morocco to cash it there.

The teller behind the grill looked at Fred's check doubtfully and asked to see his passport. He brought check and passport into an office at the back of the bank. Fred grew more and more peeved, as the time wore on and nothing was done. He was accustomed to being treated with respect, at least. The teller returned with a portly gentleman not much younger than Fred himself. He wore a striped suit with a flower in his buttonhole.

"Are you Mr. Richmon?" the gentleman asked.

"Of course I am. Look at the picture in my passport."

"I'm sorry, Mr. Richmon, but we are not able to cash this check."

"What do you mean? I've cashed checks here before. Look I've noted it down: on November 28, forty dollars; on December 1, twenty dollars."

The man shook his head. "I'm sorry, Mr. Richmon, but we are not able to cash these checks."

"I'd like to see the manager."

"I'm sorry, Mr. Richmon, it is not possible for us to cash your checks. Thank you very much." He turned to go.

"I want to see the manager!" Everybody in the bank, the tellers and the other clients, were staring at Fred, who had turned quite red.

"I am the manager," said the man in the striped suit. "Good-bye, Mr. Richmon."

"These are American Express Travellers' Checks. They're good anywhere in the world!"

The manager returned to his office, and the teller began to wait on another customer. Fred returned to the post office.

"We'll have to return here later, darling," he explained to his wife. She didn't ask why, and he didn't want to tell her.

They bought food to bring back to the hotel, since Mrs. Richmond didn't feel up to dressing for dinner.

The manager of the hotel, a thin, nervous man who wore wire-framed spectacles, was waiting at the desk to see them. Wordlessly he presented them a bill for the room.

Fred protested angrily. "We're paid up. We're paid until the twelfth of this month. What are you trying to pull?"

The manager smiled. He had gold teeth. He explained, in imperfect English, that this was the bill.

"*Nous sommes payée,*" Mrs. Richmond explained pleasantly. Then, in a diplomatic whisper to her husband, "Show him the receipt."

The manager examined the receipt. "*Non, non, non,*" he said, shaking his head. He handed Fred, instead of his receipt, the new bill.

"I'll take that receipt back, thank you very much." The manager smiled and backed away from Fred. Fred acted without thinking. He grabbed the manager's wrist and pried the receipt out of his fingers. The manager shouted words at him in Arabic. Fred took the key for their room, 216, off its hook behind the desk. Then he took his wife by the elbow and led her up the stairs. The man with the red fez came running down the stairs to do the manager's bidding.

Once they were inside the room, Fred locked the door. He was trembling and short of breath. Mrs. Richmond made him sit down and sponged his fevered brow with cold water. Five minutes later, a little slip of paper slid in under the door. It was the bill.

"Look at this!" he exclaimed. "Forty dirham a day. Eight dollars! That son of a bitch." The regular per diem rate for the room was twenty dirham, and the Richmonds, by taking it for a fortnight, had bargained it down to fifteen.

"Now, Freddy—"

"That bastard!"

"It's probably some sort of misunderstanding."

"He saw that receipt, didn't he? He made out that receipt himself.

You know why he's doing it. Because of what's happened. Now I won't be able to cash my travellers' checks here either. That son of a bitch!"

"Now, Freddy." She smoothed the ruffled strands of white hair with the wet sponge.

"Don't you now-Freddy me! I know what I'm going to do. I'm going to the American Consulate and register a complaint."

"That's a good idea, but not today, Freddy. Let's stay inside until tomorrow. We're both too tired and upset. Tomorrow we can go there together. Maybe they'll know something about Cleveland by then." Mrs. Richmond was prevented from giving further council by a new onset of her illness. She went out into the hall, but returned almost immediately. "The door into the toilet is padlocked," she said. Her eyes were wide with terror. She had just begun to understand what was happening.

That night, after a frugal dinner of olives, cheese sandwiches, and figs, Mrs. Richmond tried to look on the bright side. "Actually we're very lucky," she said, "to be here, instead of there, when it happened. At least, we're alive. We should thank God for being alive."

"If we'd of bombed them twenty years ago, we wouldn't be in this spot now. Didn't I say way back then that we should have bombed them?"

"Yes, darling. But there's no use crying over spilt milk. Try and look on the bright side, like I do."

"God-damn dirty reds."

The bourbon was all gone. It was dark, and outside, across the square, a billboard advertising Olympic Bleue cigarettes (C'est mieux!) winked on and off, as it had on all the other nights of their visit to Casablanca. Nothing here seemed to have been affected by the momentous event across the ocean.

"We're out of envelopes," Mrs. Richmond complained. She had been trying to compose a letter to her daughter.

Fred was staring out the window, wondering what it had been like: had the sky been filled with planes? Were they still fighting on the ground in India and Angola? What did Florida look like now?

He had always wanted to build a bomb shelter in their back yard in Florida, but his wife had been against it. Now it would be impossible to know which of them had been right.

"What time is it?" Mrs. Richmond asked, winding the alarm.

He looked at his watch, which was always right. "Eleven o'clock, Bulova watch time." It was an Accutron that his company, Iowa Mutual Life, had presented to him at retirement.

There was, in the direction of the waterfront, a din of shouting and clashing metal. As it grew louder, Fred could see the head of a ragged parade advancing up the boulevard. He pulled down the lath shutters over the windows till there was just a narrow slit to watch the parade through.

"They're burning something," he informed his wife. "Come see."

"I don't want to watch that sort of thing."

"Some kind of statue, or scarecrow. You can't tell who it's meant to be. Someone in a cowboy hat, looks like. I'll bet they're Commies."

When the mob of demonstrators reached the square over which the Belmonte Hotel looked, they turned to the left, toward the larger luxury hotels, the Marhaba and El Mansour. They were banging cymbals together and beating drums and blowing on loud horns that sounded like bagpipes. Instead of marching in rows, they did a sort of whirling, skipping dance step. Once they'd turned the corner, Walt couldn't see any more of them.

"I'll bet every beggar in town is out there, blowing his horn," Fred said sourly. "Every god-damn watch peddler and shoeshine boy in Casablanca."

"They sound very happy," Mrs. Richmond said. Then she began crying again.

The Richmonds slept together in the same bed that evening for the first time in several months. The noise of the demonstration continued, off and on, nearer or farther away, for several hours. This too set the evening apart from other evenings, for Casablanca was usually very quiet, surprisingly so, after ten o'clock at night.

The office of the American Consul seemed to have been bombed. The front door was broken off its hinges, and Fred entered, after some reluctance, to find all the downstairs rooms empty of furniture, the carpets torn away, the moldings pried from the walls. The files of the consulate had been emptied out and the contents burned in the center of the largest room. Slogans in Arabic had been scrawled on the walls with the ashes.

Leaving the building, he discovered a piece of typing paper nailed to the deranged door. It read: "All Americans in Morocco, whether of tourist or resident status, are advised to leave the country until the present crisis is over. The Consul cannot guarantee the safety of those who choose to remain."

A shoeshine boy, his diseased scalp inadequately concealed by a dirty wool cap, tried to slip his box under Fred's foot.

"Go away, you! *Vamoose!* This is your fault. I know what happened last night. You and your kind did this. Red beggars!"

The boy smiled uncertainly at Fred and tried again to get his shoe on the box. "*Monsieur, monsieur,*" he hissed—or, perhaps, "*Merci, merci.*"

By noonday the center of the town was aswarm with Americans. Fred hadn't realized there had been so many in Casablanca. What were they doing here? Where had they kept themselves hidden? Most of the Americans were on their way to the airport, their cars piled high with luggage. Some said they were bound for England, others for Germany. Spain, they claimed, wouldn't be safe, though it was probably safer than Morocco. They were brusque with Fred to the point of rudeness.

He returned to the hotel, where Mrs. Richmond was waiting for him. They had agreed that one of them must always be in the room. As Fred went up the stairs the manager tried to hand him another bill. "I will call the police," he threatened. Fred was too angry to reply. He wanted to hit the man in the nose and stamp on his ridiculous spectacles. If he'd been ten years younger he might have done so.

"They've cut off the water," Mrs. Richmond announced dramatically, after she'd admitted her husband to the room. "And the man with the red hat tried to get in, but I had the chain across the door, thank heaven. We can't wash or use the bidet. I don't know what will happen. I'm afraid."

She wouldn't listen to anything Fred said about the Consulate. "We've got to take a plane," he insisted. "To England. All the other Americans are going there. There was a sign on the door of the Con—"

"No, Fred. No. Not a plane. You won't make me get into an airplane. I've gone twenty years without that, and I won't start now."

"But this is an emergency. We have to."

"I refuse to talk about it. And don't you shout at *me*, Fred Richmond. We'll sail when the boat sails, and that's that! Now, let's be practical, shall we? The first thing that we have to do is for you to go out and buy some bottled water. Four bottles, and bread, and— No, you'll never remember everything. I'll write out a list."

But when Fred returned, four hours later, when it was growing dark, he had but a single bottle of soda, one loaf of hard bread, and a little box of pasteurized process cheese.

"It was all the money I had. They won't cash my checks. Not at the bank, not at the Marhaba, not anywhere." There were flecks of violet in his red, dirty face, and his voice was hoarse. He had been shouting hours long.

Mrs. Richmond used half the bottle of soda to wash off his face. Then she made sandwiches of cheese and strawberry jam, all the while maintaining a steady stream of conversation, on cheerful topics. She was afraid her husband would have a stroke.

On Thursday the twelfth, the day before their scheduled sailing, Fred went to the travel agency to find out what pier their ship had docked in. He was informed that the sailing had been canceled, permanently. The ship, a Yugoslav freighter, had been in Norfolk on December 4. The agency politely refunded the price of the tickets —in American dollars.

"Couldn't you give me dirham instead?"

"But you paid in dollars, Mr. Richmond." The agent spoke with a fussy, overprecise manner that annoyed Fred more than an honest French accent. "You paid in American Express Traveller's Checks."

"But I'd *rather* have dirham."

"That would be impossible."

"I'll give you one to one. How about that? One dirham for one dollar." He did not even become angry at being forced to make so unfair a suggestion. He had been through this same scene too many times—at banks, at stores, with people off the street.

"The government has forbidden us to trade in American money, Mr. Richmond. I am truly sorry that I cannot help you. If you would be interested to purchase an airplane ticket, however, I can accept money for that. If you have enough."

"You don't leave much choice, do you?" (He thought: *Betty will be furious.*) "What will it cost for two tickets to London?"

The agent named the price. Fred flared up. "That's highway robbery! Why, that's more than the first-class to New York City!"

The agent smiled. "We have no flights scheduled to New York, sir."

Grimly, Fred signed away his travellers' checks to pay for the tickets. It took all his checks and all but fifty dollars of the refunded money. His wife, however, had her own bundle of American Express checks that hadn't even been touched yet. He examined the tickets, which were printed in French. "What does this say here? When does it leave?"

"On the fourteenth. Saturday. At eight in the evening."

"You don't have anything tomorrow?"

"I'm sorry. You should be quite happy that we can sell you these tickets. If it weren't for the fact that our main office is in Paris, and that they've directed that Americans be given priority on all Pan-Am flights, we wouldn't be able to."

"I see. The thing is this—I'm in rather a tight spot. Nobody, not even the banks, will take American money. This is our last night at the hotel, and if we have to stay over Friday night as well . . ."

"You might go to the airport waiting room, sir."

Fred took off his Accutron wristwatch. "In America this watch would cost $120 wholesale. You wouldn't be interested . . ."

"I'm sorry, Mr. Richmond. I have a watch of my own."

Fred, with the tickets securely tucked into his passport case, went out through the thick glass door. He would have liked to have a sundae at the ice cream parlor across the street, but he couldn't afford it. He couldn't afford anything unless he was able to sell his watch. They had lived the last week out on what he'd gotten for the alarm clock and the electric shaver. Now there was nothing left.

When Fred was at the corner, he heard someone calling his name. "Mr. Richmond. Mr. Richmond, sir." It was the agent. Shyly he held out a ten dirham note and three fives. Fred took the money and handed him the watch. The agent put Fred's Accutron on his wrist beside his old watch. He smiled and offered Fred his hand to shake. Fred walked away, ignoring the outstretched hand.

Five dollars, he thought over and over again, *five dollars.* He was too ashamed to return at once to the hotel.

Mrs. Richmond wasn't in the room. Instead the man in the red fez was engaged in packing all their clothes and toilet articles into the three suitcases. "Hey!" Fred shouted. "What do you think you're doing? Stop that!"

"You must pay your bill," the hotel manager, who stood back at a safe distance in the hallway, shrilled at him. "You must pay your bill or leave."

Fred tried to prevent the man in the red fez from packing the bags. He was furious with his wife for having gone off—to the W.C. probably—and left the hotel room unguarded.

"Where is my wife?" he demanded of the manager. "This is an outrage." He began to swear. The man in the red fez returned to packing the bags.

Fred made a determined effort to calm himself. He could not risk a stroke. After all, he reasoned with himself, whether they spent one or two nights in the airport waiting room wouldn't make that much difference. So he chased the man in the red fez away and finished the packing himself. When he was done, he rang for the porter, and the man in the red fez returned and helped him carry the bags downstairs. He waited in the dark lobby, using the largest of the suitcases for a stool, for his wife to return. She had probably gone to "their" restaurant, some blocks away, where they were still allowed to use the W.C. The owner of the restaurant couldn't understand why they didn't take their meals there any more and didn't want to offend them, hoping, perhaps, that they would come back.

While he waited, Fred occupied the time by trying to remember the name of the Englishman who had been a supper guest at their house in Florida three years before. It was a strange name that was not pronounced at all the way that it was spelled. At intervals he would go out into the street to try and catch sight of his wife returning to the hotel. Whenever he tried to ask the manager, where she had gone, the man would renew his shrill complaint. Fred became desperate. She was taking altogether too long. He telephoned the restaurant. The owner of the restaurant understood enough English to be able to tell him that she had not visited his W.C. all that day.

An hour or so after sunset, Fred found his way to the police station, a wretched stucco building inside the ancient medina, the non-European quarter. Americans were advised not to venture into the medina after dark.

"My wife is missing," he told one of the gray-uniformed men. "I think she may be the victim of a robbery."

The policeman replied brusquely in French.

"My wife," Fred repeated loudly, gesturing in a vague way.

The policeman turned to speak to his fellows. It was a piece of deliberate rudeness.

Fred took out his passport and waved it in the policeman's face. "This is my passport," he shouted. "My wife is missing. My wife. Doesn't somebody here speak English? Somebody *must* speak English. *Ing-glish!*"

The policeman shrugged and handed Fred back his passport.

"My wife!" Fred screamed hysterically. "Listen to me—my wife, my wife, my wife!"

The policeman, a scrawny, moustached man, grabbed Fred by the neck of his coat and led him forcibly into another room and down a long, unlighted corridor that smelled of urine. Fred didn't realize, until he had been thrust into the room that it was a cell. The door that closed behind him was made not of bars, but of sheet metal nailed over wood. There was no light in the room, no air. He screamed, he kicked at the door and pounded on it with his fists until he had cut a deep gash into the side of his palm. He stopped, to suck the blood, fearful of blood-poisoning.

He could, when his eyes had adjusted to the darkness, see a little of the room about him. It was not much larger than Room 216 at the Belmonte, but it contained more people than Fred could count. They were heaped all along the walls, an indiscriminate tumble of rags and filth, old men and young men, a wretched assembly.

They stared at the American gentleman in astonishment.

The police released Fred in the morning, and he returned at once to the hotel, speaking to no one. He was angry but, even more, he was terrified.

His wife had not returned. The three suitcases, for a wonder, were still sitting where he had left them. The manager insisted that he leave the lobby, and Fred did not protest. The Richmonds' time at the hotel had expired, and Fred didn't have the money for another night, even at the old rate.

Outside, he did not know what to do. He stood on the curbside, trying to decide. His pants were wrinkled, and he feared (though he could not smell it himself) that he stank of the prison cell.

The traffic policeman in the center of the square began giving him funny looks. He was afraid of the policeman, afraid of being returned to the cell. He hailed a taxi and directed the driver to go to the airport.

"*Où?*" the driver asked.

"The airport, the airport," he said testily. Cabbies, at least, could be expected to know English.

But where was his wife? Where was Betty?

When they arrived at the airport, the driver demanded fifteen dirhams, which was an outrageous price in Casablanca, where cabs are pleasantly cheap. Having not had the foresight to negotiate the price in advance, Fred had no choice but to pay the man what he asked.

The waiting room was filled with people, though few seemed to be Americans. The stench of the close air was almost as bad as it had been in the cell. There were no porters, and he could not move through the crowd, so he set the suitcases down just inside the entrance and seated himself on the largest bag.

A man in an olive-drab uniform with a black beret asked, in French, to see his passport. "*Votre passeport,*" he repeated patiently, until Fred had understood. He examined each page with a great show of suspicion, but eventually he handed it back.

"Do you speak English?" Fred asked him then. He thought, because of the different uniform, that he might not be one of the city police. He answered with a stream of coarse Arabic gobbling.

Perhaps, Fred told himself, *she will come out here to look for me.* But why, after all, should she? He should have remained outside the hotel.

He imagined himself safely in England, telling his story to the American Consul there. He imagined the international repercussions it would have. What had been the name of that Englishman he knew. He had lived in London. It began with *C* or *Ch.*

An attractive middle-aged woman sat down on the other end of his suitcase and began speaking in rapid French, making sharp gestures, like karate chops, with her well-groomed hand. She was trying to explain something to him, but of course he couldn't understand her. She broke into tears. Fred couldn't even offer her his handkerchief, because it was dirty from last night.

"My wife," he tried to explain. "My—wife—is missing. My wife."

"Bee-yay," the woman said despairingly. "Vote bee-yay." She showed him a handful of dirham notes in large denominations.

"I wish I could understand what it is you want," he said.

She went away from him, as though she were angry, as though he had said something to insult her.

Fred felt someone tugging at his shoe. He remembered, with a start of terror, waking in the cell, the old man tugging at his shoes, trying to steal them but not understanding, apparently, about the laces.

It was only, after all, a shoeshine boy. He had already begun to brush Fred's shoes, which were, he could see, rather dirty. He pushed the boy away.

He had to go back to the hotel to see if his wife had returned there, but he hadn't the money for another taxi and there was no one in the waiting room that he dared trust with the bags.

Yet he couldn't leave Casablanca without his wife. Could he? But if he did stay, what was he to do, if the police would not listen to him?

At about ten o'clock the waiting room grew quiet. All that day no planes had entered or left the airfield. Everyone here was waiting for tomorrow's plane to London. How were so many people, and so much luggage, to fit on one plane, even the largest jet? Did they all have tickets?

They slept anywhere: on the hard benches, on newspapers on the concrete floor, on the narrow window ledges. Fred was one of the luckiest, because he could sleep on his three suitcases.

When he woke the next morning, he found that his passport and the two tickets had been stolen from his breast pocket. He still had his billfold, because he had slept on his back. It contained nine dirham.

Christmas morning, Fred went out and treated himself to an ice cream sundae. Nobody seemed to be celebrating the holiday in Casablanca. Most of the shops in the ancient medina (where Fred had found a hotel room for three dirham a day) were open for business, while in the European quarter one couldn't tell if the stores were closed permanently or just for the day.

Going past the Belmonte, Fred stopped, as was his custom, to ask after his wife. The manager was very polite and said that nothing was known of Mrs. Richmond. The police had her description now.

Hoping to delay the moment when he sat down before the sundae, he walked to the post office and asked if there had been any answer to his telegram to the American Embassy in London. There had not.

When at last he did have his sundae it didn't seem quite as good as he had remembered. There was so little of it! He sat down for an hour with his empty dish, watching the drizzling rain. He was alone in the ice cream parlor. The windows of the travel agency across the street were covered up by a heavy metal shutter, from which the yellow paint was flaking.

The waiter came and sat down at Fred's table. "*Il pleuve, Monsieur Richmon. It rains. Il pleuve.*"

"Yes, it does," said Fred. "It rains. It falls. Fall-out."

But the waiter had very little English. "Merry Christmas," he said. "*Joyeuse Nöel*. Merry Christmas."

Fred agreed.

When the drizzle had cleared a bit, Fred strolled to the United Nations Plaza and found a bench under a palm tree that was dry. Despite the cold and damp, he didn't want to return to his cramped hotel room and spend the rest of the day sitting on the edge of his bed.

Fred was by no means alone in the plaza. A number of figures in heavy wooden djelabas, with hoods over their heads, stood or sat on benches, or strolled in circles on the gravel paths. The djelabas made ideal raincoats. Fred had sold his own London Fog three days before for twenty dirham. He was getting better prices for his things now that he had learned to count in French.

The hardest lesson to learn (and he had not yet learned it) was to keep from thinking. When he could do that, he wouldn't become angry, or afraid.

At noon the whistle blew in the handsome tower at the end of the plaza, from the top of which one could see all of Casablanca in every direction. Fred took out the cheese sandwich from the pocket of his suitcoat and ate it, a little bit at a time. Then he took out the chocolate bar with almonds. His mouth began to water.

A shoeshine boy scampered across the graveled circle and sat down in the damp at Fred's feet. He tried to lift Fred's foot and place it on his box.

"No," said Fred. "Go away."

"*Monsieur, monsieur,*" the boy insisted. Or, perhaps, "*Merci, merci.*"

Fred looked down guiltily at his shoes. They were very dirty. He hadn't had them shined in weeks.

The boy kept whistling those meaningless words at him. His gaze was fixed on Fred's chocolate bar. Fred pushed him away with the side of his foot. The boy grabbed for the candy. Fred struck him in the side of his head. The chocolate bar fell to the gravel, not far from the boy's calloused feet. The boy lay on his side, whimpering.

"You little sneak!" Fred shouted at him.

It was a clear-cut case of thievery. He was furious. He had a right to be furious. Standing up to his full height, his foot came down accidentally on the boy's rubbishy shoe shine box. The wood splintered.

The boy began to gabble at Fred in Arabic. He scurried forward on hands and knees to pick up the pieces of the box.

"You asked for this," Fred said. He kicked the boy in the ribs. The boy rolled with the blow, as though he were not unused to such treatment. "Little beggar! Thief!" Fred screamed.

He bent forward and tried to grasp a handhold in the boy's hair, but it was cut too close to his head, to prevent lice. Fred hit him again in the face, but now the boy was on his feet and running.

There was no use pursuing him, he was too fast, too fast.

Fred's face was violet and red, and his white hair, in need of a trim, straggled down over his flushed forehead. He had not noticed, while he was beating the boy, the group of Arabs, or Moslems, or whatever they were, that had gathered around him to watch. Fred could not read the expressions on their dark, wrinkly faces.

"Did you see that?" he asked loudly. "Did you see what that little thief tried to do? Did you see him try to steal . . . my candy bar?"

One of the men, in a tan djelaba striped with brown, said something to Fred that sounded like so much gargling. Another, younger man, in European dress, struck Fred in the face. Fred teetered backward.

"Now see here!" He had not time to tell them he was an American citizen. The next blow caught him in the mouth, and he fell to the ground. Once he was lying on his back, the older men joined in in kicking him. Some kicked him in the ribs, others in his head, still others had to content themselves with his legs. Curiously, nobody went for his groin. The shoeshine boy watched from a distance, and when Fred was unconscious, came forward and removed his shoes. The young man who had first hit him removed his suitcoat and his belt. Wisely, Fred had left his billfold behind at his hotel.

When he woke he was sitting on the bench again. A policeman was addressing him in Arabic. Fred shook his head uncomprehendingly. His back hurt dreadfully, from when he had fallen to the ground. The policeman addressed him in French. He shivered. Their kicks had not damaged him so much as he had expected. Except for the young man, they had worn slippers instead of shoes. His face experienced only a dull ache, but there was blood all down the front of his shirt, and his mouth tasted of blood. He was cold, very cold.

The policeman went away, shaking his head.

At just that moment Fred remembered the name of the Englishman who had had supper in his house in Florida. It was Cholmondeley, but it was pronounced *Chum-ly*. He was still unable to remember his London address.

Only when he tried to stand did he realize that his shoes were gone. The gravel hurt the tender soles of his bare feet. Fred was mortally certain that the shoeshine boy had stolen his shoes.

He sat back down on the bench with a groan. He hoped to hell he'd hurt the god-damned little son of a bitch. He hoped to hell he had. He grated his teeth together, wishing that he could get hold of him again. The little beggar. He'd kick him this time so that he'd remember it. The god-damn dirty little red beggar. He'd kick his face in.

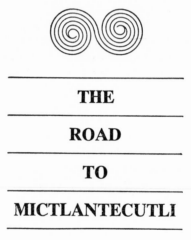

THE

ROAD

TO

MICTLANTECUTLI

The ribbon of asphalt—once black, now grey from the years of un-relenting sun—stretched out like a never-ending arrow shaft; in the distance, mirages—like dreams—sprang into life, shimmered, and silently dissolved at the approach of the speeding automobile.

Rivulets of sweat poured down from the face of Hernandez, the driver. Earlier in the day—when they had been in the good land—he had been congenial, expansive, even sympathetic. Now he drove quickly, apprehensively, almost angrily, not wanting to be caught in the bad land after sunset.

"*Semejante los buitres no tienen gordo en este distrito execrable,*"
he muttered, squinting his eyes against the glare of the late afternoon
sun.

Seated next to him, the man called Morgan smiled at the remark,
"Even the vultures are skinny in this lousy land." Hernandez had a
sense of humour; for that reason—and that reason, alone—Morgan
was sorry that it was going to be necessary to kill him. But Hernandez
was a policeman . . . a Mexican Federal cop who was taking him back
to the United States border, where Morgan would be handed over to
the criminal courts to hang, twitching, at the end of a long Texas
rope.

No, Morgan thought, and knew the thought to be true, they won't
hang me this time; next time, maybe, but not now. Hernandez was
stupid, and it would be only a matter of time before he made a mistake. Completely relaxed, Morgan dozed, his manacled hands lying
docilely in his lap . . . waiting . . . waiting . . . waiting.

It was almost five o'clock before Morgan, with all the keen instincts of the hunted, sensed his moment of freedom might be approaching. Hernandez was becoming uncomfortable—the result of
two bottles of beer after lunch. The policeman would be stopping
soon. Morgan would make his move then.

On their right, a range of gently sloping foothills gradually had
been rising from the flat surface of the desert.

Morgan asked, pretending boredom, "Anything over there?"

Hernandez sighed, "*Quien sabe?*" Who knows? The plateau on
the other side of the mountain range is supposed to be worse than
this side. *Es impossible!* No one can exist there except a few wild
Indians who speak a language that was old before the Aztecs came.
It's uncharted, untamed, uncivilized . . . ruled by Mictlantecutli.

Now, slowly, as shadows lengthened, the land was changing all
around them. For the first time since leaving Agua Lodoso, they
could see some signs of vegetation—mesquite bushes, cactus, shrub
brush. Ahead, standing like a lonely outpost sentinel, was a giant
Saguaro cactus almost fifty feet high. Hernandez slowed the car and
stopped in the shade of the cactus. "Stretch your legs if you want,
amigo, this is the last stop before Hermosillo."

Hernandez got out, walked around the car, and opened the door for his prisoner. Morgan slipped out and stood, stretching like a cat. While the Mexican was relieving himself against the cactus, Morgan walked over to what had first appeared to be a crude cross stuck in the sand. He peered at it; the cross was only a sign—weather-beaten and pock-marked by the talons of vultures who had used it as a roosting place.

Hernandez strolled over and joined him. He, too, stared at the sign, his lips pursed in puzzlement under his black moustache. "Linaculan—one hundred twenty kilometres! I did not know there was a road . . ." Then he brightened. "Ah, *si*. I remember now. This must be the old *Real Militar,* the military highway leading from the interior to the east coast."

That was all Morgan needed to know. If Linaculan was on the east coast, then Linaculan meant freedom. He yawned again, his impassive face a portrait of indifference.

"Ready, *amigo?*"

Morgan nodded. "As ready as any man is to be hung."

The Mexican laughed, coughed, and spat in the dust. "Come on then." He led the way towards the car and stood by its open door waiting for his prisoner. Morgan shambled towards him, his shoulders slumped forward as if protecting him from the oppressive heat of late afternoon. When he did move, it was as a snake strikes an unsuspecting victim. His manacled hands came down, viciously, on top of Hernandez's head. The policeman moaned and toppled to the ground. Morgan was on him immediately; his hands seeking, and finding, the gun he knew was in the Mexican's waistband. Then he stood upright—about four paces away from the figure on the ground.

Hernandez shook his head groggily, blinked his eyes, and started to rise. He had struggle to his knees when Morgan's cold voice froze him into immobility.

Morgan said, "Goodbye, Hernandez. No hard feelings."

The Mexican looked up; he saw death. "*Dios . . . dios.* No!" That was as far as he got; the .44 slug caught him above the ridge of the left eye and he was thrown ten feet backwards by the force of the bullet. He shuddered once, his legs beat a small tattoo in the dust, and then he was still.

Morgan walked over, shaking his head mournfully. "I sure had you pegged wrong. You didn't look like a coward who would beg for his life." He sighed at the dead man's lack of dignity—feeling almost as if he had been betrayed by a weak-willed friend.

He squatted and began searching the body. There was a wallet containing a badge, five hundred pesos, and a colour photograph of an overweight Mexican woman surrounded by three laughing small girls and two self-consciously grinning young boys. Morgan grunted non-committally and continued his search.

He found the handcuff keys taped to the calloused white sole of the dead man's foot.

Twilight was beginning to turn the Mexican hills to a red bronze when Morgan loaded Hernandez in the trunk of the car. He strolled back over to the road sign. After the mileage there were the words, "*Cuidado—Peligroso,*" "Take Heed—Dangerous." What a joke, he thought. Could anything be more dangerous than being hung? Or playing the part of a fox hounded by international police? He had been trapped and sentenced to die four different times in his life; and yet, he was still a free man. And . . . there could be nothing, absolutely nothing, ahead of him on this insignificant little dirt road that could match Morgan's wits, Morgan's reactions, Morgan's gun!

He got behind the wheel of the car and turned on to the road. It was rougher than it had appeared at first, but none the less, he made good time for the first thirty miles, and was able to drive fast enough that the dust remained spread out behind him like the brown tail of a comet hanging luminously in the fading light.

The sun dropped below the horizon line, but then, as Morgan began climbing the range of hills, it came back into sight once more —looking like the malevolent inflamed eye of a god angry at being awakened again.

Morgan crested the hill and began a downward ascent into a valley. Here darkness was embracing the land. He stopped once, where a *barranca* sloped down from the road, and threw over Hernandez's body. He watched it, rolling and tumbling, until it finally disappeared from sight in the black shadows beneath a strand of mesquite bushes some hundred feet below at the bottom.

Morgan drove on. He turned on the car lights as night closed in swiftly around him.

Abruptly, as he reached the valley floor, he began cursing, for the road was really no longer a road—just a scarred and broken path leading across the wilderness.

The next five kilometres took at least fifteen thousand miles out of the automobile. Morgan was forced to shift down to first gear as potholes—deep as wading pools—wrecked the front-end alignment and suspension system. Jagged hidden boulders in the middle of the road scraped at the undercarriage with a thousand steel fingers.

And dust! Dust was everywhere . . . it hung like a dark ominous cloud all about him; it coated the inside of the car as though it were beige velvet. It crept into Morgan's nostrils and throat until it became painful to breathe or swallow.

Minutes later, over the smell of dust, came the odour of hot water —steam—and he knew the cooling system had ruptured somewhere. It was then Morgan realized the car would never make it to Linaculan. By the last barely perceptible horizon glow, he searched the landscape for some evidence of life . . . and saw only the grotesque silhouettes of cactus and stunted desert brush.

The speedometer indicated they had travelled forty-four miles when his bouncing, weaving headlight picked up the solitary figure of a priest walking slowly alongside the road. Morgan's eyes narrowed as he weighed the value of offering a ride to the padre. That would be stupid, he thought—the man could be a *bandido* who would produce, and skilfully use, a knife, while Morgan was concentrating on the road.

The padre loomed up larger in the headlights. He did not turn towards the car; it seemed as though he were totally unaware of the car's approach.

Morgan passed without slowing; the figure was lost immediately in the dust and blackness of the Mexican night.

Suddenly, just as though several automatic relays had clicked open somewhere in his brain, all of Morgan's instincts were screaming at him. Something was wrong—terribly wrong. A trap of some sort had been entered. The feeling was familiar; there had been other traps before. He grinned wryly, pulled the gun from his pocket, and laid it on the seat beside him in preparation.

The next three miles seemed endless as he waited, almost eagerly, for the trap to swing shut. When nothing happened, he grew irritable and began cursing his imagination. The smell of hot oil and steam had grown humidly overpowering, and the engine was beginning to labour. Morgan glanced down at the temperature gauge and saw the needle had long since climbed into the red danger zone.

And, it was at this moment, while his attention was distracted, that the left front wheel slammed into a jagged rock which ripped through the tire's sidewall. The vehicle began bucking and weaving from side to side like a wild, enraged, injured animal. Morgan hit his brakes, knowing it was too late. The car skidded sideways on the gravel, swerved to the right, teetered for a second on an embankment, and then—almost as if it were a movie being projected in slow motion—rolled end over end down the incline.

The last thing Morgan saw was a monstrous boulder looking up in the night like some huge basalt fist of God.

For a long time after he regained consciousness, Morgan lay still with his eyes closed. Someone had wiped his forehead and spoken to him. A man! Possibly . . . the priest? He listened to the man's coarse breathing; there was no other sound. They were alone.

Morgan opened his eyes. It was dark, but not as dark as before. A little moonlight was seeping through the high thin clouds. The priest—black of clothes and dark of face—was beside him.

"*Senor,* you are all right?"

Morgan flexed his leg muscles, moved his ankles, moved his shoulders, and turned his head from side to side. There were no aches, no pains; he felt surprisingly good. Well, no sense in letting the other man know; let the priest believe Morgan had injured his back and was incapable of rapid movement . . . then, when he had to move fast, the other would be unprepared.

"I hurt my back."

"Can you stand?"

"Yes . . . I think so. Help me."

The priest reached out; Morgan took the proffered hand, and, groaning audibly, stood erect.

"You are fortunate that I came along."

"Yes. I'm grateful." Morgan felt in his pocket. The wallet was still there; the gun was gone, or had it been in his pocket? Then he remembered, it had been on the seat beside him. Well, no chance of finding it in the darkness . . . and there would be other weapons.

"Where were you going?" the priest asked.

"Linaculan."

"Oh, yes . . . a fine city." The priest was standing quite close to Morgan, staring at the American. The moon slipped in and out of the clouds. There was a moment of light, only a moment, but enough. Suddenly, for the first time in many years, Morgan was afraid . . . frightened by the padre's eyes; they were too black, too piercing, too fierce for a priest.

Morgan stepped back three paces—far enough away from the priest that the other man's eyes were lost in the darkness.

"You need not fear me," the priest said quietly. "I cannot harm you. I can only help you."

It sounded sincere. Some of Morgan's nervousness began to abate. Mentally he sniffed the wind; the odour of the trap was there, but not as strong as before. After a few moments, some of his old cockiness returned. Where do we go from here, he thought. He was at least halfway towards Linaculan, so it would seem prudent to continue on, unless . . . there would be other transportation before then.

Morgan asked, "Is Linaculan the nearest town?"

"Yes."

"Is that where you were going?"

"No."

Hopefully then, "Do you have a church near by?"

"No. But I frequently trod this road."

"For Christ's sake, why walk this miserable road?"

"For the very reason you mentioned, for Christ's sake."

Now Morgan was completely at ease. The padre was harmless. A nut, but harmless. "Well," he said almost jauntily, "I've got a long walk ahead of me. See you."

Morgan thought he saw the priest's expression soften with the remark. "I will walk part way with you."

"Suit yourself, padre. My name's . . . Dan Morgan. I'm an American."

"Yes . . . I know."

The answer surprised Morgan for a moment; then he felt his guard rising again. Obviously the priest had gone through his belongings while he was unconscious . . . and perhaps that was where the gun had gone, too.

They began walking in silence. The moon—that alien globe of cold white light—won its battle with the clouds, and now shone brightly behind them. Long slender shadows raced along the road in front of the two men. The folds of the padre's cassock made whispering noises with each stride he took; his sandals went slap-slap-slap in the thick dust of the road.

In an effort to make conversation, Morgan asked, "How far is Linaculan from here?"

"A great distance."

"But," Morgan exploded, "I thought it was only about another fifty kilometres."

"The candle lights of Linaculan are fifty-four kilometres from the point of your crash."

Well, that was nice to know anyway. With luck, Morgan could make the thirty miles by tomorrow afternoon . . . and then, it would be a simple matter to get another car. He began taking longer strides; the priest kept pace beside him.

In time, the moon was cut off by a range of hills, and their shadows disappeared. The darkness that came in around them now was a tangible thing, warm, disquieting, fearful as the interior of a locked coffin. Morgan glanced at his watch. It had stopped at 8.18, apparently something snapped when the crash occurred. He didn't know how long he had been unconscious, but they had been walking for at least two hours . . . so, perhaps, it was around midnight.

They plodded on, two dark figures—shadows almost—walking a desolate road. They climbed a short hill and were bathed in moonlight again. Morgan liked that. The darkness had been too dark; it seemed to him that there were things—unseen, unreal—out there beyond the moonlight.

They started down the other side of the hill, and the darkness crept back . . .

"Don't you have any lights at all in this God-forsaken place?" Morgan asked irritably.

The padre did not answer. Morgan repeated the question, and his voice was full of frustrated threat.

Still there was no reply. Morgan shrugged and mentally said, "To hell with you, my sullen Catholic friend. I'll take care of you later." The road led down the far side of the hill. Night—the true horribly oppressive night of the claustrophobiac—closed in menacingly.

They were in a gully for a long time before reaching another hill—this time, no moonlight greeted them; the only illumination was a hollow glow from behind the horizon clouds. It was enough though to show a fork in the road.

Morgan hesitated and asked, "Which one goes to Linaculan?"

The priest stopped. The fierce black pupils of his eyes had grown large; so large, in fact, there seemed to be no longer any white to his eyes at all. He stretched out his arms to adjust his cassock, and at that moment he looked like some evil black praying mantis about to devour a victim. Even in the semi-darkness, he cast a shadow . . . a black, elongated shadow of the cross.

And now, the cornered killer instinct took hold of Morgan. "Answer my question," he snarled. "Which way to Linaculan?"

"Have you so little faith?"

Morgan's voice was shaking in fury. "Listen, you surly bastard! You've refused to answer my questions . . . or even make conversation. What does faith have to do with it? Just tell me how much farther I have to go to get to Linaculan; that's all I want from you. No psalm singing, no preaching. Nothing! Understand?"

"You still have a great distance to go . . ." His voice trailed off, and Morgan sensed a change in the padre's attitude. A moment later, Morgan heard it too . . . the far-off drumbeat of a horse's hooves.

The moon—as if curious—parted the clouds for the last time. There was only a shadow moving across the landscape at first, but as the horse came nearer, Morgan could see the animal, its mane and tail rippling like black flags straining at their halyards. It was a magnificent beast, quite the largest he had ever seen—coal-black as the midnight and spirited as a thunderhead.

What really took Morgan's breath away, however, was the girl. She rode the animal as though she were an integral part of it. The moonlight played with her, for she was dressed completely in white, from boots and jodhpurs to the form-fitting, long-sleeved blouse and Spanish *grandee* hat. Her hair, though, was black—black as a raven's wing, and it hung like a soft ebony cloud from her shoulders.

Savagely, she reined the stallion to a halt in front of the two men. The horse reared; Morgan jumped back nervously, but the priest stood his ground.

"Well, padre," she said, smiling and—at the same time— slapping her jodhpurs with a riding whip. "I see you have taken another unfortunate under your wing." She put an odd emphasis on the word "unfortunate"; Morgan didn't know whether to be angry or puzzled. He waited, silently watching the dramatic by-play going on between the two people. Perhaps, the entire thing was elaborately staged— all part of the trap. It was of no matter—there was no immediate danger to him. So, for the moment, he was content to merely stand and enjoy the woman's proud body.

In time, the girl became aware of Morgan's stare; her own eyes, answering, were as bold and insolent as the man's. She threw back her head and laughed throatily. "You are in bad hands, my American friend. This *hombre* here"—she nodded contemptuously towards the priest—"is called 'old bad luck' among my people. Each time he is on the road, there is an accident. You have had trouble tonight . . . no?"

Morgan nodded once, then glanced sideways at the priest.

The padre, however, was watching the girl. She laughed under his scrutiny. "Don't look so angry, old man. You can't frighten me. Why don't you run along now; I'll see that our American friend reaches his destination."

The priest held out his hand to Morgan. "You must not go with her. She is evil. Evil personified." He made three crosses in the air.

There was no doubt in Morgan's mind about his decision. The padre had said she was "evil"; coming from a priest, that was a real recommendation. Besides, only an idiot would continue to walk the dark road when there was a chance to ride, a chance for pleasant conversation, a chance—really, a promise if he had correctly interpreted her look—of even more! He hesitated, still a wild, hunted animal wary of the trap.

The girl gently patted the sweating neck of her horse. "Where were you going?"

"Linaculan," Morgan answered.

"That isn't too far away. Come on, I'll give you a ride to Mictlante-cutli's ranch . . . you can call for help from there." Her lips were half parted; she seemed almost breathless as she awaited his answer.

Morgan turned to the priest. "Well, thanks for the company, padre. See you around some time."

The priest took two quick steps towards Morgan, and put out his arms, beseeching, "Stay at my side. She is evil, I say."

The girl laughed aloud. "It's two against one, churchman. You've lost another victim."

"Victim?" Morgan's eyes narrowed. He'd been right about the old devil all along. But something was ringing false. Then it came to him . . . if the padre was a thief and a murderer, why hadn't he done the job when Morgan was unconscious?

The priest gazed back over his shoulder towards the setting moon; it would be dark within seconds now. He reached inside his cassock and withdrew an ivory cross about eight or ten inches high. "The night is coming. Hold on to the cross. Believe me. Do not go to Mictlantecutli. I am your last chance."

"Go on, get away from him, you old fool," the girl shouted. "The authorities should take care of you idiots who molest and frighten travellers on this road . . . and prevent them from reaching their destination."

The priest paid no heed to the girl; he implored Morgan once again, and this time his voice was strong as he watched the last red lip of the moon disappear below the hill, "There still is time . . ."

The girl viciously pulled back on the reins and dug her spurs into the horse's flanks; it screamed in rage and reared, its front hooves blotting out the stars. When back on all fours, the stallion was between Morgan and the priest. Her face was a soft glow as she smiled and withdrew a boot from the stirrups. "Come, my friend. Place your foot here. Vault up behind me." She reached out a helping hand, and as she bent over, her blouse gaped open slightly. Morgan grinned, and took her hand. He pulled himself astride the horse. "Put your arms around me and hold on," she ordered. Morgan did

so, happily. Her body was supple, delightful to hold, and the faint
scent of some exotic perfume wafted back to him from her hair.

He gazed down at the priest; the old man's face was once more
unfathomable. "So long, padre. Don't take any wooden *pesos*."

The girl did not wait for an answer. She raked the flank of the
horse with her spurs and the beast tore out into the night. "Hold
tight," she shouted, "hold tight."

They rode at breakneck speed for almost ten minutes before she
reined the stallion to a walk. With their pace slowed, Morgan became
aware of the girl's body again, and desire built up rapidly inside
him. It had been a long time; there was no one around to stop him
. . . and the girl had shown a spirited wantonness that led him to
believe she would welcome his advances. They rode with only the
hoarse breathing and clip-clop of the horse, and the creak of their
saddle breaking the silence. Surreptitiously, his hand began to ride
higher and higher on her rib cage. She made no protest, so he became bolder. Finally, he could feel the soft flesh of her breasts beneath the silk blouse.

It was easier than Morgan had ever believed possible. She simply
reined in the horse and turned partially around. "We can stop here
. . . if you want."

Morgan's voice was guttural, his body pounding in desire, as he
said, "Yeh. I want."

She slid from the horse, and Morgan was beside her immediately.
Her arms went around his neck; their lips met in a brutal bruising
parody of love. Her fingernails dug into his shoulders as his hands
sought immediate demanding familiarity with her body. She moaned,
deep in her throat as Morgan fumbled with her clothes. And then,
with only the disinterested horse grazing near by and the brittle eyes
of the stars glittering as they watched, their bodies joined in a violent
collusion of hot, implacable lust.

Morgan could feel the lassitude of his body when he awakened.
That was his first impression. His second impression was that he was
still embracing the girl. The third—an overpowering horrible odour
of putrefaction.

He opened his eyes.

And screamed.

It was a scream wrenched involuntarily from his soul, for there, in a faint light of an approaching dawn, he could see that he was holding in his arms the rotting cadaver of a woman—a body from which the flesh was peeling in great huge strips like rotten liver, from which the death grimace revealed crooked brown teeth and eyeless sockets.

Morgan whimpered and jumped to his feet. His heart was hammering as though it were about to fly from his body like some overtaxed runaway machine that explodes into pieces. His breath came in deep animal-like pants of fright. And his eyes darted frantically around like those of a madman tormented by phantoms.

"I . . . I . . . I . . ." he panted. It was all he could say. He began running down the road. He fell twice, painfully ripping open his legs and hands on the rocky surface of the land. "I . . . I . . . I . . ." and then, the words he wanted most to say came spilling out, "Help me . . . someone! Help . . . me!"

He heard the horse's hooves behind him. It was the girl; she was alive . . . and whole! She smiled, reassuringly. "Where did you go?" she asked. And then, she grinned impishly, "Where are your clothes."

"I . . . I . . . I . . ." Morgan could not speak.

"Come," she said.

Morgan shook his head. He could not marshal his thoughts, but this much was certain; he knew he was not going with the girl.

"Come!" And this time it was an imperative command. The girl was no longer amused at his nudity, his frightened inarticulateness.

Morgan willed himself to turn and run away, but his body did not respond to his mental orders. Instead, like a mindless zombie, he mounted the horse.

"That's better," the girl said, soothingly. "Of course, you should have put on your clothes . . . but it doesn't matter." She glanced towards the east, "Night is almost gone. We must hurry. There is something I want you to see before we get to Mictlantecutli's ranch."

She slapped the stallion with her whip, and the animal began chasing the blackness of the sky.

Now, behind them, the sky was definitely beginning to lighten as dawn came to the Mexican desert. In the near light of the new day, Morgan could see a landmark that looked familiar. And then, off the road, at the bottom of the ravine, he saw his car. Gingerly, the horse picked its way down the slope until they were beside the wrecked vehicle.

Ugly, red-necked vultures screamed and flapped their wings as the horse approached. Several were fighting over what appeared to be elongated white ropes hanging out of the car windows. A few of the birds took to the air . . . the rest, arrogant and unafraid, moved over a few reluctant steps away. "But . . . but . . . what are they doing here?" Morgan asked. "There was no one in the car but me."

He could feel the girl's body shaking in silent laughter. She pointed. By squinting his eyes, Morgan could make out the figure impaled on the steering-wheel post. The cold undulating horror he had felt earlier closed in around him again. The body was familiar . . . too familiar! Morgan whimpered as the girl urged the stallion closer. The vultures had gone for the eyes first—as they usually do . . . the entrails of the dead man hung out the open window, and these had been the reason for fighting among the birds.

Morgan saw the clothes. The dead man was dressed the same as he had been. He wore the same shape wristwatch. What terrifying nightmare was this? Awaken . . . wake up . . . wake up, he mentally shouted. But the nightmare, more real than life itself, remained. The dead man was Morgan, there could be no doubt about it.

Morgan's mind was forced in a corner by the realization, his sanity backed away from the fact. He began to lose all control. He screamed, the scream of a demented lunatic.

At his cry, the girl shouted and whipped at the stallion. The horse scrambled up the side of the ravine.

There, in the roadway, stood the priest.

"Help me, Father. Help me. God help me . . ." Morgan mumbled, the saliva trickling slowly from both sides of his lax mouth.

"You made your choice. I am sorry."

"But I did not know what Mictlantecutli was."

"Mictlantecutli is known by many names: Diabolo, Satan, Devil, Lucifer, Mephistopheles. The particular name of evil is never important, for the precepts are the same in every country. You have embraced evil; you have made your last earthly choice. I am powerless now to aid you. Goodbye . . ."

He felt, then heard the girl's laughter—shrill, maniacal, satisfied.

Her whip bit into the horse's neck and her spurs drew blood. They tore down the road, galloping, galloping, galloping towards the night. The stench was back again, and shreds of the girl's flesh began sloughing off in the wind.

She turned . . . slowly, this time . . . and Morgan saw the horrible grinning expression of a skeleton.

He twisted around, unable to face the apparition, and cried out once more for the priest. Far back in the distance—as if he were viewing something in another world—Morgan could see the padre's solitary figure at the top of a hill, plodding towards the east, the rising sun, and a new day.

When Morgan turned back again, weeping and knowing now the desperate futility of hope, they had already reached the edge of night . . . and the oppressive darkness reached out to engulf them.

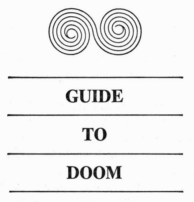

GUIDE

TO

DOOM

This way down, please. Mind your heads in the doorway, and take care on the stairs, the treads are very worn. And here we are in the courtyard again.

That concludes our tour, ladies and gentlemen. Thank you for your attention. Please keep to the paths as you cross to the gatehouse.

Yes, madam, it *is* a very little castle. Properly speaking, it's a fortified manorhouse. But it's the finest of its kind extant, and in a unique state of repair. That's what comes of being in the hands of the same family for six centuries. Yes, madam, that's how long the Chastelays have been here. And in these very walls until they built the Grace House at the far end of the grounds a hundred and fifty years ago.

189

The well, sir? You'll see the well as you cross the courtyard there. What was that sir? I didn't quite catch—

Not that well? The *other* one?

Now I wonder, sir, what should put it into your head that a small household like this—

The one where Mary Purcell drowned herself!

Hush, sir, please! Keep your voice down. Mr. Chastelay doesn't like that affair remembered. Yes, sir, I know, but we don't show the well-chamber. He wants it forgotten. No, I can't make exceptions, it's as much as my job's worth. Well, sir—very handsome of you, I'm sure. Were you, indeed? I can understand your being interested, of course, if you were one of the reporters who covered the case. You did say *Mary Purcell?*

Oh, no, sir, I wasn't in this job then. But I read the papers, like everybody else. Look, sir, if you'll wait just a moment, till I see this lot out—

That's better, now we can talk. I'm always glad to get the last party of the day through this old door, and drop the latch on 'em. Nice to hear the cars driving away down the avenue. Notice how the sound vanishes when they reach the turn where the wall begins. Quiet, isn't it? Soon we shall begin to hear the owls.

Now, sir, you want to see the well. The *other* well. The one where the tragedy occurred. I shouldn't do it, really. Mr. Chastelay would be very annoyed if he knew. No, sir, that's right, of course, he never need know.

Very well, sir, it's through here—through the great hall. After you, sir! There, fancy you turning in the right direction without being told! Mind your step, the floor's very uneven in places.

You mustn't be surprised at Mr. Chastelay not wanting that old affair dragged up again. It very nearly wrecked his life. Everybody had him down for the lover, the fellow who drove her to it. Her being his farm foreman's wife, you see, and him having been noticeably took with her, and on familiar terms with the two of them. I daresay it was only natural people should think it was him. If he could have run the rumors to their source he'd have sued, but he never could. For a year it was touch and go whether his wife divorced him, but they're over it now. After all, it's ten years and more. Nobody wants to start the tongues wagging again. No, sir, I'm sure *you* don't, or I wouldn't be doing this.

She was very beautiful, they say, this Mrs. Purcell. Very young, only twenty-one, and fair. They say the photographs didn't do justice to her coloring. Wonderful blue eyes, I believe. *Green,* were they, you say? Not blue? Well, I wouldn't argue with you, sir, you were reporting the affair, you should know. Watch out for the bottom step here, it's worn very hollow. *Green* eyes!

Oh, no, sir, I wouldn't dispute it. Wonderful trained memory you have.

Well, at any rate she was young and very pretty, and I daresay a bit simple and innocent, too, brought up country-style as she was. She was the daughter of one of the gardeners. I don't suppose you ever met him? No, he wouldn't have anything to say to the press, would he? He had a stroke afterwards, and Mr. Chastelay pensioned him off with a light job around the place. But that's neither here nor there. Mind the step into the stone gallery. Here, let me put on the lights.

Yes, gives you quite a turn, doesn't he, that halberdier standing there, with his funny-shaped knife on a stick? I keep him all burnished up like that specially, it gives the kids a thrill. Tell you the truth, when I've been going round here at night, locking up and seeing all's fast after the folks have gone, I've often borrowed his halberd and carried it round with me, just for company like. It gets pretty eerie here after dark. Makes me feel like one of the ghosts myself, trailing this thing. If it's all the same to you, sir, I'll take it along with us now.

They put a heavy cover on the well after that fatality. There's a ring in the middle, and the haft of the halberd makes a very handy lever. You'd like to look inside, I dare say. There are iron rungs down the shaft like a ladder. Her husband went down, you know, and got her out. More than most of us would like to do, but then, he felt responsible, I suppose, poor soul.

Where's her husband now? Did you never hear, sir? He cracked up, poor lad, and they had to put him away. He's still locked up.

The way I heard it, this affair of hers had been going on some time, and when she found she was expecting a child it fairly knocked her over. Made her turn and look again at what she'd let this fellow persuade her into. She went to him, and asked what to do.

And he told her not to be a fool, why should she want to do anything? She'd got a husband, hadn't she? All she had to do was hold her tongue. But he could see she didn't see it that way; she felt bad about her husband and couldn't let him father the child with his eyes shut. She was hating herself, and wanting to be honest, and wanting her lover to stand by her even in that. And wanting her husband back on the old terms, too, because I don't suppose she ever really stopped loving him, she only lost sight of him in the excitement. So this fellow put her off and said they'd talk about it again, after they'd considered it.

And he lit out the next day for I don't know where, and left her.

No, sir, you're right, of course, I wasn't in this job then, how would I know? Just reconstructing in my own mind. Maybe it wasn't like that. No, as you say, if it was Mr. Chastelay he didn't light out for anywhere; he stayed right here and got the muck thrown at him. But a lot of people think now it wasn't him, after all.

Anyhow, she went to her husband and told him the truth. All but the name, she never told anyone that. Very nearly killed him, I shouldn't wonder, if he was daft about her, as they say. He didn't rave or anything, just turned his back on her and went away. And when she followed him, crying, he couldn't bear it; he turned round and hit her.

Yes, sir, a very vivid imagination I've got, I don't deny it. So would you have if you lived in this place alone. I fairly see 'em walking, nights.

And the way I see it, she was too young and inexperienced to understand that you don't hit out at somebody who means nothing to you. She thought he was finished with her. And if he was gone, everything was gone. She didn't know enough to wait, and bear it, and hope. She ran along here, crying, and jumped into the well.

Five minutes, and he was running after her. By that time it was too late. When he got her out she was dead. Her fair hair all smeared with scum, and slime in her beautiful green eyes.

Right here, where we're standing. There's the cover they've put over it, since. Good and heavy, so's nobody can shift it easily. But if you'll stand back, sir, and let me get some leverage on this halberd—

There you are. Nobody knows quite how deep. Let's have a little more light, shall we? There, now you can see better. A girl would have to be at the end of her tether, wouldn't she, to go that way?

My sweet Mary, my little lamb!

No, sir, I didn't say anything. I thought *you* were about to speak.

What am I doing, sir? Just turning the key in the lock. Just seeing how smoothly it works. A lot of keys and wards to look after, you know, and Mr. Chastelay is very particular about this room being kept closed. No one's been here for more than three years, except me. Not until tonight. I don't suppose there'll be anyone else for the next three years, either, and if they did they wouldn't lift the well-cover. I do all the cleaning myself, you see. I'm a great one for keeping things in perfect order. Look at this halberd, now. Sharp as a butcher's knife. Here, look.

Oh, sorry, sir, did I prick you?

Mad, sir? No, sir, not me. That was her husband, remember? They put him away. All that happened to me was a stroke, and it didn't affect my co-ordination. Pensioned off with a light job I may be, but you'd be surprised how strong I still am. So I shouldn't try to rush me, if I were you, sir. It wouldn't do you any good.

It's always a mistake to know too much, sir. *Mary* Purcell, you said. Alice was her first name, the one all the papers used, did you know that? It was only her family and her intimates who called her Mary. And then, *how did you know her eyes were green?* They were shut fast enough before ever the press got near her. But her lover knew.

Yes, sir, I know you now, you were the young man who was staying with the Lovells at the farm that summer. We must have a talk about Mary. Sorry poor Tim Purcell couldn't be here to make up the party; it might have done him a power of good. But we'll spare him a thought, won't we? Now, while there's time.

Funny, isn't it? Providential, when you come to think, you walking out here from the farm, without a car or anything. And I'd stake this key and this halberd—I don't have to tell you how much I value them, do I?—that you never told a soul where you were going.

But you couldn't keep away, could you?

And I don't suppose either you or I will ever really know why you came—never dreaming you'd meet Mary's father. So I can believe it was because I've wanted you so much—*so much!*

Oh, I shouldn't scream like that, if I was you, sir, you'll only do yourself an injury. And nobody'll hear you, you know. There's nobody within half a mile but you and me. And the walls are very thick. Very thick.

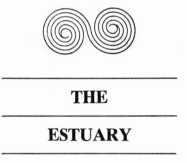

THE

ESTUARY

The best of it was that it wasn't really stealing. Everybody knew that the ships had been moored in the estuary because mooring them was cheaper than cutting them up for scrap metal would have been. There was a guard and a patrol at night, of course, but both were perfunctory and negligent. Evading them was so easy as to make abstractions seem rather more legitimate than they would have if the ships had been unguarded entirely. No wonder Pickard thought of his thefts as a sort of praiseworthy salvaging.

Night after night he scrabbled in the bowels of the rotting Liberty ships and came up with sheets of metal, parts of instruments, and lengths of brass and copper pipe. He had a friend in the boat-building business who bought most of what he appropriated, and who paid him prices which were only a shade below normal. Once in a while pictures of what would happen to him if he were caught bothered Pickard—he rather thought the ships were government property, and carried a proportionate penalty—but those apes on the patrol made so much noise on their rounds that you'd have to be deaf, dumb and blind to get caught.

Business was good. After the first three months Pickard found it expedient to hire a helper, a tall, gangling youth who wore a felt skullcap and was called Gene. He took over with no difficulty at all Pickard's belief that his occupation was, at worst, one of the slight, necessary irregularities which keep the wheels of business lubricated and revolving steadily.

He was a smart boy in other ways, too. After he had worked for Pick for three or four days, he suggested a number of improvements in the salvaging technique. They were well thought of; that week Pickard's receipts were some one hundred and twenty percent above their previous average. A modest prosperity visited the Pickard household. Estelle took to cooking with butter instead of margarine; she read advertisements for fur coats with a puckered brow and a critical eye.

"Say, Pop," Gene said hesitatingly two or three weeks after Estelle had made the down payment on a medium-priced Persian lamb greatcoat, "you ever hear anything on these boats at night? I mean, anything funny?"

Pick looked at him quizzically. The night was hazy and overcast, with a good deal of diffused light in the sky, and he could discern, though dimly, the outline of Gene's head and face beside him in the motorboat. "Don't get cold feet," he said, "that patrol won't bother us none. Those dumb bastards wouldn' know manure if they fell in it."

Gene wriggled. He was still very young. "I don't mean the patrol," he answered, "I mean something, unh, kind of funny. Something on the boats like it was following me."

Pickard laughed. "You got too much imagination, Junior," he said. (The "junior" was his revenge for Gene's calling him "Pop," which he detested.) "Nothing here but a lot of old worn-out boats. You're young and full of—"

"O.K.," Gene said. "I just—O.K."

"See if you can get some more of that little brass tubing," Pick said as they parted. He shoved a hunk of sneuss in his cheek. "Bert told me he could use any amount of it."

"O.K."

Artistically speaking, Gene should have disappeared that night. It was not until Friday, however, the he failed to show up at the motor-boat with his load of salvage and scrap.

Pick waited for him impatiently at first, then with anxiety. What could have happened to the kid? He might have got into a tangle with the patrol, of course, but Pick hadn't heard any disturbance, and sound carries well over water. The patrol always went around with lanterns and flashlights, and it made as much noise as a kaffeklatsch. But if Gene hadn't got into trouble with the patrol, where was he? Had he fallen somewhere clambering around in the dark? Was he lying unconscious in the bottom of some hold?

Before the lightening sky forced him home, Pickard hunted for the boy on a handful of ships. He found no sign of him. He hunted the next night and the next and the next (not forgetting, of course, his primary interest in salvage), until he had covered every hull in the slowly-rocking graveyard of them. No Gene. Only, on the third hull he visited on the last night he found the boy's felt skullcap floating brim-up in a sheet of filthy bilge.

Pickard was worried, more worried than he would have cared to admit. If Gene had been hauled off by the patrol, it meant trouble for Pick himself sooner or later. And if the patrol wasn't responsible for his absence, what was?

Estelle noticed his trouble and questioned him until she forced the reason for it from him. At the end of his account, she laughed.

"He was a kind of a jerk, Pick," she said comfortingly. "What happened was he got scared an' ran and then was ashamed to come back and tell you about it afterwards. Just a jerk."

"Yeh. But, what scared him?" Pickard swallowed. "I remember hearing," he said with some difficulty, "about how they was a welder got welded up in one of those ships when they was building them. They launched the ship with him in it. And then there was a man was down in the bottom of his air hose caught fire. An—"

His wife snorted. "That's a lotta horsehair, Pick, and you know it. I never heard such junk. You scared of the patrol?"

"Hunh-unh."

"Well, then! I don't know what's the matter with you. I sure never thought you'd lose your nerve . . . Mabel was telling me they laid off Reese at Selby yesterday." Estelle was thinking, Pickard knew, of the payments on her new fur coat.

Pickard slept in the daytime and worked at night and, though it was a quiet neighborhood, he never slept very well. He had been asleep three or four hours, which brought the time to 11 A.M., when he had his dream.

It started out mildly enough. He was hunting through one of the hulls for a highly salable chunk of everdur he had reason to believe was somewhere about. As he hunted he began to have a feeling, faint at first and then stronger, that something pretty unpleasant was lurking on the periphery of his vision. Two or three times he turned around abruptly, hoping to surprise it, but it moved faster than he could.

He kept on looking for the everdur. He climbed up ladders and down them again, sniffed around in the engine room and the crew's quarters. At last, in the bilge of number three hold, he saw the half-submerged piece of everdur.

As soon as he saw it, he forgot that he had been hunting it. By the strange equivalence of dreams, it was the bilge, the filthy stinking bilge, which became the object of his desire. He knelt down beside it, scooped it up in his hand and, nauseated, sick with disgust and self-loathing, began to drink.

Pick's heart was beating violently when he awoke. Of all the dumb dreams! What did a thing like that mean? What sense was there to it? His pulse was still pounding abnormally when the noon whistles blew.

He hired another helper. Fred wasn't nearly as good as Gene had been, a lazy bum in fact, and he quit after five days, saying he didn't like the noises on the hulls at night. So you can see Pick had plenty of warning before it happened to him.

It was a week later that Gene came up behind him when he was between decks on the *M.S. Blount* and pawed at him with his rotting hands. Pick screamed and screamed and tried to fight him off, but he was wholly unsuccessful. He couldn't hurt Gene; Gene was already dead. And then Pick was floundering around in the sickening stinking loathsome wonderful bilge while Gene stood over him making soft blubbering noises with his peeling, oozing lips and the other one lurked quietly in the background.

Estelle never did get finished paying for her fur coat. After a while she set up housekeeping with a man named Leon Socher who had long admired her. The ships went back to their slow job of rotting at their moorings without bothering the taxpayers. And nowadays, if you are so indiscreet as to go poking at night among the rotting hulls as they roll quietly at anchor in the estuary, you will find that they are populated by a small, select company, a company consisting of Pickard, Gene, and the welder, who is the Oldest Inhabitant.

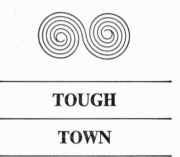

TOUGH

TOWN

Ed Dillon hesitated before the neat iron gate that barred the pathway leading to the comfortable home beyond. He shifted his battered sample case, taking no notice of the NO PEDDLERS sign hung prominently near the latch. He was tired, tired as only a door-to-door canvasser can be tired near the end of a day of doors slammed in his face. It was a hard town. A tough town.

He'd seen a constable giving him a long slow stare earlier and he'd walked jauntily on, trying to look like a well-fed tourist just stopping between bus changes, out to look the town over. But the constable hadn't been fooled. He had an eye for the cracked shoes, the shiny serge, the well-worn sample case. It had been a tough town. And only two meager sales.

He glanced at his watch and shrugged his shoulder. Just time to make his pitch here, then hustle down to the bus depot for a bite and the 5:15 on to the next town.

He opened the gate and took two steps when the dog was on him, the red red mouth, the slavering teeth. A strange horrible dog that lurked silently behind a bush and leaped savagely, growling low and deep in its throat. With the instinct of long practice he brought up his sample case and luckily, the dog's teeth only skinned his knuckles. Then the animal was behind and loping away, an eerie long-drawn howl floating back.

Ed watched it go, heart pounding, sucking his knuckles. Out of the corner of his eye he saw the agitated motions of a curtain being dropped at a window, then the door opened and a tall white-haired man stepped out. The man's quick glance raked him from head to foot, and Ed, seeing the set lines, the narrowed piercing eyes, knew there'd be no sale here. He stopped and picking up his case, opened the gate and hurried off.

"Wait!" the white-haired man yelled. "You—come back here you! Stop! Come back here!"

Ed hurried on, without looking back. He knew these towns, these mean bitter people, always anxious to slap a man in jail, to fine him for selling without a license, get his last cent and kick him out like a common bum. He know them, every miserable sooty burg, every disheveled housewife who listened with flat eyes and contemptuous smile. What was wrong with these people? Why did they hate him, sneer at him, sic their dogs at him? He did them no harm. He brought his few brushes, his kitchen gadgets, his little jokes— and they paid him with insults, threats. Behind him, the man still yelled as he turned the corner and hurried toward the bus depot, his torn knuckles burning.

Over his coffee, with still twenty minutes to go, Ed heard the commotion outside. With caution born of long experience, he picked up a newspaper and held it before his face, then he peered carefully around. There was the tall white-haired old man, talking excitedly to the constable. They walked along the covered ramp outside the depot, looking carefully at the few stragglers waiting for the big silver bus to take on the passengers.

He rose, carrying the paper and his case, walked quietly to the back of the little restaurant and out the door. He had no doubt that the white-haired man wanted him arrested for ignoring his NO

PEDDLERS sign. Probably a local merchant, outraged at his un-licensed competition.

His shoulders sagged, he felt tired and empty as he peeked around the corner and watched them enter the restaurant. So they were going to make a production of it.

He picked up his case and glanced quickly around. Down the street was a sad little park filled with straggly trees. In the center was a tiny screened summer-house, leaf-choked, empty-looking.

He started walking quickly. There was a chance, a bare chance, that he could make it to the highway and flag down the bus provided he could get out of town without being seen by the constable. He simply couldn't afford a fine—or thirty days in jail—or both. He barely had bus fare and room rent for tonight. And tomorrow, if the next town wasn't better—

He entered the park and walked along a disused path toward the summer-house. In the distance, the bus burst into sound and staccato backfires. He hesitated. Too late now.

He peered into the summer-house, at the littered floor, the dust-covered benches. He could stay there, wait until dark and then head out to catch the ten o'clock. It wasn't a pleasant prospect, but then, it was better than running into the eager-beaver constable.

He looked beyond the park, at the snug little homes, the tree-lined streets, and a vague sadness came over him. He was the eternal wanderer, peddler, an itinerant whose trade was old when the pyramids were built.

He sighed and settled himself on the bench. Tough town. Tough people. Even the damn dogs bit without warning. His knuckles hurt. He flipped open the paper and scanned the headlines quickly. LOCAL GIRL VANISHES. The subhead said: "Judy Howell Feared Victim of Foul Play." He grunted, squinting in the dimness, gave up, tucked the paper under his head and in a minute was asleep. When he awoke, it was dark.

His tongue felt thick, his head throbbed and his knuckles burned like consuming fire. He examined his watch. He just had time to ease out of town and flag down the 10:15 if he hurried. He rose and suddenly the room whirled, there was a huge roaring in his ears. He waited, strangely frightened, until his head cleared. He'd been hungry and tired before but nothing like that had ever happened. He picked up his case, wincing at the stiff pain in his scraped knuckles, cursing again the town, the dog, the white-haired man who pursued him, even through his uneasy slumber.

Unless he wanted to cut across fields, climb through or under barbed wire, he had to walk through a well-lighted section in order to get to the highway. He hesitated, but his throbbing hand gave him no choice. He was in no mood to climb fences.

Head down, clutching the rolled-up newspaper, he strode along, trying to look like a well-fed tourist out to see the town between bus stops. His feet were killing him and deep behind his eyes strange flashes came and went. It had been a long time since he'd eaten lunch, but still—

He stiffened as a man approached, staring curiously at him as most small-towners stare at strangers. The man's steps slowed as Ed approached and finally stopped, frankly waiting for Ed to come closer. With the skill born of long practice Ed sized up the stranger. Not a constable, or even a deputy. Just a local out for a stroll—and yet, the way he stared, the sudden look as of recognition—

Ed pulled his hat brim down farther and brushed by the man, forcing his aching legs to move briskly, the handle of his sample case wet in his palm.

Ed crossed the street hurriedly, glancing back. He saw the man stand irresolutely for a moment and then rush up a walk and begin pounding on the door of a house.

Suddenly he was soaked in perspiration. That man had acted as though he'd recognized him, as though his picture had been plastered all over the papers or something. Little nightmare thoughts pushed and darted about the edges of his mind. That white-haired man. Talking, telling people about him until the whole town was out to get him.

Ridiculous. For what? People in a town, even a tough town like this, didn't concern themselves about a little thing like canvassing without a license.

He averted his face as a group of laughing young girls came out of a brightly lit soda fountain. He heard one sing a brief snatch of a popular song, clear and sweet, as he passed them. And another gasped, a choked little sound that tightened his hand convulsively on the case handle.

"Did you see that man? Isn't that—it's him!"

He faltered. It was crazy. Even the kids—

"Gray suit and brown hat, carrying a suitcase—"

"It is! It is!"

Their little squeals and gasps pursued him as he crossed the street again, rounded the corner and stopped in a darkened doorway. Through the broad window opening on the street he could see them. The girls were clustered about the door of the drugstore, talking and pointing in his direction. A tall young man dressed in whites had joined them. A small boy leaped on his bike and peddled furiously up and rounded the corner, not seeing him flattened in the doorway.

The tiny bicycle light dimmed and vanished up the street, and Ed felt a terrible tremor in his neck, an uncontrollable jerking. The spasm passed and he leaned limply in the doorway, looking through the window to across the street. The man who had pounded on the door came up with several others. Cars converged on the spot. The little knot before the drugstore grew, the babble of their voices reaching him, an ominous murmur. The crowd grew, the noises it made swelled. Then they started to cross the street.

He began walking hurriedly, his head remote, the roaring returning. The street stretched endlessly, growing dim, receding into an infinite distance. Behind, he heard running footsteps, hurried explanations as others joined the group.

Something horrible had happened to this town, the people. The word of him had spread like a crown fire in a forest and they were out to get him. Why? He was no criminal. What could he possibly have done to start them off? He shifted his sample case, trying to think. And then he remembered the newspaper he'd read. The little girl. Missing. Foul-play suspected. Good God! Could it be they—?

He hurried. He realized his danger. He was The Stranger. Outsider. Beyond the sacred community pale.

He broke into a shambling staggering run. Across the street, through an empty lot, down an embankment and up the other side. There was no choice now. He had to cut across the fields, running heavily, the case banging against him, clutching the newspaper, while behind, the shouts rose. He tried to duck behind a huge oak tree but already they'd spotted him. The pursuit became bedlam.

He ran. He was every frightened man ever pursued. The night surrounded him, hideous with piercing calls. He moved spasmodically, a man in a nightmare. The town was after him, baying, slavering, with red red mouth. He should never have ignored that gigantic neon-lit NO PEDDLERS that burned and flared behind his eyes.

From all about they converged, seeing beyond the flimsy camouflage of his jaunty carriage, seeing the cracked shoes, the shining serge, the battered sample case. They knew. Canvasser. Peddler. Keep out. This is a tough town.

Suddenly he was down and they were on him, shouting, hands pulling at him.

"It's him. The guy the radio described—"

"He's the one the sheriff's after—"

"He did it. *Killer. Rapist!*"

Killer. Rapist. The words roared and crashed against his body from all angles, leaving great hurting welts. Dimly he heard a siren approaching, wailing thin and clear above the surf-sounds of the mob. Brakes squealed. There was an obscure scuffle, and still the mob pounded and pulled at him alternately.

"—not wanted for the girl!" a voice roared. "Let him go!" The voice was swallowed up in the huge murmuring. "He's been bitten by a mad dog. Stand back. In the name of the law, stand back or I'll shoot!"

"*Mad dog!* The words swept through the mob like a tremendous wave, battering and buffeting, surging back again.

"He's a mad dog!"

One voice, howling, horrible to hear rising above the others: "You heard the sheriff. He's a mad dog killer! You know what he did to Julie Howell. *What are we waiting for?*"

Another voice, lost, remote: "Stop! In the name of—"

There were shots, the mob shouted in unison, then swept forward like one kill-crazy animal. He was picked up. Hands plucked and tore at him. Faces, red, sweaty, glaring-eyed, came and went. Sounds swelled and swelled. This couldn't be real. This must be delirium, the result of the venom the mad dog had introduced into his blood. He'd heard the sheriff's words. He understood at last. It would be all right. This was fever. Soon, they'd put him between cool sheets and kind nurses would bathe his hot forehead.

He tried to move his broken mouth, to tell them this. He'd misjudged the people, the town. They weren't tough. Not really. It was just that he'd been bitten by a mad dog and they'd wanted to find him, to help him. They meant him no harm. All this, the noises, the battering blows, the mob—this wasn't really happening. Not really. It was the delirium.

Brilliant lights flared in his face. He opened his swollen eyes, squinting against the glare. Above was the massive outline of a great tree. An oak tree. Something moved up there, then came dropping toward him, alien, sinuous, like a brown hairy snake.

It dangled before his face and he smiled at it while lights flared and diminished in his eyes. It looked like a rope, it felt harsh when they put it around his neck, but it couldn't be a rope. Not really. The crowd screamed, a strangely feminine sound that lifted him up, up on a shrill crest of unbelievable sound, then suddenly he felt himself dropping, dropping.

It was just part of the nightmare. They meant him no harm. Soon they'd put him between cool sheets and kind nur—

◎ BY T. H. WHITE

THE

TROLL

"My father," said Mr. Marx, "used to say that an experience like the one I am about to relate was apt to shake one's interest in mundane matters. Naturally he did not expect to be believed, and he did not mind whether he was or not. He did not himself believe in the supernatural, but the thing happened, and he proposed to tell it as simply as possible. It was stupid of him to say that it shook his faith in mundane affairs, for it was just as mundane as anything else. Indeed the really frightening part about it was the horribly tangible atmosphere in which it took place. None of the outlines wavered in the least. The creature would have been less remarkable if it had been less natural. It seemed to overcome the usual laws without being immune to them.

"My father was a keen fisherman, and used to go to all sorts of places for his fish. On one occasion he made Abisko his Lapland

207

base, a comfortable railway hotel, one hundred and fifty miles within the Arctic circle. He travelled the prodigious length of Sweden (I believe it is as far from the South of Sweden to the North, as it is from the South of Sweden to the South of Italy) in the electric railway, and arrived tired out. He went to bed early, sleeping almost immediately, although it was bright daylight outside; as it is in those parts throughout the night at that time of the year. Not the least shaking part of his experience was that it should all have happened under the sun.

"He went to bed early, and slept, and dreamt. I may as well make it clear at once, as clear as the outlines of that creature in the northern sun, that his story did not turn out to be a dream in the last paragraph. The division between sleeping and waking was abrupt, although the feeling of both was the same. They were both in the same sphere of horrible absurdity, though in the former he was asleep and in the latter almost terribly awake. He tried to be asleep several times.

"My father always used to tell one of his dreams, because it somehow seemed of a piece with what was to follow. He believed that it was a consequence of the thing's presence in the next room. My father dreamed of blood.

"It was the vividness of the dreams that was impressive, their minute detail and horrible reality. The blood came through the keyhole of a locked door which communicated with the next room. I suppose the two rooms had originally been designed *en suite*. It ran down the door panel with a viscous ripple, like the artificial one created in the conduit of Trumpingdon Street. But it was heavy, and smelt. The slow welling of it sopped the carpet and reached the bed. It was warm and sticky. My father woke up with the impression that it was all over his hands. He was rubbing his first two fingers together, trying to rid them of the greasy adhesion where the fingers joined.

"My father knew what he had got to do. Let me make it clear that he was now perfectly wide awake, but he knew what he had got to do. He got out of bed, under this irresistible knowledge, and looked through the keyhole into the next room.

"I suppose the best way to tell the story is simply to narrate it, without an effort to carry belief. The thing did not require belief. It was not a feeling of horror in one's bones, or a misty outline, or anything that needed to be given actuality by an act of faith. It was as solid as a wardrobe. You don't have to believe in wardrobes. They are there, with corners.

"What my father saw through the keyhole in the next room was a Troll. It was eminently solid, about eight feet high, and dressed in brightly ornamented skins. It had a blue face, with yellow eyes, and on its head there was a woolly sort of nightcap with a red bobble on top. The features were Mongolian. Its body was long and sturdy, like the trunk of a tree. Its legs were short and thick, like the elephant's feet that used to be cut off for umbrella stands, and its arms were wasted: little rudimentary members like the forelegs of a kangaroo. Its head and neck were very thick and massive. On the whole, it looked like a grotesque doll.

"That was the horror of it. Imagine a perfectly normal golliwog (but without the association of a Christie minstrel) standing in the corner of a room, eight feet high. The creature was as ordinary as that, as tangible, as stuffed, and as ungainly at the joints: but it could move itself about.

"The Troll was eating a lady. Poor girl, she was tightly clutched to its breast by those rudimentary arms, with her head on a level with its mouth. She was dressed in a nightdress which had crumpled up under her armpits, so that she was a pitiful naked offering, like a classical picture of Andromeda. Mercifully, she appeared to have fainted.

"Just as my father applied his eye to the keyhole, the Troll opened its mouth and bit off her head. Then, holding the neck between the bright blue lips, he sucked the bare meat dry. She shrivelled, like a squeezed orange, and her heels kicked. The creature had a look of thoughtful ecstasy. When the girl seemed to have lost succulence as an orange she was lifted into the air. She vanished in two bites. The Troll remained leaning against the wall, munching patiently and casting its eyes about it with a vague benevolence. Then it leant forward from the low hips, like a jack-knife folding in half, and opened its mouth to lick the blood up from the carpet. The mouth was incandescent inside, like a gas fire, and the blood evaporated before its tongue, like dust before a vacuum cleaner. It straightened itself, the arms dangling before it in patient uselessness, and fixed its eyes upon the keyhole.

"My father crawled back to bed, like a hunted fox after fifteen miles. At first it was because he was afraid that the creature had seen him through the hole, but afterwards it was because of his reason. A man can attribute many night-time appearances to the imagination, and can ultimately persuade himself that creatures of the dark did not exist. But this was an appearance in a sunlit room, with all the solidity of a wardrobe and unfortunately almost none of its possibility. He spent the first ten minutes making sure that he was awake, and the rest of the night trying to hope that he was asleep. It was either that, or else he was mad.

"It is not pleasant to doubt one's sanity. There are no satisfactory tests. One can pinch oneself to see if one is asleep, but there are no means of determining the other problem. He spent some time opening and shutting his eyes, but the room seemed normal and remained unaltered. He also soused his head in a basin of cold water, without result. Then he lay on his back, for hours, watching the mosquitoes on the ceiling.

"He was tired when he was called. A bright Scandinavian maid admitted the full sunlight for him and told him that it was a fine day. He spoke to her several times, and watched her carefully, but she seemed to have no doubts about his behaviour. Evidently, then, he was not badly mad: and by now he had been thinking about the matter for so many hours that it had begun to get obscure. The outlines were blurring again, and he determined that the whole thing must have been a dream or a temporary delusion, something temporary, anyway, and finished with; so that there was no good in thinking about it longer. He got up, dressed himself fairly cheerfully, and went down to breakfast.

"These hotels used to be run extraordinary well. There was a hostess always handy in a little office off the hall, who was delighted to answer any questions, spoke every conceivable language, and generally made it her business to make the guests feel at home. The particular hostess at Abisko was a lovely creature into the bargain. My father used to speak to her a good deal. He had an idea that when you had a bath in Sweden one of the maids was sent to wash you. As a matter of fact this sometimes used to be the case, but it was always an old maid and highly trusted. You had to keep yourself under water and this was supposed to confer a cloak of invisibility. If you popped your knee out she was shocked. My father had a dim sort of hope that the hostess would be sent to bath him one day: and I dare say he would have shocked her a good deal. However, this is beside the point. As he passed through the hall something prompted him to ask about the room next to his. Had anybody, he enquired, taken number 23?

" 'But, yes,' said the lady manager with a bright smile, '23 is taken by a doctor professor from Upsala and his wife, such a charming couple!'

"My father wondered what the charming couple had been doing, whilst the Troll was eating the lady in the nightdress. However, he decided to think no more about it. He pulled himself together, and went in to breakfast. The Professor was sitting in an opposite corner (the manageress had kindly pointed him out), looking mild and shortsighted, by himself. My father thought he would go out for a long climb on the mountains, since exercise was evidently what his constitution needed.

"He had a lovely day. Lake Torne blazed a deep blue below him, for all its thirty miles, and the melting snow made a lacework of filigree round the tops of the surrounding mountain basin. He got away from the stunted birch trees, and the mossy bogs with the reindeer in them, and the mosquitoes, too. He forded something that might have been a temporary tributary of the Abiskojokk, having to take off his trousers to do so and tucking his shirt up round his neck. He wanted to shout, bracing himself against the glorious tug of the snow water, with his legs crossing each other involuntarily as they passed, and the boulders turning under his feet. His body made a bow wave in the water, which climbed and feathered on his stomach, on the upstream side. When he was under the opposite bank a stone turned in earnest, and he went in. He came up, shouting with laughter, and made out loud a remark which has since become a classic in my family, 'Thank God,' he said, 'I rolled up my sleeves.' He wrung out everything as best he could, and dressed again in the wet clothes, and set off up the shoulder of Niakatjavelk. He was dry and warm again in half a mile. Less than a thousand feet took him over the snow line, and there, crawling on hands and knees, he came face to face with what seemed to be the summit of ambition. He met an ermine. They were both on all fours, so that there was a sort of equality about the encounter, especially as the ermine was higher up than he was. They looked at each other for a fifth of a second, without saying anything, and then the ermine vanished. He searched for it everywhere in vain, for the snow was only patchy. My father sat down on a dry rock, to eat his well-soaked luncheon of chocolate and rye bread.

"Life is such unutterable hell, solely because it is sometimes beautiful. If we could only be miserable all the time, if there could be no such things as love or beauty or faith or hope, if I could be absolutely certain that my love would never be returned: how much more simple life would be. One could plod through the Siberian salt mines of existence without being bothered about happiness. Unfortunately the happiness is there. There is always the chance (about eight hundred and fifty to one) that another heart will come to mine. I can't help hoping, and keeping faith, and loving beauty. Quite frequently I am not so miserable as it would be wise to be. And there, for my poor father sitting on his boulder above the snow, was stark happiness beating at the gates.

"The boulder on which he was sitting had probably never been sat upon before. It was a hundred and fifty miles within the Arctic circle, on a mountain five thousand feet high, looking down on a blue lake. The lake was so long that he could have sworn it sloped away at the ends, proving to the naked eye that the sweet earth was round. The railway line and the half-dozen houses of Abisko were hidden in the trees. The sun was warm on the boulder, blue on the snow, and his body tingled smooth from the spate water. His mouth watered for the chocolate, just behind the tip of his tongue.

"And yet, when he had eaten the chocolate—perhaps it was heavy on his stomach—there was the memory of the Troll. My father fell suddenly into a black mood, and began to think about the supernatural. Lapland was beautiful in the summer, with the sun sweeping round the horizon day and night, and the small tree leaves twinkling. It was not the sort of place for wicked things. But what about the winter? A picture of the Arctic night came before him, with the silence and the snow. Then the legendary wolves and bears snuffled at the far encampments, and the nameless winter spirits moved on their darkling courses. Lapland had always been associated with sorcery, even by Shakespeare. It was at the outskirts of the world that the Old Things accumulated, like driftwood round the edges of the sea. If one wanted to find a wise woman, one went to the rims of the Hebrides; on the coast of Brittany one sought the mass of St. Secaire. And what an outskirt Lapland was! It was an outskirt not only of Europe, but of civilisation. It had no boundaries. The Lapps went with the reindeer, and where the reindeer were was Lapland. Curiously indefinite region, suitable to the indefinite things. The Lapps were not Christians. What a fund of power they must have had behind them, to resist the march of mind. All through the missionary centuries they had held to something: something had stood behind them, a power against Christ. My father realised with a shock that he was living in the age of the reindeer, a period contiguous to the mammoth and the fossil.

"Well, this was not what he had come out to do. He dismissed the nightmares with an effort, got up from his boulder, and began the scramble back to his hotel. It was impossible that a professor from Abisko could become a troll.

"As my father was going in to dinner that evening the manageress stopped him in the hall.

" 'We have had a day so sad,' she said. 'The poor Dr. Professor has disappeared his wife. She has been missing since last night. The Dr. Professor is inconsolable.'

"My father then knew for certain that he had lost his reason.

"He went blindly to dinner, without making any answer, and began to eat a thick sour-cream soup that was taken cold with pepper and sugar. The Professor was still sitting in his corner, a sandy-headed man with thick spectacles and a desolate expression. He was looking at my father, and my father, with the soup spoon half-way to his mouth, looked at him. You know that eye-to-eye recognition, when two people look deeply into each other's pupils, and burrow to the soul? It usually comes before love. I mean the clear, deep, milk-eyed recognition expressed by the poet Donne. Their eyebeams twisted and did thread their eyes upon a double string. My father recognised that the Professor was a Troll, and the Professor recognised my father's recognition. Both of them knew that the Professor had eaten his wife.

"My father put down his soup spoon, and the Professor began to grow. The top of his head lifted and expanded, like a great loaf rising in an oven; his face went red and purple, and finally blue; the whole ungainly upperworks began to sway and topple towards the ceiling. My father looked about him. The other diners were eating unconcernedly. Nobody else could see it, and he was definitely mad at last. When he looked at the Troll again, the creature bowed. The enormous superstructure inclined itself towards him from the hips, and grinned seductively.

"My father got up from his table experimentally, and advanced towards the Troll, arranging his feet on the carpet with excessive care. He did not find it easy to walk, or to approach the monster, but it was a question of his reason. If he was mad, he was mad; and it was essential that he should come to grips with the thing, in order to make certain.

"He stood before it like a small boy, and held out his hand, saying, 'Good-evening.'

" 'Ho! Ho!' said the Troll, 'little mannikin. And what shall I have for my supper to-night?'

"Then it held out its wizened furry paw and took my father by the hand.

"My father went straight out of the dining-room, walking on air. He found the manageress in the passage and held out his hand to her.

" 'I am afraid I have burnt my hand,' he said. 'Do you think you could tie it up?'

"The manageress said, 'But it is a very bad burn. There are blisters all over the back. Of course, I will bind it up at once.'

"He explained that he had burnt it on one of the spirit lamps at the sideboard. He could scarcely conceal his delight. One cannot burn oneself by being insane.

" 'I saw you talking to the Dr. Professor,' said the manageress, as she was putting on the bandage. 'He is a sympathetic gentleman, is he not?'

"The relief about his sanity soon gave place to other troubles. The Troll had eaten its wife and given him a blister, but it had also made an unpleasant remark about its supper that evening. It proposed to eat my father. Now very few people can have been in a position to decide what to do when a troll earmarks them for its next meal. To begin with, although it was a tangible Troll in two ways, it had been invisible to the other diners. This put my father in a difficult position. He could not, for instance, ask for protection. He could scarcely go to the manageress and say, 'Professor Skål is an odd kind of werewolf, ate his wife last night, and proposes to eat me this evening.' He would have found himself in a looney-bin at once. Besides, he was too proud to do this, and still too confused. Whatever the proofs and blisters, he did not find it easy to believe in professors that turned into Trolls. He had lived in the normal world all his life, and, at his age, it was difficult to start learning afresh. It would have been quite easy for a baby, who was still co-ordinating the world, to cope with the Troll situation: for my father, not. He kept trying to fit it in somewhere, without disturbing the universe. He kept telling himself that it was nonsense: one did not get eaten by professors. It was like having a fever, and telling oneself that it was all right, really, only a delirium, only something that would pass.

"There was that feeling on the one side, the desperate assertion of all the truths that he had learned so far, the tussle to keep the world from drifting, the brave but intimidated refusal to give in or to make a fool of himself.

"On the other side there was stark terror. However much one struggled to be merely deluded, or hitched up momentarily in an odd pocket of space-time, there was panic. There was the urge to go away as quickly as possible, to flee the dreadful Troll. Unfortunately the last train had left Abisko, and there was nowhere else to go.

"My father was not able to distinguish these trends of thought. For him they were at the time intricately muddled together. He was in a whirl. A proud man, and an agnostic, he stuck to his muddled guns alone. He was terribly afraid of the Troll, but he could not afford to admit its existence. All his mental processes remained hung up, whilst he talked on the terrace, in a state of suspended animation, with an American tourist who had come to Abisko to photograph the midnight sun.

"The American told my father that the Abisko railway was the northernmost electric railway in the world, that twelve trains passed through it every day travelling between Upsala and Narvik, that the population of Abo was 12,000 in 1862, and that Gustavus Adolphus ascended the throne of Sweden in 1611. He also gave some facts about Greta Garbo.

"My father told the American that a dead baby was required for the mass of St. Secaire, that an elemental was a kind of mouth in space that sucked at you and tried to gulp you down, that homeopathic magic was practised by the aborigines of Australia, and that a Lapland woman was careful at her confinement to have no knots or loops about her person, lest these should make the delivery difficult.

"The American, who had been looking at my father in a strange way for some time, took offense at this and walked away; so that there was nothing for it but to go to bed.

"My father walked upstairs on will power alone. His faculties seemed to have shrunk and confused themselves. He had to help himself with the banister. He seemed to be navigating himself by wireless, from a spot about a foot above his forehead. The issues that were involved had ceased to have any meaning, but he went on doggedly up the stairs, moved forward by pride and contrariety. It was physical fear that alienated him from his body, the same fear that he had felt as a boy, walking down long corridors to be beaten. He walked firmly up the stairs.

"Oddly enough, he went to sleep at once. He had climbed all day and been awake all night and suffered emotional extremes. Like a condemned man, who was to be hanged in the morning, my father gave the whole business up and went to sleep.

"He was woken at midnight exactly. He heard the American on the terrace below his window, explaining excitedly that there had been a cloud on the last two nights at 11:58, thus making it impossible to photograph the midnight sun. He heard the camera click.

"There seemed to be a sudden storm of hail and wind. It roared at his window-sill, and the window curtains lifted themselves taut, pointing horizontally into the room. The shriek and rattle of the tempest framed the window in a crescendo of growing sound, an increasing blizzard directed towards himself. A blue paw came over the sill.

"My father turned over and hid his head in the pillow. He could feel the domed head dawning at the window and the eyes fixing themselves upon the small of his back. He could feel the places physically, about four inches apart. They itched. Or else the rest of his body itched, except those places. He could feel the creature growing into the room, glowing like ice, and giving off a storm. His mosquito curtains rose in its afflatus, uncovering him, leaving him defenceless. He was in such an ecstasy of terror that he almost enjoyed it. He was like a bather plunging for the first time into freezing water and unable to articulate. He was trying to yell, but all he could do was to throw a series of hooting noises from his paralysed lungs. He became a part of the blizzard. The bedclothes were gone. He felt the Troll put out its hands.

"My father was an agnostic, but, like most idle men, he was not above having a bee in his bonnet. His favourite bee was the psychology of the Catholic Church. He was ready to talk for hours about psycho-analysis and the confession. His greatest discovery had been the rosary.

"The rosary, my father used to say, was intended solely as a factual occupation which calmed the lower centres of the mind. The automatic telling of the beads liberated the higher centres to meditate upon the mysteries. They were a sedative, like knitting or counting sheep. There was no better cure for insomnia than a rosary. For several years he had given up deep breathing or regular counting. When he was sleepless he lay on his back and told his beads, and there was a small rosary in the pocket of his pyjama coat.

"The Troll put out its hands, to take him round the waist. He became completely paralysed, as if he had been winded. The Troll put its hand upon the beads.

"They met, the occult forces, in a clash above my father's heart. There was an explosion, he said, a quick creation of power. Positive and negative. A flash, a beam. Something like the splutter with which the antenna of a tram meets its overhead wires again, when it is being changed about.

"The Troll made a high squealing noise, like a crab being boiled, and began rapidly to dwindle in size. It dropped my father and turned about, and ran wailing, as if it had been terribly burnt, for the window. Its colour waned as its size decreased. It was one of those air-toys now, that expire with a piercing whistle. It scrambled over the window-sill, scarcely larger than a little child, and sagging visibly.

"My father leaped out of bed and followed it to the window. He saw it drop on the terrace like a toad, gather itself together, stumble off, staggering and whistling like a bat, down the valley of the Abiskojokk.

"My father fainted.

"In the morning the manageress said, 'There has been such a terrible tragedy. The poor Dr. Professor was found this morning in the lake. The worry about his wife had certainly unhinged his mind.'

"A subscription for a wreath was started by the American, to which my father subscribed five shillings; and the body was shipped off next morning, on one of the twelve trains that travel between Upsala and Narvik every day."

◎ BY ROBERT SOMERLOTT

EVENING

AT

THE

BLACK

HOUSE

His eyes widened and his big hands holding the sherry bottle trembled slightly, causing a brown trickle to run down the side of the goblet.

"Are you certain, Eric?"

"Yes," I said. "I've been around enough to know when something's up."

"Tell me exactly what happened. It may be important."

219

"It was just getting dark when I left the hotel. I walked along, thinking how good Frieda's sauerbraten was going to taste after eating tortillas and chili most of the week. I didn't pay any attention to the pair when I passed them in the plaza. It was three blocks before I realized they were following me."

Henry Black's hands were under control as he offered me the sherry. He sat quietly in the leather chair opposite me, his face calm, but the pale blue eyes glancing uneasily toward the living room windows with their drawn drapes and barred shutters. He tilted his close-cropped head, as though listening for some unfamiliar sound outside. I heard nothing but a patter of rain and the whining of Inga, the more nervous of his two Doberman pinschers. I pictured the restless dogs prowling between the house and the barb-topped fence that encircled it. Loki, the male, was more powerful. But Inga was tautly alert, tense with suspicion. Months before, during my first evenings at Henry Black's, I had felt like an explorer sitting down with cannibals. Would the dogs lunge for my throat if I reached for a fork? They were completely unused to strangers. In the house, they never left Henry's side. It had taken two months and a dozen visits before they would trust me to walk across the room. Now, patrolling in the yard, they probed the night for a warning scent, a muffled footfall.

"What did these men look like?" Henry asked.

"Like a couple of Mexican drunks," I said. "When I realized they were following me, I figured they were out to sandbag and roll an American tourist. Then I felt—I don't know—they just didn't *walk* like Mexicans. I suppose that's ridiculous, but—"

"No, Eric, it's not!" His sudden excitement carried him to his feet. "Every race, every nationality moves differently. Like breeds of dogs —each has its own gait. Some people would never notice the difference, but you and I would."

"Anyway," I said, "there was something odd about them. I decided if I was going to have trouble, I'd better have it in the village instead of on this deserted country road. So I stopped and waited. They didn't pass me, but turned into one of those courtyards. I would have forgotten the whole thing if I hadn't seen them later near your gate."

"What were they doing?"

"This black car was parked in the road and they were talking to the driver. They watched me for a minute, and when they saw me turn toward your gate, they got in the car. They took off down the road heading away from town. Oh, yes, the car had an American license."

Henry slammed his hard fist into his palm. "Took off for where? That road leads to a couple of adobe huts and a pig farm three miles away. You should have told me at once, Eric."

I chuckled, trying to ease the tension in the room. "Did you want me to ruin Frieda's dinner with a story about being watched by mysterious strangers? Besides, nothing happened. They just looked peculiar, and I can't figure out how they got here ahead of me without my seeing them on the road. Oh, hell, I think they just wanted to grab a few American dollars and changed their minds."

"Perhaps. Perhaps."

Frieda entered so suddenly that I had a feeling she had been standing just outside the dining room archway, listening.

"Nutses," she announced, displaying a carved wooden tray. "*Und* cheeses."

"*And* cheeses," Henry corrected.

"*Ja.*" Frieda's round face had a dumpling-fed smile, but there was a strained look around her eyes. Her plump fingers, weighted by gold rings, were fidgety as she set the tray on the coffee table. The dishes brimmed with after-dinner tidbits.

"When I break down and get married—Lord help me—it's going to be a German girl like Frieda."

"*Ja,*" she smiled, "but a younger."

"She's a good wife," said Henry. A long look passed between them, a half smile of devotion and appreciation—but at the same time there was sadness.

"You have been a good husband," she said. Every syllable carried a weight of doom, making her words sound like a good-bye whispered beside a new grave. Henry patted her hand, his fingers touching the beautiful gold bracelet she wore proudly. Frieda was so plain, so housewifely, that her fascination with gold ornaments seemed like a child's. She delighted equally in the really lovely bracelet and the cheap, gypsy hoops that dragged at the lobes of her pierced ears.

Outside, Inga barked sharply. Henry crossed the room in three strides. Jerking back the drapes, he flung open the window and pressed his face against the shutter slats. He was well past fifty, but he moved like a tiger, power and balance in every step.

"What is it?" I asked.

His tense body slowly relaxed. "Nothing. I heard Inga bark."

"I'll go out to take a look around."

Before I could take a step toward the door, he stopped me with a snapped military command. "No, Eric!"

I faced him. "Look, Henry, all evening you've acted like you expected a bomb to come through the window. It started long before I mentioned being followed. At dinner you were jumpy as a cat. It's not like you. Now you think something's outside. Well, I'm going to find out."

"Go ahead. It's better to know."

At the door, the dogs raced to me. "Good boy, Loki," I said, petting him. I did not touch Inga. Together, we slowly circled the house.

The place was a fortress, or perhaps more like a concentration camp, with the high wire fence and cleared strip between it and the surrounding jungle. The fence, powerfully electrified, claimed a daily toll of birds which perched on its deadly strands. Even in this remote part of Mexico, where the rich always topped their walls with jagged glass and kept guard dogs, such precautions as Henry Black had taken were extraordinary.

I had met Henry five months before, shortly after my arrival in the village of San Xavier. He was an arresting figure, striding through the plaza with Inga at his side and Hugo, the square-faced valet, at his heels. For a second, he paused to glance at the painting I was struggling with. Nodding curtly to me, he moved on, his back as military as the revolver holstered at his side.

During the next two weeks he passed me every morning on his way to and from the post office, never speaking, but always glancing curiously. Finally, his fascination with painting and his love of the

flowers that were my constantly repeated subject overcame his aloof-
ness.

After the first brief conversation our friendship developed rapidly,
since he was an amateur painter himself. We played chess together;
we were evenly matched. Our similar backgrounds overcame the
twenty-year difference in our ages. I had seen a lot of the world during my thirty years. Henry and I had both fought in wars, knew odd
countries and remembered certain twisting streets in Singapore or
Barcelona.

"What a relief to talk to an intelligent man again!" he said. "How
did you happen to come to this hellhole?"

"No accident," I said. "I'd made inquiries from friends and connections in Mexico for three years before I decided on this town.
For me, it's ideal."

I did not question him about his reasons for choosing San Xavier
as a retirement spot. Something about Henry warded off inquiry.

A week later, I met Frieda. "I found her in Germany," he said,
"when I was on a military mission. Eric, you should have seen her
thirty years ago!"

Henry was always on guard. But his watchfulness had increased
during the last six weeks. I became aware of new shadows under his
eyes, a tension in his manner. He took to glancing over his shoulder
in the street. I realized one day that he was deliberately varying his
arrival time at the post office.

Now, as the dogs and I turned the fourth corner of the house and
were once again in the front yard, I felt that he was close to a
breaking point. Through the shutter slits I could see him watching
me, straining to see into the night.

Reaching the window, I stopped suddenly, my shoulders stiffening.
Loki barked as my hand touched him. The dogs, sensing an uneasiness in me, growled viciously, sniffing as near the fence as they
dared go.

I returned quickly to the house.

"What was it?" Henry asked.

"Nothing."

"No, Eric! You saw something. I watched through the shutter.
You were startled by something in the jungle."

"Just a light," I said. "It came on twice, then vanished. For a moment I thought it was some kind of signal, but probably it was just some Mexican carrying an open lantern that the rain put out. It's plenty wet out there."

Henry looked doubtful. I felt uncomfortable as he stared at me without speaking.

"What is this?" I asked, taking off my dampened coat. "Why did Hugo come this morning and ask me to come here tonight instead of Friday as usual? It's not like you to change plans suddenly."

He continued to stare at me, inner conflict apparent on his face.

"I'm your friend," I told him. "You and Frieda have meant a lot to me in the past months. Sometime I hope I can show you how much. If you need help, I'm here, and I'm not easy to scare. But I have to know what it's all about."

"Sit down, Eric." He took a long time lighting cigarettes for himself and me. "I once swore I'd never speak to a living soul. But now I need help. I have to protect Frieda no matter what the risk is." His eyes were intent on my face, boring into me. "Eric, will you swear before God that no matter what I tell you—no matter what you think of me afterward—you'll guard her for twenty-four hours, if I'm not around to do it?"

I hesitated, then made up my mind. "Of course I will. You knew I would before you asked."

"You swear?"

"Yes." I said. "But with a condition. Whatever you tell me, make it the truth. Otherwise, don't count on me."

"Always a chess player," he said. "I agree. It is an oath between friends. First, you tell me some things. How much have you figured out about me?"

"All right," I said. "Don't blame me if I'm wrong. To start with, you're not really an American. Your accent's almost perfect, but wrong in little ways. Then there's the way you sit at the dinner table, the way you reach out when you move a chess piece. Right so far?"

"Exactly," he said. "You're sharp, and I think there's a ruthless streak in you. Perhaps that's why I trust you."

"I know you're hiding from something," I continued. "This house is ready for a siege. Yet you're not a crook and I don't think you've ever been one."

Frieda was in the archway. "Come in, *Liebchen,*" he said. She knelt beside his chair. "You're correct on all counts, Eric. Now, it's my turn to speak."

"*Nein, nein,*" came Frieda's terrified whisper. "No one—"

"We must have help, Frieda." It was the curt tone he used when speaking to Inga. Frieda stifled a sob and was silent.

"My name is Heinrich Schwartz," he said. "I am in Mexico illegally, passing myself off as a retired American, which is not difficult for me. As a child I lived for eight years in the town of Milwaukee. Later I had training in 'American' at a German military establishment."

Outside, the rain increased. I could hear the wind began to rise as Black left his chair, moving slowly across the room, twisting his hands together.

"I was a major in the German Army. Young for the assignments they gave me, but I come from an important family. We were not Nazis! No matter what they say, we were not! True, we had Party connections. Frieda had important contacts. Who didn't have? But I was an Army man, decorated three times, once in Poland, twice in Africa."

Hugo entered, carrying a wooden box that I took to be a gun chest. Henry did not seem to notice him.

"I went to the school in Bavaria where we learned to impersonate Americans, to create disorder, to sabotage. Then a shrapnel wound from Africa began to cripple me again. They took me from active duty and put me in charge of a transport depot near the Belgian border. Hugo was my orderly then. He still is." The valet bowed his head dumbly.

"Part of my job was transportation of Jew fugitives caught in Holland, but it was a small part of my work. Just providing guards, clearing facilities for removal to the interior. There weren't many of them. Less than a hundred a week. It was a nuisance, but I never paid much attention. Dull, routine work. But at least Frieda could be with me there.

"Then everything started to collapse. I had fourteen prisoners on my hands and the Americans were almost upon us. There was no more transport." His fist crashed down on the coffee table. "What was I to do? Turn the prisoners loose to sabotage what was left of our Army?" His voice rose to a shout. "*I had orders!* I was a soldier. Hugo and I carried them out." His eyes wandered to the windows. "It was raining that night," he said. "Just like this."

I tried to see the pictures that were before the eyes of my three companions. Did they see a pitiful procession of captives, starved faces hardly more than skin-covered skulls? I pictured Hugo and Henry standing near a stalled boxcar, waiting for the final line to be formed. Was Frieda, in her mind, now hearing methodical, evenly spaced Luger shots? The last whimpers of the victims? No, she was listening for a nearer danger. Something outside in the night.

"Later they tried me at Nuremberg," Henry said dully. "They proved nothing. There was a rumor that two children with that group had escaped. So they kept me in jail for months while they searched for imaginary witnesses. They failed. They even dragged poor Frieda into it, accusing her of being a ghoul who robbed the dead bodies. *Mein Gott!* Horrible! They proved nothing, but I spent five years in Landsberg prison.

"The week after they released me, we fled here. We knew as long as we could be found, vengeance would follow. At last, they have caught up with us. Look." Reaching into his pocket, he drew out an envelope with a Mexico City postmark.

Inside was a page from a desk calendar, bearing today's date. The drawing on it was crude, almost childish. Three bodies, one in a skirt, dangled grotesquely from a tree. *Tonight, Major* was scribbled across the bottom in German.

"Other things came before," he said. "Starting six weeks ago. First a package with a gold bracelet—like the one Frieda wears. The devils had wrapped a rubber snake around it. That time the note said, *Soon, Major, but not too soon.*"

Frieda's breathing was harsh, rapid. "Then the toy gun," she cried. "With red paint—like on it was blood. Another time a book it was."

"Yes," said Henry. "A book about Adolf Eichmann. They wrote, *You will join him this month,* on the inside."

I looked at the three of them on the opposite side of the room. "That's why you asked me here tonight," I said. "You think they won't strike if there's a stranger in the house."

"I don't know, Eric," he said. "They won't harm you. You're an American, and it would cause trouble for them. They're careful. Read the Eichmann story!" A deep frown crossed his face. "Yet this isn't like it was with Eichmann. These warnings that have come to torture us. It's personal somehow. Fiendish!" Henry put his hand on my shoulder. "Hugo and I can take care of ourselves. We've got guns and plenty of ammunition. But I've got to get Frieda to Mexico City. You swore you'd do it."

I couldn't look into his eyes. "I promised," I said. "I'll do it. Whatever you've done, it isn't her fault. And if things get rough here tonight, I'll help you. No matter what I think of your story, I won't stand by while you're shot by some cowards out there in the dark."

"Thank you, Eric." His voice almost broke. Frieda came to my side. Standing on tiptoe, she kissed my cheek.

As the wind drove rain against the shutters, there was a *rata-tat-tat* outside. Inga, Loki barked wildly. *Rata-tat*. The noise was high-pitched, metallic. We seized guns from the box that Hugo opened. I checked the Luger in my hand, finding it ready for action.

"Frieda!" She came to attention at Henry's command. "The lights. *Aus*."

Moving militarily, trained by long drill, Frieda took her assigned place at the light switches. She reversed the first two, plunging the house into darkness but lighting up the yard as much as was possible in the driving rain. *Rata-tat!* It seemed closer. "Stay by the door," I told Henry. "Hugo and I'll go out back and circle around through the cane."

"*Ja*." The terror in the brief word told me that Henry was trembling in the darkness. We slipped through the kitchen door, Hugo reaching to the left to switch off the current to the back gate. The dogs found us instantly, but Hugo silenced them with a soft command. As a gust of wind bearing a sheet of water struck our faces, we heard the metallic noise again.

The blinding rain and tangled jungle of cane shoots and banana palms battled against us as we tried to move carefully over concealed

roots and fallen branches. At this season in San Xavier, a windborne
storm came almost every night at the same hour. Obviously this was
part of the plan—to strike during the worst of it. Nothing had been
left to chance.

Fifty yards from the house we found the source of the noise—a
simple device attached to a tree trunk operated by the wind like a
schoolboy's tick-tack, a wooden beater striking a metal pan. Cursing, Hugo ripped it from the tree. "A trick," I said, "to get us to this
side. Get back fast." We started for the house, even more cautious
now, neither of us knowing exactly what lay ahead.

We were almost to the rear gate when Hugo seemed to sense
something. He halted abruptly. I suddenly realized what he saw.
"Hugo!" I yelled as he threw himself to the ground—too late. A shot
rang out in the darkness. There was no cry from the dead valet.

Crouching low, I raced through the gate, pushing aside the yelping
dogs, now roused to frenzy by the gunshot. For a terrible second I
thought Inga would attack me in her confusion, but she let me pass.

Slamming open the kitchen door, I stumbled through the dark interior. "Henry!" I yelled. "They got Hugo. He's dead."

"*Mein Gott!* Where are they now? How many?"

"Coming round front, I think. I couldn't tell how many. Maybe
three. Maybe four."

In the streaked light between the shutter slats, I saw Frieda still
at her post near the switches. Henry's revolver dangled at his side
as he peered into the yard. With one swift movement, I knocked it
from his hand and shoved Frieda aside. Light flooded the room.

"There's only one, Major," I said. "And he's not out there. He's
here. It was stupid of you to let those two children escape."

The terror on their faces was all I had dreamed it would be. It was
worth waiting for through all those years, then through the last
months when, finally, I had found them. I stood quietly a moment,
enjoying it, letting every detail stamp itself on my memory. I would
have to recall every expression, every pleading look for my sister
who was waiting in Mexico City.

"It's raining tonight, Major," I said in German. "Just as it was
then."

I killed Frieda first, so he would be alive to see it happen. Then I shot Heinrich through the head as he lunged for the revolver on the floor. The few minor things I had to do in the house—planting the death gun on Heinrich, removing the other guns and disposing of my sherry glass—did not take much time. Besides, no one would miss the trio for a couple of days. By then, my sister and I would be happily back in New York.

Before leaving, I took the gold bracelet from Frieda's wrist. On the back I found my mother's initials—as I knew I would. I remembered the bracelet so clearly. It had been the last of our wealth and we had thought someday we might barter it for our lives. I remember how, as I lay in the mud pretending death, Frieda had ripped it from its hiding place on my mother's wet, lifeless body.

The time I took doing these things gave the dogs a chance to quiet down. Their greeting was almost friendly as I went toward the gate.

"*Shalom*, Loki," I said. "*Shalom*, Inga."

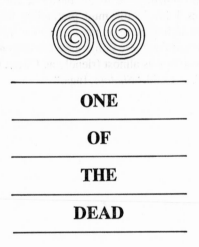

ONE

OF

THE

DEAD

We couldn't have been more pleased. Deep in Clay Canyon we came upon the lot abruptly at a turn in the winding road. There was a crudely lettered board nailed to a dead tree which read, LOT FOR SALE—$1500 OR BEST OFFER, and a phone number.

"Fifteen hundred dollars—in Clay Canyon? I can't believe it," Ellen said.

"Or best offer," I corrected.

"I've heard you can't take a step without bumping into some movie person here."

"We've come three miles already without bumping into one. I haven't seen a soul."

"But there are the houses." Ellen looked about breathlessly.

There indeed were the houses—to our left and our right, to our front and our rear—low, ranch-style houses, unostentatious, prosaic, giving no hint of the gay and improbable lives we imagined went on inside them. But as the houses marched up the gradually climbing road there was not a single person to be seen. The cars— the Jaguars and Mercedeses and Cadillacs and Chryslers—were parked unattended in the driveways, their chrome gleaming in the sun; I caught a glimpse of one corner of a pool and a white diving board, but no one swam in the turquoise water. We climbed out of the car, Ellen with her rather large, short-haired head stooped forward as if under a weight. Except for the fiddling of a cicada somewhere on the hill, a profound hush lay over us in the stifling air. Not even a bird moved in the motionless trees.

"There must be something wrong with it," Ellen said.

"It's probably already been sold, and they just didn't bother to take down the sign. . . . There was something here once, though." I had come across several ragged chunks of concrete that lay about randomly as if heaved out of the earth.

"A house, do you think?"

"It's hard to say. If it was a house it's been gone for years."

"Oh, Ted," Ellen cried. "It's perfect! Look at the view!" She pointed up the canyon toward the round, parched hills. Through the heat shimmering on the road they appeared to be melting down like wax.

"Another good thing," I said. "There won't be much to do to get the ground ready except for clearing the brush away. This place has been graded once. We save a thousand dollars right there."

Ellen took both my hands. Her eyes shone in her solemn face. "What do you think, Ted? What do you think?"

Ellen and I had been married four years, having both taken the step relatively late—in our early thirties—and in that time had lived in two different places, first an apartment in Santa Monica, then, when I was promoted to office manager, in a partly furnished house in the Hollywood Hills, always with the idea that when our first child came we would either buy or build a larger house of our own. But the child had not come. It was a source of anxiety and sadness to us both and lay between us like an old scandal for which each of us took on the blame.

Then I made an unexpected killing on the stock market and Ellen suddenly began agitating in her gentle way for the house. As we shopped around she dropped hints along the way—"This place is really too small for us, don't you think?" or "We'd have to fence off the yard of course"—that let me know that the house had become a talisman for her; she had conceived the notion that perhaps, in some occult way, if we went ahead with our accommodations for a child the child might come. The notion gave her happiness. Her face filled out, the gray circles under her eyes disappeared, the quiet gaiety, which did not seem like gaiety at all but a form of peace, returned.

As Ellen held on to my hands, I hesitated. I am convinced now that there was something behind my hesitation—something I felt then only as a quality of silence, a fleeting twinge of utter desolation. "It's so safe," she said. "There's no traffic at all."

I explained that. "It's not a through street. It ends somewhere up in the hills."

She turned back to me again with her bright, questioning eyes. The happiness that had grown in her during our months of house-hunting seemed to have welled into near rapture.

"We'll call the number," I said, "but don't expect too much. It must have been sold long ago."

We walked slowly back to the car. The door handle burned to the touch. Down the canyon the rear end of a panel truck disappeared noiselessly around a bend.

"No," Ellen said, "I have a feeling about this place. I think it was meant to be ours."

And she was right, of course.

Mr. Carswell Deeves, who owned the land, was called upon to do very little except take my check for $1500 and hand over the deed to us, for by the time Ellen and I met him we had already sold ourselves. Mr. Deeves, as we had suspected from the unprofessional sign, was a private citizen. We found his house in a predominantly Mexican section of Santa Monica. He was a chubby, pink man of indeterminate age dressed in white ducks and soft white shoes, as if he had had a tennis court hidden away among the squalid, asphalt-shingled houses and dry kitchen gardens of his neighbors. "Going to live in Clay Canyon, are you?" he said. "Ros Russell lives up there, or used to." So, we discovered, did Joel McCrea, Jimmy Stewart and Paula Raymond, as well as a cross-section of producers, directors and character actors. "Oh, yes," said Mr. Deeves, "it's an address that will look extremely good on your stationery."

Ellen beamed and squeezed my hand.

Mr. Deeves turned out to know very little about the land other than that a house had been destroyed by fire there years ago and that the land had changed hands many times since. "I myself acquired it in what may strike you as a novel way," he said as we sat in his parlor—a dark, airless box which smelled faintly of camphor and whose walls were obscured with yellowing autographed photographs of movie stars. "I won it in a game of hearts from a makeup man on the set of *Quo Vadis*. Perhaps you remember me. I had a close-up in one of the crowd scenes."

"That was a number of years ago, Mr. Deeves," I said. "Have you been trying to sell it all this time?"

"I've nearly sold it dozens of times," he said, "but something always went wrong somehow."

"What kind of things?"

"Naturally, the fire-insurance rates up there put off a lot of people. I hope you're prepared to pay a high premium——"

"I've already checked into that."

"Good. You'd be surprised how many people will let details like that go till the last minute."

"What other things have gone wrong?"

Ellen touched my arm to discourage my wasting any more time with foolish questions.

Mr. Deeves spread out the deed before me and smoothed it with his forearm. "Silly things, some of them. One couple found some dead doves. . . ."

"Dead doves?" I handed him the signed article. With one pink hand Mr. Deeves waved it back and forth to dry the ink. "Five of them, if I remember correctly. In my opinion they'd sat on a wire and were electrocuted somehow. The husband thought nothing of it, of course, but his wife became so hysterical that we had to call off the transaction."

I made a sign at Mr. Deeves to drop this line of conversation. Ellen loves animal and birds of all kinds with a devotion that turns the loss of a household pet into a major tragedy, which is why, since the death of our cocker spaniel, we have had no more pets. But Ellen appeared not to have heard; she was watching the paper in Mr. Deeves's hand fixedly, as if she were afraid it might vanish.

Mr. Deeves sprang suddenly to his feet. "Well!" he cried. "It's all yours now. I know you'll be happy there."

Ellen flushed with pleasure. "I'm sure we will," she said, and took his pudgy hand in both of hers.

"A prestige address," called Mr. Deeves from his porch as we drove away. "A real prestige address."

Ellen and I are modern people. Our talk in the evenings is generally on issues of the modern world. Ellen paints a little and I do some writing from time to time—mostly on technical subjects. The house that Ellen and I built mirrored our concern with present-day aesthetics. We worked closely with Jack Salmanson, the architect and a friend, who designed a steel module house, low and compact and private, which could be fitted into the irregularities of our patch of land for a maximum of space. The interior *décor* we left largely up to Ellen, who combed the home magazines and made sketches as if she were decorating a dozen homes.

I mention these things to show that there is nothing Gothic about my wife and me: We are as thankful for our common sense as for our sensibilities, and we flattered ourselves that the house we built achieved a balance between the aesthetic and the functional. Its lines were simple and clean; there were no dark corners, and it was surrounded on three sides by houses, none of which were more than eight years old.

There were, however, signs from the very beginning, ominous signs which can be read only in retrospect, though it seems to me now that there were others who suspected but said nothing. One was the Mexican who cut down the tree.

As a money-saving favor to us, Jack Salmanson agreed to supervise the building himself and hire small, independent contractors to do the labor, many of whom were Mexicans or Negroes with dilapidated equipment that appeared to run only by some mechanical miracle. The Mexican, a small, forlorn workman with a stringy moustache, had already burned out two chain-saw blades and still had not cut halfway through the tree. It was inexplicable. The tree, the same one on which Ellen and I had seen the original FOR SALE sign, had obviously been dead for years, and the branches that already lay scattered on the ground were rotted through.

"You must have run into a batch of knots," Jack said. "Try it again. If the saw gets too hot, quit and we'll pull it down with the bulldozer." As if answering to its name, the bulldozer turned at the back of the lot and lumbered toward us in a cloud of dust, the black shoulders of the Negro operator gleaming in the sun.

The Mexican need not have feared for his saw. He had scarcely touched it to the tree when it started to topple of its own accord. Startled, he backed away a few steps. The tree had begun to fall toward the back of the lot, in the direction of his cut, but now it appeared to arrest itself, its naked branches trembling as if in agitation; then with an awful rending sound it writhed upright and fell back on itself, gaining momentum and plunging directly at the bulldozer. My voice died in my throat, but Jack and the Mexican shouted, and the operator jumped and rolled on the ground just as the tree fell high on the hood, shattering the windshield to bits. The bulldozer, out of control and knocked off course, came directly at us, gears whining and gouging a deep trough in the earth. Jack and I jumped one way, the Mexican the other; the bulldozer lurched between us and ground on toward the street, the Negro sprinting after it.

"The car!" Jack shouted. "The car!"

Parked in front of the house across the street was a car, a car which was certainly brand-new. The bulldozer headed straight for it, its blade striking clusters of sparks from the pavement. The Mexican waved his chain saw over his head like a toy and shouted in Spanish. I covered my eyes with my hands and heard Jack grunt softly, as if he had been struck in the mid-section, just before the crash.

Two women stood on the porch of the house across the street and gaped. The car had caved in at the center, its steel roof wrinkled like tissue paper; its front and rear ends were folded around the bulldozer as if embracing it. Then, with a low whoosh, both vehicles were enveloped in creeping blue flame.

"Rotten luck," Jack muttered under his breath as we ran into the street. From the corner of my eye I caught the curious sight of the Mexican on the ground, praying, his chain saw lying by his knees.

In the evening Ellen and I paid a visit to the Sheffits', Sondra and Jeff, our neighbors across the canyon road, where we met the owner of the ruined car, Joyce Castle, a striking blonde in lemon-colored pants. The shock of the accident itself wore off with the passing of time and cocktails, and the three of them treated it as a tremendous joke.

Mrs. Castle was particularly hilarious. "I'm doing better," she rejoiced. "The Alfa-Romeo only lasted two days, but I held on to this one a whole six weeks. I even had the permanent plates on."

"But you mustn't be without a car, Mrs. Castle," Ellen said in her serious way. "We'd be glad to loan you our Plymouth until you can—"

"I'm having a new car delivered tomorrow afternoon. Don't worry about me. A Daimler, Jeff, you'll be interested to know. I couldn't resist after riding in yours. What about the poor bulldozer man? Is he absolutely wiped out?"

"I think he'll survive," I said. "In any case he has two other 'dozers."

"Then you won't be held up," Jeff said.

"I wouldn't think so."

Sondra chuckled softly. "I just happened to look out the window," she said. "It was just like a Rube Goldberg cartoon. A chain reaction."

"And there was my poor old Cadillac at the end of it," Mrs. Castle sighed.

Suey, Mrs. Castle's dog, who had been lying on the floor beside his mistress glaring dourly at us between dozes, suddenly ran to the front door barking ferociously, his red mane standing straight up.

"Suey!" Mrs. Castle slapped her knee. "Suey! Come here!"

The dog merely flattened its ears and looked from his mistress toward the door again as if measuring a decision. He growled deep in his throat.

"It's the ghost," Sondra said lightly. "He's behind the whole thing." Sondra sat curled up in one corner of the sofa and tilted her head to one side as she spoke, like a very clever child.

Jeff laughed sharply. "Oh, they tell some very good stories."

With a sigh Mrs. Castle rose and dragged Suey back by his collar. "If I didn't feel so self-conscious about it I'd take him to an analyst," she said. "Sit, Suey! Here's a cashew nut for you."

"I'm very fond of ghost stories," I said, smiling.

"Oh, well," Jeff murmured, mildly disparaging.

"Go ahead, Jeff," Sondra urged him over the rim of her glass. "They'd like to hear it."

Jeff was a literary agent, a tall, sallow man with dark oily hair that he was continually pushing out of his eyes with his fingers. As he spoke he smiled lopsidedly as if defending against the probability of being taken seriously. "All I know is that back in the late seventeenth century the Spanish used to have hangings here. The victims are supposed to float around at night and make noises."

"Criminals?" I asked.

"Of the worst sort," said Sondra. "What was the story Guy Relling told you, Joyce?" She smiled with a curious inward relish that suggested she knew the story perfectly well herself.

"Is that Guy Relling, the director?" I asked.

"Yes," Jeff said. "He owns those stables down the canyon."

"I've seen them," Ellen said. "Such lovely horses."

Joyce Castle hoisted her empty glass into the air. "Jeff, love, will you find me another?"

"We keep straying from the subject," said Sondra gently. "Fetch me another too, darling"—she handed her glass to Jeff as he went by—"like a good boy. . . . I didn't mean to interrupt, Joyce. Go on." She gestured toward us as the intended audience. Ellen stiffened slightly in her chair.

"It seems that there was one *hombre* of outstanding depravity," Joyce Castle said languidly. "I forgot the name. He murdered, stole, raped . . . one of those endless Spanish names with a 'Luis' in it, a nobleman I think Guy said. A charming sort. Mad, of course, and

completely unpredictable. They hanged him at last for some un-
savory escapade in a nunnery. You two are moving into a neighborhood rich with tradition."

We all laughed.

"What about the noises?" Ellen asked Sondra. "Have you heard
anything?"

"Of course," Sondra said, tipping her head prettily. Every inch of
her skin was tanned to the color of coffee from afternoons by the
pool. It was a form of leisure that her husband, with his bilious
coloring and lank hair, apparently did not enjoy.

"Everywhere I've ever lived," he said, his grin growing crookeder
and more apologetic, "there were noises in the night that you
couldn't explain. Here there are all kinds of wildlife—foxes, coons,
possums—even coyotes up on the ridge. They're all active after sundown."

Ellen's smile of pleasure at this news turned to distress as Sondra
remarked in her offhand way, "We found our poor kitty-cat positively torn to pieces one morning. He was all blood. We never did
find his head."

"A fox," Jeff put in quickly. Everything he said seemed hollow.
Something came from him like a vapor. I thought it was grief.

Sondra gazed smugly into her lap as if hugging a secret to herself.
She seemed enormously pleased. It occurred to me that Sondra was
trying to frighten us. In a way it relieved me. She was enjoying herself too much, I thought, looking at her spoiled, brown face, to be
frightened herself.

After the incident of the tree everything went well for some
weeks. The house went up rapidly. Ellen and I visited it as often as
we could, walking over the raw ground and making our home in our
mind's eye. The fireplace would go here, the refrigerator here, our
Picasso print there. "Ted," Ellen said timidly, "I've been thinking.
Why don't we fix up the extra bedroom as a children's room?"

I waited.

"Now that we'll be living out here our friends will have to stay
overnight more often. Most of them have young children. It would
be nice for them."

I slipped my arm around her shoulders. She knew I understood.

It was a delicate matter. She raised her face and I kissed her between her brows. Signal and countersignal, the keystones of our life together—a life of sensibility and tact.

"Hey, you two!" Sondra Sheffits called from across the street. She stood on her front porch in a pink bathing suit, her skin brown, her hair nearly white. "How about a swim?"

"No suits!"

"Come on, we've got plenty."

Ellen and I debated the question with a glance, settled it with a nod.

As I came out onto the patio in one of Jeff's suits, Sondra said, "Ted, you're pale as a ghost. Don't you get any sun where you are?" She lay in a chaise longue behind huge elliptical sunglasses encrusted with glass gems.

"I stay inside too much, writing articles," I said.

"You're welcome to come here any time you like"—she smiled suddenly, showing me a row of small, perfect teeth—"and swim."

Ellen appeared in her borrowed suit, a red one with a short, limp ruffle. She shaded her eyes as the sun, glittering metallically on the water, struck her full in the face.

Sondra ushered her forward as if to introduce my wife to me. "You look much better in that suit than I ever did." Her red nails flashed on Ellen's arm. Ellen smiled guardedly. The two women were about the same height, but Ellen was narrower in the shoulders, thicker through the waist and hips. As they came toward me it seemed to me that Ellen was the one I did not know. Her familiar body became strange. It looked out of proportion. Hairs that on Sondra were all but invisible except when the sun turned them to silver, lay flat and dark on Ellen's pallid arm.

As if sensing the sudden distance between us, Ellen took my hand. "Let's jump in together," she said gaily. "No hanging back."

Sondra retreated to the chaise longue to watch us, her eyes invisible behind her outrageous glasses, her head on one side.

Incidents began again and continued at intervals. Guy Relling, whom I never met but whose pronouncements on the supernatural reached me through others from time to time like messages from an oracle, claims that the existence of the living dead is a particularly excruciating one as they hover between two states of being. Their memories keep the passions of life forever fresh and sharp, but they are able to relieve them only at a monstrous expense of will and energy which leaves them literally helpless for months or sometimes even years afterward. This was why materializations and other forms of tangible action are relatively rare. There are of course exceptions, Sondra, our most frequent translator of Relling's theories, pointed out one evening with the odd joy that accompanied all of her remarks on the subject; some ghosts are terrifically active—particularly the insane ones who, ignorant of the limitations of death as they were of the impossibilities of life, transcend them with the dynamism that is exclusively the property of madness. Generally, however, it was Relling's opinion that a ghost was more to be pitied than feared. Sondra quoted him as having said, "The notion of a haunted house is a misconception semantically. It is not the house but the soul itself that is haunted."

On Saturday, August 6, a workman laying pipe was blinded in one eye by an acetylene torch.

On Thursday, September 1, a rockslide on the hill behind us dumped four tons of dirt and rock on the half-finished house and halted work for two weeks.

On Sunday, October 9—my birthday, oddly enough—while visiting the house alone, I slipped on a stray screw and struck my head on a can of latex paint which opened up a gash requiring ten stitches. I rushed across to the Sheffits'. Sondra answered the door in her bathing suit and a magazine in her hand. "Ted?" She peered at me. "I scarcely recognized you through the blood. Come in, I'll call the doctor. Try not to drip on the furniture, will you?"

I told the doctor of the screw on the floor, the big can of paint. I did not tell him that my foot had slipped because I had turned too quickly and that I had turned too quickly because the sensation had grown on me that there was someone behind me, close enough to touch me, perhaps, because something hovered there, fetid and damp and cold and almost palpable in its nearness; I remember shivering violently as I turned, as if the sun of this burning summer's day had been replaced by a mysterious star without warmth. I did not tell the doctor this nor anyone else.

In November Los Angeles burns. After the long drought of summer the sap goes underground and the baked hills seem to gasp in pain for the merciful release of either life or death—rain or fire. Invariably fire comes first, spreading through the outlying parts of the country like an epidemic, till the sky is livid and starless at night and overhung with dun-colored smoke during the day.

There was a huge fire in Tujunga, north of us, the day Ellen and I moved into our new house—handsome, severe, aggressively new on its dry hillside—under a choked sky the color of earth and a muffled, flyspeck sun. Sondra and Jeff came over to help, and in the evening Joyce Castle stopped by with Suey and a magnum of champagne.

Ellen clasped her hands under her chin. "What a lovely surprise!"

"I hope it's cold enough. I've had it in my refrigerator since four o'clock. Welcome to the canyon. You're nice people. You remind me of my parents. God, it's hot. I've been weeping all day on account of the smoke. You'll have air conditioning I suppose?"

Jeff was sprawled in a chair with his long legs straight in front of him in the way a cripple might put aside a pair of crutches. "Joyce, you're an angel. Excuse me if I don't get up. I'm recuperating."

"You're excused, doll, you're excused."

"Ted," Ellen said softly. "Why don't you get some glasses?"

Jeff hauled in his legs. "Can I give you a hand?"

"Sit still, Jeff."

He sighed. "I hadn't realized I was so out of shape." He looked more cadaverous than ever after our afternoon of lifting and shoving. Sweat had collected in the hollows under his eyes.

"Shall I show you in the house, Joyce? While Ted is in the kitchen?"

"I love you, Ellen," Joyce said. "Take me on the whole tour."

Sondra followed me into the kitchen. She leaned against the wall and smoked, supporting her left elbow in the palm of her right hand. She didn't say a word. Through the open door I could see Jeff's outstretched legs from the calves down.

"Thanks for all the help today," I said to Sondra in a voice unaccountably close to a whisper. I could hear Joyce and Ellen as they moved from room to room, their voices swelling and dying: "It's all steel? You mean everything? Walls and all? Aren't you afraid of lightning?"

"Oh, we're all safely grounded, I think."

Jeff yawned noisily in the living room. Wordlessly Sondra put a tray on the kitchen table as I rummaged in an unpacked carton for the glasses. She watched me steadily and coolly, as if she expected me to entertain her. I wanted to say something further to break a silence which was becoming unnatural and oppressive. The sounds around us seemed only to isolate us in a ring of intimacy. With her head on one side Sondra smiled at me. I could hear her rapid breathing.

"What's this, a nursery? Ellen, love!"

"No, no! It's only for our friends' children."

Sondra's eyes were blue, the color of shallow water. She seemed faintly amused, as if we were sharing in a conspiracy—a conspiracy I was anxious to repudiate by making some prosaic remark in a loud voice for all to hear, but a kind of pain developed in my chest as the words seemed dammed there, and I only smiled at her foolishly. With every passing minute of silence, the more impossible it became to break through and the more I felt drawn in to the intrigue of which, though I was ignorant, I was surely guilty. Without so much as a touch she had made us lovers.

Ellen stood in the doorway, half turned away as if her first impulse had been to run. She appeared to be deep in thought, her eyes fixed on the steel, cream-colored doorjamb.

Sondra began to talk to Ellen in her dry, satirical voice. It was chatter of the idlest sort, but she was destroying, as I had wished to destroy, the absurd notion that there was something between us. I could see Ellen's confusion. She hung on Sondra's words, watching her lips attentively, as if this elegant, tanned woman, calmly smoking and talking of trifles, were her savior.

As for myself, I felt as if I had lost the power of speech entirely. If I joined in with Sondra's carefully innocent chatter I would only be joining in the deception against my wife; if I proclaimed the truth and ended everything by bringing it into the open. . . . but what truth? What was there in fact to bring into the open? What was there to end? A feeling in the air? An intimation? The answer was nothing, of course. I did not even like Sondra very much. There was something cold and unpleasant about her. There was nothing to proclaim because nothing had happened. "Where's Joyce?" I asked finally, out of a dry mouth. "Doesn't she want to see the kitchen?"

Ellen turned slowly toward me, as if it cost her a great effort. "She'll be here in a minute," she said tonelessly, and I became aware of Joyce's and Jeff's voices from the living room. Ellen studied my face, her pupils oddly dilated under the pinkish fluorescent light, as if she were trying to penetrate to the bottom of a great darkness that lay beneath my chance remark. Was it a code of some kind, a new signal for her that I would shortly make clear? What did it mean? I smiled at her and she responded with a smile of her own, a tentative and formal upturning of her mouth, as if I were a familiar face whose name escaped her for the moment.

Joyce came in behind Ellen. "I hate kitchens. I never go into mine." She looked from one to the other of us. "Am I interrupting something?"

At two o'clock in the morning I sat up in bed, wide awake. The bedroom was bathed in the dark red glow of the fire which had come closer in the night. A thin, autumnal veil of smoke hung in the room. Ellen lay on her side, asleep, one hand cupped on the pillow next to her face as if waiting for something to be put in it. I had no idea why I was so fully awake, but I threw off the covers and went to the window to check on the fire. I could see no flame, but the hills stood out blackly against a turgid sky that belled and sagged as the wind blew and relented.

Then I heard the sound.

I am a person who sets store by precision in the use of words—in the field of technical writing this is a necessity. But I can think of no word to describe that sound. The closest I can come with a word of my own invention is "vlump." It came erratically, neither loud nor soft. It was, rather, pervasive and without location. It was not a *solid* sound. There was something vague and whispering about it, and from time to time it began with the suggestion of a sigh—a shuffling dissipation in the air that seemed to take form and die in the same instant. In a way I cannot define, it was mindless, without will or reason, yet implacable. Because I could not explain it immediately I went to seek an explanation.

I stepped into the hall and switched on the light, pressing the noiseless button. The light came down out of a fixture set flush into the ceilings and diffused through a milky plastic-like Japanese rice paper. The clean, indestructible walls rose perpendicularly around me. Through the slight haze of smoke came the smell of the newness, sweet and metallic—more like a car than a house. And still the sound went on. It seemed to be coming from the room at the end of the hall, the room we had designed for our friends' children. The door was open and I could see a gray patch that was a west window. Vlump . . . vlump . . . vlumpvlump. . . .

Fixing on the gray patch, I moved down the hall while my legs made themselves heavy as logs, and all the while I repeated to myself, "The house is settling. All new houses settle and make strange noises." And so lucid was I that I believed I was not afraid. I was walking down the bright new hall of my new steel house to investigate a noise, for the house might be settling unevenly, or an animal might be up to some mischief—raccoons regularly raided the garbage cans, I had been told. There might be something wrong with the plumbing or with the radiant-heating system that warmed our steel and vinyl floors. And now, like the responsible master of the house, I had located the apparent center of the sound and was going responsibly toward it. In a second or two, very likely, I would know. Vlump vlump. The gray of the window turned rosy as I came near enough to see the hillside beyond it. That black was underbrush and that pink the dusty swath cut by the bulldozer before it had run amok. I had watched the accident from just about the spot where I stood now, and the obliterated hole where the tree had been, laid firmly over with the prefabricated floor of the room whose darkness I would eradicate by touching with my right hand the light switch inside the door.

"Ted?"

Blood boomed in my ears. I had the impression that my heart had burst. I clutched at the wall for support. Yet of course I knew it was Ellen's voice, and I answered her calmly. "Yes, it's me."

"What's the matter?" I heard the bedclothes rustle.

"Don't get up, I'm coming right in." The noise had stopped. There was nothing. Only the almost inaudible hum of the refrigerator, the stirring of the wind.

Ellen was sitting up in bed. "I was just checking on the fire," I said. She patted my side of the bed and in the instant before I turned out the hall light I saw her smile.

"I was just dreaming about you," she said softly, as I climbed under the sheets. She rolled against me. "Why, you're trembling."

"I should have worn my robe."

"You'll be warm in a minute." Her fragrant body lay against mine, but I remained rigid as stone and just as cold, staring at the ceiling, my mind a furious blank. After a moment she said, "Ted?" It was her signal, always hesitant, always tremulous, that meant I was to roll over and take her in my arms.

Instead I answered, "What?" just as if I had not understood.

For a few seconds I sensed her struggling against her reserve to give me a further sign that would pierce my peculiar distraction and tell me she wanted love. But it was too much for her—too alien. My coldness had created a vacuum she was too unpracticed to fill—a coldness sudden and inexplicable, unless . . .

She withdrew slowly and pulled the covers up under her chin. Finally she asked, "Ted, is there something happening that I should know about?" She had remembered Sondra and the curious scene in the kitchen. It took, I knew, great courage for Ellen to ask that question, though she must have known my answer.

"No, I'm just tired. We've had a busy day. Good-night, dear." I kissed her on the cheek and sensed her eyes, in the shadow of the fire, searching mine, asking the question she could not give voice to. I turned away, somehow ashamed because I could not supply the answer that would fulfill her need. Because there was no answer at all.

The fire was brought under control after burning some eight hundred acres and several homes, and three weeks later the rains came. Jack Salmanson came out one Sunday to see how the house was holding up, checked the foundation, the roof and all the seams and pronounced it tight as a drum. We sat looking moodily out the glass doors onto the patio—a flatland of grayish mud which threatened to swamp with a thin ooze of silt and gravel the few flagstones I had set in the ground. Ellen was in the bedroom lying down; she had got into the habit of taking a nap after lunch, though it was I, not she, who lay stark awake night after night explaining away sounds that became more and more impossible to explain away. The gagging sound that sometimes accompanied the vlump and the strangled expulsion of air that followed it were surely the result of some disturbance in the water pipes; the footsteps that came slowly down the hall and stopped outside our closed door and then went away again with something like a low chuckle were merely the night contracting of our metal house after the heat of the day. Through all this Ellen slept as if in a stupor; she seemed to have become addicted to sleep. She went to bed at nine and got up at ten the next morning; she napped in the afternoon and moved about lethargically the rest of the time with a Mexican shawl around her shoulders, complaining of the cold. The doctor examined her for mononucleosis but found nothing. He said perhaps it was her sinuses and that she should rest as much as she wanted.

After a protracted silence Jack put aside his drink and stood up. "I guess I'll go along."

"I'll tell Ellen."

"What the hell for? Let her sleep. Tell her I hope she feels better." He turned to frown at the room of the house he had designed and built. "Are you happy here?" he asked suddenly.

"Happy?" I repeated the word awkwardly. "Of course we're happy. We love the house. It's . . . just a little noisy at night, that's all." I stammered it out, like the first word of a monstrous confession, but Jack seemed hardly to hear it. He waved a hand. "House settling." He squinted from one side of the room to the other. "I don't know. There's something about it. . . . It's not right. Maybe it's just the weather . . . the light. . . . It could be friendlier, you know what I mean? It seems cheerless."

I watched him with a kind of wild hope, as if he might magically fathom my terror—do for me what I could not do for myself, and permit it to be discussed calmly between two men of temperate mind. But Jack was not looking for the cause of the gloom but the cure for it. "Why don't you try putting down a couple of orange rugs in this room?" he said.

I stared at the floor as if two orange rugs were an infallible charm. "Yes," I said, "I think we'll try that."

Ellen scuffed in, pushing back her hair, her face puffy with sleep. "Jack," she said, "when the weather clears and I'm feeling livelier, you and Anne and the children must come and spend the night."

"We'd like that. After the noises die down," he added satirically to me.

"Noises? What noises?" A certain blankness came over Ellen's face when she looked at me now. The expression was the same, but what had been open in it before was now merely empty. She had put up her guard against me; she suspected me of keeping things from her.

"At night," I said. "The house is settling. You don't hear them."

When Jack had gone, Ellen sat with a cup of tea in the chair where Jack had sat, looking out at the mud. Her long purple shawl hung all the way to her knees and made her look armless. There seemed no explanation for the two white hands that curled around the teacup in her lap. "It's a sad thing," she said tonelessly. "I can't help but feel sorry for Sondra."

"Why is that?" I asked guardedly.

"Joyce was here yesterday. She told me that she and Jeff have been having an affair off and on for six years." She turned to see how I would receive this news.

"Well, that explains the way Joyce and Sondra behave toward each other," I said, with a pleasant glance straight into Ellen's eyes; there I encountered only the reflection of the glass doors, even to the rain trickling down them, and I had the eerie sensation of having been shown a picture of the truth, as if she were weeping secretly in the depths of a soul I could no longer touch. For Ellen did not believe in my innocence; I'm not sure I still believed in it myself; very likely Jeff and Joyce didn't either. It is impossible to say what Sondra believed. She behaved as if our infidelity were an accomplished fact. In its way it was a performance of genius, for Sondra never touched me except in the most accidental or impersonal way; even her glances, the foundation on which she built the myth of our liaison, had nothing soft in them; they were probing and sly and were always accompanied by a furtive smile, as if we merely shared some private joke. Yet there was something in the way she did it—in the tilt of her head perhaps—that plainly implied that the joke was at everyone else's expense. And she had taken to calling me "darling."

"Sondra and Jeff have a feebleminded child off in an institution somewhere," Ellen said. "That set them against each other, apparently."

"Joyce told you all this?"

"She just mentioned it casually as if it were the most natural thing in the world—she assumed we must have known. . . . But I don't want to know things like that about my friends."

"That's show biz, I guess. You and I are just provincials at heart."

"Sondra must be a very unhappy girl."

"It's hard to tell with Sondra."

"I wonder what she tries to do with her life. . . . If she looks for anything—outside."

I waited.

"Probably not," Ellen answered her own question. "She seems very self-contained. Almost cold . . ."

I was treated to the spectacle of my wife fighting with herself to delay a wound that she was convinced would come home to her sooner or later. She did not want to believe in my infidelity. I might have comforted her with lies. I might have told her that Sondra and I rendezvoused downtown in a cafeteria and made love in a second-rate hotel on the evenings when I called to say that I was working late. Then the wound would be open and could be cleaned and cured. It would be painful of course, but I would have confided in her again and our old system would be restored. Watching Ellen torture herself with doubt, I was tempted to tell her those lies. The truth never tempted me: To have admitted that I knew what she was thinking would have been tantamount to an admission of guilt. How could I suspect such a thing unless it were true? And was I to explain my coldness by terrifying her with vague stories of indescribable sounds which she never heard?

And so the two of us sat on, dumb and chilled, in our watertight house as the daylight began to go. And then a sort of exultation seized me. What if my terror were no more real than Ellen's? What if both our ghosts were only ghosts of the mind which needed only a little

common sense to drive them away? And I saw that if I could drive
away my ghost, Ellen's would soon follow, for the secret that shut
me away from her would be gone. It was a revelation, a triumph of
reason.

"What's that up there?" Ellen pointed to something that looked
like a leaf blowing at the top of the glass doors. "It's a tail, Ted.
There must be some animal on the roof."

Only the bushy tip was visible. As I drew close to it I could see
raindrops clinging as if by a geometrical system to each black hair.
"It looks like a raccoon tail. What would a coon be doing out so
early?" I put on a coat and went outside. The tail hung limply over
the edge, ringed with white and swaying phlegmatically in the breeze.
The animal itself was hidden behind the low parapet. Using the ship's
ladder at the back of the house I climbed up to look at it.

The human mind, just like other parts of the anatomy, is an organ
of habit. Its capabilities are bounded by the limits of precedent; it
thinks what it is used to thinking. Faced with a phenomenon beyond
its range it rebels, it rejects, sometimes it collapses. My mind, which
for weeks had steadfastly refused to honor the evidence of my senses
that there was Something Else living in the house with Ellen and me,
something unearthly and evil, largely on the basis of insufficient evidence, was now forced to the subsequent denial by saying, as Jeff
had said, "fox." It was of course, ridiculous. The chances of a fox's
winning a battle with a raccoon were very slight at best, let alone
what had been done to this raccoon. The body lay on the far side of
the roof. I didn't see the head at all until I had stumbled against it
and it had rolled over and over to come to rest against the parapet
where it pointed its masked, ferret face at me.

Only because my beleaguered mind kept repeating, like a voice,
"Ellen mustn't know, Ellen mustn't know," was I able to take up
the dismembered parts and hurl them with all my strength onto the
hillside and answer when Ellen called out, "What is it, Ted?" "Must
have been a coon. It's gone now," in a perfectly level voice before I
went to the back of the roof and vomited.

I recalled Sondra's mention of their mutilated cat and phoned Jeff
at his agency. "We will discuss it over lunch," I told myself. I had
a great need to talk, an action impossible within my own home,

where every day the silence became denser and more intractable. Once or twice Ellen ventured to ask, "What's the matter, Ted?" but I always answered, "Nothing." And there our talk ended. I could see it in her wary eyes: I was not the man she had married; I was cold, secretive, The children's room, furnished with double bunks and wallpaper figured with toys, stood like a rebuke. Ellen kept the door closed most of the time though once or twice, in the late afternoon, I had found her in there moving about aimlessly, touching objects as if half in wonder that they should still linger on after so many long, sterile months; a foolish hope had failed. Neither did our friends bring their children to stay. They did not because we did not ask them. The silence had brought with it a profound and debilitating inertia. Ellen's face seemed perpetually swollen, the features cloudy and amorphous, the eyes dull; her whole body had become bloated, as if an enormous cache of pain had backed up inside her. We moved through the house in our orbits like two sleepwalkers, going about our business out of habit. Our friends called at first, puzzled, a little hurt, but soon stopped and left us to ourselves. Occasionally we saw the Sheffitses. Jeff was looking seedier and seedier, told bad jokes, drank too much and seemed always ill at ease. Sondra did most of the talking, chattering blandly on indifferent subjects and always hinting by gesture, word or glance at our underground affair.

Jeff and I had lunch at the Brown Derby on Vine Street under charcoal caricatures of show folk. At a table next to ours an agent was eulogizing an actor in a voice hoarse with trumped-up enthusiasm to a large, purple-faced man who was devoting his entire attention to a bowl of vichyssoise.

"It's a crazy business," Jeff said to me. "Be glad you're not in it."

"I see what you mean," I replied. Jeff had not the faintest idea of why I had brought him there, nor had I given him any clue. We were "breaking the ice." Jeff grinned at me with that crooked trick of his mouth, and I grinned back. "We are friends"—presumably that is the message we were grinning at each other. Was he my friend? Was I his friend? He lived across the street; our paths crossed perhaps once a week; we joked together; he sat always in the same chair in our living room twisting from one sprawl to another; there was a straight white chair in his living room that I preferred. Friendships have been founded on less, I suppose. Yet he had an idiot child locked off in an asylum somewhere and a wife who amused herself with infidelity by suggestion; I had a demon loose in my house and a wife gnawed with suspicion and growing remote and old because of it. And I had said, "I see what you mean." It seemed insufferable. I caught Jeff's eye. "You remember we talked once about a ghost?" My tone was bantering; perhaps I meant to make a joke.

"I remember."

"Sondra said something about a cat of yours that was killed."

"The one the fox got."

"That's what you said. That's not what Sondra said."

Jeff shrugged. "What about it?"

"I found a dead raccoon on our roof."

"Your roof!"

"Yes. It was pretty awful."

Jeff toyed with his fork. All pretense of levity was at an end. "No head?"

"Worse."

For a few moments he was silent. I felt him struggle with himself before he spoke. "Maybe you'd better move out, Ted," he said.

He was trying to help—I knew it. With a single swipe he had tried to push through the restraint that hung between us. He was my friend; he was putting out his hand to me. And I suppose I must have known what he'd suggest. But I could not accept it. It was not what I wanted to hear. "Jeff, I can't do that," I said tolerantly, as if he had missed my point. "We've only been living there five months. It cost me twenty-two thousand to build that place. We have to live in it at least a year under the GI loan."

"Well, you know best, Ted." The smile dipped at me again.

"I just wanted to talk," I said, irritated at the ease with which he had given in. "I wanted to find out what you knew about this ghost business."

"Not very much. Sondra knows more than I do."

"I doubt that you would advise me to leave a house I had just built for no reason at all."

"There seems to be some sort of jinx on the property, that's all. Whether there's a ghost or not I couldn't tell you," he replied, annoyed in his turn at the line the conversation was taking. "How does Ellen feel about this?"

"She doesn't know."

"About the raccoon?"

"About anything."

"You mean there's more?"

"There are noises—at night. . . ."

"I'd speak to Sondra if I were you. She's gone into this business much more deeply than I. When we first moved in, she used to hang around your land a good deal . . . just snooping . . . particularly after that cat was killed. . . ." He was having some difficulty with his words. It struck me that the conversation was causing him pain. He was showing his teeth now in a smiling grimace. Dangling an arm over the back of his chair he seemed loose to the point of collapse. We circled warily about his wife's name.

"Look, Jeff," I said, and took a breath, "about Sondra . . ."

Jeff cut me off with a wave of his hand. "Don't worry, I know Sondra."

"Then you know there's nothing between us?"

"It's just her way of amusing herself. Sondra's a strange girl. She does the same thing with me. She flirts with me but we don't sleep together." He picked up his spoon and stared at it unseeingly. "It started when she became pregnant. After she had the boy, everything between us stopped. You knew we had a son? He's in a sanitarium in the Valley."

"Can't you do anything?"

"Sure. Joyce Castle. I don't know what I'd have done without her."

"I mean divorce."

"Sondra won't divorce me. And I can't divorce her. No grounds." He shrugged as if the whole thing were of no concern at all to him. "What could I say? I want to divorce my wife because of the way she looks at other men? She's scrupulously faithful."

"To whom, Jeff? To you? To whom?"

"I don't know—to herself, maybe," he mumbled.

Whether with encouragement he might have gone on I don't know, for I cut him off. I sensed that with this enigmatic remark he was giving me my cue and that if I had chosen to respond to it he would have told me what I had asked him to lunch to find out—and all at once I was terrified; I did not want to hear it; I did not want to hear it at all. And so I laughed in a quiet way and said, "Undoubtedly, undoubtedly," and pushed it behind the closed door of my mind where I had stored all the impossibilities of the last months—the footsteps, the sounds in the night, the mutilated raccoon—or else, by recognizing them, go mad.

Jeff suddenly looked me full in the face; his cheeks were flushed, his teeth clamped together. "Look, Ted," he said, "can you take the afternoon off? I've got to go to the sanitarium and sign some papers. They're going to transfer the boy. He has fits of violence and does . . . awful things. He's finally gotten out of hand."

"What about Sondra?"

"Sondra's signed already. She likes to go alone to visit him. She seems to like to have him to herself. I'd appreciate it, Ted—the moral support. . . . You don't have to come in. You can wait in the car. It's only about thirty miles from here, you'd be back by dinner-time. . . ." His voice shook, tears clouded the yellow-stained whites of his eyes. He looked like a man with fever. I noticed how shrunken his neck had become as it revolved in his collar, how his head caved in sharply at the temples. He fastened one hand on my arm, like a claw. "Of course I'll go, Jeff," I said. "I'll call the office. They can get along without me for one afternoon."

He collected himself in an instant. "I'd appreciate it, Ted. I promise you it won't be so bad."

The sanitarium was in the San Fernando Valley, a complex of new stucco buildings on a newly seeded lawn. Everywhere there were signs that read, PLEASE KEEP OFF, FOLKS. Midget saplings stood in discs of powdery earth along the cement walks angling white and hot through the grass. On these walks, faithfully observing the signs, the inmates strolled. Their traffic, as it flowed somnolently from one avenue to another, was controlled by attendants stationed at inter-sections, conspicuous in white uniforms and pith helmets.

After a time it became unbearably hot in the car, and I climbed out. Unless I wished to pace in the parking lot among the cars, I had no choice but to join the inmates and their visitors on the walks. I chose a nearly deserted walk and went slowly toward a building that had a yard attached to it surrounded by a wire fence. From the slide and the junglegym in it I judged it to be for the children. Then I saw Jeff come into it. With him was a nurse pushing a kind of cart railed around like an oversized toddler. Stropped into it was "the boy."

He was human, I suppose, for he had all the equipment assigned to humans, yet I had the feeling that if it were not for the cart the creature would have crawled on his belly like an alligator. He had the eyes of an alligator too—sleepy, cold and soulless—set in a swarthy face and a head that seemed to run in a horizontal direction rather than the vertical, like an egg lying on its side. The features were devoid of any vestige of intelligence; the mouth hung open and the chin shone with saliva. While Jeff and the nurse talked, he sat under the sun, inert and repulsive.

I turned on my heel and bolted, feeling that I had intruded on a disgrace. I imagined that I had been given a glimpse of a diseased universe, the mere existence of which constituted a threat to my life; the sight of that monstrous boy with his cold, bestial eyes made me feel as if, by stumbling on this shame I somehow shared in it with Jeff. Yet I told myself that the greatest service I could do him was to pretend that I had seen nothing, knew nothing, and not place on him the hardship of talking about something which obviously caused him pain.

He returned to the car pale and shaky and wanting a drink. We stopped first at a place called Joey's on Hollywood Way. After that it was Cherry Lane on Vine Street, where a couple of girls propositioned us, and then a stop at the Brown Derby again, where I had left my car. Jeff downed the liquor in a joyless, businesslike way and talked to me in a rapid, confidential voice about a book he had just sold to Warner Brothers Studio for an exorbitant sum of money— trash in his opinion, but that was always the way—the parasites made it. Pretty soon there wouldn't be any good writers left: "There'll only be competent parasites and incompetent parasites." This was perhaps the third time we had had this conversation. Now Jeff repeated it mechanically, all the time looking down at the table where he was painstakingly breaking a red swizzle stick into ever tinier pieces.

When we left the restaurant, the sun had gone down, and the evening chill of the desert on which the city had been built had settled in. A faint pink glow from the vanished sun still lingered on the top of the Broadway Building. Jeff took a deep breath, then fell into a fit of coughing. "Goddam smog," he said. "Goddam city. I can't think of a single reason why I live here." He started toward his Daimler, tottering slightly.

"How about driving home with me?" I said. "You can pick your car up tomorrow."

He fumbled in the glove compartment and drew out a packet of small cigars. He stuck one between his teeth where it jutted unlit toward the end of his nose. "I'm not going home tonight, Ted friend," he said. "If you'll just drop me up the street at the Cherry Lane I'll remember you for life."

"Are you sure? I'll go with you if you want."

Jeff shook a forefinger at me archly. "Ted, you're a gentleman and a scholar. But my advice to you is to go home and take care of your wife. No, seriously. Take care of her, Ted. As for myself I shall go quietly to seed in the Cherry Lane Café." I had started toward my car when Jeff called out to me again. "I just want to tell you, Ted friend. . . . My wife was once just as nice as your wife. . . ."

I had gone no more than a mile when the last glimmer of light left the sky and night fell like a shutter. The sky above the neon of Sunset Boulevard turned jet black, and a sickly half-moon rose and was immediately obscured by thick fog that lowered itself steadily as I traveled west, till at the foot of Clay Canyon it began to pat my windshield with little smears of moisture.

The house was dark, and at first I thought Ellen must have gone out, but then seeing her old Plymouth in the driveway I felt the grip of a cold and unreasoning fear. The events of the day seemed to crowd around and hover at my head in the fog; and the commonplace sight of that car, together with the blackness and silence of the house, sent me into a panic as I ran for the door. I pushed at it with my shoulder as if expecting it to be locked, but it swung open easily and I found myself in the darkened living room with no light anywhere and the only sound the rhythm of my own short breathing. "Ellen!" I called in a high, querulous voice I hardly recognized. "Ellen!" I seemed to lose my balance; my head swam; it was as if this darkness and silence were the one last iota that the chamber of horrors in my mind could not hold, and the door snapped open a crack, emitting a cloudy light that stank of corruption, and I saw the landscape of my denial, like a tomb. It was the children's room. Rats nested in the double bunks, mold caked the red wallpaper, and in it an insane Spanish don hung by his neck from a dead tree, his heels vlumping against the wall, his foppish clothes rubbing as he revolved slowly in invisible currents of bad air. And as he swung toward me, I saw his familiar reptile eyes open and stare at me with loathing and contempt.

I conceded: It is here and It is evil, and I have left my wife alone in the house with It, and now she has been sucked into that cold eternity where the dumb shades store their plasms against an anguished centenary of speech—a single word issuing from the petrified throat, a scream or a sigh or a groan, syllables dredged up from a lifetime of eloquence to slake the bottomless thirst of living death.

And then a light went on over my head, and I found myself in the hall outside the children's room. Ellen was in her nightgown, smiling at me. "Ted? Why on earth are you standing here in the dark? I was just taking a nap. Do you want some dinner? Why don't you say something? Are you all right?" She came toward me; she seemed extraordinarily lovely; her eyes, a deeper blue than Sondra's, looked almost purple; she seemed young and slender again; her old serenity shone through like a restored beacon.

"I'm all right," I said hoarsely. "Are you sure you are?"

"Of course I am," she laughed. "Why shouldn't I be? I'm feeling much, much better." She took my hand and kissed it gaily. "I'll put on some clothes and then we'll have our dinner." She turned and went down the hall to our bedroom, leaving me with a clear view into the children's room. Though the room itself was dark, I could see by the hall light that the covers on the lower bunk had been turned back and that the bed had been slept in. "Ellen," I said. "Ellen, were you sleeping in the children's room?"

"Yes," she said, and I heard the rustle of a dress as she carried it from the closet. "I was in there mooning around, waiting for you to come home. I got sleepy and lay down on the bunk. What were *you* doing, by the way? Working late?"

"And nothing happened?"

"Why? What should have happened?"

I could not answer; my head throbbed with joy. It was over—whatever it was, it was over. All unknowing Ellen had faced the very heart of the evil and had slept through it like a child, and now she was herself again without having been tainted by the knowledge of what she had defeated; I had protected her by my silence, by my refusal to share my terror with this woman whom I loved. I reached inside and touched the light button; there was the brave red wallpaper scattered over with toys, the red-and-white curtains, the blue-and-red bedspreads. It was a fine room. A fine, gay room fit for children.

Ellen came down the hall in her slip. "Is anything wrong, Ted? You seem so distraught. Is everything all right at the office?"

"Yes, yes," I said. "I was with Jeff Sheffits. We went to see his boy in the asylum. Poor Jeff; he leads a rotten life." I told Ellen the whole story of our afternoon, speaking freely in my house for the first time since we had moved there. Ellen listened carefully as she always did, and wanted to know, when I had finished, what the boy was like.

"Like an alligator," I said with disgust. "Just like an alligator."

Ellen's face took on an unaccountable expression of private glee. She seemed to be looking past me into the children's room, as if the source of her amusement lay there. At the same moment I shivered in a breath of profound cold, the same clammy draft that might have warned me on my last birthday had I been other than what I am. I had a sense of sudden dehydration, as if all the blood had vanished from my veins. I felt as if I were shrinking. When I spoke, my voice seemed to come from a throat rusty and dry with disuse. "Is that funny?" I whispered.

And my wife replied, "Funny? Oh, no, it's just that I'm feeling so much better. I think I'm pregnant, Ted." She tipped her head to one side and smiled at me.

◎ BY ROBERT SPECHT

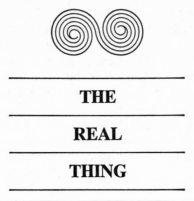

THE

REAL

THING

They took Charlie Atkinson and Tad Winters off to the madhouse on the same day. Charlie went real quiet—being a half-wit, one place to sleep was just as good as another to him. Not Tad, though. When they took him away he was howling like a run-over dog.

Every small town has its village idiot and its practical joker. And it seems that the first is always going to be made a fool of by the second. That was Charlie and Tad. Charlie never seemed to mind, though. No matter what kind of trick Tad played on him, he'd smile that fool's smile of his and say, "That Tad's funny. He's sure funny."

Charlie slept in a little room in back of Mr. Eakin's funeral parlor. He kept the place neat and swept up once in a while. Mister Eakins let him do little chores like that so Charlie wouldn't feel he was getting charity. Charlie liked his little room, not minding at all that most of the time there was somebody dead lying out in the parlor.

Came April, though, the main water line that led into town burst. The seepage turned the graveyard into pure mud, and until the water could be pumped out, Eakins' Funeral Parlor had three people laid out and waiting to make the final trip. Charlie was forced to share his little room with the Dayton girl, who'd died of pneumonia a few days before.

As soon as Tad heard about it he couldn't resist ribbing Charlie. "Hear you got company, Charlie, is that right?"

Charlie looked at him quizzically.

"I mean that pretty little girl you got stayin' with you."

"Shucks, Tad, that's the Dayton girl. You know that." Charlie looked around at Tad's cronies to see if they were smiling. He still wasn't sure his leg was being pulled.

"You mean she ain't your wife?"

"Tad, that girl's *dead*. She couldn't be nobody's wife. You sure are a card you are."

Some of the fellows were ready to laugh, but Tad gave them a quick look that shut them up. He had an idea. "Charlie . . . you ever see that girl get up and wander around at night?"

"Now I know you're foolin'."

"I ain't foolin' you at all," Tad said darkly. "All I can tell you is you better make sure that lid's on tight."

The faces around Charlie took on serious expressions. "Why should I better make sure?" he asked.

"Talk's around town that girl was bitten by a wolf before she died." Tad put his face close to Charlie's. "But not by no *ordinary* wolf. A werewolf. You know what that makes her, don't you?"

"A vampire?"

Charlie had got his legends mixed, but Tad let it go. "That's right. Sure enough you're going to be asleep some night and the next thing you know that gal's teeth'll be in your throat, suckin' you dry as a bone." With that, Tad walked away with his friends, leaving Charlie to think about it alone.

Later Charlie asked Mr. Eakins about vampires and Mr. Eakins told him all he knew. Before he could ask Charlie why he wanted to know, a customer came in and Eakins forgot about it.

It was too bad he did, because that same night Tad and his pals were gathered at the back of the funeral parlor outside of Charlie's room. A few of the merchants in town paid Charlie fifty cents a week to check their doors before he went to sleep, and that's what the group outside his room were waiting for him to do.

Tad turned to Susan, the one girl among them. He was due to be married to her shortly, but the way her face was made up that night even Tad couldn't help but be a little frightened looking at it. Her eyes were ringed in black and her lips were painted scarlet. The rest of her face was painted chalk-white, except for some streaks of black that hollowed her cheeks. "Tad, I don't like doing this," she whispered.

"Now, honey, it's all in fun . . ."

"Yeah, but I don't like the idea of gettin' into that casket."

"You won't be in there but for a few minutes until Charlie gets back. Like I said, we're gonna put you in the one Eakins keeps in the front room for a sample, then switch it with the one in Charlie's room. When he comes back you give out with a few moans, open the casket, and it's all a laugh."

"Suppose he gets a heart attack or something?"

"Aw, he's too dumb for that. He'll let out a yell and high-tail it for the county line—be there in two minutes."

Susan giggled.

"Sshh," a voice said. It belonged to someone who was peering around the edge of the building, towards the front. "He's gone. Let's go."

The group stole forward, and when Charlie disappeared up the street they hurried through the unlocked door of the shop. A few minutes later, when Charlie returned, the men were once more waiting outside the back of the shop.

"Give me a boost," Tad said. With one man holding each of his legs Tad was slowly raised until he could see into Charlie's room through a little transom-like window. "He's comin' in," Tad whispered to the men below. "He's settin' down on the cot takin' his shoes off."

Tad didn't have to report what happened next, for even from where they were the moan that came from the wicker casket could be heard. Within the little room Charlie sat bolt upright. Another moan issued from the casket and Charlie gripped the edge of his cot. At the same time Tad held onto the edge of the window sill with one hand while he tried to stifle his laughter with the other.

"What's happening?" a voice below him asked.

"Wait." He giggled. "The casket's opening. She's comin' up. God, she looks like the real thing! I think Charlie's gon—" He broke off as Charlie suddenly came to life. He moved swiftly—not for the door as Tad thought he would, but straight for the casket. Susan, too, was surprised, Tad saw. She offered no resistance as in almost one motion Charlie sprang, pushed her back in the casket and shoved the lid down on her.

"What's goin' on, Tad?" someone hissed.

Tad was almost too amazed to answer. "I don't know. . . . He locked her in. Now he's gettin' somethin' out from under his cot. Looks like— Oh my God! *Oh my God, NO!*"

The horror in his voice cut through the suppressed laughter of his friends. One of the men holding his legs shifted suddenly and Tad fell to the ground, yelling. Before the men could untangle themselves an unearthly shriek came from within Charlie's room, cutting through Tad's frantic cries and freezing everyone where he stood. It was the shriek of a woman in mortal agony, and it was followed by another, louder than the first.

Tad scrambled to his feet and dashed around the building. When his friends caught up with him he was already hurling himself against the heavy front door in a frenzy. One of the men kept his wits about him. Warning the others away, he picked up a chair that stood in front of the plateglass window and heaved it. Tad was the first one through when the glass stopped falling. The shrieks from Charlie's room had reached a peak. They died suddenly as the men reached his door.

Tad was the first one in the room, and what he saw forced a groan from him. The wicker casket still straddled the two sawhorses on which it had been placed only a few minutes before. Charlie stood before it with a mallet in his hand. A soft gurgling sound came from the casket and the long wooden stake that had been driven through its woven fibres moved a little as the remains of the woman within shuddered once and then were still. Blood had begun to drip to the floor.

Tad began to scream.

Later on, after the authorities took Tad and Charlie away everybody agreed it was Tad's fault. Everybody except Mister Eakins. He stayed drunk for a week, saying that he was the damn fool who told Charlie that the way to kill a vampire was with a stake through its heart.

◎ BY DONALD E. WESTLAKE

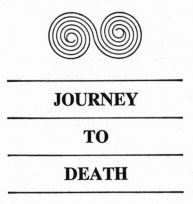

JOURNEY

TO

DEATH

Although ocean voyages are not new to me, I have never grown accustomed to the sway and roll of ships, especially at night. For that reason, I normally get very little sleep while crossing the Atlantic, not being able to close my eyes until I have reached such a point of exhaustion that it is no longer possible for me to keep them open. Since business often makes it necessary for me to journey to America, my wife has urged me, from time to time, to go by air, but I'm afraid I'm much too cowardly for that. The rolling of a ship at sea causes uneasiness in both my stomach and mind, but the mere thought of traveling through the air terrifies me. A sea voyage, then, is the lesser of two evils, and I face my insomnia, after all these years, with the calm of old resignation.

And yet, it is impossible to merely lie in bed awake, eyes staring at the ceiling, through all the long rolling nights between Dover and New York, and even reading begins, at last, to pall. On so many voyages, I have been reduced to aimless pacing of the deck, watching the million moons reflected in the waves surrounding me.

I was delighted, therefore, on this last and latest crossing, to discover, the third night out, a fellow-sufferer, an isomniac like myself, named Cowley. Cowley was an American, a businessman, younger than me, perhaps forty-five or fifty. A direct and sensible man I found him, and enjoyed his company, late at night, when all the other passengers slept and we were alone in an empty and silent sea. I found no fault in him at all, save for an occasional example of rather grim and tasteless humor, a reference to the decaying bodies in Davy Jones's locker, or some such thing.

The nights were spent in conversation, in strolls about the decks, or in billiards, a game which we both loved but which neither had ever mastered. Being of equal incompetence in the sport, we contentedly wiled away many hours in the large billiard room located on the same deck as my cabin.

The eighth night of the voyage was spent in this room, where we puffed happily at cigars, played with our normal lack of skill, and waited patiently for dawn. It was a brisk and chilly night, with a cold wet wind scampering across the waves like a chilled and lonely ghost searching for land, and we had closed every door and window in the room, preferring an atmosphere polluted by cigar smoke to being chilled to the bone.

It was only fifteen minutes after thus sealing ourselves into the room that the catastrophe struck. I don't know what it could have been, an explosion in the huge and mysterious engines somewhere in the bowels of the ship, perhaps unexpected contact with a mine still unreclaimed from the Second World War. Whatever it was, the silence of the night was suddenly torn apart by a tremendous and powerful *sound,* a roar, a crash that dulled the senses and paralyzed the body, and the whole ship, the *Aragon,* shuddered and trembled with a violent jerking spasm. Cowley and I were both thrown to the floor, and on all the tables, the billiard balls clacked and rolled, as though their hysteria and fear were equal to our own.

And then the ship seemed to poise, to stop and hold itself immobile while time flashed by, and I struggled to my feet, hearing the hum of absolute silence, of a broken world suddenly without time or movement.

I turned toward the main door, leading out to the deck, and saw there, staring in, a wild and terrified face, a woman, still in her nightgown, whose mouth was open and who was screaming. I started toward her, staring at her through the glass in the door, and time began again. The ship lurched, bent, and as I struggled to keep my balance, I saw her torn away, out to the emptiness, and eager waves dashed against the window panes.

It was like an elevator gone mad, hurtling down from the uppermost story. The water boiled and fumed outside the window, and I clung to the wall, sick and terrified, knowing that we were sinking, we were sinking, and in a matter of seconds I would surely be dead.

A final jolt, and all movement stopped. The ship lay at a slight angle, the floor was at a slant, and we were at the bottom of the sea.

A part of my mind screamed in horror and fear, but another part of me was calm, as though outside myself, separate, a brain not dependent upon this frail and doomed body. It—this part of my mind that I had never known before—it thought, it conjectured, it reasoned. The ship was lying on the sea floor, that much was obvious. But how far down, how far from the surface? Not too far, surely, or the pressure of the water would have burst the glass of the windows. Was the surface close enough for me to dare to leave the ship, this room, this pocket of trapped air? Could I hope to fight my way to the surface before my lungs burst, before my need for air drove open my mouth and let the water in to kill me?

I couldn't take the chance. We had fallen for so long, and I was not a young man. I couldn't take the chance.

A groan reminded me of Cowley. I turned and saw him lying on the floor against one wall, apparently rolled there when the ship sank. He moved now, feebly, and touched his hand to his head.

I hurried to him and helped him to his feet. At first, he had no idea what had happened. He had heard the explosion, had stumbled, his head had hit the edge of a billiard table, that was all he knew. I told him of our situation, and he stared at me, unbelieving.

"Underwater?" His face was pale with shock, pale and stiff as dry clay. He turned and hurried to the nearest window. Outside, the feeble light from our prison faintly illuminated the swirling waters around us. Cowley faced me again. "The lights—" he said.

I shrugged. "Perhaps there are other rooms still sealed off," I said, and as I finished speaking, the lights flickered and grew dim.

I had expected Cowley to panic, as I had done, but he smiled instead, sardonically, and said, "What a way to die."

"We may not die," I told him. "If there were survivors—"

"Survivors? What if there were? We aren't among them."

"They'll be rescued," I said, suddenly full of hope. "They'll know where the ship went down. And divers will come."

"Divers? Why?"

"They always do. At once. To salvage what they can, to determine the cause of the sinking. They'll send divers. We may yet be saved."

"If there were survivors," said Cowley. "And, if not?"

I sat down, heavily. "Then we are dead men."

"You suggest we wait, is that it?"

I looked at him, surprised. "What else can we do?"

"We can get it over with. We can open the door."

I stared at him. He seemed calm, the faint smile was still on his lips. "Can you give up so easily?"

The smile broadened. "I suppose not," he said, and once more the lights flickered. We looked up, staring at the dimming bulbs. Yet a third time they flickered, and all at once they went out. We were in the dark, in pitch blackness, alone beneath the sea.

In the blackness, Cowley said, "I suppose you're right. There's nothing to lose but our sanity. We'll wait."

I didn't answer him. I was lost in my own thoughts, of my wife, of my children and their families, of my friends on both continents, of land and air and life. We were both silent. Unable to see one another, unable to see anything at all, it seemed impossible to converse.

How long we sat there I don't know, but suddenly I realized that it was not quite so dark any more. Vaguely, I could make out shapes within the room, I could see the form of Cowley sitting in another chair.

He stirred. "It must be daylight," he said. "A sunny day. On the surface."

"How long," I asked him, "how long do you suppose the air will last?"

"I don't know. It's a large room, there's only two of us. Long enough for us to starve to death, I suppose."

"Starve?" I realized, all at once, just how hungry I was. This was a danger I hadn't thought about. Keeping the water out, yes. The amount of air we had, yes. But it hadn't occurred to me, until just now, that we were completely without food.

Cowley got to his feet and paced about the dim room, stretching and roaming restlessly. "Assuming survivors," he said, as though our earlier conversation were still going on, as though there had been no intervening silence, "assuming survivors, and assuming divers, how long do you suppose it will take? Perhaps the survivors will be rescued today. When will the divers come? Tomorrow? Next week? Two months from now?"

"I don't know."

Cowley laughed suddenly, a shrill and harsh sound in the closed room, and I realized that he wasn't as calm as he had seemed. "If this were fiction," he said, "they would come at the last minute. In the nick of time. Fiction is wonderful that way. It is full of last minutes. But in life there is only one last minute. The minute before death."

"Let's talk about other things," I said.

"Let's not talk at all," said Cowley. He stopped by one of the tables and picked up a billiard ball. In the gloom, I saw him toss the ball into the air, catch it, toss it and catch it, and then he said, "I could solve our problem easily. Merely throw this ball through the window there."

I jumped to my feet. "Put it down! If you care nothing for your own life, at least remember that *I* want to live!"

Again he laughed, and dropped the ball onto the table. He paced again for a while, then sank at last into a chair. "I'm tired," he said. "The ship is very still now. I think I could sleep."

I was afraid to go to sleep, afraid that Cowley would wait until I was dozing and would then open the door after all, or throw the billiard ball through the window. I sat and watched him for as long as I could, but my eyelids grew heavy and at last, in spite of my fears, my eyes closed and I slept.

When I awoke, it was dark again, the dark of a clouded midnight, the dark of blindness. I stirred, stretched my cramped limbs, then subsided. I could hear Cowley's measured breathing. He slumbered on.

He woke as it was again growing light, as the absolute blackness was once again dispelled by a gray and murky gloom, the look of late evening, a frustrating half-light that made the eyes strain to see details where there were only shapes and vague forms and half-seen mounds.

Cowley grumbled and stirred and came slowly to consciousness. He got to his feet and moved his arms in undefined and meaningless arcs. "I'm hungry," he muttered. "The walls are closing in on me."

"Maybe they'll come today," I said.

"And maybe they'll never come." Once more, he paced around the room. At length, he stopped. "I once read," he said, as though to himself, "that hunger is always the greatest after the first meal missed. That after a day or two without food, the hunger pains grow less."

"I think that's right. I don't think I'm as hungry now as I was yesterday."

"I am," he said, petulantly, as though it were my fault. "I'm twice as hungry. My stomach is full of cramps. And I'm thirsty." He stood by a window, looking out. "I'm thirsty," he said again. "Why don't I open the window and let some water in?"

"Stay away from there!" I hurried across the room and pulled him away from the window. "Cowley, for God's sake get hold of yourself! If we're calm, if we're patient, if we have the self-reliance and strength to wait, we may yet be saved. Don't you *want* to live?"

"Live?" He laughed at me. "I died the day before yesterday." He flung away from me, hurled himself into his chair. "I'm dead," he said bitterly, "dead and my stomach doesn't know it. Oh, *damn* this pain! Martin, believe me, I could stand anything, I could be as calm and solid as a rock, except for these terrible pains in my stomach. I have to eat, Martin. If I don't get food soon, I'll go out of my mind. I know I will."

I stood watching him, helpless to say or do a thing.

His moods changed abruptly, instantaneously, without rhyme or reason. Now, he suddenly laughed again, that harsh and strident laugh that grated on my spine, that was more terrible to me than the weight of the water outside the windows. He laughed, and said, "I have read of men, isolated, without food, who finally turned to the last solution to the problem of hunger."

I didn't understand him. I said, "What is that?"

"Each other."

I stared at him, and a chill breath of terror touched my throat and dried it. I tried to speak, but my voice was hoarse, and I could only whisper, "Cannibalism? Good God, Cowley, you can't mean—"

Again, he laughed. "Don't worry, Martin. I don't think I could. If I could *cook* you, I might consider it. But raw? No, I don't believe I'll ever get *that* hungry." His mood changed again, and he cursed. "I'll be eating the rug soon, my own clothing, anything!"

He grew silent, and I sat as far from him as I could get. I meant to stay awake now, no matter how long it took, no matter what happened. This man was insane, he was capable of anything. I didn't dare sleep, and I looked forward with dread to the coming blackness of night.

The silence was broken only by an occasional muttering from Cowley across the room, unintelligible, as he mumbled to himself of horrors I tried not to imagine. Blackness came, and I waited, straining to hear a sound, waiting to hear Cowley move, for the attack I knew must come. His breathing was regular and slow, he seemed to be asleep, but I couldn't trust him. I was imprisoned with a madman, my only hope of survival was in staying awake, watching him every second until the rescuers came. And the rescuers must come. I couldn't have gone through all this for nothing. They would come, they must come.

My terror and need kept me awake all night long and all through the next day. Cowley slept much of the time, and when he was awake he contented himself with low mumbling or with glowering silence.

But I couldn't stay awake forever. As darkness returned again, as the third day ended without salvation, a heavy fog seemed to lower around me, and although I fought it, although I could feel the terror in my vitals, the fog closed in and I slept.

I woke suddenly. It was day again, and I couldn't breathe. Cowley stood over me, his hands around my neck, squeezing, shutting off the air from my lungs, and I felt as though my head were about to burst. My eyes bulged, my mouth opened and closed helplessly. Cowley's face, indistinct above me, gleamed with madness, his eyes bored into me and his mouth hung open in a hideous laugh.

I pulled at his hands, but they held me tight, I couldn't move them, I couldn't get air, air. I flailed away at his face, and my heart pounded in fear as I struggled. My fingers touched his face, perspiring face, slid away, I lunged at his eyes. My finger drove into his eye, and he screamed and released me. He fell back, his hands against his face, and I felt the warm jelly of his eye on my finger.

I stumbled out of the chair, looking madly for escape, but the room was sealed, we were prisoners together. He came at me again, his clutching hands reaching out for me, his face terrible now with the bloody wound where his left eye had been. I ran, and the breath rattled in my throat as I gulped in air. Choking, sobbing, I ran from him, my arms outstretched in the gloom, and I fell against one of the billiard tables. My hands touched a cuestick, I picked it up, turned, swung at Cowley with it. Cowley fell back, howling like an animal, but then came on again. Screaming, I jabbed the cuestick full into his open mouth.

The stick snapped in two, part of it still in my hands, part jutting out of his mouth, and he started a shriek that ended in a terrible gurgling wail. He toppled face forward to the floor, driving the piece of stick through the back of his head.

I turned away and collapsed over a table. I was violently ill, my stomach jerking spasmodically, my throat heaving and retching. But it had been so long since I had eaten that I could bring nothing up, but could only lie helplessly, coughing and shaking and terribly, terribly sick.

That was three days ago, and still they haven't come. They must come soon now. The air is growing foul in here, I can hardly breathe any more. And I find that I am talking to myself, and every once in a while I will pick up a billiard ball and look longingly at the window. I am coming to long for death, and I know that that is madness. So they must come soon.

And the worst thing is the hunger. Cowley is gone, now, all gone, and I am hungry again.

◎ By Algis Budrys

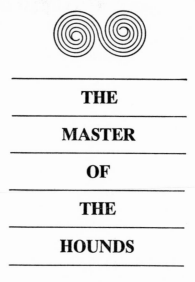

THE
MASTER
OF
THE
HOUNDS

The white sand road led off the state highway through the sparse pines. There were no tire tracks in the road, but, as Malcolm turned the car onto it, he noticed the footprints of dogs, or perhaps of only one dog, running along the middle of the road toward the combined general store and gas station at the intersection.

"Well, it's far enough away from everything, all right," Virginia said. She was lean and had dusty black hair. Her face was long, with high cheekbones. They had married ten years ago, when she had been girlish and very slightly plump.

"Yes," Malcolm said. Just days ago, when he'd been turned down for a Guggenheim Fellowship that he'd expected to get, he had quit his job at the agency and made plans to spend the summer, somewhere as cheap as possible, working out with himself whether he was really an artist or just had a certain commercial talent. Now they were here.

He urged the car up the road, following a line of infrequent and weathered utility poles that carried a single strand of power line. The real-estate agent already had told them there were no telephones. Malcolm had taken that to be a positive feature, but somehow he did not like the looks of that one thin wire sagging from pole to pole. The wheels of the car sank in deeply on either side of the dog prints, which he followed like a row of bread crumbs through a forest.

Several hundred yards farther along, they came to a sign at the top of a hill:

Marine View Shores! New Jersey's Newest, Fastest-Growing Residential Community. Welcome Home! From $9,990. No Dn Pyt for Vets.

Below them was a wedge of land—perhaps ten acres altogether that pushed out into Lower New York Bay. The road became a gullied, yellow gravel street, pointing straight toward the water and ending in three concrete posts, one of which had fallen and left a gap wide enough for a car to blunder through. Beyond that was a low drop-off where the bay ran northward to New York City and, in the other direction, toward the open Atlantic.

On either side of the roughed-out street, the bulldozed land was overgrown with scrub oak and sumac. Along the street were rows of roughly rectangular pits—some with half-finished foundation walls in them—piles of excavated clay, and lesser quantities of sand, sparsely weed-grown and washed into ravaged mounds like Dakota Territory. Here and there were houses with half-completed frames, now silvered and warped.

There were only two exceptions to the general vista. At the end of the street, two identically designed, finished houses faced each other. One looked shabby. The lot around it was free of scrub, but weedy and unsodded. Across the street from it stood a house in excellent repair. Painted a charcoal gray and roofed with dark asphalt shingles, it sat in the center of a meticulously green and level lawn, which was in turn surrounded by a wire fence approximately four feet tall and splendid with fresh aluminum paint. False shutters, painted stark white, flanked high, narrow windows along the side Malcolm could see. In front of the house, a line of whitewashed stones the size of men's heads served as curbing. There wasn't a thing about the house and its surroundings that couldn't have been achieved with a straight string, a handsaw, and a three-inch brush. Malcolm saw a chance to cheer things up. "There now, Marthy!" he said to Virginia. "I've led you safe and sound through the howlin' forest to a snug home right in the shadder of brave Fort Defiance."

"It's orderly," Virginia said. "I'll bet it's no joke, keeping up a place like that out here."

As Malcolm was parking the car parallel to where the curb would have been in front of their house, a pair of handsome young Doberman pinschers came out from behind the gray house across the street and stood together on the lawn with their noses just short of the fence, looking out. They did not bark. There was no movement at the front window, and no one came out into the yard. The dogs simply stood there, watching, as Malcolm walked over the clay to his door.

The house was furnished—that is to say, there were chairs in the living room, although there was no couch, and a chromium-and-plastic dinette set in the area off the kitchen. Though one of the bedrooms was completely empty, there was a bureau and a bed in the other. Malcolm walked through the house quickly and went back out to the car to get the luggage and groceries. Nodding toward the dogs, he said to Virginia, "Well! The latest thing in iron deer." He felt he had to say something light, because Virginia was staring across the street.

He knew perfectly well, as most people do and he assumed Virginia did, that Doberman pinschers are nervous, untrustworthy, and vicious. At the same time, he and his wife did have to spend the whole summer here. He could guess how much luck they'd have trying to get their money back from the agent now.

"They look streamlined like that because their ears and tails are trimmed when they're puppies," Virginia said. She picked up a bag of groceries and carried it into the house.

When Malcolm had finished unloading the car, he slammed the trunk lid shut. Although they hadn't moved until then, the Dobermans seemed to regard this as a sign. The turned smoothly, the arc of one inside the arc of the other, and keeping formation, trotted out of sight behind the gray house.

Malcolm helped Virginia put things away in the closets and in the lone bedroom bureau. There was enough to do to keep both of them busy for several hours, and it was dusk when Malcolm happened to look out through the living-room window. After he had glanced that way, he stopped.

Across the street, floodlights had come on at the four corners of the gray house. They poured illumination downward in cones that lighted the entire yard. A crippled man was walking just inside the fence, his legs stiff and his body bent forward from the waist, as he gripped the projecting handles of two crutch-canes that supported his weight at the elbows. As Malcolm watched, the man took a precise square turn at the corner of the fence and began walking along the front of his property. Looking straight ahead, he moved regularly and purposefully, his shadow thrown out through the fence behind the composite shadow of the two dogs walking at his pace immediately ahead of him. None of them was looking in Malcolm's direction. He watched as the man made another turn, followed the fence toward the back of his property, and disappeared behind the house.

Later Virginia served cold cuts in the little dining alcove. Putting the house in order seemed to have had a good effect on her morale.

"Listen, I think we're going to be all right here, don't you?" Malcolm said.

"Look," she said reasonably, "any place you can get straightened out is fine with me."

This wasn't quite the answer he wanted. He had been sure in New York that the summer would do it—that in four months a man would come to *some* decision. He had visualized a house for them by the ocean, in a town with a library and a movie and other diversions. It had been a shock to discover how expensive summer rentals were and how far in advance you had to book them. When the last agent they saw described this place to them and told them how low the rent was, Malcolm had jumped at it immediately. But so had Virginia, even though there wasn't anything to do for distraction. In fact, she had made a point of asking the agent again about the location of the house, and the agent, a fat, gray man with ashes on his shirt, had said earnestly, "Mrs. Lawrence, if you're looking for a place where nobody will bother your husband from working, I can't think of anything better." Virginia had nodded decisively.

It had bothered her, his quitting the agency; he could understand that. Still, he wanted her to be happy, because he expected to be surer of what he wanted to do by the end of the summer. She was looking at him steadily now. He cast about for something to offer her that would interest her and change the mood between them. Then he remembered the scene he had witnessed earlier that evening. He told her about the man and his dogs, and this did raise her eyebrows.

"Do you remember the real-estate agent telling us anything about him?" she asked. "I don't."

Malcolm, searching through his memory, did recall that the agent had mentioned a custodian they could call on if there were any problems. At the time he had let it pass, because he couldn't imagine either agent or custodian really caring. Now he realized how dependent he and Virginia were out here if it came to things like broken plumbing or bad wiring, and the custodian's importance altered accordingly. "I guess he's the caretaker," he said.

"Oh."

"It makes sense—all this property has got to be worth something. If they didn't have someone here, people would just carry stuff away or come and camp or something."

"I suppose they would. I guess the owners let him live here rent-free, and with those dogs he must do a good job."

"He'll get to keep it for a while, too," Malcolm said. "Whoever started to build here was a good ten years ahead of himself. I can't see anybody buying into these places until things have gotten completely jammed up closer to New York."

"So, he's holding the fort," Virginia said, leaning casually over the table to put a dish down before him. She glanced over his shoulder toward the living-room window, widened her eyes, and automatically touched the neckline of her housecoat, and then snorted at herself.

"Look, he can't possibly see in here," Malcolm said. "The living room, yes, but to look in here he'd have to be standing in the far corner of his yard. And he's back inside his house." He turned his head to look, and it was indeed true, except that one of the dogs was standing at that corner looking toward their house, eyes glittering. Then its head seemed to melt into a new shape, and it was looking down the road. It pivoted, moved a few steps away from the fence, turned, soared, landed in the street, and set off. Then, a moment later, it came back down the street running side by side with its companion, whose jaws were lightly pressed together around the rolled-over neck of a small paper bag. The dogs trotted together companionably and briskly, their flanks rubbing against one another, and when they were a few steps from the fence they leaped over it in unison and continued across the lawn until they were out of Malcolm's range of vision.

"For heaven's sake! He lives all alone with those dogs!" Virginia said.

Malcolm turned quickly back to her. "How do you come to think that?"

"Well, it's pretty plain. You saw what they were doing out there just now. They're his servants. He can't get around himself, so they run errands for him. If he had a wife, she would do it."

"You learned all that already?"

"Did you notice how happy they were?" Virginia asked. "There was no need for that other dog to go meet its friend. But it wanted to. They can't be anything but happy." Then she looked at Malcolm, and he saw the old, studying reserve coming back into her eyes.

"For Pete's sake! They're only dogs—what do they know about anything?" Malcolm said.

"They know about happiness," Virginia said. "They know what they do in life."

Malcolm lay awake for a long time that night. He started by think-ing about how good the summer was going to be, living here and working, and then he thought about the agency and about why he didn't seem to have the kind of shrewd, limited intuition that let a man do advertising work easily. At about four in the morning he wondered if perhaps he wasn't frightened, and had been frightened for a long time. None of this kind of thinking was new to him, and he knew that it would take him until late afternoon the following day to reach the point where he was feeling pretty good about him-self.

When Virginia tried to wake him early the next morning he asked her to please leave him alone. At two in the afternoon, she brought him a cup of coffee and shook his shoulder. After a while, he walked out to the kitchen in his pajama pants and found that she had scrambled up some eggs for the two of them.

"What are your plans for the day?" Virginia said when he had fin-ished eating.

He looked up. "Why?"

"Well, while you were sleeping, I put all your art things in the front bedroom. I think it'll make a good studio. With all your gear in there now, you can be pretty well set up by this evening."

At times she was so abrupt that she shocked him. It upset him that she might have been thinking that he wasn't planning to do anything at all today. "Look," he said, "you know I like to get the feel of a new thing."

"I know that. I didn't set anything up in there. I'm no artist. I just moved it all in."

When Malcolm had sat for a while without speaking, Virginia cleared away their plates and cups and went into the bedroom. She came out wearing a dress, and she had combed her hair and put on lipstick. "Well, you do what you want to," she said. "I'm going to go across the street and introduce myself."

A flash of irritability hit him, but then he said, "If you'll wait a minute, I'll get dressed and go with you. We might as well both meet him."

He got up and went back to the bedroom for a T-shirt and blue jeans and a pair of loafers. He could feel himself beginning to react to pressure. Pressure always made him bind up; it looked to him as if Virginia had already shot the day for him.

They were standing at the fence, on the narrow strip of lawn between it and the row of whitewashed stones, and nothing was happening. Malcolm saw that although there was a gate in the fence, there was no break in the little grass border opposite it. And there was no front walk. The lawn was lush and all one piece, as if the house had been lowered onto it by helicopter. He began to look closely at the ground just inside the fence, and when he saw the regular pock-marks of the man's crutches, he was comforted.

"Do you see any kind of bell or anything?" Virginia asked.

"No."

"You'd think the dogs would bark."

"I'd just as soon they didn't."

"Will you look?" she said, fingering the gate latch. "The paint's hardly scuffed. I'll bet he hasn't been out of his yard all summer." Her touch rattled the gate lightly, and at that the two dogs came out from behind the house. One of them stopped, turned, and went back. The other dog came and stood by the fence, close enough for them to hear its breathing, and watched them with its head cocked alertly.

The front door of the house opened. At the doorway there was a wink of metal crutches, and then the man came out and stood on his front steps. When he had satisfied himself as to who they were, he nodded, smiled, and came toward them. The other dog walked beside him. Malcolm noticed that the dog at the fence did not distract himself by looking back at his master.

The man moved swiftly, crossing the ground with nimble swings of his body. His trouble seemed to be not in the spine, but in the legs themselves, for he was trying to help himself along with them. It could not be called walking, but it could not be called total help-lessness either.

Although the man seemed to be in his late fifties, he had not gone to seed any more than his property had. He was wiry and clean-boned, and the skin on his face was tough and tanned. Around his small blue eyes and at the corners of his thin lips were many fine, deep-etched wrinkles. His yellowish-white hair was brushed straight back from his temples in the classic British military manner. And he even had a slight mustache. He was wearing a tweed jacket with leather patches at the elbows, which seemed a little warm for this kind of day, and a light flannel pale-gray shirt with a pale-blue bow tie. He stopped at the fence, rested his elbows on the crutches, and held out a firm hand with short nails the color of old bones.

"How do you do," he said pleasantly, his manner polished and well-bred. "I have been looking forward to meeting my new neighbors. I am Colonel Ritchey." The dogs stood motionless, one to each side of him, their sharp black faces pointing outward.

"How do you do," Virginia said. "We are Malcolm and Virginia Lawrence."

"I'm very happy to meet you," Colonel Ritchey said. "I was prepared to believe Cortelyou would fail to provide anyone this season."

Virginia was smiling. "What beautiful dogs," she said. "I was watching them last night."

"Yes. Their names are Max and Moritz. I'm very proud of them."

As they prattled on, exchanging pleasantries, Malcolm wondered why the Colonel had referred to Cortelyou, the real-estate agent, as a provider. There was something familiar, too, about the colonel.

Virginia said, "You're the famous Colonel Ritchey."

Indeed he was, Malcolm now realized, remembering the big magazine series that had appeared with the release of the movie several years before.

Colonel Ritchey smiled with no trace of embarrassment. " I am the famous Colonel Ritchey, but you'll notice I certainly don't look much like that charming fellow in the motion picture."

"What in hell are you doing *here?*" Malcolm asked.

Ritchey turned his attention to him. "One has to live somewhere, you know."

Virginia said immediately, "I was watching the dogs last night, and they seemed to do very well for you. I imagine it's pleasant having them to rely on."

"Yes, it is, indeed. They're quite good to me, Max and Moritz. But it is much better with people here now. I had begun to be quite disappointed in Cortelyou."

Malcolm began to wonder whether the agent would have had the brass to call Ritchey a custodian if the colonel had been within earshot.

"Come in, please," the colonel was saying. The gate latch resisted him momentarily, but he rapped it sharply with the heel of one palm and then lifted it. "Don't be concerned about Max and Moritz— they never do anything they're not told."

"Oh, I'm not the least bit worried about them," Virginia said.

"Ah, to some extent you should have been," the colonel said. "Dobermans are not to be casually trusted, you know. It takes many months before one can be at all confident in dealing with them."

"But you trained them yourself, didn't you?" Virginia said.

"Yes, I did," Colonel Ritchey said, with a pleased smile. "From imported pups." The voice in which he now spoke to the dogs was forceful, but as calm as his manner had been to Virginia. "Kennel," he said, and Max and Moritz stopped looking at Malcolm and Virginia and smoothly turned away.

The colonel's living room, which was as neat as a sample, contained beautifully cared for, somewhat old-fashioned furniture. The couch, with its needle-point upholstery and carved framing, was the sort of thing Malcolm would have expected in a lady's living room. Angling out from one wall was a Morris chair, placed so that a man might relax and gaze across the street or, with a turn of his head, rest his eyes on the distant lights of New York. Oil paintings in heavy gilded frames depicted landscapes, great eye-stretching vistas of rolling, open country. The furniture in the room seemed sparse to Malcolm until it occurred to him that the colonel needed extra clearance to get around in and had no particular need to keep additional chairs for visitors.

"Please do sit down," the colonel said. "I shall fetch some tea to refresh us."

When he had left the room, Virginia said, "Of all people! Neighborly, too."

Malcolm nodded. "Charming," he said.

The colonel entered holding a silver tray perfectly steady, its edges grasped between his thumbs and forefingers, his other fingers curled around each of the projecting black-rubber handgrips of his crutches. He brought tea on the tray and, of all things, homemade cookies.

"I must apologize for the tea service," he said, "but it seems to be the only one I have."

When the colonel offered the tray, Malcolm saw that the utensils were made of the common sort of sheet metal used to manufacture food cans. Looking down now into his cup, he saw it had been enameled over its original tinplate, and he realized that the whole thing had been made literally from a tin can. The teapot—handle, spout, vented lid, and all—was the same. "Be damned—you made this for yourself at the prison camp, didn't you?"

"As a matter of fact, I did, yes. I was really quite proud of my handiwork at the time, and it still serves. Somehow, living as I do, I've never brought myself to replace it. It's amazing, the fuddy-duddy skills one needs in a camp and how important they become to one. I find myself repainting these poor objects periodically and still taking as much smug pleasure in it as I did when that attitude was quite necessary. One is allowed to do these things in my position, you know. But I do hope my *ersatz* Spode isn't uncomfortably hot in your fingers."

Virginia smiled. "Well, of course, it's trying to be." Malcolm was amazed. He hadn't thought Virginia still remembered how to act so coquettish. She hadn't grown apart from the girl who'd always attracted a lot of attention at other people's gallery openings; she had simply put that part of herself away somewhere else.

Colonel Ritchey's blue eyes were twinkling in response. He turned to Malcolm. "I must say, it will be delightful to share this summer with someone as charming as Mrs. Lawrence."

"Yes," Malcolm said, preoccupied now with the cup, which was distressing his fingers with both heat and sharp edges. "At least, I've always been well satisfied with her," he added.

"I've been noticing the inscription here," Virginia said quickly, indicating the meticulous freehand engraving on the tea tray. She read out loud, " 'To Colonel David N. Ritchey, R.M.E., from his fellow officers at *Oflag* XXXI*b,* on the occasion of their liberation, May 14, 1945. Had he not been there to lead them, many would not have been present to share of this heartfelt token.' " Virginia's eyes shone, as she looked up at the colonel. "They must all have been very fond of you."

"Not all," the colonel said, with a slight smile. "I was senior officer over a very mixed bag. Mostly younger officers gathered from every conceivable branch. No followers at all—just budding leaders, all personally responsible for having surrendered once already, some apathetic, others desperate. Some useful, some not. It was my job to weld them into a disciplined, responsive body, to choose whom we must keep safe and who was best suited to keeping the Jerries on the jump. And we were in, of course, from the time of Dunkirk to the last days of the war, with the strategic situation in the camp constantly changing in various ways. All most of them understood was tactics—when they understood at all."

The colonel grimaced briefly, then smiled again. "The tray was presented by the survivors, of course. They'd had a tame Jerry pinch it out of the commandant's sideboard a few days earlier, in plenty of time to get the inscription on. But even the inscription hints that not all survived."

"It wasn't really like the movie, was it?" Virginia said.

"No, and yet—" Ritchey shrugged, as if remembering a time when he had accommodated someone on a matter of small importance. "That was a question of dramatic values, you must realize, and the need to tell an interesting and exciting story in terms recognizable to a civilian audience. Many of the incidents in the motion picture are literally true—they simply didn't happen in the context shown. The Christmas tunnel was quite real, obviously. I did promise the men I'd get at least one of them home for Christmas if they'd pitch in and dig it. But it wasn't a serious promise, and they knew it wasn't. Unlike the motionpicture actor, I was not being fervent; I was being ironic.

"It was late in the war. An intelligent man's natural desire would be to avoid risk and wait for liberation. A great many of them felt exactly that way. In fact, many of them had turned civilian in their own minds and were talking about their careers outside, their families —all that sort of thing. So by couching in sarcasm trite words about Christmas tunnels, I was reminding them what and where they still were. The tactic worked quite well. Through devices of that sort, I was able to keep them from going to seed and coming out no use to anyone." The colonel's expression grew absent. "Some of them called me 'The Shrew,' " he murmured. "*That* was in the movie, too, but they were all shown smiling when they said it."

"But it was your duty to hold them all together any way you could," Virginia said encouragingly.

Ritchey's face twisted into a spasm of tension so fierce that there might have been strychnine in his tea. But it was gone at once. "Oh, yes, yes, I held them together. By lying and cajoling and tricking them. But the expenditure of energy was enormous. And demeaning. It ought not to have made any difference that we were cut off from higher authority. If we had all still been home, there was not a man among the prisoners who would have dared not jump to my simplest command. But in the camp they could shilly-shally and evade; they could settle down into little private ambitions. People will do that. People will not hold true to common purposes unless they are shown discipline." The colonel's uncompromising glance went from Virginia to Malcolm. It's no good telling people what they ought to do. The only surety is in being in a position to tell people what they *must* do."

"Get some armed guards to back you up. That the idea, Colonel? Get permission from the Germans to set up your own machine-gun towers inside the camp?" Malcolm liked working things out to the point of absurdity.

The colonel appraised him imperturbably. "I was never quite that much my own man in Germany. But there is a little story I must tell you. It's not altogether off the point." He settled back, at ease once again.

"You may have been curious about Max and Moritz. The Germans, as you know, have always been fond of training dogs to perform all sorts of entertaining and useful things. During the war the Jerries were very much given to using Dobermans for auxiliary guard duty at the various prisoner-of-war camps. In action, Mr. Lawrence, or simply in view, a trained dog is far more terrifying than any soldier with a machine pistol. It takes an animal to stop a man without hesitation, no matter if the man is cursing or praying.

"Guard dogs at each camp were under the charge of a man called the *Hundführer*—the master of the hounds, if you will—whose function, after establishing himself with the dogs as their master and director, was to follow a few simple rules and to take the dogs to wherever they were needed. The dogs had been taught certain patrol routines. It was necessary only for the *Hundführer* to give simple commands such as 'Search' or 'Arrest,' and the dogs would know what to do. Once we had seen them do it, they were very much on our minds, I assure you.

"A Doberman, you see, has no conscience, being a dog. And a trained Doberman has no discretion. From the time he is a puppy, he is bent to whatever purpose has been preordained for him. And the lessons are painful—and autocratic. Once an order has been given, it must be enforced at all costs, for the dog must learn that all orders are to be obeyed unquestioningly. That being true, the dog must also learn immediately and irrevocably that only the orders from one particular individual are valid. Once a Doberman has been trained, there is no way to retrain it. When the American soldiers were seen coming, the Germans in the machine-gun towers threw down their weapons and tried to flee, but the dogs had to be shot. I watched from the hospital window, and I shall never forget how they continued to leap at the kennel fencing until the last one was dead. Their *Hundführer* had run away. . . ."

Malcolm found that his attention was wandering, but Virginia asked, as if on cue, "How did you get into the hospital—was that the Christmas tunnel accident?"

"Yes," the colonel said to Virginia, gentleman to lady. "The sole purpose of the tunnel was, as I said, to give the men a focus of attention. The war was near enough its end. It would have been foolhardy to risk actual escape attempts. But we did the thing up brown, of course. We had a concealed shaft, a tunnel lined with bed slats, a trolley for getting to and from the tunnel entrance, fat lamps made from shoe-blacking tins filled with margarine—all the normal appurtenances. The Germans at that stage were quite experienced in ferreting out this sort of operation, and the only reasonable assurance of continued progress was to work deeply and swiftly. Tunneling is always a calculated risk—the accounts of that sort of operation are biased in favor of the successes, of course.

"At any rate, by the end of November, some of the men were audibly thinking it was my turn to pitch in a bit, so one night I went down and began working. The shoring was as good as it ever was, and the conditions weren't any worse than normal. The air was breathable, and as long as one worked—ah—unclothed, and brushed down immediately on leaving the tunnel, the sand was not particularly damaging to one's skin. Clothing creates chafes in those circumstances. Sand burns coming to light at medical inspections were one of the surest signs that such an operation was under way.

"However that may be, I had been down there for about an hour and a half, and was about to start inching my way back up the tunnel, feetfirst on the trolley like some Freudian symbol, when there was a fall of the tunnel roof that buried my entire chest. It did not cover my face, which was fortunate, and I clearly remember my first thought was that now none of the men would be able to feel the senior officer hadn't shared their physical tribulations. I discovered, at once, that the business of clearing the sand that had fallen was going to be extremely awkward. First, I had to scoop some extra clearance from the roof over my face. Handfuls of sand began falling directly on me, and all I could do about that was to thrash my head back and forth. I was becoming distinctly exasperated at that when there was another slight fall behind the original collapse. This time, the fat lamp attached to the shoring loosened from its fastenings and spilled across my thighs. The hot fat was quite painful. What made it rather worse was that the string wick was not extinguished by the fall, and accordingly, the entire lower part of my body between navel and knees, having been saturated with volatile fat. . . ." The colonel grimaced in embarrassment.

"Well, I was immediately in a very bad way, for there was nothing I could do about the fire until I had dug my way past the sand on my chest. In due course, I did indeed free myself and was able to push my way backward up the tunnel after extinguishing the flames. The men at the shaft head had seen no reason to become alarmed—tunnels always smell rather high and sooty, as you can imagine. But they did send a man down when I got near the entrance shaft and made myself heard.

"Of course, there was nothing to do but tell the Jerries, since we had no facilities whatever for concealing my condition or treating it. They put me in the camp hospital, and there I stayed until the end of the war with plenty of time to lie about and think my thoughts. I was even able to continue exercising some control over my men. I shouldn't be a bit surprised if that hadn't been in the commandant's mind all along. I think he had come to depend on my presence to moderate the behavior of the men.

"That is really almost the end of the story. We were liberated by the American Army, and the men were sent home. I stayed in military hospitals until I was well enough to travel home, and there I dwelt in hotels and played the retired, invalided officer. After that journalist's book was published and the dramatic rights were sold, I was called to Hollywood to be the technical adviser for the movie. I was rather grateful to accept the employment, frankly—an officer's pension is not particularly munificent—and what with selectively lending my name and services to various organizations while my name was still before the public, I was able to accumulate a sufficient nest egg.

"Of course, I cannot go back to England, where the Inland Revenue would relieve me of most of it, but, having established a relationship with Mr. Cortelyou and acquired and trained Max and Moritz, I am content. A man must make his way as best he can and do whatever is required for survival." The colonel cocked his head brightly and regarded Virginia and Malcolm. "Wouldn't you say?"

"Y—es," Virginia said slowly. Malcolm couldn't decide what the look on her face meant. He had never seen it before. Her eyes were shining, but wary. Her smile showed excitement and sympathy, but tension too. She seemed caught between two feelings.

"Quite!" the colonel said, smacking his hands together. "It is most important to me that you fully understand the situation." He pushed himself up to his feet and, with the same move, brought the crutches out smoothly and positioned them to balance him before he could fall. He stood leaning slightly forward, beaming. "Well, now, having heard my story, I imagine the objectives of this conversation are fully attained, and there is no need to detain you here further. I'll see you to the front gate."

"That won't be necessary," Malcolm said.

"I insist," the colonel said in what would have been a perfectly pleasant manner if he had added the animated twinkle to his eyes. Virginia was staring at him, blinking slowly.

"Please forgive us," she said. "We certainly hadn't mean to stay long enough to be rude. Thank you for the tea and cookies. They were very good."

"Not at all, my dear," the colonel said. "It's really quite pleasant to think of looking across the way, now and then, and catching glimpses of someone so attractive at her domestic preoccupations. I cleaned up thoroughly after the last tenants, of course, but there are always little personal touches one wants to apply. And you will start some plantings at the front of the house, won't you? Such little activities are quite precious to me—someone as charming as you, in her summer things, going about her little fussings and tendings, resting in the sun after weeding—that sort of thing. Yes, I expect a most pleasant summer. I assume there was never any question you wouldn't stay all summer. Cortelyou would hardly bother with anyone who could not afford to pay him that much. But little more, eh?" The urbane, shrewd look returned to the colonel's face. "Pinched resources and few ties, eh? Or what would you be doing here, if there were somewhere else to turn to?"

"Well, good afternoon, Colonel," Virginia said with noticeable composure. "Let's go, Malcolm."

"Interesting conversation, Colonel," Malcolm said.

"Interesting and necessary, Mr. Lawrence," the colonel said, following them out onto the lawn. Virginia watched him closely as she moved toward the gate, and Malcolm noticed a little downward twitch at the corners of her mouth.

"Feeling a bit of a strain, Mrs. Lawrence?" the colonel asked solicitously. "Please believe that I shall be as considerate of your sensibilities as intelligent care of my own comfort will permit. It is not at all in my code to offer offense to a lady, and in any case—" the colonel smiled deprecatingly "—since the mishap of the Christmas tunnel, one might say the spirit is willing but . . ." The colonel frowned down absently at his canes. "No, Mrs. Lawrence," he went on, shaking his head paternally, "is a flower the less for being breathed of? And is the cultivated flower, tended and nourished, not more fortunate than the wild rose that blushes unseen? Do not regret your present social situation too much, Mrs. Lawrence—some might find it enviable. Few things are more changeable than points of view. In the coming weeks your viewpoint might well change."

"Just what the hell are you saying to my wife?" Malcolm asked.

Virginia said quickly, "We can talk about it later."

The colonel smiled at Virginia. "Before you do that, I have something else to show Mr. Lawrence." He raised his voice slightly: "Max! Moritz! Here!"—and the dogs were there. "Ah, Mr. Lawrence, I would like to show you first how these animals respond, how discriminating they can be." He turned to one of the dogs. "Moritz," he said sharply, nodding toward Malcolm. "Kill."

Malcolm couldn't believe what he had heard. Then he felt a blow on his chest. The dog was on him, its hind legs making short, fast, digging sounds in the lawn as it pressed its body against him. It was inside the arc of his arms, and the most he could have done was to clasp it closer to him. He made a tentative move to pull his arms back and then push forward against its rib cage, but the minor shift in weight made him stumble, and he realized if he completed the gesture he would fall. All this happened in a very short time, and then the dog touched open lips with him. Having done that, it dropped down and went back to stand beside Colonel Ritchey and Max.

"You see, Mr. Lawrence?" the colonel asked conversationally. "A dog does not respond to literal meaning. It is conditioned. It is trained to perform a certain action when it hears a certain sound. The cues one teaches a dog with pain and patience are not necessarily cues an educated organism can understand. Pavlov rang a bell and a dog salivated. Is a bell food? If he had rung a different bell, or said, 'Food, doggie,' there would have been no response. So, when I speak in a normal tone, rather than at command pitch, 'kill' does not mean 'kiss,' even to Moritz. It mean nothing to him—unless I raise my voice. And I could just as easily have conditioned him to perform that sequence in association with some other command—such as, oh, say, 'gingersnaps'—but then you might not have taken the point of my little, instructive jest. There is no way anyone but myself can

operate these creatures. Only when I command do they respond.
And now you respond, eh, Mr. Lawrence? I dare say. . . . Well,
good day. As I said, you have things to do."

They left through the gate, which the colonel drew shut behind
them. "Max," he said, "watch," and the dog froze in position.
"Moritz, come." The colonel turned, and he and the other dog
crossed the lawn and went into his house.

Malcolm and Virginia walked at a normal pace back to the rented
house, Malcolm matching his step to Virginia's. He wondered if she
were being so deliberate because she wasn't sure what the dog would
do if she ran. It had been a long time since Virginia hadn't been
sure of something.

In the house, Virginia made certain the door was shut tight, and
then she went to sit in the chair that faced away from the window.
"Would you make me some coffee, please?" she said.

"All right, sure. Take a few minutes. Catch your breath a little."

"A few minutes is what I need," she said. "Yes, a few minutes, and
everything will be fine." When Malcolm returned with the coffee,
she continued, "He's got some kind of string on Cortelyou, and I bet
those people at the store down at the corner aren't too happy about
those dogs walking in and out of there all the time. He's got us.
We're locked up."

"Now, wait," Malcolm said, "there's the whole state of New
Jersey out there, and he can't—"

"Yes, he can. If he thinks he can get away with it, and he's got
good reasons for thinking he can. Take it on faith. There's no bluff
in *him*."

"Well, look," he said, "just what can he do to us?"

"Any damn thing he pleases."

"That can't be right." Malcolm frowned. "He's got us pretty well
scared right now, but we ought to be able to work out some way
of—"

Virginia said tightly, "The dog's still there, right?" Malcolm
nodded. "Okay," she said. "What did it feel like when he hit you?
It looked awful. It looked like he was going to drive you clear onto
your back. Did it feel that way? What did you *think?*"

"Well, he's a pretty strong animal," Malcolm said. "But, to tell you the truth, I didn't have time to believe it. You know, a man just saying 'kill' like that is a pretty hard thing to believe. Especially just after tea and cookies."

"He's very shrewd," Virginia said. "I can see why he had the camp guards running around in circles. He deserved to have a book written about him."

"All right, and then they should have thrown him into a padded cell."

"Tried to throw," Virginia amended.

"Oh, come on. This is his territory, and he dealt the cards before we even knew we were playing. But all he is is a crazy old cripple. If he wants to buffalo some people in a store and twist a two-bit real-estate salesman around his finger, fine—if he can get away with it. But he doesn't own us. We're not in his army."

"We're inside his prison camp," Virginia said.

"Now, look," Malcolm said. "When we walk in Cortelyou's door and tell him we know all about the colonel, there's not going to be any trouble about getting the rent back. We'll find someplace else, or we'll go back to the city. But whatever we do to get out of this, it's going to work out a lot smoother if the two of us think about it. It's not like you to be sitting there and spending a lot of time on how we can't win."

"Well, Malcolm. Being a prisoner certainly brings out your initiative. Here you are, making noises just like a senior officer. Proposing escape committees and everything."

Malcolm shook his head. Now of all times, when they needed each other so much, she wouldn't let up. The thing to do was to move too fast for her.

"All right," he said, "let's get in the car." There was just the littlest bit of sweat on his upper lip.

"*What?*" He had her sitting up straight in the chair, at least. "Do you imagine that that dog will let us get anywhere near the car?"

"You want to stay here? All right. Just keep the door locked. I'm going to try it, and once I'm out I'm going to come back here with a nice healthy state cop carrying a nice healthy riot gun. And we're either going to do something about the colonel and those two dogs, or we're at least going to move you and our stuff out of here."

He picked up the car keys, stepped through the front door very quickly, and began to walk straight for the car. The dog barked sharply, once. The front door of Ritchey's house opened immediately, and Ritchey called out, "Max! Hold!" The dog on the lawn was over the fence and had its teeth thrust carefully around Malcolm's wrist before he could take another eight steps, even though he had broken into a run. Both the dog and Malcolm stood very still. The dog was breathing shallowly and quietly, its eyes shining. Ritchey and Moritz walked as far as the front fence. "Now, Mr. Lawrence," Ritchey said, "in a moment I am going to call to Max, and he is to bring you with him. Do not attempt to hold back, or you will lacerate your wrist. Max! Bring here!"

Malcolm walked steadily toward the colonel. By some smooth trick of his neck, Max was able to trot alongside him without shifting his grip. "Very good, Max," Ritchey said soothingly when they had reached the fence. "Loose now," and the dog let go of Malcolm's wrist. Malcolm and Ritchey looked into each other's eyes across the fence, in the darkening evening. "Now, Mr. Lawrence," Ritchey said, "I want you to give me your car keys." Malcolm held out the keys, and Ritchey put them into his pocket. "Thank you." He seemed to reflect on what he was going to say next, as a teacher might reflect on his reply to a child who has asked why the sky is blue. "Mr. Lawrence, I want you to understand the situation. As it happens, I also want a three-pound can of Crisco. If you will please give me all the money in your pocket, this will simplify matters."

"I don't have any money on me," Malcolm said. "Do you want me to go in the house and get some?"

"No, Mr. Lawrence, I'm not a thief. I'm simply restricting your radius of action in one of the several ways I'm going to do so. Please turn out your pockets."

Malcolm turned out his pockets.

"All right, Mr. Lawrence, if you will hand me your wallet and your address book and the thirty-seven cents, they will all be returned to you whenever you have a legitimate use for them." Ritchey put the items away in the pockets of his jacket. "Now, a three-pound can of Crisco is ninety-eight cents. Here is a dollar bill. Max will walk with you to the corner grocery store, and you will buy the Crisco for me and bring it back. It is too much for a dog to carry in a bag, and it is three days until my next monthly delivery of staples. At the store you will please tell them that it will not be necessary for them to come here with monthly deliveries any longer—that you will be in to do my shopping for me from now on. I expect you to take a minimum amount of time to accomplish all this and to come back with my purchase, Mr. Lawrence. Max!" The colonel nodded toward Malcolm. "Guard. Store." The dog trembled and whined. "Don't stand still, Mr. Lawrence. Those commands are incompatible until you start toward the store. If you fail to move, he will grow increasingly tense. Please go now. Moritz and I will keep Mrs. Lawrence good company until you return."

The store consisted of one small room in the front of a drab house. On unpainted pine shelves were brands of goods that Malcolm had never heard of. "Oh! You're with one of those nice dogs," the tired, plump woman behind the counter said, leaning down to pat Max, who had approached her for that purpose. It seemed to Malcolm that the dog was quite mechanical about it and was pretending to itself that nothing caressed it at all. He looked around the place, but he couldn't see anything or anyone that offered any prospect of alliance with him.

"Colonel Ritchey wants a three-pound can of Crisco," he said, bringing the name out to check the reaction.

"Oh, you're helping him?"

"You could say that."

"Isn't he brave?" the woman said in low and confidential tones, as if concerned that the dog could overhear. "You know, there are some people who would think you shoud feel sorry for a man like that, but I say it would be a sin to do so. Why, he gets along just fine, and he's got more pride and spunk than any whole man I've ever seen. Makes a person proud to know him. You know, I think it's just wonderful the way these dogs come and fetch little things for him. But I'm glad he's got somebody to look out for him now. 'Cept for us, I don't think he sees anybody from one year to the next—'cept summers, of course."

She studied Malcolm closely. "You're summer people too, aren't you? Well, glad to have you, if you're doin' some good for the colonel. Those people last year were a shame. Just moved out one night in September, and neither the colonel nor me or my husband seen hide nor hair of them since. Owed the colonel a month's rent, he said when we was out there."

"Is he the landlord?" Malcolm asked.

"Oh, sure, yes. He owns a lot of land around here. Bought it from the original company after it went bust."

"Does he own this store, too?"

"Well, we lease it from him now. Used to own it, but we sold it to the company and leased it from them. Oh, we was all gonna be rich. My husband took the money from the land and bought a lot across the street and was gonna set up a real big gas station there—figured to be real shrewd—but you just can't get people to live out here. I mean, it isn't as if this was *ocean*-front property. But the colonel now, he's got a head on his shoulders. Value's got to go up someday, and he's just gonna hold on until it does."

The dog was getting restless, and Malcolm was worried about Virginia. He paid for the can of Crisco, and he and Max went back up the sand road in the dark. There really, honestly, didn't seem to be much else to do.

At his front door, he stopped, sensing that he should knock. When Virginia let him in, he saw that she had changed to shorts and a halter. "Hello," she said, and then stood aside quietly for him and Max. The colonel, sitting pertly forward on one of the chairs, looked up. "Ah, Mr. Lawrence, you're a trifle tardy, but the company has been delightful, and the moments seemed to fly."

Malcolm looked at Virginia. In the past couple of years, a little fat had accumulated above her knees, but she still had long, good legs. Colonel Ritchey smiled at Malcolm. "It's a rather close evening. I simply suggested to Mrs. Lawrence that I certainly wouldn't be offended if she left me for a moment and changed into something more comfortable."

It seemed to Malcolm that she could have handled that. But apparently she hadn't.

"Here's your Crisco," Malcolm said. "The change is in the bag."

"Thank you very much," the colonel said. "Did you tell them about the grocery deliveries?"

Malcolm shook his head. "I don't remember. I don't think so. I was busy getting an earful about how you owned them, lock, stock, and barrel."

"Well, no harm. You can tell them tomorrow."

"Is there going to be some set time for me to run your errands every day, Colonel? Or are you just going to whistle whenever something comes up?"

"Ah, yes. You're concerned about interruptions in your mood. Mrs. Lawrence told me you were some sort of artist. I'd wondered at your not shaving this morning." The colonel paused and then went on crisply. "I'm sure we'll shake down into whatever routine suits best. It always takes a few days for individuals to hit their stride as a group. After that, it's quite easy—regular functions, established duties, that sort of thing. A time to rise and wash, a time to work, a time to sleep. Everything and everyone in his proper niche. Don't worry, Mr. Lawrence, you'll be surprised how comfortable it becomes. Most people find it a revelation." The colonel's gaze grew distant for a moment. "Some do not. Some are as if born on another planet, innocent of human nature. Dealing with that sort, there comes a point when one must cease to try; at the camp, I found that the energy for over-all success depended on my admitting the existence of the individual failure. No, some do not respond. But we needn't dwell on what time will tell us."

Ritchey's eyes twinkled. "I have dealt previously with creative people. Most of them need to work with their hands; do stupid, dull, boring work that leaves their minds free to soar in spirals and yet forces them to stay away from their craft until the tension is nearly unbearable." The colonel waved in the direction of the unbuilt houses. "There's plenty to do. If you don't know how to use a hammer and saw as yet, I know how to teach that. And when from time to time I see you've reached the proper pitch of creative frustration, then you shall have what time off I judge will best serve you artistically. I think you'll be surprised how pleasingly you'll take to your studio. From what I gather from your wife, this may well be a very good experience for you."

Malcolm looked at Virginia. "Yes. Well, that's been bugging her for a long time. I'm glad she's found a sympathetic ear."

"Don't quarrel with your wife, Mr. Lawrence. That sort of thing wastes energy and creates serious morale problems." The colonel got to his feet and went to the door. "One thing no one could ever learn to tolerate in a fellow *Kriegie* was pettiness. That sort of thing was always weeded out. Come, Max. Come, Moritz. Good night." He left.

Malcolm went over to the door and put the chain on. "Well?" he said.

"All right, now, look—"

Malcolm held up one finger. "Hold it. Nobody likes a quarrelsome *Kriegie*. We're not going to fight. We're going to talk, and we're going to think." He found himself looking at her halter and took his glance away. Virginia blushed.

"I just want you to know it was exactly the way he described it," she said. "He said he wouldn't think it impolite if I left him alone in the living room while I went to change. And I wasn't telling him our troubles. We were talking about what you did for a living, and it didn't take much for him to figure out—"

"I don't want you explaining," Malcolm said. "I want you to help me tackle this thing and get it solved."

"How are you going to solve it? This is a man who always uses everything he's got! He never quits! How is somebody like *you* going to solve that?"

All these years, it occurred to Malcolm, at a time like this, now, she finally had to say the thing you couldn't make go away.

When Malcolm did not say anything at all for a while but only walked around frowning and thinking, Virginia said she was going to sleep. In a sense, he was relieved; a whole plan of action was forming in his mind, and he did not want her there to badger him.

After she had closed the bedroom door, he went into the studio. In a corner was a carton of his painting stuff, which he now approached, detached but thinking. From this room he could see the floodlights on around the colonel's house. The colonel had made his circuit of the yard, and one of the dogs stood at attention, looking across the way. The setting hadn't altered at all from the night before.

Setting, no, Malcolm thought, bouncing a jar of brown tempera in his hand; mood, *si*. His arm felt good all the way down from his shoulder, into the forearm, wrist, and fingers.

When Ritchey had been in his house a full five minutes, Malcolm said to himself aloud, "Do first, analyze later." Whipping open the front door, he took two steps forward on the bare earth to gather momentum and pitched the jar of paint in a shallow arc calculated to end against the aluminum fence.

It was going to fall short, Malcolm thought, and it did, smashing with a loud impact against one of the whitewashed stones and throwing out a fan of gluey, brown spray over the adjacent stones, the fence, and the dog, which jumped back but, lacking orders to charge, stood its ground, whimpering. Malcolm stepped back into his open doorway and leaned in it. When the front door of Ritchey's house opened he put his thumbs to his ears and waggled his fingers, "*Gute Nacht, Herr Kommandant*," he called, then stepped back inside and slammed and locked the door, throwing the spring-bolt latch. The dog was already on its way. It loped across the yard and scraped its front paws against the other side of the door. Its breath sounded like giggling.

Malcolm moved over to the window. The dog sprang away from the door with a scratching of toenails and leaped upward, glancing off the glass. It turned, trotted away for a better angle, and tried again. Malcolm watched it; this was the part he'd bet on.

The dog didn't make it. Its jaws flattened against pane, and the whole sheet quivered, but there was too much going against success. The window was pretty high above the yard, and the dog couldn't get a proper combination of momentum and angle of impact. If he did manage to break it, he'd never have enough momentum left to clear the break; he'd fall on the sharp edges of glass in the frame while other chunks fell and cut his neck, and then the colonel would be down to one dog. One dog wouldn't be enough; the system would break down somewhere.

The dog dropped down, leaving nothing on the glass but a wet brown smear.

It seemed to Malcolm equally impossible for the colonel to break the window himself. He couldn't stride forward to throw a small

298))) Alfred Hitchcock Presents

stone hard enough to shatter the pane, and he couldn't balance well enough to heft a heavy one from nearby. The lock and chain would prevent him from entering through the front door. No, it wasn't efficient for the colonel any way you looked at it. He would rather take a few days to think of something shrewd and economical. In fact, he was calling the dog back now. When the dog reached its master, he shifted one crutch and did his best to kneel while rubbing the dog's head. There was something rather like affection in the scene. Then the colonel straightened up and called again. The other dog came out of the house and took up its station at the corner of the yard. The colonel and the dirty dog went back into the colonel's house.

Malcolm smiled, then turned out the lights, double-checked the locks, and went back through the hall to the bedroom. Virginia was sitting up in bed, staring in the direction from which the noise had come.

"What did you do?" she asked.

"Oh, changed the situation a little," Malcolm said, grinning. "Asserted my independence. Shook up the colonel. Smirched his neatness a little bit. Spoiled his night's sleep for him, I hope. Standard *Kriegie* tactics. I hope he likes them."

Virginia was incredulous. "Do you know what he could do to you with those dogs if you step outside this house?"

"I'm not going to step outside. Neither are you. We're just going to wait a few days."

"What do you mean?" Virginia said, looking at him as if he were the maniac.

"Day after tomorrow, maybe the day after that," Malcolm explained, "he's due for a grocery delivery I didn't turn off. Somebody's going to be here with a car then, lugging all kinds of things. I don't care how beholden those storekeepers are to him; when we come out the door, he's not going to have those dogs tear us to pieces right on the front lawn in broad daylight and with a witness. We're going to get into the grocery car, and sooner or later we're going to drive out in it, because *that* car and driver have to turn up in the outside world again."

Virginia sighed. "Look," she said with obvious control, "all he has to do is send a note with the dogs. He can stop the delivery that way."

Malcolm nodded. "Uh-huh. And so the groceries don't come. Then what? He starts trying to freight flour and eggs in here by dog back? By remote control? What's he going to do? All right, so it doesn't work out so neatly in two or three days. But we've got a fresh supply of food, and he's almost out. Unless he's planning to live on Crisco, he's in a bad way. And even so, he's only got three pounds of that." Malcolm got out of his clothes and lay down on the bed. "Tomorrow's another day, but I'll be damned if I'm going to worry any more about it tonight. I've got a good head start on frustrating the legless wonder, and tomorrow I'm going to have a nice clear mind, and I'm going to see what other holes I can pick in his defense. I learned a lot of snide little tricks from watching jolly movies about clever prisoners and dumb guards." He reached up and turned out the bed light. "Good night, love," he said. Virginia rolled away from him in the dark. "Oh, my God," she said in a voice with a brittle edge around it.

It was a sad thing for Malcolm to lie there thinking that she had that kind of limitation in her, that she didn't really understand what had to be done. On the other hand, he thought sleepily, feeling more relaxed than he had in years, he had his own limitations. And she had put up with them for years. He fell asleep wondering pleasantly what tomorrow would bring.

He woke to a sound of rumbling and crunching under the earth, as if there were teeth at the foundations of the house. Still sleeping in large portions of his brain, he cried out silently to himself with a madman's lucidity, "Ah, of course, he's been tunneling!" And his mind gave him all the details—the careful transfer of supporting timber from falling houses, the disposal of the excavated clay in the piles beside the other foundations. Perhaps there were tunnels leadings toward those other foundations, too, for when the colonel had more people. . . .

Now one corner of the room showed a jagged line of yellow, and Malcolm's hands sprang to the light switch. Virginia jumped from sleep. In the corner was a trap door, its uneven joints concealed by boards of different lengths. The trap door crashed back, releasing a stench of body odor and soot.

A dog popped up through the opening and scrambled into the bedroom. Its face and body were streaked, and it shook itself to get the sand from its coat. Behind it, the colonel dragged himself up, naked, and braced himself on his arms, half out of the tunnel mouth. His hair was matted down with perspiration over his narrow-boned skull. He was mottled yellow-red with dirt, and half in the shadows. Virginia buried her face in her hands, one eye glinting out between spread fingers, and cried to Malcolm, "Oh my God, what have you done to us?"

"Don't worry, my dear," the colonel said crisply to her. Then he screamed at Malcolm, "I will not be abused!" Trembling with strain as he hung on one corded arm, he said to the dog at command pitch, pointing at Malcolm, "Kiss!"

◎ BY HENRY SLESAR

THE

CANDIDATE

"A man's worth can be judged by the calibre of his enemies." Burton Grunzer, encountering the phrase in a pocket-sized biography he had purchased at a newsstand, put the book in his lap and stared reflectively from the murky window of the commuter train. Darkness silvered the glass and gave him nothing to look at but his own image, but it seemed appropriate to his line of thought. How many people were enemies of that face, of the eyes narrowed by a myopic squint denied by vanity that correction of spectacles, of the nose he secretly called patrician, of the mouth that was soft in relaxation and hard when animated by speech or smiles or frowns? How many enemies? Grunzer mused. A few he could name, others he could guess. But it was their calibre that was important. Men like Whitman Hayes, for instance, there was a 24-carat opponent for you. Grunzer smiled, darting a sidelong glance at the seat-sharer beside him, not wanting to be caught indulging in a secret thought. Grunzer was thirty-four; Hayes was twice as old, his white hairs synonymous with experience, an enemy to be proud of. Hayes knew the food business, all right, knew it from every angle: he'd been a wagon jobber for six years, a broker for ten, a food company executive for twenty before the old man had brought him into the organization to sit on his right hand. Pinning Hayes to the mat wasn't easy, and that made Grunzer's small but increasing triumphs all the sweeter. He congratulated himself. He had twisted Hayes's advantages into drawbacks, had made his long years seem tantamount to senility and outlived usefulness; in meetings, he had concentrated his questions on the new supermarket and suburbia phenomena to demonstrate to the old man that times had changed, that the past was dead, that new merchandising tactics were needed, and that only a younger man could supply them. . . .

Suddenly, he was depressed. His enjoyment of remembered victories seemed tasteless. Yes, he'd won a minor battle or two in the company conference room; he'd made Hayes' ruddy face go crimson, and seen the old man's parchment skin wrinkle in a sly grin. But what had been accomplished? Hayes seemed more self-assured than ever, and the old man more dependent upon his advice. . . .

When he arrived home, later than usual, his wife Jean didn't ask questions. After eight years of a marriage in which, childless, she knew her husband almost too well, she wisely offered nothing more than a quiet greeting, a hot meal, and the day's mail. Grunzer flipped through the bills and circulars, and found an unmarked letter. He slipped it into his hip pocket, reserving it for private perusal, and finished the meal in silence.

After dinner, Jean suggested a movie and he agreed; he had a passion for violent action movies. But first, he locked himself in the bathroom and opened the letter. Its heading was cryptic: *Society for United Action.* The return address was a post office box. It read:

Dear Mr. Grunzer:

Your name has been suggested to us by a mutual acquaintance. Our organization has an unusual mission which cannot be described in this letter, but which you may find of exceeding interest. We would be gratified by a private discussion at your earliest convenience. If I do not hear from you to the contrary in the next few days, I will take the liberty of calling you at your office.

It was signed, *Carl Tucker, Secretary*. A thin line at the bottom of the page read: *A Non-Profit Organization*.

His first reaction was a defensive one; he suspected an oblique attack on his pocketbook. His second was curiosity: he went to the bedroom and located the telephone directory, but found no organization listed by the letterhead name. *Okay, Mr. Tucker,* he thought wryly, *I'll bite.*

When no call came in the next three days, his curiosity was increased. But when Friday arrived, he forgot the letter's promise in the crush of office affairs. The old man called a meeting with the bakery products division. Grunzer sat opposite Whitman Hayes at the conference table, poised to pounce on fallacies in his statements. He almost had him once, but Eckhardt, the bakery products manager, spoke up in defense of Hayes's views. Eckhardt had only been with the company a year, but he had evidently chosen sides already. Grunzer glared at him, and reserved a place for Eckhardt in the hate chamber of his mind.

At three o'clock, Carl Tucker called.

"Mr. Grunzer?" The voice was friendly, even cheery. "I haven't heard from you, so I assume you don't mind me calling today. Is there a chance we can get together sometime?"

"Well, if you could give me some idea, Mr. Tucker—"

The chuckle was resonant. "We're not a charity organization, Mr. Grunzer, in case you got that notion. Nor do we sell anything. We're more or less a voluntary service group: our membership is over a thousand at present."

"To tell you the truth," Grunzer frowned, "I never heard of you."

"No, you haven't, and that's one of the assets. I think you'll understand when I tell you about us. I can be over at your office in fifteen minutes, unless you want to make it another day."

Grunzer glanced at his calendar. "Okay, Mr. Tucker. Best time for me is right now."

"Fine! I'll be right over."

Tucker was prompt. When he walked into the office, Grunzer's eyes went dismayed at the officious briefcase in the man's right hand. But he felt better when Tucker, a florid man in his early sixties with small, pleasant features, began talking.

"Nice of you to take the time, Mr. Grunzer. And believe me, I'm not here to sell you insurance or razor blades. Couldn't if I tried; I'm a semi-retired broker. However, the subject I want to discuss is rather—intimate, so I'll have to ask you to bear with me on a certain point. May I close the door?"

"Sure," Grunzer said, mystified.

Tucker closed it, hitched his chair closer, and said:

"The point is this. What I have to say must remain in the strictest confidence. If you betray that confidence, if you publicize our society in any way, the consequences could be most unpleasant. Is that agreeable?"

Grunzer, frowning, nodded.

"Fine!" The visitor snapped open the briefcase and produced a stapled manuscript. "Now, the society has prepared this little spiel about our basic philosophy, but I'm not going to bore you with it. I'm going to go straight to the heart of our argument. You may not agree with our first principle at all, and I'd like to know that now."

"How do you mean, first principle?"

"Well . . ." Tucker flushed slightly. "Put in the crudest form, Mr. Grunzer, the Society for United Action believes that—*some* people are just not fit to live." He looked up quickly, as if anxious to gauge the immediate reaction. "There, I've said it," he laughed, somewhat in relief. "Some of our members don't believe in my direct approach; they feel the argument has to be broached more discreetly. But frankly, I've gotten excellent results in this rather crude manner. How do you feel about what I've said, Mr. Grunzer?"

"I don't know. Guess I never thought about it much."

"Were you in the war, Mr. Grunzer?"

"Yes. Navy." Grunzer rubbed his jaw. "I suppose I didn't think the Japs were fit to live, back then. I guess maybe there are other cases. I mean, you take capital punishment, I believe in that. Murderers, rape-artists, perverts, hell, I certainly don't think *they're* fit to live."

"Ah," Tucker said. "So you really accept our first principle. It's a question of category, isn't it?"

"I guess you could say that."

"Good. So now I'll try another blunt question. Have you—personally—ever wished someone dead? Oh, I don't mean those casual, fleeting wishes everybody has. I mean a real, deep-down, uncomplicated wish for the death of someone *you* thought was unfit to live. Have you?"

"Sure." Grunzer said frankly. "I guess I have."

"There are times, in your opinion, when the removal of someone from this earth would be beneficial?"

Grunzer smiled. "Hey, what is this? You from Murder, Incorporated or something?"

Tucker grinned back. "Hardly, Mr. Grunzer, hardly. There is absolutely no criminal aspect to our aims or our methods. I'll admit we're a 'secret' society, but we're no Black Hand. You'd be amazed at the quality of our membership; it even includes members of the legal profession. But suppose I tell you how the society came into being?

"It began with two men; I can't reveal their names just now. The year was 1949, and one of these men was a lawyer attached to the district attorney's office. The other man was a state psychiatrist. Both of them were involved in a rather sensational trial, concerning a man accused of a hideous crime against two small boys. In their opinion, the man was unquestionably guilty, but an unusually persuasive defense counsel, and a highly suggestible jury, gave him his freedom. When the shocking verdict was announced, these two, who were personal friends as well as colleagues, were thunderstruck and furious. They felt a great wrong had been committed, and they were helpless to right it . . .

"But I should explain something about this psychiatrist. For some years, he had made studies in a field which might be called anthropological psychiatry. One of these researches related to the Voodoo practice of certain groups, the Haitian in particular. You've probably heard a great deal about Voodoo, or Obeah as they call it in Jamaica, but I won't dwell on the subject lest you think we hold tribal rites and stick pins in dolls . . . But the chief feature of his study was the uncanny *success* of certain strange practices. Naturally, as a scientist, he rejected the supernatural explanation and sought the rational one. And of course, there was only one answer. When the Vodun priest decreed the punishment or death of a malefactor, it was the malefactor's own convictions concerning the efficacy of the death-wish, his own faith in the Voodoo power, that eventually made the wish come true. Sometimes, the process was organic—his body reacted psychosomatically to the Voodoo curse, and he would sicken and die. Sometimes, he would die by 'accident'—an accident prompted by the secret belief that once cursed, he *must* die. Eerie, isn't it?"

"No doubt," Grunzer said, dry-lipped.

"Anyway, our friend, the psychiatrist, began wondering aloud if *any* of us have advanced so far along the civilized path that we couldn't be subject to this same sort of 'suggested' punishment. He proposed that they experiment on this choice subject, just to see.

"How they did it was simple," he said. "They went to see this man, and they announced their intentions. They told him they were going to *wish him dead*. They explained how and why the wish would become reality, and while he laughed at their proposal, they could see the look of superstitious fear cross his face. They promised him that regularly, every day, they would be wishing for his death, until he could no longer stop the mystic juggernaut that would make the wish come true."

Grunzer shivered suddenly, and clenched his fist. "That's pretty silly," he said softly.

"The man died of a heart attack two months later."

"Of course. I knew you'd say that. But there's such a thing as coincidence."

"Naturally. And our friends, while intrigued, weren't satisfied. *So they tried it again.*"

"Again?"

"Yes, again. I won't recount who the victim was, but I will tell you that this time they enlisted the aid of four associates. This little band of pioneers was the nucleus of the society I represent today."

Grunzer shook his head. "And you mean to tell me there's a *thousand* now?"

"Yes, a thousand and more, all over the country. A society whose one function is to *wish people dead*. At first, membership was purely voluntary, but now we have a system. Each new member of the Society for United Action joins on the basis of submitting one potential victim. Naturally, the society investigates to determine whether the victim is deserving of his fate. If the case is a good one, the *entire* membership then sets about to *wish him dead*. Once the task has been accomplished, naturally, the new member must take part in all future concerted action. That and a small yearly fee, is the price of membership."

Carl Tucker grinned.

"And in case you think I'm not serious, Mr. Grunzer—" He dipped into the briefcase again, this time producing a blue-bound volume of telephone directory thickness. "Here are the facts. To date, two hundred and twenty-nine victims were named by our selection committee. Of those, *one hundred and four* are no longer alive. Coincidence, Mr. Grunzer?

"As for the remaining one hundred and twenty-five—perhaps that indicates that our method is not infallible. We're the first to admit that. But new techniques are being developed all the time. I assure you, Mr. Grunzer, *we will get them all*."

He flipped through the blue-bound book.

"Our members are listed in this book, Mr. Grunzer. I'm going to give you the option to call one, ten, or a hundred of them. Call them and see if I'm not telling the truth."

He flipped the manuscript toward Grunzer's desk. It landed on the blotter with a thud. Grunzer picked it up.

"Well?" Tucker said. "Want to call them?"

"No." He licked his lips. "I'm willing to take your word for it, Mr. Tucker. It's incredible, but I can see how it works. *Just knowing* that a thousand people are wishing you dead is enough to shake hell out of you." His eyes narrowed. "But there's one question. You talked about a 'small' fee—"

"It's fifty dollars, Mr. Grunzer."

"Fifty, huh? Fifty times a thousand, that's pretty good money, isn't it?"

"I assure you, the organization is not motivated by profit. Not the kind you mean. The dues merely cover expenses, committee work, research, and the like. Surely you can understand that?"

"I guess so," he grunted.

"Then you find it interesting?"

Grunzer swiveled his chair about to face the window.

God! he thought.

God! if it *really* worked!

But how could it? If wishes became deeds, he would have slaughtered dozens in his lifetime. Yet, that was different. His wishes were always secret things, hidden where no man could know them. But this method was different, more practical, more terrifying. Yes, he could see how it might work. He could visualize a thousand minds burning with the single wish of death, see the victim sneering in disbelief at first, and then slowly, gradually, surely succumbing to the tightening, constricting chain of fear that it *might* work, that so many deadly thoughts could indeed emit a mystical, malevolent ray that destroyed life.

Suddenly, ghost-like, he saw the ruddy face of Whitman Hayes before him.

He wheeled about and said:

"But the victim has to *know* all this, of course? He has to know the society exists, and has succeeded, and is wishing for *his* death? That's essential, isn't it?"

"Absolutely essential," Tucker said, replacing the manuscripts in his briefcase. "You've touched on the vital point, Mr. Grunzer. The victim must be informed, and that, precisely, is what I have done." He looked at his watch. "Your death wish began at noon today. The society has begun to work. I'm very sorry."

At the doorway, he turned and lifted both hat and briefcase in one departing salute.

"Goodbye, Mr. Grunzer," he said.

◎ BY JOHN WYNDHAM

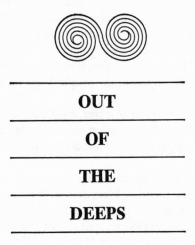

OUT

OF

THE

DEEPS

PHASE 1

I'm a reliable witness, you're a reliable witness, practically all God's
children are reliable witnesses in their own estimation—which
makes it funny how such different ideas of the same affair get about.
Almost the only people I know who agree word for word on what
they saw on the night of July fifteenth are Phyllis and I. And as
Phyllis happens to be my wife, people said, in their kindly way be-

309

hind our backs, that I "overpersuaded" her, a thought that could proceed only from someone who did not know Phyllis.

The time was 11:15 P.M.; the place, latitude thirty-five, some twenty-four degrees west of Greenwich; the ship, the *Guinevere;* the occasion, our honeymoon. About these facts there is no dispute. The cruise had taken us to Madeira, the Canaries, Cape Verde Islands, and had then turned north to show us the Azores on our way home. We, Phyllis and I, were leaning on the rail, taking a breather. From the saloon came the sound of the dance continuing, and the crooner yearning for somebody. The sea stretched in front of us like a silken plain in the moonlight. The ship sailed as smoothly as if she were on a river. We gazed out silently at the infinity of sea and sky. Behind us the crooner went on baying.

"I'm so glad I don't feel like him; it must be devastating," Phyllis said. "Why, do you suppose, do people keep on mass-producing these dreary moanings?"

I had no answer ready for that one, but I was saved the trouble of trying to find one when her attention was suddenly caught elsewhere.

"Mars is looking pretty angry tonight, isn't he? I hope it isn't an omen," she said.

I looked where she pointed at a red spot among myriads of white ones, and with some surprise. Mars does look red, of course, though I had never seen him look quite as red as that—but then, neither were the stars, as seen at home, quite as bright as they were here. Being practically in the tropics might account for it.

"Certainly a little inflamed," I agreed.

We regarded the red point for some moments. Then Phyllis said: "That's funny. It seems to be getting bigger."

I explained that that was obviously an hallucination formed by staring at it. We went on staring, and it became quite indisputably bigger. Moreover: "There's another one. There can't be two Marses," said Phyllis.

And sure enough there was. A smaller red point, a little up from, and to the right of, the first. She added: "*And* another. To the left. See?"

She was right about that, too, and by this time the first one was glowing as the most noticeable thing in the sky.

"It must be a flight of jets of some kind, and that's a cloud of luminous exhaust we're seeing," I suggested.

We watched all three of them slowly getting brighter and also sinking lower in the sky until they were little above the horizon line, and reflecting in a pinkish pathway across the water toward us.

"Five now," said Phyllis.

We've both of us been asked many times since to describe them, but perhaps we are not gifted with such a precise eye for detail as some others. What we said at the time, and what we still say, is that on this occasion there was no real shape visible. The center was solidly red, and a kind of fuzz round it was less so. The best suggestion I can make is that you imagine a brilliantly red light as seen in a fairly thick fog so that there is a strong halation, and you will have something of the effect.

Others besides ourselves were leaning over the rail, and in fairness I should perhaps mention that between them they appear to have seen cigar-shapes, cylinders, discs, ovoids, and, inevitably, saucers. We did not. What is more, we did not see eight, nine, or a dozen. We saw five.

The halation may or may not have been due to some kind of jet drive, but it did not indicate any great speed. The things grew in size quite slowly as they approached. There was time for people to go back into the saloon and fetch their friends out to see, so that presently a line of us leaned all along the rail, looking at them and guessing.

With no idea of scale we could have no judgment of their size or distance; all we could be sure of was that they were descending in a long glide which looked as if it would take them across our wake.

When the first one hit the water a great burst of steam shot up in a pink plume. Then, swiftly, there was a lower, wider spread of steam which had lost the pink tinge, and was simply a white cloud in the moonlight. It was beginning to thin out when the sound of it reached us in a searing hiss. The water round the spot bubbled and seethed and frothed. When the steam drew off, there was nothing to be seen there but a patch of turbulence, gradually subsiding.

Then the second of them came in, in just the same way, on almost the same spot. One after another all five of them touched down on the water with great whooshes and hissings of steam. Then the vapor cleared, showing only a few contiguous patches of troubled water.

Aboard the *Guinevere,* bells clanged, the beat of the engines changed, we started to change course, crews turned out to man the boats, men stood by to throw lifebelts.

Four times we steamed slowly back and forth across the area, searching. There was no trace whatever to be found. But for our own wake, the sea lay all about us in the moonlight, placid, empty, unperturbed . . .

The next morning I sent my card in to the captain. In those days I had a staff job with the E.B.C., and I explained to him that they would be pretty sure to take a piece from me on the previous night's affair. He gave the usual response: "You mean *B*.B.C.?"

The E.B.C. was comparatively young then. People long accustomed to the B.B.C.'s monopoly of the British air were still finding it difficult to become used to the idea of a competitive radio service. Life would have been a great deal simpler, too, if somebody had not had the idea in the early days of sailing as near the wind as possible by calling us the English Broadcasting Company. It was one of those pieces of foolishness that becomes more difficult to undo as time goes on, and led continually to one's explaining as I did now: "Not the *B*.B.C.; the *E*.B.C. Ours is the largest all-British commercial radio network . . ." etc. And when I was through with that I added:

"Our news-service is a stickler for accuracy, and as every passenger has his own version of this business, I hoped you would let me check mine against your official one."

He nodded approval of that.

"Go ahead and tell me yours," he invited me.

When I had finished, he showed me his own entry in the log. Substantially we were agreed; certainly in the view that there had been five, and on the impossibility of attributing a definite shape to them. His estimates of speed, size, and position were, of course, technical matters. I noticed that they had registered on the radar screens, and were tentatively assumed to have been aircraft of an unknown type.

"What's your own private opinion?" I asked him. "Did you ever see anything at all like them before?"

"No, I never did," he said, but he seemed to hesitate.

"But what—?" I asked.

"Well, but not for the record," he said, "I've heard of two instances, almost exactly similar, in the last year. One time it was three of the things by night; the other, it was half a dozen of them by daylight—even so, they seem to have looked much the same; just a kind of red fuzz. They were in the Pacific, though, not over this side."

"Why 'not for the record'?" I asked.

"In both cases there were only two or three witnesses—and it doesn't do a seaman any good to get a reputation for seeing things, you know. The stories just get around professionally, so to speak—among ourselves we aren't quite as skeptical as landsmen: some funny things can still happen at sea, now and then."

"You can't suggest an explanation I can quote?"

"On professional grounds I'd prefer not. I'll just stick to my official entry. But reporting it is a different matter this time. We've a couple of hundred witnesses and more."

"Do you think it'd be worth a search? You've got the spot pinpointed."

He shook his head. "It's deep there—over three thousand fathoms. That's a long way down."

"There wasn't any trace of wreckage in those other cases, either?"

"No. That would have been evidence to warrant an inquiry. But they had no evidence."

We talked a little longer, but I could not get him to put forward any theory. Presently I went away, and wrote up my account. Later, I got through to London, and dictated it to an E.B.C. recorder. It went out on the air the same evening as a filler, just an oddity which was not expected to do more than raise a few eyebrows.

So it was by chance that I was a witness of that early stage—almost the beginning, for I have not been able to find any references to identical phenomena earlier than those two spoken of by the captain. Even now, years later, though I am certain enough in my own mind that this was the beginning, I can still offer no *proof* that it was not an unrelated phenomenon. What the end that will eventually follow this beginning may be, I prefer not to think too closely. I would also prefer not to dream about it, either, if dreams were within my control.

It began so unrecognizably. Had it been more obvious—and yet it is difficult to see what could have been done effectively even if we had recognized the danger. Recognition and prevention don't necessarily go hand in hand. We recognized the potential dangers of atomic fission quickly enough—yet we could do little about them. If we had attacked immediately—well, perhaps. But until the danger was well established we had no means of knowing that we *should* attack—and then it was too late.

However, it does no good to cry over our shortcomings. My purpose is to give as good a brief account as I can of how the present situation arose—and, to begin with, it arose very scrappily . . .

In due course the *Guinevere* docked at Southampton without being treated to any more curious phenomena. We did not expect any more, but the event had been memorable; almost as good, in fact, as having been in a position to say, upon some remote future occasion: "When your grandmother and I were on our honeymoon we saw a sea serpent," though not quite. Still, it was a wonderful honeymoon, I never expect to have a better; and Phyllis said something to much the same effect as we leaned on the rail, watching the bustle below.

"Except," she added, "that I don't see why we shouldn't have one nearly as good, now and then."

So we disembarked, sought our brand-new home in Chelsea, and I turned up at the E.B.C. offices the following Monday morning to discover that *in absentia* I had been rechristened Fireball Watson. This was on account of the correspondence. They handed it to me in a large sheaf, and said that since I had caused it, I had better do something about it. One letter, referring to a recent experience off the Philippines, I identified with fair certainty as being a confirmation of what the captain of the *Guinevere* had told me. One or two others seemed worth following up, too—particularly a rather cagey approach which invited me to meet the writer at La Plume D'Or, where lunch is always worth having.

I kept that appointment a week later. My host turned out to be a

man two or three years older than myself who ordered four glasses
of Tio Pepe, and then opened up by admitting that the name under
which he had written was not his own, and that he was a Flight
Lieutenant, R.A.F.

"It's a bit tricky, you see," he said. "At the moment I am considered to have suffered some kind of hallucination, but if enough
evidence turns up to show that it was *not* a hallucination, then they're
almost certain to make it an official secret. Awkward, you see."

I agreed that it must be.

"Still," he went on, "the thing worries me, and if you're collecting
evidence, I'd like you to have it—though maybe not to make direct
use of it. I mean, I don't want to find myself on the carpet."

I nodded understandingly. He went on:

"It was about three months ago. I was flying one of the regular
patrols, a couple of hundred miles or so east of Formosa—"

"I didn't know we—" I began.

"There are a number of things that don't get publicity, though
they're not particularly secret," he said. "Anyway, there I was. The
radar picked these things up when they were still out of sight behind
me, but coming up fast from the west."

He had decided to investigate, and climbed to intercept. The
radar continued to show the craft on a straight course behind and
above him. He tried to communicate, but couldn't raise them. By the
time he was getting the ceiling of them they were in sight, as three
red spots, quite bright, even by daylight, and coming up fast though
he was doing close to five hundred himself. He tried again to radio
them, but without success. They just kept on coming, steadily over-
taking him.

"Well," he said, "I was there to patrol. I told base that they were
a completely unknown type of craft—if they were craft at all—and
as they wouldn't talk I proposed to have a pip at them. It was either
that, or just let 'em go—in which case I might as well not have been
patrolling at all. Base agreed, kind of cautiously.

"I tried them once more, but they didn't take a damn bit of notice
of either me or my signals. And as they got closer I was doubtful
whether they were craft at all. They were just as you said on the radio
—a pink fuzz, with a deeper red center: might have been miniature

red suns for all I could tell. Anyway, the more I saw of them the less I liked 'em, so I set the guns to radar-control, and let 'em get on ahead.

"I reckoned they must be doing seven hundred or more as they passed me. A second or two later the radar picked up the foremost one, and the guns fired.

"There wasn't any lag. The thing seemed to blow up almost as the guns went off. And, boy, did it blow! It suddenly swelled immensely, turning from red to pink to white, but still with a few red spots here and there—and then my aircraft hit the concussion, and maybe some of the debris too. I lost quite a lot of seconds, and probably had a lot of luck, because when I got sorted out I found that I was coming down fast. Something had carried away three-quarters of my starboard wing, and messed up the tip of the other. So I reckoned it was time to try the ejector, and rather to my surprise it worked."

He paused reflectively. Then he added: "I don't know that it gives you a lot besides confirmation, but there are one or two points. One is that they are capable of traveling a lot faster than those you saw. Another is that, whatever they are, they are highly vulnerable."

And that, as we talked it over in detail, was about all the additional information he did provide—that, and the fact that when they hit they did not disintegrate into sections, but exploded completely, which should, perhaps, have conveyed more than it seemed to at the time.

During the next few weeks several more letters trickled in without adding much, but then it began to look as if the whole affair were going the way of the Loch Ness Monster. What there was came to me because it was generally conceded at E.B.C. that fireball stuff was my pigeon. Several observatories confessed themselves puzzled by detecting small red bodies traveling at high speeds, but were extremely guarded in their statements. None of the newspapers really played it because, in editorial opinion, the whole thing was suspect in being too similar to the flying saucer business, and their readers would prefer more novelty in their sensations. Nevertheless, bits and pieces did slowly accumulate—though it took nearly two years before they acquired serious publicity and attention.

This time it was a flight of thirteen. A radar station in the north of Finland picked them up first, estimating their speed as fifteen hundred miles per hour, and their direction as approximately southwest. In passing the information on they described them simply as "unidentified aircraft." The Swedes picked them up as they crossed their territory, and managed to spot them visually, describing them as small red dots. Norway confirmed, but estimated the speed at under thirteen hundred miles per hour. A Scottish station logged them as traveling at a thousand miles per hour, and just visible to the naked eye. Two stations in Ireland reported them as passing directly overhead, on a line slightly west of southwest. The more southerly station gave their speed as eight hundred and claimed that they were "clearly visible." A weather ship at about 65 degrees North, gave a description which tallied exactly with that of the earlier fireballs, and calculated a speed close to 500 m.p.h. They were not sighted again.

There was a sudden spate of fireball observation after that. Reports came in from so far and wide that it was impossible to do more than sort out the more wildly imaginative and put the rest aside to be considered at more leisure, but I noticed that among them were several accounts of fireballs descending into the sea that tallied well with my own observation—so well, indeed, that I could not be absolutely sure that they did not derive from my own broadcast. All in all, it appeared to be such a muddle of guesswork, tall stories, thirdhand impressions, and thoroughgoing invention that it taught me little. One negative point, however, did strike me—not a single observer claimed to have seen a fireball descend on land. Ancillary to that, not a single one of those descending on water had been observed from the shore: all had been noticed from ships, or from aircraft well out to sea.

For a couple of weeks reports of sightings in groups large or small continued to pour in. The skeptics were weakening; only the most obstinate still maintained that they were hallucinations. Nevertheless, we learned nothing more about them than we had known before. No pictures. So often it seemed to be a case of the things you see when you don't have a gun. But then a flock of them came up against a fellow who did have a gun—literally.

The fellow in this case happened to be the U.S.S. *Tuskegee,* a carrier. The message from Curaçao that a flight of eight fireballs was headed directly toward her reached her when she was lying off San Juan, Puerto Rico. The captain breathed a short hope that they would commit a violation of the territory, and made his preparations. The fireballs, true to type, kept on in a dead straight line which would bring them across the island, and almost over the ship herself. The captain watched their approach on his radar with great satisfaction. He waited until the technical violation was indisputable. Then he gave the word to release six guided missiles at three-second intervals, and went on deck to watch, against the darkling sky.

Through his glasses he watched six of the red dots change as they burst, one after another, into big white puffs.

"Well, that's settled them," he observed, complacently. "Now it's going to be mighty interesting to see who beefs," he added, as he watched the two remaining red dots dwindle away to the northward.

But the days passed, and nobody beefed. Nor was there any decrease in the number of fireball reports.

For most people such a policy of masterly silence pointed only one way, and they began to consider the responsibility as good as proved.

In the course of the following week, two more fireballs that had been incautious enough to pass within range of the experimental station at Woomera paid for that temerity, and three others were exploded by a ship off Kodiak after flying across Alaska.

Washington, in a note of protest to Moscow regarding repeated territorial violations, ended by observing that in several cases where drastic action had been taken it regretted the distress that must have been caused to the relatives of the crews aboard the craft, but that responsibility lay at the door not of those who dealt with the craft, but with those who sent them out under orders which transgressed international agreements.

The Kremlin, after a few days of gestation, produced a rejection of the protest. It proclaimed itself unimpressed by the tactics of attributing one's own crime to another, and went on to state that its own weapons, recently developed by Russian scientists for the defense of peace, had now destroyed more than twenty of these craft over Soviet territory, and would, without hesitation, give the same treatment to any others detected in their work of espionage . . .

The situation thus remained unresolved. The non-Russian world was, by and large, divided sharply into two classes—those who believed every Russian pronouncement, and those who believed none. For the first class no question arose; their faith was firm. For the second, interpretation was less easy. Was one to deduce, for instance, that the whole thing was a lie? Or merely that when the Russians claimed to have accounted for twenty fireballs, they had only, in fact, exploded five or so?

An uneasy situation, constantly punctuated by an exchange of notes, drew out over months. Fireballs were undoubtedly more numerous than they had been, but just how much more numerous, or more active, or more frequently reported was difficult to assess. Every now and then a few more were destroyed in various parts of the world, and from time to time, too, it would be announced that numbers of capitalistic fireballs had been effectively shown the penalties that awaited those who conducted espionage upon the territory of the only true People's Democracy.

Public interest must feed to keep alive; and as novelty waned, an era of explaining-away set it.

Nevertheless, in Admiralty and Air Force Headquarters all over the world these notes and reports came together. Courses were plotted on charts. Gradually a pattern of a kind began to emerge.

At E.B.C. I was still regarded as the natural sifting place for anything to do with fireballs, and although the subject was dead mutton for the moment, I kept up my files in case it should revive. Meanwhile, I contributed in a small way to the building up of the bigger picture by passing along to the authorities such snippets of information as I thought might interest them.

In due course I found myself invited to the Admiralty to be shown some of the results.

It was a Captain Winters who welcomed me there, explaining that while what I should be shown was not exactly an official secret, it was preferred that I should not make public use of it yet. When I had agreed to that, he started to bring out maps and charts.

The first one was a map of the world hatched over with fine lines, each numbered and dated in minute figures. At first glance it looked as if a spider's web had been applied to it; and, here and there, there were clusters of little red dots, looking much like the monkey spiders who had spun it.

Captain Winters picked up a magnifying glass and held it over the the area southeast of the Azores.

"There's your first contribution," he told me.

Looking through it, I presently distinguished one red dot with a figure 5 against it, and the date and time when Phyllis and I had leaned over the *Guinevere*'s rail watching the fireballs vanish in steam. There were quite a number of other red dots in the area, each labeled, and more of them were strung out to the northeast.

"Each of these dots represents the descent of a fireball?" I asked.

"One or more," he told me. "The lines, of course, are only for those on which we have had good enough information to plot the course. What do you think of it?"

"Well," I told him, "my first reaction is to realize that there must have been a devil of a lot more of them than I ever imagined. The second is to wonder why in thunder they should group in spots, like that."

"Ah!" he said. "Now stand back from the map a bit. Narrow your eyes, and get a light and shade impression."

I did, and saw what he meant.

"Areas of concentration," I said.

He nodded. "Five main ones, and a number of lesser. A dense one to the southwest of Cuba; another, six hundred miles south of the Cocos Islands; heavy concentrations off the Philippines, Japan, and the Aleutians. I'm not going to pretend that the proportions of density are right—in fact, I'm pretty sure that they are not. For instance, you can see a number of courses converging toward an area northeast of the Falklands, but only three red dots there. It very likely means simply that there are precious few people around those parts to observe them. Anything else strike you?"

I shook my head, not seeing what he was getting at. He produced a bathymetric chart, and laid it beside the first. I looked at it.

"All the concentrations are in deep water areas?" I suggested.

"Exactly. There aren't many reports of descents where the depth is less than four thousand fathoms, and none at all where it is less than two thousand."

I thought that over, without getting anywhere.

"So—just what?" I inquired.

"Exactly," he said again. "So what?"

We contemplated the proposition awhile.

"All descents," he observed. "No reports of any coming up."

He brought out maps on a large scale of the various main areas. After we had studied them a bit I asked: "Have you any idea at all what all this means—or wouldn't you tell me if you had?"

"On the first part of that, we have only a number of theories, all unsatisfactory for one reason or another, so the second doesn't really arise."

"What about the Russians?"

"Nothing to do with them. As a matter of fact, they're a lot more worried about it than we are. Suspicion of capitalists being part of their mother's milk, they simply can't shake themselves clear of the idea that we must be at the bottom of it somehow, and they just can't figure out, either, what the game can possibly be. But what both we and they are perfectly satisfied about is that the things are not natural phenomena, nor are they random."

"And you'd know if it were any other country pulling it?"

"Bound to—not a doubt of it."

We considered the charts again in silence.

"The other obvious question is, of course, what do they seem to be doing?"

"Yes," he said.

"Meaning, no clue?"

"They come," he said. "Maybe they go. But certainly they come. That's about all."

I looked down at the maps, the crisscrossing lines, and the red-dotted areas.

"Are you doing anything about it? Or shouldn't I ask?"

"Oh, that's why you're here. I was coming round to that," he told me. "We're going to try an inspection. Just at the moment it is not considered to be a matter for a direct broadcast, nor even for publica-

tion, but there ought to be a record of it, and we shall need one ourselves. So if your people happened to feel interested enough to send
you along with some gear for the job . . ."

"Where would it be?" I inquired.

He circled his finger round an area.

"Er—my wife has a passionate devotion to tropical sunshine, the
West Indian kind in particular," I said.

"Well, I seem to remember that your wife has written some pretty
good documentary scripts," he remarked.

"And it's the kind of thing E.B.C. might be very sorry about afterwards if they'd missed it," I reflected.

Not until we had made our last call and were well out of sight of
land were we allowed to see the large object which rested in a specially constructed cradle aft. When the Lieutenant Commander in
charge of technical operations ordered the shrouding tarpaulin to be
removed, there was quite an unveiling ceremony. But the mystery
revealed was something of an anticlimax: it was simply a sphere of
metal some ten feet in diameter. In various parts of it were set
circular, porthole-like windows; at the top it swelled into a protuberance which formed a massive lug. The Lieutenant Commander, after
regarding it a while with the eye of a proud mother, addressed us in
the manner of a lecturer.

"This instrument that you now see," he said, impressively, "is what
we call the Bathyscope." He allowed an interval for appreciation.

"Didn't Beebe—?" I whispered to Phyllis.

"No," she said. "That was the bathysphere."

"Oh," I said.

"It has been constructed," he went on, "to resist a pressure approaching two tons to the square inch, giving it a theoretical floor
of fifteen hundred fathoms. In practice we do not propose to use it at
a greater depth than twelve hundred fathoms, thus providing for a
safety factor of something over six hundred pounds to the square
inch. Even at this it will considerably surpass the achievements of
Dr. Beebe who descended a little over five hundred fathoms, and
Barton who reached a depth of seven hundred and fifty fathoms . . ."

He continued in this vein for a time, leaving me somewhat behind. When he seemed to have run down for a bit I said to Phyllis,

"I can't think in all these fathoms. What is it in God's feet?"

She consulted her notes.

"The depth they intend to go to is seven thousand, two hundred feet; the depth they *could* go to is nine thousand feet."

"Either of them sounds an awful lot of feet," I said.

Phyllis is, in some ways, more precise and practical.

"Seven thousand, two hundred feet is just over a mile and a third," she informed me. "The pressure will be a little more than a ton and a third."

"That's my continuity-girl," I said. "I don't know where I'd be without you." I looked at the bathyscope. "All the same—" I added doubtfully.

"What?" she asked.

"Well, that chap at the Admiralty, Winters; he was talking in terms of four or five tons pressure—meaning, presumably, four or five miles down." I turned to the Lieutenant Commander. "How deep is it where we're bound for?" I asked him.

"It's an area called the Cayman Trench, between Jamaica and Cuba," he said. "In parts it reaches nearly four thousand."

"But—" I began, frowning.

"Fathoms, dear," said Phyllis. "Getting on for twenty-four thousand feet."

"Oh," I said. "That'll be—er—something like four and a half miles?"

"Yes," she said.

"Oh," I said, again.

He returned to his public address manner.

"That," he told the assembled crowd of us, "is the present limit of our ability to make direct visual observations. However—" He paused to make a gesture somewhat in the manner of a conjuror towards a party of sailors, and watched while they pulled the tarpaulin from another, similar, but smaller sphere. "—here," he continued, "we have a new instrument with which we hope to be able to make observations at something like twice the depth attainable by the bathyscope, perhaps even more. It is entirely automatic. In addition to registering pressures, temperature, currents, and so on, and transmitting the readings to the surface, it is equipped with five small television cameras, four of them giving all round horizontal coverage, and one transmitting the view vertically beneath the sphere."

"This instrument," continued another voice in good imitation of his own, "we call the telebath."

Facetiousness could not put a man like the Commander off his stroke. He continued his lecture. But the instrument had been christened, and the telebath it remained.

The three days after we reached our position were occupied with tests and adjustments of both the instruments. In one test Phyllis and I were allowed to make a dive of three hundred feet or so, cramped up in the bathyscope, "just to get the feel of it." It gave us no envy of anyone making a deeper dive. Then, with all the gear fully checked, the real descent was announced for the morning of the fourth day.

Soon after sunrise we were clustering round the bathyscope where it rested in its cradle. The two naval technicians, Wiseman and Trant, who were to make the descent, wriggled themselves in through the narrow hole that was the entrance. The warm clothing they would need in the depths was handed in after them, for they could never have squeezed in wearing it. Then followed the packets of food and the vacuum flasks of hot drinks. They made their final checks, gave their okays. The circular entrance-plug was swung over by the hoist, screwed gradually down into its seating, and bolted fast. The bathyscope was hoisted outboard, and hung there, swinging slightly. One of the men inside switched on his hand television camera, and we ourselves, as seen from within the instrument, appeared on the screen.

"Okay," said a voice from the loudspeaker, "lower away now."

The winch began to turn. The bathyscope descended, and the water lapped at it. Presently it had disappeared from sight beneath the surface.

The descent was a long business which I do not propose to describe in detail. Frankly, as seen on the screen in the ship, it was a pretty boring affair to the noninitiate. Life in the sea appears to exist in fairly well-defined levels. In the better-inhabited strata the water is full of plankton which behaves like a continuous dust storm and obscures everything but creatures that approach very closely. At other levels where there is no plankton for food, there are consequently few fish. In addition to the tediousness of very limited views or dark emptiness, continuous attention to a screen that is linked with a slightly swinging and twisting camera has a dizzying effect. Both Phyllis and I spent much of the time during the descent with our eyes shut, relying on the loud-speaking telephone to draw our attention to anything interesting. Occasionally we slipped on deck for a cigarette.

There could scarcely have been a better day for the job. The sun beat fiercely down on decks that were occasionally sluiced with water to cool them off. The ensign hung limp, barely stirring. The sea stretched out flat to meet the dome of the sky which showed only one low bank of cloud, to the north, over Cuba, perhaps. There was scarcely a sound, either, except for the muffled voice of the loud-speaker in the mess, the quiet drone of the winch, and from time to time the voice of a deck hand calling the tally of fathoms.

The group sitting in the mess scarcely spoke; they left that to the men now far below.

At intervals, the Commander would ask: "All in order, below there?"

And, simultaneously two voices would reply: "Aye, aye, sir!"

Once a voice inquired: "Did Beebe have an electrically heated suit?"

Nobody seemed to know.

"I take my hat off to him if he didn't," said the voice.

The Commander was keeping a sharp eye on the dials as well as watching the screen.

"Half-mile coming up. Check," he said.

The voice from below counted:

"Four thirty-eight . . . Four thirty-nine . . . *Now!* Half mile, sir."

The winch went on turning. There wasn't much to see. Occasional glimpses of schools of fish hurrying off into the murk. A voice complained: "Sure as I get the camera to one window a damn great fish comes and looks in at another."

"Five hundred fathoms. You're passing Beebe now," said the Commander.

"Bye-bye, Beebe," said the voice. "But it goes on looking much the same."

Presently the same voice said: "More life around just here. Plenty of squid, large and small. You can probably see 'em. There's something out this way, keeping on the edge of the light. A big thing. I can't quite—might be a giant squid—no! my God! It *can't* be a whale! Not down here!"

"Improbable, but not impossible," said the Commander.

"Well, in that case—oh, it's sheered off now, anyway. Gosh! We mammals do get around a bit, don't we?"

In due course the moment arrived when the Commander announced: "Passing Barton now," and then added with an unexpected change of manner. "From now on it's all yours, boys. Sure you're quite happy there? If you're not perfectly satisfied you've only to say."

"That's all right, sir. Everything functioning okay. We'll go on."

Up on deck the winch droned steadily.

"One mile coming up," announced the Commander. When that had been checked he asked, "How are you feeling now?"

"What's the weather like up there?" asked a voice.

"Holding well. Flat calm. No swell."

The two down below conferred.

"We'll go on, sir. Could wait weeks for conditions like this again."

"All right—if you're both sure."

"We are, sir."

"Very good. About three hundred fathoms more to go then."

There was an interval. Then: "Dead," remarked the voice from below. "All black and dead now. Not a thing to be seen. Funny thing the way these levels are quite separate. Ah, now we can begin to see something below . . . Squids again . . . luminous fish . . . Small shoal there, see? . . . There's . . . Gosh! Gosh—"

He broke off, and simultaneously a nightmare fishy horror gaped at us from the screen.

"One of nature's careless moments," he remarked.

He went on talking, and the camera continued to give us glimpses of unbelievable monstrosities, large and small.

Presently the Commander announced: "Stopping you now. Twelve hundred fathoms." He picked up the telephone and spoke to the deck. The winch slowed and then ceased to turn.

"That's all, boys," he said.

"Huh," said the voice from below, after a pause. "Well, whatever it was we came here to find, we've not found it."

The Commander's face was expressionless. Whether he had expected tangible results or not I couldn't tell. I imagined not. In fact, I wondered if any of us there really had. After all, these centers of activity were all Deeps. And from that it would seem to follow that the reason must lie at the bottom. The echogram gave the bottom hereabouts as still three miles or so below where the two men now dangled . . .

"Hullo, there, bathyscope," said the Commander. "We're going to start you up now. Ready?"

"Aye, aye, sir! All set," said the two voices.

The Commander picked up his telephone.

"Haul away there!"

We could hear the winch start, and slowly gather speed.

"On your way now. All okay?"

"All correct, sir."

There was an interval without talk for ten minutes or more. Then a voice said: "There's something out there. Something big—can't see it properly. Keeps just on the fringe of the light. Can't be that whale again—not at this depth. Try to show you."

The picture on the screen switched and then steadied. We could see the light-rays streaming out through the water, and the brilliant speckles of small organisms caught in the beam. At the very limits there was a suspicion of a faintly lighter patch. It was hard to be sure of it.

"Seems to be circling us. We're spinning a bit, too, I think. I'll try —ah, got a bit better glimpse of it then. It's not the whale, anyway. There, see it now?"

This time we could undoubtedly make out a lighter patch. It was roughly oval, but indistinct, but there was nothing to give it scale.

"H'm," said the voice from below. "That's certainly a new one. Could be a fish—or maybe something else kind of turtle-shaped. Monstrous-sized brute, anyway. Circling a bit closer now, but I still can't make out any details. Keeping pace with us."

Again the camera showed us a glimpse of the thing as it passed one of the bathyscope's ports, but we were little wiser; the definition was too poor for us to be sure of anything about it.

"It's going up now. Rising faster than we are. Getting beyond our angle of view. Ought to be a window in the top of this thing . . . Lost it now. Gone somewhere up above us. Maybe it'll—"

The voice cut off dead. Simultaneously, there was a brief, vivid flash on the screen, and it, too, went dead. The sound of the winch outside altered as it speeded up.

We sat looking at one another without speaking. Phyllis's hand sought mine, and tightened on it.

The Commander started to stretch his hand towards the telephone, changed his mind, and went out without a word. Presently the winch speeded up still more.

It takes quite a time to reel in more than a mile of heavy cable. The party in the mess dispersed awkwardly. Phyllis and I went up into the bows and sat there without talking much.

After what seemed a very long wait the winch slowed down. By common consent we got up, and moved aft together.

At last, the end came up. We all, I suppose, expected to see the end of the wire rope unraveled, with the strands splayed out, brush-like.

They were not. They were melted together. Both the main and the communication cables ended in a blob of fused metal.

We all stared at them, dumbfounded.

In the evening the Captain read the service, and three volleys were fired over the spot.

The weather held, and the glass was steady. At noon the next day the Commander assembled us in the mess. He looked ill, and very tired. He said, briefly, and unemotionally: "My orders are to proceed with the investigation, using our automatic instrument. If our arrangements and tests can be completed in time, and providing the weather remains favorable, we shall conduct the operation tomorrow morning, commencing as soon after dawn as possible. I am instructed to lower the instrument to the point of destruction, so there will be no other opportunity for observation."

The arrangement in the mess the following morning was different from that on the former occasion. We sat facing a bank of five television screens, four for the quadrants about the instrument, and one viewing vertically beneath it. There was also a movie camera photographing all five screens simultaneously for the record.

Again we watched the descent through the ocean layers, but this time instead of a commentary we had an astonishing assortment of chirrupings, raspings, and gruntings picked up by externally-mounted microphones. The deep sea is, in its lower inhabited strata, it seems, a place of hideous cacophony. It was something of a relief when at about three-quarters of a mile down silence fell, and somebody muttered: "Huh! Said those mikes'd never take the pressure."

The display went on. Squids sliding upwards past the cameras, shoals of fish darting nervously away, other fish attracted by curiosity —monstrosities, grotesques, huge monsters dimly seen. On and on. A mile down, a mile and a half, two miles, two and a half . . . And then, at about that point, something came into view which quickened all attention on the screens. A large, uncertain, oval shape at the extreme of visibility that moved from screen to screen as it circled round the descending instrument. For three or four minutes it continued to show on one screen or another, but always tantalizingly ill-defined, and never quite well enough illuminated for one to be certain even of its shape. Then, gradually, it drifted towards the upper edges of the screen, and presently it was left behind.

Half a minute later all the screens went blank . . .

Why not praise one's wife? Phyllis can write a thundering good feature script—and this was one of her best. It was too bad that it was not received with the immediate enthusiasm it deserved.

When it was finished, we sent it round to the Admiralty for checking. A week later we were asked to call. It was Captain Winters who received us. He congratulated Phyllis on the script, as well he might, even if he had not been so taken with her as he so obviously was. Once we were settled in our chairs, however, he shook his head regretfully.

"Nevertheless," he said, "I'm afraid I'm going to have to ask you to hold it up for a while."

Phyllis looked understandably disappointed; she had worked hard on that script. Not just for cash, either. She had tried to make it a tribute to the two men, Wiseman and Trant, who had vanished with the bathyscope. She looked down at her toes.

"I'm sorry," said the Captain, "but I did warn your husband that it wouldn't be for immediate release."

Phyllis looked up at him. "Why?" she asked.

That was something I was equally anxious to know about. My own recordings of the preparations, of the brief descent we had both made in the bathyscope, and of various aspects that were not on the official tape record of the dive, had been put into cold storage, too.

"I'll explain what I can. We certainly owe you that," agreed Captain Winters. He sat down and leaned forward, elbows on knees, fingers interlaced between them, and looked at us both in turn.

"The crux of the thing—and of course you will both of you have realized that long ago—is those fused cables," he said. "Imagination staggers a bit at the thought of a creature capable of snapping through steel hawsers—all the same, it might just conceivably admit the possibility. When, however, it comes up against the suggestion that there is a creature capable of cutting through them like an oxyacetylene flame, it recoils. It recoils, and definitely rejects.

"Both of you saw what had happened to those cables, and I think you must agree that their condition opens a whole new aspect. A thing like that is not just a hazard of deep-sea diving—and we want to know more about just what kind of hazard it is before we give a release on it."

We talked it over for a little time. The Captain was apologetic and understanding, but he had his orders.

"Honestly, Captain Winters—and off the record, if you like— have you any idea what can have done it?"

He shook his head. "On or off the record, Mrs. Watson, I can think of no explanation that approaches being possible—and, though this is not for publication, I doubt whether anyone else in the Service has an idea, either."

And so, with the affair left in that unsatisfactory state, we parted.

The prohibition, however, lasted a shorter time than we expected. A week later, just as we were sitting down to dinner, he telephoned. Phyllis took the call.

"Oh, hullo, Mrs. Watson. I'm glad it's you. I have some good news for you," Captain Winters' voice said. "I've just been talking to your E.B.C. people, and giving them the okay, so far as we are concerned, to go ahead with that feature of yours, and the whole story."

Phyllis thanked him for the news. "But what's happened?" she added.

"The story's broken, anyway. You'll hear it on the nine o'clock news tonight, and see it in tomorrow's papers. In the circumstances it seemed to me that you ought to be free to take your chance as soon as possible. Their Lordships saw the point—in fact, they would like your feature to go out as soon as possible. So there it is. And the best of luck to you."

Phyllis thanked him again, and hung up. "Now what do you suppose can have happened?" she inquired.

We had to wait until nine o'clock to find that out. The notice on the news was scanty, but sufficient from our point of view. It reported simply that an American naval unit conducting research into deep-sea conditions somewhere off the Philippines had suffered the loss of a depth chamber, with its crew of two men.

Almost immediately afterwards E.B.C. came through on the telephone with a lot of talk about priorities, and altered program schedules, and available cast.

Audio-assessment told us later that the feature had rated an excellent reception figure. Coming so soon after the American announcement, we hit the peak of popular interest. Their Lordships were pleased too. It gave them the opportunity of showing that they did not always have to follow the American lead—though I still think there was no need to make the U.S. a present of the first publicity. Anyway, in view of what has followed, I don't suppose it greatly matters.

Phyllis rewrote a part of the script, making greater play with the fusing of the cables than before. A flood of correspondence came in, but when all the tentative explanations and suggestions had been winnowed none of us was any wiser than before.

Perhaps it was scarcely to be expected that we should be. Our listeners had not even seen the maps, and at this stage it had not occurred to the general public that there could be any link between the diving catastrophes and the somewhat *démodé* topic of fireballs.

But if, as it seemed, the Royal Navy was disposed simply to sit still for a time and ponder the problem theoretically, the U.S. Navy was not. Deviously we heard that they were preparing to send a second expedition to the same spot where their loss had occurred. We promptly applied to be included, and were refused. How many other people applied, I don't know, but enough for them to allocate a second small craft. We couldn't get a place on that either. All space was reserved for their own correspondents and commentators who would cover for Europe, too.

Well, it was their own show. They were paying for it. All the same, I'm sorry we missed it because, though we did think it likely they would lose their apparatus again, it never crossed our minds that they might lose their ship as well . . .

About a week after it happened one of the N.B.C. men who had been covering it came over. We more or less shanghaied him for lunch and the personal dope.

"Never saw anything like it," he said, "but if ever lightning were to strike upwards from the sea, I guess that'd be about the way it'd look. The sparks ran around all over the ship for a few seconds. Then she blew up."

"I never heard of anything like that," Phyllis said.

"It certainly isn't on the record," he agreed. "But there has to be a first time."

"Not very satisfactory," Phyllis commented.

He looked us over. "Seeing that you two were on that British fishing party, do I take it you know why we were there?"

"I'd not be surprised," I told him.

He nodded. "Well, look," he said, "I'm told it isn't possible to persuade a high charge, say a few million volts to run up an uninsulated hawser in sea water, so I must accept that; it's not my department. All I say is that *if* it were possible, then I guess the effect might be quite a bit like what we saw."

"There'd be insulated cables, too—to the cameras, microphones, thermometers and things," Phyllis said.

"Sure. And there was an insulated cable relaying the TV to our ship; but it couldn't carry that charge, and burned out—which was a darned good thing for us. That would make it look to me like it followed the main hawser—if it didn't so happen that the physics boys won't have it."

"They've no alternative suggestions?" I asked.

"Oh, sure. Several. Some of them could sound quite convincing —to a fellow who hadn't seen it happen."

"If you are right, this is very queer indeed," Phyllis said, reflectively.

The N.B.C. man looked at her. "A nice British understatement —but it's queer enough, even without me," he said, modestly. "However they explain this away, the physics boys are still stumped on those fused cables, because, whatever this may be, those cable severances *couldn't* have been accidental."

"On the other hand, all that way down, all that pressure. . . ?" Phyllis said.

He shook his head. "I'm making no guesses. I'd want more data than we've got, even for that. Could be we'll get it before long."

We looked questioning.

He lowered his voice. "Seeing you're in this too, but strictly under your hats, they've got a couple more probes lined up right now. But no publicity this time—the last lot had a nasty taste."

"Where?" we asked, simultaneously.

"One off the Aleutians, some place. The other in a deep spot in the Guatemala Basin. What're your folks doing?"

"We don't know," we said honestly.

He shook his head. "Always kinda close, your people," he said, sympathetically.

And close they remained. During the next few weeks we kept our ears uselessly wide open for news of either of the two new investigations, but it was not until the N.B.C. man was passing through London again a month later that we learned anything. We asked him what had happened.

He frowned. "Off Guatemala they drew a blank," he said. "The ship south of the Aleutians was transmitting by radio while the dive was in progress. It cut out suddenly. She's reported as lost with all hands."

Official cognizance of these matters remained underground—if that can be considered an acceptable term for their deep-sea investigations. Every now and then we would catch a rumor which showed that the interest had not been dropped, and from time to time a few apparently isolated items could, when put in conjunction, be made to give hints. Our naval contacts preserved an amiable evasiveness, and we found that our opposite numbers across the Atlantic were doing little better with their naval sources. The consoling aspect was that had they been making any progress we should most likely have heard of it, so we took silence to mean that they were stalled.

Public interest in fireballs was down to zero, and few people troubled to send in reports of them any more. I still kept my files going though they were not so unrepresentative that I could not tell how far the apparently low incidence was real.

As far as I knew, the two phenomena had never so far been publicly connected, and presently both were allowed to lapse unexplained, like any silly-season sensation.

In the course of the next three years we ourselves lost interest almost to vanishing point. Other matters occupied us. There was the birth of our son, William—and his death, eighteen months later. To help Phyllis to get over that I wangled myself a traveling-correspondent series, sold the house, and for a time we roved.

In theory, the appointment was simply mine; in practice, most of the gloss and finish on the scripts which pleased the E.B.C., were Phyllis's, and most of the time when she wasn't dolling up my stuff she was working on scripts of her own. When we came back home, it was with enhanced prestige, a lot of material to work up, and a feeling of being set on a smooth, steady course.

Almost immediately, the Americans lost a cruiser off the Marianas.

The report was scanty, an Agency message, slightly blown up locally; but there was a something about it—just a kind of feeling. When Phyllis read it in the newspaper, it struck her, too. She pulled out the atlas, and considered the Marianas.

"It's pretty deep round three sides of them," she said.

"That report's not handled quite the regular way. I can't exactly put my finger on it. But the approach is a bit off the line, somehow," I agreed.

"We'd better try the grapevine," Phyllis decided.

We did, without result. It wasn't that our sources were holding out on us; there seemed to be a blackout somewhere. We got no further than the official handout: this cruiser, the *Keweenaw,* had, in fair weather, simply gone down. Twenty survivors had been picked up. There would be an official inquiry.

Possibly there was: I never heard the outcome. The incident was somehow overlayed by the inexplicable sinking of a Russian ship, engaged on some task never specified, to eastward of the Kurils, that string of islands to the south of Kamchatka. Since it was axiomatic that any Soviet misadventure must be attributable in some way to capitalist jackals or reactionary fascist hyenas, this affair assumed an importance which quite eclipsed the American loss, and the acrimonious innuendoes went on echoing for some time. In the noise of vituperation the mysterious disappearance of the survey vessel *Utskarpen,* in the Southern Ocean, went almost unnoticed outside her native Norway.

Several others followed, but I no longer have my records to give me the details. It is my impression that quite half a dozen vessels, all seemingly engaged in ocean research in one way or another had vanished before the Americans suffered again, off the Philippines. This time they lost a destroyer, and with it, their patience.

The ingenuous announcement that since the water about Bikini was too shallow for a contemplated series of deep-water atomic-bomb tests the locale of these experiments would be shifted west-wards by a little matter of a thousand miles or so, may possibly have deceived a portion of the general public, but in radio and newspaper circles it touched off a scramble for assignments.

Phyllis and I had better standing now, and we were lucky, too. We flew out there, and a few days later we formed part of the complement of a number of ships lying at a strategic distance from the point where the *Keweenaw* had gone down off the Marianas.

I can't tell you what that specially designed depth bomb looked like, for we never saw it. All we were allowed to see was a raft supporting a kind of semispherical, metal hut which contained the bomb itself, and all we were told was that it was much like one of the more regular types of atomic bomb, but with a massive casing that would resist the pressure at five miles deep, if necessary.

At first light on the day of the test a tug took the raft in tow, and chugged away over the horizon with it. From then on we had to observe by means of unmanned television cameras mounted on floats. In this way we saw the tug cast off the raft, and put on full speed. Then there was an interval while the tug hurried out of harm's way and the raft pursued a calculated drift towards the exact spot where the *Keweenaw* had disappeared. The hiatus lasted for some three hours, with the raft looking motionless on the screens. Then a voice through the loudspeakers told us that the release would take place in approximately thirty minutes. It continued to remind us at intervals until the time was short enough for it to start counting in reverse, slowly and calmly. There was a complete hush as we stared at the screens and listened to the voice: "—three—two—one —*NOW!*"

On the last word a rocket sprang from the raft, trailing red smoke as it climbed.

"Bomb away!" said the voice.

We waited.

For a long time, as it seemed, everything was intensely still. Around the vision screens no one spoke. Every eye was on one or another of the frames which showed the raft calmly afloat on the blue, sunlit water. There was no sign that anything had occurred there, save the plume of red smoke drifting slowly away. For the eye and the ear there was utter serenity; for the feelings, a sense that the whole world held its breath.

Then it came. The placid surface of the sea suddenly belched into a vast white cloud which spread, and boiled as it writhed upwards. A tremor passed through the ship.

We left the screens, and rushed to the ship's side. Already the cloud was above our horizon. It still writhed and convolved upon itself in a fashion that was somehow obscene as it climbed monstrously up the sky. Only then did the sound reach us, in a buffeting roar. Much later, amazingly delayed, we saw the dark line which was the first wave of turbulent water rushing toward us.

That night we shared a dinner table with Mallarby of *The Tidings* and Bennell of *The Senate*. This was Phyllis's show, and she had them more or less where she wanted them between the entree and the roast. They argued a while along familiar lines, but after a while the name Bocker began to crop up with increasing frequency and some acrimony. Apparently this Bocker had some theory about deep-sea disturbances which had not come our way, and did not seem to be held in great repute by either party.

Phyllis was on it like a hawk. One would never have guessed that she was utterly in the dark, from the judicial way she said: "Surely the Bocker line can't be altogether dismissed?" frowning a little as she spoke.

It worked. In a little time we were adequately briefed on the Bocker view, and without either of them guessing that as far as we were concerned he had come into it for the first time.

The name of Alastair Bocker was not, of course, entirely unknown to us: it was that of an eminent geographer, a name customarily followed by several groups of initials. However, the information on him that Phyllis now prompted forth was something quite new to us. When reordered and assembled it amounted to this: Almost a year earlier Bocker had presented a memorandum to the Admiralty in London. Because he was Bocker it succeeded in getting itself read at some quite important levels although the gist of its argument was as follows: The fused cables and electrification of certain ships must be regarded as indisputable evidence of intelligence at work in certain deeper parts of the oceans.

Conditions, such as pressure, temperature, perpetual darkness, etc., in those regions made it inconceivable that any intelligent form of life could have evolved there—and this statement he backed with several convincing arguments.

It was to be assumed that no nation was capable of constructing mechanisms that could operate at such depths as indicated by the evidence, nor would they have any purpose in attempting to do so.

But, if the intelligence in the depths were not indigenous, then it must have come from elsewhere. Also, it must be embodied in some form able to withstand a pressure of tons to the square inch— two tons certainly from present evidence, probably five or six tons, even seven tons if it was capable of existing in the very deepest Deeps. Now, was there anywhere else on Earth where a mobile form could find conditions of such pressure to evolve in? Clearly, there was not.

Very well, then if it could not have evolved on Earth, it must have evolved somewhere else—say, on a large planet where the pressures were normally very high. If so, how did it cross space and arrive here?

Bocker then recalled attention to the fireballs which had aroused so much speculation a few years ago, and were still occasionally to be seen. None of these had been known to descend on land; none, indeed, had been known to descend anywhere but in areas of very deep water. Moreover, such of them as had been struck by missiles had exploded with such violence as to suggest that they had been retaining a very high degree of pressure.

It was significant, also, that these fireball globes invariably sought the only regions of the Earth in which high-pressure conditions compatible with movement were available.

Therefore, Bocker deduced, we were in the process, while almost unaware of it, of undergoing a species of interplanetary immigration. If he were to be asked the source of it, he would point to Jupiter as being most likely to fulfill the conditions of pressure.

His memorandum had concluded with the observation that such an incursion need not necessarily be regarded as hostile. It seemed to him that the interests of a type of creation which existed at fifteen pounds to the square inch were unlikely to overlap seriously with those of a form which required several tons per square inch. He advocated, therefore, that the greatest efforts should be made to develop some means of making a sympathetic approach to the new dwellers in our depths, with the aim of facilitating an exchange of science, using the word in its widest sense.

The views expressed by Their Lordships upon these elucidations and suggestions are not publicly recorded. It is known, however, that no long interval passed before Bocker withdrew his memorandum from their unsympathetic desks, and shortly afterwards presented it for the personal consideration of the Editor of *The Tidings.* Undoubtedly *The Tidings,* in returning it to him, expressed itself with its usual tact. It was only for the benefit of his professional brethren that the Editor remarked: "This newspaper has managed to exist for more than one hundred years without a comic strip, and I see no reason to break that tradition now."

In due course, the memorandum appeared in front of the Editor of *The Senate,* who glanced at it, called for a synopsis, lifted his eyebrows, and dictated an urbane regret.

Subsequently it ceased to circulate, and was known only by word of mouth within a small circle.

"The best you can say of it," said Mallarby, "is that he does include more factors than anyone else has—and that anything that includes even most of the factors is bound to be fantastic. We may decry it but, for all that, until something better turns up, it's the best we have."

"That's true," said Bennell. "But whatever the top naval men may think about Bocker, it is clear enough that they too must have been assuming for some time that there *is* something intelligent down there. You don't design and make a special bomb like that all in five minutes, you know. Anyway, whether the Bocker theory is sheer hot-air or not, he's lost his main point. This bomb was not the amiable and sympathetic approach that he advocated."

Mallarby paused, and shook his head. "I've met Bocker several times. He's a civilized, liberal-minded man—with the usual trouble of liberal-minded men; that they think others are, too. He has an interested, inquiring mind. He has never grasped that the average mind when it encounters something new is scared, and says: "Better smash it, or suppress it, quick." Well, he's just had another demonstration of the average mind at work.' "

"But," Bennell objected, "if, as you say, it is officially believed that these ship losses have been caused by an intelligence, then there's something to be scared about, and you *can't* put today's affair down as nothing stronger than retaliation."

Mallarby shook his head again. "My dear Bennell, I not only can, but I do. Suppose, now, that something were to come dangling down to us on a rope out of space; and suppose that that thing was emitting rays on a wave length that acutely discomforted us, perhaps even caused us physical pain. What should we do? I suggest that the first thing we should do would be to snip the rope, and put it out of action. Then we should examine the strange object and find out what we could about it. And if more of the same followed, we should forthwith take what steps we could to discourage them. This might be done simply in the spirit of ending a nuisance, or it might be done with some animosity, and regarded as—retaliation. Now, would it be we, or the thing above, that was to blame?

"It is difficult to imagine any kind of intelligence that would not resent what we've just done. If this were the only Deep where trouble has occurred, there might well be no intelligence left to resent it— but this *isn't* the only place, as you know; not by any means. So, what form that very natural resentment will take remains for us to see."

"You think there really will be some kind of response, then?" Phyllis asked.

He shrugged. "To take up my analogy again: suppose that some violently destructive agency were to descend from space upon one of our cities. What should we do?"

"Well, what *could* we do?" asked Phyllis, reasonably enough.

"We could turn the backroom boys on to it. And if it happened a few times more, we should soon be giving the backroom boys full priorities. No," he shook his head, "no, I'm afraid Bocker's idea of fraternization never had the chance of a flea in a furnace."

That was, I think, very likely as true as Mallarby made it sound; but if there ever had been any chance at all, it was gone by the time we reached home. Somehow, and apparently overnight, the public had put several twos together at last. The halfhearted attempt to represent the depth bomb as one of a series of tests had broken down altogether. The vague fatalism with which the loss of the *Keweenaw* and the other ships had been received was succeeded by a burning sense of outrage, a satisfaction that the first step in vengeance had been taken, and a demand for more.

The atmosphere was similar to that at a declaration of war. Yesterday's phlegmatics and skeptics were, all of a sudden, fervid preachers of a crusade against the—well, against whatever it was that had had the insolent temerity to interfere with the freedom of the seas. Agreement on that cardinal point was virtually unanimous, but from that hub speculation radiated in every direction, so that not only fireballs, but every other unexplained phenomenon that had occurred for years was in some way attributed to, or at least connected with, the mystery in the Deeps.

The wave of world-wide excitement struck us when we stopped off for a day at Karachi on our way home. The place was bubbling with tales of sea serpents and visitations from space, and it was clear that whatever restrictions Bocker might have put on the circulation of his theory, a good many million people had now arrived at a similar explanation by other routes. This gave me the idea of telephoning to the E.B.C. in London to find out if Bocker himself would now unbend enough for an interview.

They told me that others had had the same idea, and that Bocker would be giving a restricted press conference on Friday. They would do their best to get us in on it. They did, and we arrived back in London with a couple of hours to spare before it took place.

Alastair Bocker was recognizable from his photographs, but they had not done him justice. The main facial architecture, with its rather full, middle-aged-infant quality, the broad eyebrows, the lock of gray hair tending to stray forward, the shapes of the nose and mouth, were all familiar; but the camera by its inability to convey the liveliness of his eyes, the mobility of the mouth and the whole face, the sparrow-like quality of his movements, had falsified him.

"One of those so unrestful small-boys-grown-up," observed Phyllis, studying him before the affair began.

For some minutes longer people continued to arrive and settle down, then Bocker stepped up to the table in front. The way he did it managed to convey that he had not come there to conciliate. When the babble had died he stood looking us over for some seconds. Then he spoke, without script or notes.

"I don't suppose for a moment that this meeting is going to be useful," he began. "However I did not call it, and I am not concerned now whether I get a good press or not.

"A couple of years ago I should have welcomed the chance of this publicity. One year ago I attempted to achieve it, though my hopes that we might be able to deflect the probable course of events were no more than slight, even then. I find it somewhat ironical, therefore, that you should honor me in this way now that they have become nonexistent.

"A version of my arguments, very likely a garbled one, may have reached you, but I will summarize them now so that at least we shall know what we are talking about."

The summary differed little from the version we had already heard. At the end of it he paused. "Now. Your questions," he said.

At this distance in time I cannot pretend to remember who asked what questions, but I recall that the few first fatuous ones were slapped down pretty sharply. Then someone asked: "Doctor Bocker, I seem to recall that originally you made some deliberate play with the word "immigration," but just now you spoke of "invasion." You have changed your mind?"

"It has been changed for me," Bocker told him. "For all I know, it may have been, in intention, just a peaceful immigration—but the evidence is that it is not so now."

"So," said somebody else, "you are telling us that this is our old blood-chiller, the interplanetary war, come at last."

"It might be put that way—by the facetious," agreed Bocker, calmly. "It is certainly an invasion, and from some place unknown." He paused. "Almost equally remarkable," he went on, "is the fact that in this sensation-seeking world it has managed to take place almost unrecognized for what it is. Only now, several years after its inception, is it starting to be taken seriously."

"It doesn't look like an interplanetary war to me now, whatever it is," a voice remarked.

"That," remarked Bocker, "I would ascribe to two main causes. First, constipation of the imagination; and, secondly, the influence of the late Mr. H. G. Wells.

"One of the troubles about writing a classic is that it sets a pattern of thinking. Everybody reads it, with the result that everybody thinks he knows exactly the form which an interplanetary invasion not only ought to, but must, take. If a mysterious cylinder were to land close to London or Washington tomorrow, we should all of us immediately recognize it as a right and proper subject for alarm. It seems to have been overlooked that Mr. Wells was simply employing one of a number of devices that he might have used for a work of fiction, so one might point out that he did not pretend to be laying down a law for the conduct of interplanetary campaigns. And the fact that his choice remains the only prototype for the occurrence in so many minds is a better compliment to his skill in writing than it is to those minds' skill in thinking.

"There could be quite a large variety of invasions against which it would be no good to call out the marines. This one is much more difficult to come to grips with than Mr. Wells' Martians were. It still remains to be seen whether the weapons we shall have to face will be more or less effective than those he imagined."

Somebody put in: "All right. Say, for purposes of discussion, that this is an invasion. Now why, would you say, have we been invaded?"

Bocker regarded him for a long moment, then he said: "I imagine that 'Why?' to have been the cry of every invaded party throughout history."

"But there must be some reason," the questioner persisted.

"Must there?—Well, I suppose, in the widest sense there must. But it does not follow from that that it is a reason we should understand, even if we knew it. I do not suppose the original Americans had much understanding of the reasons why they were being invaded by the Spaniards . . .

"But what you are, in fact, asking is that I should explain to you the motives that are animating an alien form of intelligence. In modesty I must decline to make that much of a fool of myself. The way to have found out, if not to have understood perhaps, would have been to get into communication with these things in our Deeps. But it would appear that whatever chance there may once have been of that, we have now very surely spoiled it."

The questioner was not satisfied with that. "But if we can't assign a reason," he said, "then surely the whole thing becomes very little different from a natural disaster—something like, say, an earthquake or a cyclone?"

"True enough," agreed Bocker. "And why not? I imagine that it is just so that the bird appears to the insect. Also, for the common people involved in a great war its distinction from a natural disaster is not very sharp. I know that you have all taught your readers to expect oversimplified explanations of everything, not excluding God Himself, in words of one syllable, so go ahead, and satisfy their lust for wisdom; no one can contradict you. But if you try to hang your explanations on me, I'll sue you.

"I'll go just as far as this: I can think of just two *human* motives for migration across space, if it were possible, on any scale. One would be simple expansion and aggrandizement; the other, flight from intolerable conditions on the home planet. But those things in the Deeps are certainly not human, whatever they may be; therefore, their reasons and motives may, but much more likely will not, be similar to human motives."

He paused and looked round again. "You know," he said, "this 'Why?' business is a waste of breath. If we were to go to another planet, and the people we found there promptly threw bombs at us, the 'Why?' of our going there wouldn't make the least difference; we should simply assume that if we did not take steps to stop it, we should be exterminated. And there, possibly, we do have some common ground with these things in the Deeps—the life-force, in whatever shape it is embodied, must have, collectively or individually, the will to survive, or it will soon cease to be."

"Then it is definitely your opinion that this is a *hostile* invasion?" someone asked.

Bocker regarded him with interest. "You know, you'd better stay after class. What I say is that it *is* an invasion, that it *is* hostile now, but it *may* not have been hostile in intention."

"And now," he concluded, "all I ask is that you convince your readers that this is no stunt, but a very serious matter—those of you whom editorial and proprietorial policies permit, of course."

What happened, in point of fact, was that almost all reports presented Bocker as a crackpot, with the kind of implied comment: "This is the sort of thing you might believe if you were a crackpot, too—but of course you are not, you are a sensible man."

There were signs that the playing-down was not accidental. The public was in a mood in which it would have taken anything, but there was pointed neglect of the opportunity to exploit the situation. Nor, just then, did anything sensational occur to interrupt the soothing process.

Then, by degrees, a feeling got about that this was not at all the way anyone had expected an interplanetary war to be; so very likely it was not an interplanetary war after all. From there, of course, it was only a step to deciding that it must be the Russians.

The Russians had all along encouraged, within their dictatorate, suspicion of capitalistic warmongers. When whispers of the interplanetary notion did in some way penetrate their curtain, they were countered by the statements that, (a) it was all a lie, a verbal smoke screen to cover the preparations of warmongers, (b) that it was true; and the capitalists, true to type, had immediately attacked the unsuspecting strangers with atom bombs, and, (c) whether it was true or not, the U.S.S.R. would fight unswervingly for Peace with all the weapons it possessed, except germs.

The swing continued. People were heard to say: "Huh—that interplanetary stuff? Don't mind telling you that I very nearly fell for it at the time. But, of course, when you start to actually *think* about it—! Wonder what the Russian game really is? Must've been something pretty big to make 'em use A-bombs on it." Thus, in quite a short time, the *status quo ante bellum hypotheticum* was restored, and we were back on the familiar comprehensible basis of international suspicion. The only lasting result was that marine insurance stayed up one per cent.

A couple of weeks later we had a little dinner party—with Captain Winters sitting at Phyllis's right hand. They looked to be getting on very well. Afterward, in our domestic privacy, I inquired: "If you aren't too sleepy, how did it go? What did the Captain have to say?"

"Oh, lots of nice things. Irish blood there, I think."

"But, passing from the really important to matters of mere worldwide interest—?" I suggested, patiently.

"He wouldn't let go of much, but what he did say wasn't encouraging. Some of it was rather horrid."

"Tell me."

"Well, the main situation doesn't seem to have altered a lot on the surface, but they're getting increasingly worried about what's happening below. He didn't actually *say* that investigation has made no progress, either, but what he did say implied it.

"He says for instance that atomic bombs are out, for the moment at any rate. You can only use them in isolated places, and even then the radioactivity spreads widely. The fisheries experts on both sides of the Atlantic have been raising hell, and saying that it's because of the bombings that some shoals have been failing to turn up in the proper places at the proper times. They've been blaming the bombs for upsetting the ecology, whatever that is, and affecting the migratory habits. But a few of them are saying that the data isn't sufficient to be absolutely sure that it is the bombs that have done it, but something certainly has, and it may have serious effects on food supplies. And so, as nobody seems to be quite clear what the bombs were expected to do, and all they do do is to kill and bewilder lots of fish at great expense, they've become unpopular just now.

"And here's something else. Two of those bombs they've sent down haven't gone off."

"Oh," I said, "and what do we infer from that?"

"I don't know. But it has them worried, very worried. You see, the way they are set to operate is by the pressure at a given depth; simple and pretty accurate."

"Meaning that they never reached the right pressure zone? Must have got hung up somewhere on the way down?"

Phyllis nodded. "It's made them extremely anxious."

"Understandably, too. I'd not feel too happy myself if I'd mislaid a couple of live atom bombs," I admitted. "What else?"

"Three cable-repair ships have unaccountably disappeared. One of them was cut off in the middle of a radio message. She was known to be grappling for a defective cable at the time."

"When was this?"

"One about six months ago, one about three weeks ago, and one last week."

"They might not have anything to do with it."

"They *might* not—but everyone's pretty sure they have."

"No survivors to tell what happened?"

"None."

Presently I asked: "Anything more?"

"Let me see. Oh, yes. They are developing some kind of guided depth missile which will be high-explosive, not atomic. But it hasn't been tested yet."

I turned to look at her admiringly. "That's the stuff, darling. The real Mata Hari touch."

Phyllis ignored that one. "The most important thing is that he is going to give me an introduction to Dr. Matet, the oceanographer."

I sat up. "But, darling, the Oceanographical Society has more or less threatened to excommunicate anybody who deals with us after that last script—it's part of their anti-Bocker line."

"Well, Dr. Matet happens to be a friend of the Captain's. He's seen his fireball-incidence maps, and he's a half-convert. Anyway, we're not convinced Bockerites, are we?"

"What we think we are isn't necessarily what other people think we are. Still, if he's willing—when can we see him?"

"*I* hope to see him in a few days' time, darling."

"Don't you think I should—"

"No. But it's sweet of you not to trust me still."

"But—"

"No. And now it's time we went to sleep," she said, firmly.

The beginning of Phyllis's interview was, she reported, almost standard: "*E*.BC.?" said Doctor Matet, raising eyebrows like miniature door mats. "I thought Captain Winters said *B*.B.C."

He was a man with a large frame sparingly covered, which gave his head the appearance of properly belonging to a still larger frame. His tanned forehead was high, and well polished back to the crown. He gave one, Phyllis said, a feeling of being overhung.

She sighed inwardly, and started on the routine justification of the English Broadcasting Company's existence, and worked him round gradually until he had reached the position of considering us nice-enough people striving manfully to overcome the disadvantages of being considered a slightly second-class oracle. Then, after making it quite clear that any material he might supply was strictly anonymous in origin, he opened up a bit.

The trouble from Phyllis's point of view was that he did it on a pretty academic level, full of strange words and instances which she had to interpret as best she could. The gist of what he had to tell her, however, seemed to be this: A year ago there had begun to be reports of discolorations in certain ocean currents. The first observation of the kind had been made in the Kuroshio current in the North Pacific—an unusual muddiness flowing northeast, becoming less discernible as it gradually widened out along the West Wind Drift until it was no longer perceptible to the naked eye.

"Samples were taken and sent for examination, of course, and what do you think the discoloration turned out to be?" said Dr. Matet.

Phyllis looked properly expectant. He told her: "Mainly radiolarian ooze, but with an appreciable percentage of diatomaceous ooze."

"How very remarkable!" Phyllis said, safely. "Now what on earth could produce a result like that?"

"Ah," said Dr. Matet, "that is the question. A disturbance on a quite remarkable scale—even in samples taken on the other side of the ocean, off the coast of California, there was still quite a heavy impregnation of both these oozes."

He went on and on, until Phyllis finally managed to interrupt him.

"Something, then," she said, "not only was, but still is, going on down there?"

"Something is," he agreed, looking at her. Then, with a sudden descent to the vernacular, he added: "But, to be honest with you, Lord knows what it is."

"Too much geography," said Phyllis, "and too much oceanography, and too much bathyography: too much of all the ographies, and lucky to escape ichthyology."

"Tell me," I said.

She did, with notes. "And," she concluded, "I'd like to see anyone scribe a script out of that lot."

"H'm," I said.

"There's no 'H'm' about it. Some kind of ographer might give a talk on it to high brows and low listening-figures, but even if he were intelligible, where'd it get anybody?"

"That," I remarked, "is the key question each time. But little by little the bits do accumulate. This is another bit. You didn't really expect to come back with the stuff for a whole script, anyway. He didn't suggest how this might link up with the rest of it?"

"No. I said it was sort of funny how everything seemed to be happening down in the most inaccessible parts of the ocean lately, and a few things like that, but he didn't rise. Very cautious. I think he was rather wishing he had not agreed to see me, so he stuck to verifiable facts. Eminently nonwheedlable—at first meeting, anyhow. He admitted that might send his reputation the way Bocker's has gone."

"Look," I said. "Bocker must have got to know about this as soon as anyone did. He ought to have some views on it, and it might be worth trying to find out what they are. The select press conference of his that we went to was almost an introduction."

"He went very coy after that," she said doubtfully. "Not surprising, really. Still, we weren't among the ones who panned him publicly —in fact, we were very objective."

"Toss you which of us rings him up," I offered.

"I'll do it," she said.

So I leaned back comfortably in my chair, and listened to her going through the opening ceremony of making it clear that she was the *E*.B.C.

I will say for Bocker that having proposed his mouthful of a theory and then sold it to himself, he had not backed out of the deal when he found it unpopular. At the same time he had no great desire to be involved in a further round of controversy when he would be pelted with cheap cracks and drowned in the noise from empty vessels. He made that quite clear when we met. He looked at us earnestly, his head a little one one side, the lock of gray hair hanging slightly forward, his hands clasped together. He nodded thoughtfully, and then said: "You want a theory from me because nothing you can think of will explain this phenomenon. Very well, you shall have one. I don't suppose you'll accept it, but I do ask you if you use it at all to use it anonymously. When people come round to my view again, I shall be ready, but I prefer not to be thought of as keeping my name before the public by letting out sensational driblets —is that quite clear?"

We nodded. We are becoming used to this general desire for anonymity.

"What we are trying to do," Phyllis explained, "is to fit a lot of bits and pieces into a puzzle. If you can show us where one of them should go, we'll be very grateful. If you would rather not have the credit for it, well, that is your own affair."

"Exactly. Well, you already know my theory of the origin of the deepwater intelligences, so we'll not go into that now. We'll deal with their present state, and I deduce that to be this: having settled into the environment best suited to them, these creatures' next thought would be to develop that environment in accordance with their ideas of what constitutes a convenient, orderly, and, eventually, civilized condition. They are, you see, in the position of—well, no, they are *actually* pioneers, colonists. Once they have safely arrived they set about improving and exploiting their new territory. What we have been seeing are the results of their having started work on the job."

"By doing what?" I asked.

He shrugged his shoulders. "How can we possibly tell? But judging by the way we have received them, one would imagine that their primary concern would be to provide themselves with some form of defense against us. For this they would presumably require metals. I suggest to you, therefore, that somewhere down in the Mindanao Trench, and also somewhere in the Deep in the southeast of the Cocos-Keeling Basin, you would, if you could go there, find mining operations now in progress."

I glimpsed the reason of his demand for anonymity. "Er—but the working of metals in such conditions—?" I said.

"How can we guess what technology they may have developed? We ourselves have plenty of techniques for doing things which would at first thought appear impossible in an atmospheric pressure of fifteen pounds per square inch; there are also a number of unlikely things we can do under water."

"But, with a pressure of tons, and in continual darkness, and—" I began, but Phyllis cut across me with that decisiveness which warns me to shut up and not argue.

"Dr. Bocker," she said, "you named two particular Deeps then, why was that?"

He turned from me to her. "Because that seems to me the only reasonable explanation where those two are concerned. It may be, as Mr. Holmes once remarked to your husband's illustrious namesake, 'a capital mistake to theorize before one has data,' but it is mental suicide to funk the data one has. I know of nothing, and can imagine nothing, that could produce the effect Dr. Matet spoke of except some exceedingly powerful machine for continuous ejection."

"But," I said, a little firmly, for I get rather tired of being dogged by the ghost of Mr. Holmes, "if it is mining as you suggest, then why is the discoloration due to ooze, and not grit?"

"Well, firstly there would be a great deal of ooze to be shifted before one could get at the rock, immense deposits, most likely, and secondly the density of the ooze is little more than that of water, whereas the grit, being heavy, would begin to settle long before it got anywhere near the surface, however fine it might be."

Before I could pursue that, Phyllis cut me off again: "What about the other places, Doctor. Why mention just those two?"

"I don't say that the others don't also signify mining, but I suspect, from their locations, that they may have another purpose."

"Which is—?" prompted Phyllis, looking at him, all girlish expectation.

"Communications, I think. You see, for instance, close to, though far below, the area where discoloration begins to occur in the equatorial Atlantic lies the Romanche Trench. It is a gorge through the submerged mountains of the Atlantic Ridge. Now, when one considers the fact that it forms the only deep link between the eastern and western Atlantic Basins, it seems more than just a coincidence that signs of activity should show up there. In fact, it strongly suggests to me that something down below is not satisfied with the natural state of that Trench. It is quite likely that it is blocked here and there by falls of rock. It may be that in some parts it is narrow and awkward; almost certainly, if there were a prospect of using it, it would be an advantage to clear it of ooze deposits down to a solid bottom. I don't *know,* of course, but the fact that something is undoubtedly taking place in that strategic Trench leaves me with little doubt that whatever is down there is concerned to improve its methods of getting about in the depths—just as we have improved our ways of getting about on the surface."

There was a silence while we took in that one, and its implications. Phyllis rallied first. "Er—and the other two main places—the Caribbean one, and the one west of Guatemala?" she asked.

Dr. Bocker offered us cigarettes, and lit one himself.

"Well, now," he remarked, leaning back in his chair, "doesn't it strike you as probable that, for a creature of the depths, a tunnel connecting the Deeps on either side of the isthmus would offer advantages almost identical with those that we ourselves obtain from the existence of the Panama Canal?"

People may say what they like about Bocker, but they can never truthfully claim that the scope of his ideas is mean or niggling. What is more, nobody has ever actually *proved* him wrong. His chief trouble was that he usually provided such large, indigestible slabs that they stuck in all gullets—even mine, and I would class myself as a fairly wide-gulleted type. That, however, was a subsequent reflection. At the climax of the interview I was chiefly occupied with trying to convince myself that he really meant what he had said, and finding nothing but my own resistance to suggest that he did not.

Before we left, he gave us one more thing to think about, too. He said: "Since you are following this along, you've probably heard of two atomic bombs that failed to go off?"

We told him we had.

"And have you heard that there was an unsponsored atomic explosion yesterday?"

"No. Was it one of them?" Phyllis asked.

"I should very much hope so—because I should hate to think it could be any other," he replied. "But the odd thing is that though one was lost off the Aleutians, and the other in the process of trying to give the Mindanao Trench another shake up, the explosion took place not so far off Guam—a good twelve hundred miles from Mindanao."

PHASE 2

We made an early start the next morning. The car, ready loaded, had stood out all night, and we were away a few minutes after five, with the intention of putting as much of southern England behind us as we could before the roads got busy. It was two hundred and sixty-eight point eight (when it wasn't point seven or point nine) miles to the door of the cottage that Phyllis had bought with a small legacy from her Aunt Helen.

I had rather favored the idea of a cottage a mere fifty miles or so away from London, but it was Phyllis's aunt who was to be commemorated with what was now Phyllis's money, so we became the proprietors of Rose Cottage, Penllyn, Nr. Constantine, Cornwall, Telephone Number: Navasgan 333. It was a gray stone, five-roomed cottage set on a southeasterly sloping, heathery hillside, with its almost eaveless roof clamped down tight on it in true Cornish manner. Straight before us we looked across the Helford River, and on toward the Lizard where, by night, we could see the flashing of the lighthouse. To the left was a view of the coast stretching raggedly away on the other side of Falmouth Bay, and if we walked a hundred yards ahead, and so out of the lee of the hillside which protected us from the southwesterly gales, we could look across Mount's Bay, towards the Scilly Isles, and the open Atlantic beyond. Falmouth, seven miles; Helston, nine; elevation 332 feet above sea level; several, though not all, mod. con.

We used it in a migratory fashion. When we had enough commissions and ideas on hand to keep us going for a time we would withdraw there to drive our pens and bash our typewriters in pleasant, undistracting seclusion for a few weeks. Then we would return to London for a while, market our wares, cement relations, and angle for commissions until we felt the call to go down there again with another accumulated batch of work—or we might, perhaps, simply declare a holiday.

That morning, I made pretty good time. It was still only half-past eight when I removed Phyllis's head from my shoulder and woke her up to announce: "Breakfast, darling." I left her trying to pull herself together to order breakfast intelligibly while I went to get some newspapers. By the time I returned she was functioning better, and had already started on the cereal. I handed over her paper, and looked at mine. The main headline in both was given to a shipping disaster. That this should be so when the ship concerned was Japanese suggested that there was little news from elsewhere.

I glanced at the story below the picture of the ship. From a welter of human interest I unearthed the fact that the Japanese liner, *Yatsushiro,* bound from Nagasaki to Amboina, in the Moluccas, had sunk. Out of some seven hundred people on board, only five survivors had ben found.

Before I could settle down to the story, however, Phyllis interrupted with an exclamation. I looked across. Her paper carried no picture of the vessel; instead, it printed a small sketch-map of the area, and she was intently studying the spot marked "X."

"What is it?" I asked.

She put her finger on the map. "Speaking from memory, and always supposing that the cross was made by somebody with a conscience," she said, "doesn't that put the scene of this sinking pretty near our old friend the Mindanao Trench?"

I looked at the map, trying to recall the configuration of the ocean floor around there.

"It can't be far off," I agreed.

I turned back to my own paper, and read the account there more carefully. "Women," apparently, "screamed when—" "Women in night attire ran from their cabins," "Women, wide-eyed with terror, clutched their children—," "Women" this and "Women" that when "death struck silently at the sleeping liner." When one had swept all this woman jargon, and the London Office's repertoire of phrases suitable for trouble at sea, aside, the skeleton of a very bare Agency message was revealed—so bare that for a moment I wondered why two large newspapers had decided to splash it instead of giving it just a couple of inches. Then I perceived the real mystery angle which lay submerged among all the phoney dramatics. It was that the *Yatsushiro* had, without warning, and for no known reason, suddenly gone down like a stone.

I got hold of a copy of this Agency message later, and I found its starkness a great deal more alarming and dramatic than this business of dashing about in "night attire." Nor had there been much time for that kind of thing, for, after giving particulars of the time, place, etc., the message concluded laconically: "Fair weather, no (no) collision, no (no) explosion, cause unknown. Foundered less one (one) minute alarm. Owners state quote impossible unquote."

So there can have been very few shrieks that night. Those unfortunate Japanese women—and men— had time to wake, and then, perhaps, a little time to wonder, bemused with sleep, and then the water came to choke them: there were no shrieks, just a few bubbles as they sank down, down, down in their nineteen-thousand-ton steel coffin.

When I read what there was I looked up. Phyllis was regarding me, chin on hands, across the breakfast table. Neither of us spoke for a moment. Then she said: "It says here: '—in one of the deepest parts of the Pacific Ocean.' Do you think this can be *it*, Mike—so soon?"

I hesitated. "It's difficult to tell. So much of this stuff's obviously synthetic—If it actually was only one minute—No, I suspend judgment, Phyl. We'll see *The Times* tomorrow and find what really happened—if anyone knows."

We drove on, making poorer time on the busier roads, stopped to lunch at the usual little hotel on Dartmoor, and finally arrived in the late afternoon—two hundred and sixty-eight point seven, this time. We were sleepy and hungry again, and though I did remember when I telephoned to London to ask for cuttings on the sinking to be sent, the fate of the *Yatsushiro* on the other side of the world seemed as remote from the concerns of a small gray Cornish cottage as the loss of the *Titanic*.

The Times noticed the affair the next day in a cautious manner which gave an impression of the staff pursing their lips and staying their hands rather than mislead their readers in any way. Not so, however, the reports in the first batch of cuttings which arrived on the afternoon of the following day. We put the stack between us, and drew from it. Facts were evidently still meager, and comments curiously similar.

"All got a strong dose of not-before-the-children this time," I said, as we finished. "And not altogether surprising, seeing the hell the advertisers would raise."

Phyllis said coldly: "Mike, this isn't a game, you know. After all, a big ship *has* gone down, and seven hundred poor people have been drowned. That is a terrible thing. I dreamed last night that I was shut up in one of those little cabins when the water came bursting in."

"Yesterday——" I began, and then stopped. I had been about to say that Phyllis had poured a kettle of boiling water down a crack in order to kill a lot more than seven hundred ants, but thought better of it. "Yesterday," I amended, "a lot of people were killed in road accidents, a lot will be today."

"I don't see what that has to do with it," she said.

She was right. It was not a very good amendment—but neither had it been the right moment to postulate the existence of a menace that might think no more of us than we, of ants.

"As a race," I said, "we have allowed ourselves to become accustomed to the idea that the proper way to die is in bed, at a ripe age. It is a delusion. The normal end for all creatures comes suddenly. The——"

But that wasn't the right thing to say at that time, either. She withdrew, using those short, brisk, hard-on-the heel steps.

I was sorry. I was worried, too, but it takes me differently.

Later, I found her staring out of the living room window. From where she stood, at the side of it, she had a view of the blue water stretching to the horizon.

"Mike," she said, "I'm sorry about this morning. The thing—this ship going down like that—suddenly got me. Until now this has been a sort of guessing game, a puzzle. Losing the bathyscope with poor Weisman and Trant was bad, and so was losing the naval ships. But this—well, it suddenly seemed to put it into a different category— a big liner full of ordinary, harmless men, women, and children peacefully asleep, to be wiped out in a few seconds in the middle of the night! It's somehow a different *class* of thing altogether. Do you see what I mean? Naval people are always taking risks doing their jobs—but these people on a liner hadn't anything to do with it. It made me feel that those things down there had been a working hypothesis that I had hardly believed in, and now, all at once, they had become horribly real. I don't like it, Mike. I suddenly started to feel afraid. I don't quite know why."

I went over and put my arm round her. "I know what you mean," I said. "I think it is part of it—the thing is not to let it get us down."

She turned her head. "Part of what?" she asked, puzzled.

"Part of the process we are going through—the instinctive reaction. The idea of an alien intelligence here *is* intolerable to us, we *must* hate and fear it. We can't help it—even our own kind of intelligence when it goes a bit off the rails in drunks and crazies alarms us not very rationally."

"You mean I'd not be feeling quite the same way about it if I knew that it had been done by—well, the Chinese, or somebody?"

"Do you think you would?"

"I—I'm not sure."

"Well, for myself, I'd say I'd be roaring with indignation. Knowing that it was somebody hitting well below the belt, I'd at least have a glimmering of who, how, and why, to give me focus. As it is, I've only the haziest impressions of the who, no idea about the how, and a feeling about the why that makes me go cold inside, if you really want to know."

She pressed her hand on mine. "I'm glad to know that, Mike. I was feeling pretty lonely this morning."

"My protective coloration isn't intended to deceive you, my sweet. It is intended to deceive me."

She thought. "I must remember that," she said, with an air of extensive implication that I am not sure I have fully understood yet.

A pleasant month followed as we settled down to our tasks— Phyllis to the search for something which had not already been said about Beckford of Fonthill. I, to the less literary occupation of framing a series on royal love matches, to be entitled provisionally either, "The Heart of Kings" or "Cupid Wears a Crown."

The outer world intruded little. Phyllis finished the Beckford script, and two more, and picked up the threads of the novel that never seemed to get finished. I went steadily ahead with the task of straining the royal love-lives free from any political contaminations, and writing an article or two in between, to clear the air a bit. On days that we thought were too good to be wasted we went down to the coast and bathed, or hired a sailing dinghy. The newspapers forgot about the *Yatsushiro.* The deep sea and all our speculations concerning it, seemed very far away.

Then, on a Wednesday night, the nine o'clock bulletin announced that the *Queen Anne* had been lost at sea . . .

The report was very brief. Simply the fact, followed by: "No details are available as yet, but it is feared that the list of the missing may prove to be very heavy indeed." There was silence for fifteen seconds, then the announcer's voice resumed: "The *Queen Anne,* the current holder of the Transatlantic record, was a vessel of ninety thousand tons displacement. She was built . . ."

I leaned forward, and turned it off. We sat looking at one another. Tears came into Phyllis's eyes. The tip of her tongue appeared, wetting her lips.

"The *Queen Anne!*—Oh, God!" she said.

She searched for a handkerchief. "Oh, Mike. That lovely ship!"

I crossed to sit beside her. For the moment she was seeing simply the ship as we had last seen her, putting out from Southampton. A creation that had been somewhere between a work of art and a living thing, shining and beautiful in the sunlight, moving serenely out towards the high seas, leaving a flock of little tugs bobbing behind. But I knew enough of my wife to realize that in a few minutes she would be on board, dining in the fabulous restaurant, or dancing in the ballroom, or up on one of the decks, watching it happen, feeling what they must have felt there. I put both my arms around her, and held her close.

I am thankful that such imagination as I, myself, have is more prosaic, and seated further from the heart.

Half an hour later the telephone rang. I answered it, and recognized the voice with some surprise.

"Oh, hullo, Freddy, What is it?" I asked, for nine-thirty in the evening was not a time that one expected to be called by the E.B.C.'s Director of Talks & Features.

"Good. 'Fraid you might be out, You've heard the news?"

"Yes."

"Well, we want something from you on this deep-sea menace of yours, and we want it quick. Half-hour feature."

"But, look here, the last thing I was told was to lay off any hint——"

"This has altered all that. It's a *must,* Mike. You don't want to be too sensational, but you *do* want to be convincing. Make 'em really believe there is something down there."

"Look here, Freddy, if this is some kind of legpull——"

"It isn't. It's an urgent commission."

"That's all very well, but for over a year now I've been regarded as the dumb coot who can't let go of an exploded crackpot theory. Now you suddenly ring me at about the time when a fellow might have made a fool bet at a party, and say——"

"Hell, I'm not at a party. I'm at the office, and likely to be here all night."

"You'd better explain," I told him.

"It's like this. There's a rumor running wild here that the Russians did it. Somebody launched that one off within a few minutes of the news coming through on the tape. Why the hell anybody'd think they would want to start anything that way, heavens knows, but you know how it is when people are emotionally worked up; they'll swallow anything for a bit. My own guess is that it is the let's-have-a-showdown-now school of thought seizing the opportunity, the damn fools. Anyway, it's got to be stopped. If it isn't there might be enough pressure worked up to force the Government out, or make it send an ultimatum, or something. So stopped it's damned well going to be, and the line is your deep-sea menace. Tomorrow's papers are using it, the Admiralty is willing to play, we've got several big scientific names already, the B.B.C.'s next bulletin, and ours, will have good strong hints in order to start the ball rolling, the American networks have started already, and some of their evening editions are coming on the streets with it. So if you want to put in your own penny-worth towards stopping the atom bombs falling, get cracking right away." I hung up and turned to Phyllis. "Work for us, darling."

The next morning, with one accord, we decided to go back to London. The first thing we did upon reaching the flat was to switch on the radio. We were just in time to hear of the sinking of the aircraft carrier *Meritorious*, and the liner *Carib Princess*.

The *Meritorious*, it will be recalled, went down in mid-Atlantic, eight hundred miles southwest of the Cape Verde Islands: the *Carib Princess* not more than twenty miles from Santiago de Cuba: both sank in a matter of two or three minutes, and from each very few survived. It is difficult to say whether the British were the more shocked by the loss of a brand-new naval unit, or the Americans by their loss of one of their best cruise liners with her load of wealth and beauty; both had already been somewhat stunned by the *Queen Anne*, for in the great Atlantic racers there was community of pride. Now, the language of resentment differed, but both showed the characteristics of a man who had been punched in the back in a crowd, and is looking round, both fists clenched, for someone to hit.

The American reaction appeared more extreme for, in spite of the violent nervousness of the Russians existing there, a great many found the idea of the deep-sea menace easier to accept than did the British, and a clamor for drastic, decisive action swelled up, giving a lead to a similar clamor at home. The Americans decided to make the placating gesture of depth-bombing the Cayman Trench close to the point where the *Carib Princess* had vanished—they can scarcely have expected any decisive result from the random bombing of a Deep some fifty miles wide and four hundred miles long.

The occasion was well-publicized on both sides of the Atlantic. American citizens were proud that their forces were taking the lead in reprisals: British citizens, though vocal in their dissatisfaction at being left standing at the post when the recent loss of two great ships should have given them the greater incentive to swift action, decided to applaud the occasion loudly, as a gesture of reproof to their own leaders. The flotilla of ten vessels commissioned for the task was reported as carrying a number of H. E. bombs specially designed for great depth, as well as two atomic bombs. It put out from Chesapeake Bay amid an acclamation which entirely drowned the voice of Cuba plaintively protesting at the prospect of atomic bombs on her doorstep.

None of those who heard the broadcast put out from one of the vessels as the task force neared the chosen area will ever forget the sequel. The voice of the announcer when it suddenly broke off from his description of the scene to say sharply: "Something seems to be ——my God! She's blown up!" and the the boom of the explosion. The announcer gabbling incoherently, then a second boom. A clatter, a sound of confusion and voices, a clanging of bells, then the announcer's voice again: breath short, sounding unsteady, talking fast: "That explosion you heard—the first one—was the destroyer, *Cavort*. She has entirely disappeared. Second explosion was the frigate, *Redwood*. She has disappeared, too. The *Redwood* was carrying one of our two atomic bombs. It's gone down with her. It is constructed to operate by pressure at five miles depth——

"The other eight ships of the flotilla are dispersing at full speed to get away from the danger area. We shall have a few minutes to get clear. I don't know how long. Nobody here can tell me. A few minutes, we think. Every ship in sight is using every ounce of power to get away from the area before the bomb goes off. The deck is shuddering under us. We're going full speed . . . Everyone's looking back at the place where the *Redwood* went down——Hey, doesn't anybody here know how long it'll take that thing to sink five miles ——? Hell, *somebody must* know——We're pulling away, pulling away for all we're worth——All the other ships, too. All getting the hell out of it, fast as we can make it——Anybody know what the area of the main spout's reckoned to be——? For crysake! Doesn't anybody know any damn thing around here? We're pulling off now, pulling off—Maybe we *will* make it——wish I knew how long——? Maybe——maybe——Faster, now faster, for heaven's sake——Pull the guts out of her, what's it matter?—— Hell, slog her to bits——Cram her along——

"Five minutes now since the *Redwood* sank——How far'll she be down in five minutes——? For God's sake, somebody: *How long does that damn thing take to sink*——?

"Still going——Still keeping going——Still beating it for all we're worth——Surely to heaven we must be beyond the main spout area by now——Must have a chance now——We're keeping it up—— Still going——Still going full speed——Everybody looking astern ——Everybody watching and waiting for it——And we're still going ——How can a thing be sinking all this time?——But thank God it is——Over seven minutes now——Nothing yet——Still going ——And the other ships, with great white wakes behind them—— Still going——Maybe it's a dud——Or maybe the bottom isn't five miles around here——Why can't somebody tell us how long it *ought* to take——? Must be getting clear of the worst now——Some of the other ships are just black dots on white spots now——still going ——We're still hammering away——Must have a chance now—— I guess we've really got a chance now——Everybody still staring aft——Oh, God! The whole sea's——"

And there it cut off.

But he survived, that radio announcer. His ship and five others out of the flotilla of ten came through, a bit radioactive, but otherwise unharmed. And I understand that the first thing that happened to him when he reported back to his office after treatment was a reprimand for the use of overcolloquial language which had given offense to a number of listeners by its neglect to the Third Commandment.

That was the day on which argument stopped, and propaganda became unnecessary. Two of the four ships lost in the Cayman Trench disaster had succumbed to the bomb, but the end of the other two had occurred in a glare of publicity that routed the skeptics and the cautious alike. As last it was established beyond doubt that there was something—and a highly dangerous something, too—down there in the Deeps.

Such was the wave of alarmed conviction spreading swiftly round the world that even the Russians sufficiently overcame their national reticence to admit that they had lost one large freighter and one unspecified naval vessel, both, again, off the Kurils, and one more survey craft off eastern Kamchatka. In consequence of this, they were, they said, willing to co-operate with other powers in putting down this menace of the cause of world Peace.

The following day the British Government proposed that an International Naval Conference should meet in London to make a preliminary survey of the problem. A disposition among some of those invited to quibble about the locale was quenched by the unsympathetically urgent mood of the public. The conference assembled in Westminster within three days of the announcement, and, as far as England was concerned, none too soon. In those three days cancelations of sea passages had been wholesale, overwhelmed airline companies had been forced to apply priority schedules, the Government had clamped down fast on the sales of oils of all kinds, and was rushing out a rationing system for essential services.

On the day before the conference opened Phyllis and I met for lunch.

"You ought to see Oxford Street," she said. "Talk about panic-buying! Cottons particularly. Every hopeless line is selling out at double prices, and they're scratching one another's eyes out for things they wouldn't have been seen dead in last week."

"From what they tell me of the City," I told her, "it's about as good there. Sounds as if you could get control of a shipping line for a few bob, but you couldn't buy a single share in anything to do with aircraft for a fortune. Steel's all over the place; rubbers are, too; plastics are soaring; distilleries are down; about the only thing that's holding its own seems to be breweries."

"I saw a man and a woman loading two sacks of coffee beans into a Rolls, in Piccadilly. And there were—" She broke off suddenly as though what I had been saying had just registered. "You *did* get rid of Aunt Mary's shares in those Jamaican Plantations?" she inquired, with the expression that she applies to the monthly housekeeping accounts.

"Some time ago," I reassured her. "The proceeds went, oddly enough, into airplane engines, and plastics."

She gave an approving nod, rather as if the instructions had been hers. Then another thought occurred to her. "What about the press tickets for tomorrow?" she asked.

"There aren't any for the conference proper," I told her. "There will be a statement afterwards."

She stared at me. "*Aren't any?* For heaven's sake! How do they expect us to do our job?" she exclaimed, and sat there brooding.

When Phyllis said "our job" the words did not connote exactly what they would have implied a few days before. The job somehow changed quality under our feet. The task of persuading the public of the reality of the unseen, indescribable menace had turned suddenly into one of keeping up morale in the face of a menace which everyone now accepted to the point of panic. E.B.C. ran a feature called "News-Parade" in which we appeared to have assumed the roles of special oceanic correspondents, without being quite sure how it had occurred. In point of fact, Phyllis had never been on the E.B.C. staff, and I had technically left it when I ceased, officially, to have an office there some two years before. Nobody, however, seemed to be aware of this except the accounts department which now paid by the piece instead of by the month. All the same, there was not going to be much freshness of treatment in our assignment if we could get no nearer to the sources than official handouts. Phyllis was still brooding about it when I left her to go back to the office I officially didn't have in E.B.C.

We did our best during the next few days to play our part in putting across the idea of firm hands steady on the wheel, and of the backroom boys who had produced radar, asdic, and other marvels nodding confidently, and saying, in effect: "Sure. Just give us a few days to think, and we'll knock together something that will settle this lot!" There was a satisfactory feeling that confidence was gradually being restored.

Perhaps the main stabilizing factor, however, emerged from a difference of opinion on one of the technical committees.

General agreement had been reached that a torpedolike weapon designed to give submerged escort to a vessel could profitably be developed to counter the assumed mine form of attack. The motion was accordingly put that all should pool information likely to help in the development of such a weapon.

The Russian delegates demurred. Remote control of missiles, they pointed out was, of course, a Russian invention in any case. Moreover, Russian scientists, zealous in the fight for Peace, had already developed such control to a degree greatly in advance of that achieved by the capitalist-ridden science of the West. It could scarcely be expected of the Soviets that they should make a present of their discoveries to warmongers.

The Western spokesman replied that, while respecting the intensity of the fight for Peace and the fervor with which it was being carried on in every department of Soviet science except, of course, the biological, the West would remind the Soviets that this was a conference of peoples faced by a common danger and resolved to meet it by cooperation.

The Russian leader responded frankly that he doubted whether, if the West had happened to possess a means of controlling a submerged missile by radio, such as had been invented by Russian engineers, they would care to share such knowledge with the Soviet people.

The Western spokesman assured the Soviet representative that since the West had called the conference for the purpose of cooperation, it felt in duty bound to state that it had indeed perfected such a means of control as the Soviet delegate had mentioned.

Following a hurried consultation, the Russian delegate announced that *if* he believed such a claim to be true, he would also know that it could only have come about through theft of the work of Soviet scientists by capitalist hirelings. And, since neither a lying claim, nor the admission of successful espionage showed that disinterest in national advantage which the conference had professed, his delegation was left with no alternative but to withdraw.

This action, with its reassuring ring of normality, exerted a valuable tranquilizing influence.

Amid the widespread satisfaction and resuscitating confidence, the voice of Bocker, dissenting, rose almost alone: It was late, he proclaimed, but it still might not be too late to make some last attempt at a pacific approach to the sources of the disturbance. They had already been shown to possess a technology equal to, if not superior to, our own. In an alarming short time they had been able not only to establish themselves, but to produce the means of taking effective action for their self-defense. In the face of such a beginning one was justified in regarding their powers with respect and, for his part, with apprehension.

The very differences of environment that they required made it seem unlikely that human interests and those of these xenobathetic intelligences need seriously overlap. Before it should be altogether too late, the very greatest efforts should be made to establish communication with them in order to promote a state of compromise which would allow both parties to live peacefully in their separate spheres.

Very likely this was a sensible suggestion—though whether the attempt would ever have produced the desired result is a different matter. Where there was no will whatever to compromise, however, the only evidence that his appeal had been noticed at all was that the word, "xenobathetic," and a derived noun, "xenobath," and its diminutive, "bathy," began to be used in print.

"More honored in the dictionary than in the observance," remarked Bocker, with some bitterness. "If it is Greek words they are interested in, there are others—Cassandra, for instance."

Hard on Bocker's words, but with a significance that was not immediately recognized, came the news first from Saphira, and then from April Island.

Saphira, a Brazilian island in the Atlantic, lies a little south of the Equator and some four hundred miles southeast of the larger island of Fernando de Noronha. In that isolated spot a population of a hundred or so lived in primitive conditions, largely on its own produce, content to get along in its own way, and little interested in the rest of the world. It is said that the original settlers were a small party who, arriving on account of a shipwreck sometime in the eighteenth century, remained perforce. By the time they were discovered they had settled to the island life and already become interestingly inbred. In due course, and without knowing or caring much about it, they had ceased to be Portuguese and become technically Brazilian citizens, and a token connection with their foster mother country was maintained by a ship which called at roughly six-month intervals to do a little barter.

Normally, the visiting ship had only to sound its siren, and the Saphirans would come hurrying out of their cottages down to the minute quay where their few fishing boats lay, to form a reception committee which included almost the entire population. On this occasion, however, the hoot of the siren echoed emptily back and forth in the little bay, and set the sea birds wheeling in flocks, but no Saphiran appeared at the cottage doors. The ship hooted again . . .

The coast of Saphira slopes steeply. The ship was able to approach to within a cable's length of the shore, but there was nobody to be seen—nor, still more ominously, was there any trace of smoke from the cottages' chimneys.

A boat was lowered and a party, with the mate in charge, rowed ashore. They made fast to a ringbolt and climbed the stone steps up to the little quay. They stood there in a bunch, listening and wondering. There was not a sound to be heard but the cries of the sea birds and the lapping of the water.

"Must've made off, the lot of 'em. Their boat's gone," said one of the sailors, uneasily.

"Huh!" said the mate. He took a deep breath, and gave a mighty hail, as though he had greater faith in his own lungs than in the ship's siren.

They listened for an answer, but none came save the sound of the mate's voice echoing faintly back across the bay.

"Huh!" said the mate again. "Better take a look."

The uneasiness which had come over the party kept them together. They followed him in a bunch as he strode towards the nearest of the small, stone-built cottages. The door was standing half-open. He pushed it back.

"Phew!" he said.

Several putrid fish decomposing on a dish accounted for the smell. Otherwise the place was tidy and, by Saphiran standards, reasonably clean. There were no signs of disorder or hasty packing-up. In the inner room the beds were made up, ready to be slept in. The occupant might have been gone only a matter of a few hours, but for the fish and the lack of warmth in the turf-fire ashes.

In the second and third cottages there was the same air of unpremeditated absence. In the fourth they found a dead baby in its cradle in the inner room. The party returned to the ship, puzzled and subdued.

The situation was reported by radio to Rio. Rio in its reply suggested a thorough search of the island. The crew started on the task with reluctance and a tendency to keep in close groups, but, as nothing fearsome revealed itself, gradually gained confidence.

On the second day of their three-day search they discovered a party of four women and six children in two caves on a hillside. All had been dead for some weeks, apparently from starvation. By the end of the third day they were satisfied that if there were any living person left, he must be deliberately hiding. It was only then, on comparing notes, that they realized also that there could not be more than a dozen sheep and two or three dozen goats left out of the island's normal flocks of some hundreds.

They buried the bodies they had found, radioed a full report to Rio, and then put to sea again, leaving Saphira, with its few surviving animals, to the sea birds.

In due course the news came through from the Agencies and won an inch or two of space here and there, but no one at the time inquired further into the matter.

The April Island affair was set in quite a different key and might have continued undiscovered for some time but for the coincidence of official interest in the place.

The interest stemmed from the existence of a group of Javanese malcontents variously described as smugglers, terrorists, communists, patriots, fanatics, gangsters, or merely rebels who, whatever their true affiliations, operated upon a troublesome scale. For many years they had dropped out of sight, but recently an informer had managed to reach the authorities with the news that they had taken over April Island. The authorities set out immediately to capture them.

In order to minimize the risk to a number of innocent people who were being held hostage by the criminals, the approach to April Island was made by night. Under starlight the gunboat stole quietly into a little-used bay which was masked from the main village by a headland. There, a well-armed party, accompanied by the informant who was to act as their guide, was put ashore with the task of taking the village by surprise. The gunboat then drew off, moved a little way along the coast, and lay in lurk behind the point of the headland until the landing party should summon her to come in and dominate the situation.

Three-quarters of an hour had been the length of time estimated for the party's crossing of the isthmus, and then perhaps another ten or fifteen minutes for its disposal of itself about the village. It was, therefore, with concern that after only forty minutes had passed the men aboard the gunboat heard the first burst of automatic fire, succeeded presently by several more.

With the element of surprise lost, the Commander ordered full speed ahead, but even as the boat surged forward the sound of firing was drowned by a dull, reverberating boom. The crew of the gunboat looked at one another with raised eyebrows: the landing party had carried no higher forms of lethalness than automatic rifles and grenades. There was a pause, then the hammering of the automatic rifles started again. This time, it continued longer in intermittent bursts until it was ended again by a similar boom.

The gunboat rounded the headland. In the dim light it was impossible to make out anything that was going on in the village two miles away. For the moment all there was dark. Then a twinkling broke out, and another, and the sound of firing reached them again. The gunboat, continuing at full speed, switched on her searchlight. The village and the trees behind it sprang into sudden miniature existence. No figures were visible among the houses. The only sign of activity was some froth and commotion in the water, a few yards out from the edge. Some claimed afterwards to have seen a dark, humped shape showing above the water a little to the right of it.

As close inshore as she dared go the gunboat put her engines astern, and hove to in a flurry. The searchlight played back and forth over the huts and their surroundings. Everything lit by the beam had hard lines, and seemed endowed with a curious glistening quality. The man on the oerlikons followed the beam, his fingers steady on the triggers. The light made a few more slow sweeps and then stopped. It was trained on several submachine guns lying on the sand, closer to the water's edge.

A stentorian voice from the hailer called the landing party from cover. Nothing stirred. The searchlight roved again, prying between the huts, among the trees. Nothing moved there. The patch of light slid back across the beach and steadied upon the abandoned arms. The silence seemed to deepen.

The Commander refused to allow landing until daylight. The gunboat dropped anchor. She rode there for the rest of the night, her searchlight making the village look like a stage-set upon which at any moment the actors might appear, but never did.

When there was full daylight the First Officer, with a party of five armed men rowed cautiously ashore under cover from the ship's oerlikons. They landed close to the abandoned arms, and picked them up to examine them. All the weapons were covered with a thin slime. The men put them in the boat, and then washed their hands clean of the stuff.

The beach was scored in four places by broad furrows leading from the water's edge towards the huts. They were something over eight feet wide, and curved in section. The depth in the middle was five or six inches; the sand at the edges was banked a trifle above the level of the surrounding beach. Some such track, the First Officer thought, might have been left if a large boiler had been dragged across the foreshore. Examining them more closely he decided from the lie of the sand that though one of the tracks led towards the water, the other three undoubtedly emerged from it. It was a discovery which caused him to look at the village with increased wariness. As he did so, he became aware that the scene which had glistened oddly in the searchlight was still glistening oddly. He regarded it curiously for some minutes. Then he shrugged. He tucked the butt of his submachine gun comfortably under his right arm, and slowly, with his eyes flicking right and left for the least trace of movement, led his party up the beach.

The village was formed of a semicircle of huts of various sizes fringing upon an open space, and as they drew closer the reason for the glistening look became plain. The ground, the huts themselves, and the surrounding trees, too, all had a thin coating of the slime which had been on the guns.

The party kept steadily, slowly on until they reached the center of the open space. There they paused, bunched together, facing outwards, examining each foot of cover closely. There was no sound, no movement but a few fronds stirring gently in the morning breeze. The men began to breathe more evenly.

The First Officer removed his gaze from the huts, and examined the ground. It was littered with a wide scatter of small metal fragments, most of them curved, all of them shiny with the slime. He turned one over curiously with the toe of his boot, but it told him nothing. He looked about them again, and decided on the largest hut. "We'll search that," he said.

The whole front of it glistened stickily. He pushed the unfastened door open with his foot, and led the way inside. There was little disturbance; only a couple of overturned stools suggested a hurried exit. No one, alive or dead, remained in the place.

They came out again. The First Officer glanced at the next hut, then he paused, and looked at it more closely. He went round to examine the side of the hut they had already entered. The wall there was quite dry and clear of slime. He considered the surroundings again. "It looks," he said, "as if everything had been sprayed with this muck by something in the middle of the clearing."

A more detailed examination supported the idea, but took them little further.

"But how?" the officer asked, meditatively. "Also what? And why?"

"Something came out of the sea," said one of his men, looking back uneasily toward the water.

"Some things—three of them," the First Officer corrected him.

They returned to the middle of the open semicircle. It was clear that the place was deserted, and there did not seem to be much more to be learned there at present.

"Collect a few of these bits of metal—they may mean something to somebody," the officer instructed.

He himself went across to one of the huts, found an empty bottle, scraped some of the slime into it, and corked it up. "This stuff's beginning to stink now the sun's getting at it," he said, on his return. "We might as well clear out. There's nothing we can do here."

Back on board, he suggested that a photographer should take pictures of the furrows on the beach, and showed the Commander his trophies, now washed clean of the slime. "Queer stuff," he said, holding a piece of the thick, dull metal. "A shower of it around." He tapped it with a knuckle. "Sounds like lead; weighs like feathers. Cast, by the look of it. Ever seen anything like that, sir?"

The Commander shook his head. He observed that the world seemed to be full of strange alloys these days.

Presently the photographer came rowing back from the beach. The Commander decided: "We'll give 'em a few blasts on the siren. If nobody shows up we'd better make a landing some other place and find a local inhabitant who can tell us what the hell goes on."

A couple of hours later the gunboat cautiously nosed her way into a bay on the northeast coast of April Island. A similar though smaller village stood there in a clearing, close to the water's edge. The similarity was uncomfortably emphasized by an absence of life as well as by a beach displaying four broad furrows to the water's edge.

Closer investigation, however, showed some differences: of these furrows, two had been made by some objects ascending to the beach; the other two, apparently, the same objects *de*scending it. There was no trace of the slime either in or about the deserted village.

The Commander frowned over his charts. He indicated another bay. "All right. We'll try there, then," he said.

This time there were no furrows to be seen on the beach, though the village was just as thoroughly deserted. Again the gunboat's siren gave a forlorn, unheeded wail. They examined the scene through glasses, then the First Officer, scanning the neighborhood more widely, gave an exclamation. "There's a fellow up on that hill there, sir. Waving a shirt, or something."

The Commander turned his own glasses that way. "Two or three others, a bit to the left of him, too."

The gunboat gave a couple of hoots, and moved closer inshore. The boat was lowered.

"Stand off a bit till they come," the Commander directed. "Find out whether there's been an epidemic of some kind before you try to make contact."

He watched from his bridge. In due course a party of natives, eight or nine strong appeared from the trees a couple of hundred yards east of the village, and hailed the boat. It moved in their direction. Some shouting and countershouting between the two parties ensued, then the boat went in and grounded on the beach. The First Officer beckoned the natives with his arm, but they hung back in the fringe of the trees. Eventually he jumped ashore and walked across the strand to talk to them. An animated discussion took place. Clearly an invitation to some of them to visit the gunboat was being declined with vigor. Presently the First Officer descended the beach alone, and the landing party headed back.

"What's the trouble there?" the Commander inquired as the boat came alongside.

The First Officer looked up. "They won't come, sir."

"What's the matter with them?"

"They're okay themselves, sir, but they say the sea isn't safe."

"They can see it's safe enough for us. What do they mean?"

"They say several of the shore villages have been attacked, and they think theirs may be at any moment."

"Attacked! What by?"

"Er—perhaps if you'd come and talk to them yourself, sir—?"

"I sent a boat so that they could come to me—that ought to be good enough for them."

"I'm afraid they'll not come, short of force, sir."

The Commander frowned. "*That* scared are they? What's been doing this attacking?"

The First Officer moistened his lips; his eyes avoided his commander's. "They—er, they say—whales, sir."

The Commander stared at him. "They say—*what?*" he demanded.

The First Officer looked unhappy. "Er—I know, sir. But that's what they keep on *saying.* Er—whales, and er—giant jellyfish. I think that if you'd speak to them yourself, sir . . . ?"

The news about April Island did not exactly "break" in the accepted sense. Curious goings on on an atoll which could not even be found in most atlases had, on the face of it, little news value, and the odd line or two which recorded the matter was allowed to slip past. Possibly it would not have attracted attention nor been remembered until much later, if at all, but for the chance that an American journalist who happened to be in Jakarta discovered the story for himself, took a speculative trip to April Island, and wrote the affair up for a weekly magazine.

A pressman, reading it, recalled the Saphira incident, linked the two, and splashed a new peril across a Sunday newspaper. It happened that this preceded by one day the most sensational communiqué yet issued by the Standing Committee for Action, with the result that the Deeps had the big headlines once more. Moreover, the term "Deeps" was more comprehensive than formerly, for it was announced that shipping losses in the last month had been so heavy, that the areas in which they had occurred so much more extensive that, pending the development of a more efficient means of defense, all vessels were strongly advised to avoid crossing deep water and keep, as far as was practicable, to the areas of the continental shelves.

It was obvious that the Committee would not have dealt such a blow to a confidence in shipping which had been recovering, without the gravest reasons. Nevertheless, the answering outburst of indignation from the shipping interests accused it of everything from sheer alarmism to a vested interest in airlines. To follow such advice, they protested, would mean routing transatlantic liners into Iceland and Greenland waters, creeping coastwise down the Bay of Biscay and the West African coast, etc. Transpacific commerce would become impossible, and Australia and New Zealand, isolated. It showed a shocking and lamentable lack of a sense of responsibility that the Committee should be allowed to advise in this way, without full consultation of all interested parties, these panic-inspired measures which would, if heeded, bring the maritime commerce of the world virtually to a stop. Advice which could never be implemented, should never have been given.

The Committee hedged slightly under the attack. It had not ordered, it said. It had simply suggested that wherever possible vessels should attempt to avoid crossing any extensive stretch of water where the depth was greater than two thousand fathoms, and thus avoid exposing itself to danger unnecessarily.

This, retorted the shipowners, curtly, was virtually putting the same thing in different words; and their case, though not their cause, was upheld by the publication in almost every newspaper of sketch-maps showing hurried and somewhat varied impressions of the two-thousand fathom line.

Before the Committee was able to re-express itself in still different words the Italian liner, *Sabina,* and the German liner, *Vorpommern,* disappeared on the same day—the one in mid-Atlantic, the other in the South Pacific—and reply became superfluous.

The news of the latest sinkings was announced on the 8 A.M. news bulletin on a Saturday. The Sunday papers took full advantage of their opportunity. At least six of them slashed at official incompetence with almost eighteenth century gusto, and set the pitch for the dailies.

On the Wednesday I rang up Phyllis.

It used to come upon her periodically when we had had a longer spell than usual in London that she could not stand the works of civilization any longer without a break for refreshment. If it happened that I were free, I was allowed along, too; if not, she went off to commune with nature on her own. As a rule, she returned

spiritually refurbished in the course of a week or so. This time, however, the communion had already been going on for almost a fortnight, and there was still no sign of the postcard which customarily
preceded her return by a short head, when it did not come on the
following day.

The telephone down in Rose Cottage rang forlornly for some time.
I was on the point of giving up when she answered it.

"Hullo, darling!" said her voice.

"I might have been the butcher, or the income tax man," I re-
proved her.

"They'd have given up more quickly. Sorry if I've been long answering. I was busy outside."

"Digging the garden?" I asked hopefully.

"No, as a matter of fact. I was bricklaying."

"This line's not good. It sounded like bricklaying."

"It was, darling."

"Oh," I said. "Bricklaying."

"It's very fascinating when you get into it. Did you know there are
all kinds of bonds and things; Flemish Bond, and English Bond, and
so on? And you have things called "headers" and other things
called——"

"What is this, darling? A tool shed, or something?"

"No. Just a wall, like Balbus and Mr. Churchill. I read somewhere
that in moments of stress Mr. Churchill used to find that it gave him
tranquility, and I thought that anything that could tranquilize Mr.
Churchill was probably worth following up."

"Well, I hope it has cured the stress."

"Oh, it has. It's very soothing. I love the way when you put the
brick down the mortar squidges out at the sides and you——"

"Darling, the minutes are ticking up. I rang you to say that you
are wanted here."

"That's sweet of you, darling. But leaving a job half——"

"It's not me—I mean—it is me, but not only. The E.B.C. want a
word with us."

"What about?"

"I don't really know. They're being cagey, but insistent."

"Oh. When do they want to see us?"

"Freddy suggested dinner on Friday. Can you manage that?"

There was a pause. "Yes. I think I'll be able to finish—All right. I'll be on that train that gets into Paddington about six."

"Good. I'll meet it. There is the other reason, too, Phyl."

"It being?"

"The running sand, darling. The unturned coverlet. The tarnished thimble. The dull, unflavored drops from life's clepsydra. The—"

"Mike, you've been rehearsing."

"What else had I to do?"

We were only twenty minutes late, but Freddy Whittier might have been desiccating for some hours from the urgency with which we were swept into the bar. He disappeared into the mob round the counter with a nicely controlled violence and presently emerged with a selection of double and single sherries on a tray.

"Doubles first," he said.

Soon his mind broadened out of the single track. He looked more himself, and noticed things. He even noticed Phyllis's hands; the abraded knuckles on the right, the large piece of plaster on the left. He frowned and seemed about to speak, but thought better of it. I observed him covertly examining my face, and then my hands.

"My wife," I explained, "has been down in the country. The start of the bricklaying season, you know."

He looked relieved rather than interested. "Nothing wrong with the old team spirit?" he inquired, with a casual air.

We shook our heads.

"Good," he said, "because I've got a job for two."

He went on to expound. It seemed that one of E.B.C.'s favorite sponsors had put a proposition to them. This sponsor had apparently been feeling for some time that a description, some photographs, and definite evidence of the nature of the Deeps creatures was well overdue.

"A man of perception," I said. "For the last five or six years—"

"Shut up, Mike," said my dear wife, briefly.

"Things," Freddy went on, "have in his opinion now reached a pass where he might as well spend some of his money while it still has value, and might even bring in some valuable information. At the same time, he doesn't see why he shouldn't get some benefit out of the information if it is forthcoming. So he proposes to fit out and send out an expedition to find out what it can—and of course the whole thing will be tied up with exclusive rights and so on. By the way, this is highly confidential: we don't want the B.B.C. to get on to it first."

"Look, Freddy," I said. "For several years now everybody has been trying to get on it, let alone the B.B.C. What the—?"

"Expedition where to?" asked Phyllis, practically.

"That," said Freddy, "was naturally our first question. But he doesn't know. The whole decision on a location is in Bocker's hands."

"Bocker!" I exclaimed. "Is he becoming un-untouchable, or something?"

"His stock has recovered quite a bit," Freddy admitted. "And, as this fellow, the sponsor, said: 'If you leave out all the outer-space nonsense, the rest of Bocker's pronouncements have had a pretty high score'—higher than anyone else's, anyway. So he went to Bocker, and said: 'Look here. These things that came up on Saphira and April Island; where do you think they are most likely to appear next—or, at any rate, soon?' Bocker wouldn't tell him, of course. But they talked; and the upshot was that the sponsor will subsidize an expedition led by Bocker to a region to be selected by Bocker. What is more, Bocker also selects the personnel. And part of the selection, with E.B.C.'s blessing and your approval, could be you two."

"He was always my favorite ographer," said Phyllis. "When do we start?"

"Wait a minute," I put in. "Once upon a time an ocean voyage used to be recommended for health. Recently, however, so far from being healthy—"

"Air," said Freddy. "Exclusively air. People have doubtless got a lot of personal information about the things the other way, but we would prefer you to be in a position to bring it back."

Phyllis wore an abstracted air at intervals during the evening. When we got home I said: "If you'd rather not take this up—"

"Nonsense. Of course we're going," she said. "But do you think 'subsidize' means we can get suitable clothes and things on expenses?"

"I like idleness—in the sun," said Phyllis.

From where we sat at an umbrella-ed table in front of the mysteriously named Grand Hotel Britannia y la Justicia it was possible to direct idle contemplation on tranquility or activity. Tranquility was on the right. Intensely blue water glittered for miles until it was ruled off by a hard, straight horizon line. The shore, running round like a bow, ended in a palm-tufted headland which trembled miragewise in the heat. A backcloth which must have looked just the same when it formed a part of the Spanish Main.

To the left was a display of life as conducted in the capital, and only town of the island of Escondida.

The island's name derived, presumably, from erratic seamanship in the past which had caused ships to arrive mistakenly at one of the Caymans, but through all the vicissitudes of those parts it had managed to retain it, and much of its Spanishness, too. The houses looked Spanish, the temperament had a Spanish quality, in the language there was more Spanish than English, and, from where we were sitting at the corner of the open space known indifferently as the Plaza, or the Square, the church at the far end with the bright market-stalls in front of it looked positively picture-book Spanish. The population, however, was somewhat less so, and ranged from sunburnt-white to coal-black. Only a bright-red British mailbox prepared one for the surprise of learning that the place was called Smithtown—and even that took on romance when one learned also that the Smith commemorated had been a pirate in a prosperous way.

Behind us, and therefore behind the hotel, one of the two mountains which made Escondida climbed steeply, emerging far above as a naked peak with a scarf of greenery about its shoulders. Between the mountain's foot and the sea stretched a tapering rocky shelf, with the town clustered on its wider end.

And there, also, had clustered for five weeks the Bocker Expedition.

Bocker had contrived a probability-system all his own. Eventually his eliminations had given him a list of ten islands as likely to be

attacked, and the fact that four of them were in the Caribbean area
had settled our course.

That was about as far as he cared to go simply on paper, and it
landed us all at Kingston, Jamaica. There we stayed a week in company with Ted Jarvey, the cameraman; Leslie Bray, the recordist;
and Muriel Flynn, one of the technical assistants while Bocker himself and his two male assistants flew about in an armed coastal-patrol
aircraft put at his disposal by the authorities, and considered the rival
attractions of Grand Cayman, Little Cayman, Cayman Brac, and
Escondida. The reasoning which led to their final choice of Escondida was no doubt very nice, so that it seemed a pity that two days
after the aircraft had finished ferrying us and our gear to Smithtown
it should have been a large village on Grand Cayman which suffered
the first visitation in those parts.

But if we were disappointed, we were also impressed. It was clear
that Bocker really had been doing something more than a high-class
eeny meeny miney mo, and had brought off a very near miss.

The plane took four of us over there as soon as he had the news.
Unfortunately we learned little. There were grooves on the beach,
but they had been greatly trampled by the time we arrived. Out of
two hundred and fifty villagers about a score had got away by fast
running. The rest had simply vanished. The whole affair had taken
place in darkness, so that no one had seen much. Each survivor felt
an obligation to give any inquirer his money's worth, and the whole
thing was almost folklore already.

Bocker announced that we should stay where we were. Nothing
would be gained by dashing hither and thither; we should be just as
likely to miss the occasion as to find it. Even more likely, for
Escondida in addition to its other qualities had the virtue of being a
one-town island so that when an attack did come (and he was sure
that sooner or later it would) Smithtown must almost certainly be
the objective.

We hoped he knew what he was doing, but in the next two weeks
we doubted it. The radio brought reports of a dozen raids—all, save
one small affair in the Azores, were in the Pacific. We began to have
a depressed feeling that we were in the wrong hemisphere.

When I say "we," I must admit I mean chiefly me. The others

continued to analyze the reports and go stolidly ahead with their preparations. One point was that there was no record of an assault taking place by day; lights, therefore, would be necessary. Once the town council had been convinced that it would cost them nothing we were all impressed into the business of fixing improvised flood-lights on trees, posts and the corners of buildings all over Smithtown, though with greater proliferation toward the waterside, all of which, in the interests of Ted's cameras had to be wired back to a switch-board in his hotel room.

The inhabitants assumed that a fiesta of some kind was in prep-aration, the council considered it a harmless form of lunacy, but were pleased to be paid for the extra current we consumed. Most of us were slowly growing more cynical, until the affair at Gallows Island which, though Gallows was in the Bahamas, unnerved the whole Caribbean, nevertheless.

Port Anne, the chief town on Gallows, and three large coastal villages there were raided the same night. About half the popula-tion of Port Anne, and a much higher proportion from the villages disappeared entirely. Those who survived had either shut themselves in their houses or run away, but this time there were plenty of people who agreed that they had seen things like tanks—like military tanks, they said, but larger—emerge from the water and come sliding up the beaches. Owing to the darkness, the confusion, and the speed with which most of the informants had either made off or hidden themselves, there were only imaginative reports of what these tanks from the sea had then done. The only verifiable fact was that from the four points of attack more than a thousand people in all had vanished during the night.

All around there was a prompt change of heart. Every islander in every island shed his indifference and sense of security, and was immediately convinced that his own home would be the next scene of assault. Ancient, uncertain weapons were dug out of cupboards, and cleaned up. Patrols were organized, and for the first night or two of their existence went on duty with a fine swagger. Talks on an inter-island flying defense system were proposed.

When, however, the next week went by without trace of further trouble anywhere in the area enthusiasm waned. Indeed, for that week there was a pause in subsea activity all over. The only report of a raid came from the Kurils, for some Slavonic reason, undated, and therefore assumed to have spent some time under microscopic examination from every security angle.

By the tenth day after the alarm Escondida's natural spirit of *mañana* had fully reasserted itself. By night and siesta it slept soundly; the rest of the time it drowsed, and we with it. It was difficult to believe that we shouldn't go on like that for years, so we were settling down to it, some of us. Muriel explored happily among the island flora; Johnny Tallton, the pilot, who was constantly standing by, did most of it in a café where a charming *señorita* was teaching him the patois; Leslie had also gone native to the extent of acquiring a guitar which we could now hear tinkling through the open window above us; Phyllis and I occasionally told one another about the scripts we might write if we had the energy; only Bocker and his two closest assistants, Bill Weyman and Alfred Haig, retained an air of purpose. If the sponsor could have seen us he might well have felt dubious about his money's worth.

I began to feel that I had had about enough of it. There was a suggestion of the Anglo-Saxon draining out, and the tropical Latin seeping in, and, while the sensation was not unpleasant, I felt it was a bit early in my life to let myself get fixed that way.

"This can't continue indefinitely," I said to Phyllis. "I suggest we give Bocker a time limit—a week from now to produce his phenomenon."

"Well—" she began reluctantly. "Yes, I suppose you're right."

"I'm damned sure I am," I told her. "In fact, I'm not at all sure that even another week may not prove fatal."

Which was, in an unintended way, truer than I knew.

"Darling, stop worrying that moon now, and come to bed."

"No soul—that's the trouble. I often wonder why I married you."

So I got up and joined her at the window.

"See?" she said. " 'A ship, an isle, a sickle moon . . .' So fragile, so eternal—isn't it lovely?"

We gazed out, across the empty Plaza, past the sleeping houses, over the silvered sea.

"I want it. It's one of the things I'm putting away to remember," she said.

Faintly from behind the opposite houses, down by the waterfront, came the tinkling of a guitar.

"*El amor tonto—y dulce,*" she sighed.

And then, suddenly, the distant player dropped his guitar, with a clang.

Down by the waterfront a voice called out, unintelligible but alarming. Then other voices. A woman screamed. We turned to look at the houses that hid the little harbor.

"Listen!" said Phyllis. "Mike, do you think—?" She broke off at the sound of a couple of shots. "It must be! Mike, they must be coming!"

There was an increasing hubbub in the distance. In the Square itself windows were opening, people calling questions from one to another. A man ran out of a door, round the corner, and disappeared down the short street that led to the water. There was more shouting now, more screaming, too. Among it the crack of three or four more shots. I turned from the window and thumped on the wall which separated us from the next room.

"Hey, Ted!" I shouted. "Turn up your lights! Down by the waterfront, man. Lights!"

I heard his faint okay. He must have been out of bed already, for almost as I turned back to the window the lights began to go on in batches.

There was nothing unusual to be seen except a dozen or more men pelting across the Square towards the harbor. Quite abruptly the noise which had been rising in crescendo was cut off. Ted's door slammed. His boots thudded along the corridor past our room. Beyond the houses the yelling and screaming broke out again, louder than before, as if it had gained force from being briefly dammed.

"I must—" I began, and then stopped when I found that Phyllis was no longer beside me.

I looked across the room, and saw her in the act of locking the door. I went over. "I must go down there. I must see what's—"

"No!" she said.

She turned and planted her back firmly against the door. She looked rather like a severe angel barring a road, except that angels are assumed to wear respectable cotton night dresses, not nylon.

"But, Phyl—it's the job. It's what we're here for."

"I don't care. We wait a bit."

She stood without moving, severe angel expression now modified by that of mutinous small girl. I held out my hand. "Phyl. Please give me that key."

"No!" she said, and flung it across the room, through the window. It clattered on the cobbles outside. I gazed after it in astonishment. That was not at all the kind of thing one associated with Phyllis. All over the now floodlit Square people were now hurriedly converging towards the street on the opposite side. I turned back.

"Phyl. Please get away from that door."

She shook her head. "Don't be a fool, Mike. You've got a job to do."

"That's just what I—"

"No, it isn't. Don't you see? The only reports we've had at all were from the people who *didn't* rush to find out what was happening. The ones who either hid, or ran away."

I was angry with her, but not too angry for the sense of that to reach me and make me pause. She followed up: "It's what Freddy said—the point of our coming at all is that we should be able to go back and tell them about it."

"That's all very well, but—"

"No! Look there." She nodded towards the window.

People were still converging upon the streets that led to the waterside; but they were no longer going into it. A solid crowd was piling up at the entrance. Then, while I still looked, the previous scene started to go into reverse. The crowd backed, and began to break up at its edges. More men and women came out of the street, thrusting it back until it was dispersing all over the Square.

I went closer to the window to watch. Phyllis left the door and came and stood beside me. Presently we spotted Ted, turret-lensed movie camera in hand, hurrying back.

"What is it?" I called down.

"God knows. Can't get through. There's a panic up the street there. They all say it's coming this way, whatever it is. If it does, I'll get a shot from my window. Can't work this thing in that mob." He glanced back, and then disappeared into the hotel doorway below us.

People were still pouring into the Square, and breaking into a run when they reached a point where there was room to run. There had been no further sound of shooting, but from time to time there would be another outbreak of shouts and screams somewhere at the hidden far end of the short street.

Among those headed back to the hotel came Dr. Bocker himself, and the pilot, Johnny Talton. Bocker stopped below, and shouted up. Heads popped out of various windows. He looked them over. "Where's Alfred?" he asked.

No one seemed to know.

"If anyone sees him, call him inside," Bocker instructed. "The rest of you stay where you are. Observe what you can, but don't expose yourselves till we know more about it. Ted, keep all your lights on. Leslie—"

"Just on my way with the portable recorder, Doc," said Leslie's voice.

"No, you're not. Sling the mike outside the window if you like, but keep under cover yourself. And that goes for everyone, for the present."

"But, Doc, what is it? What's—"

"We don't know. So we keep inside until we find out why it makes people scream. Where the hell's Miss Flynn? Oh, you're there. Right. Keep watching, Miss Flynn."

He turned to Johnny, and exchanged a few inaudible words with him. Johnny nodded, and made off round the back of the hotel. Bocker himself looked across the Square again, and then came in, shutting the door behind him.

Running, or at least hurrying, figures were still scattering over the Square in all directions, but no more were emerging from the street. Those who had reached the far side turned back to look, hovering close to doorways or alleys into which they could jump swiftly if necessary. Half a dozen men with guns or rifles laid themselves down on the cobbles, their weapons all aimed at the mouth of the street. Everything was much quieter now. Except for a few sounds of sobbing, a tense, expectant silence held the whole scene. And then, in the background, one became aware of a grinding, scraping noise; not loud, but continuous.

The door of a small house close to the church opened. The priest, in a long black robe, stepped out. A number of people nearby ran towards him, and then knelt around him. He stretched out both arms as though to encompass and guard them all.

The noise from the narrow street sounded like the heavy dragging of metal upon stone.

Three or four rifles fired suddenly, almost together. Our angle of view still stopped us from seeing what they fired at, but they let go a number of rounds each. Then the men jumped to their feet and ran further back, almost to the further side of the Square. There they turned round, and reloaded.

From the street came a noise of crackling timbers and falling bricks and glass.

Then we had our first sight of a "sea-tank." A curve of dull, gray metal sliding into the Square, carrying away the lower corner of a housefront as it came.

Shots cracked at it from half a dozen different directions. The bullets splattered or thudded against it without effect. Slowly, heavily, with an air of inexorability, it came on, grinding and scraping across the cobbles. It was inclining slightly to its right, away from us and toward the church, carrying away more of the corner house, unaffected by the plaster, bricks and beams that fell on it and slithered down its sides.

More shots smacked against it or ricocheted away whining, but it kept steadily on, thrusting itself into the Square at something under three miles an hour, massively indeflectable. Soon we were able to see the whole of it.

Imagine an elongated egg which has been halved down its length and set flat side to the ground, with the pointed end foremost. Consider this egg to be between thirty and thirty-five feet long, of a drab, lusterless leaden color, and you will have a fair picture of the "sea-tank" as we saw it pushing into the Square.

There was no way of seeing how it was propelled; there may have been rollers beneath, but it seemed, and sounded, simply to grate forward on its metal belly with plenty of noise, but none of machinery. It did not jerk to turn, as a tank does, but neither did it steer like a car. It simply moved to the right on a diagonal, still pointing forwards. Close behind it followed another, exactly similar contrivance which slanted its way to the left, in our direction, wrecking the housefront on the nearest corner of the street as it came. A third kept straight ahead into the middle of the Square, and then stopped.

At the far end the crowd that had knelt about the priest scrambled to its feet, and fled. The priest himself stood his ground. He barred the thing's way. His right hand held a cross extended against it, his left was raised, fingers spread and palm outward, to halt it. The thing moved on, neither faster nor slower, as if he had not been there. Its curved flank pushed him aside a little as it came. Then it, too, stopped.

A few seconds later the one at our end of the Square reached what was apparently its appointed position and also stopped.

"Troops will establish themselves at first objective in extended order," I said to Phyllis as we regarded the three evenly spaced out in the Square. "This isn't haphazard. Now what?"

For almost half a minute it did not appear to be now anything. There was a little more sporadic shooting, some of it from windows which, all round the Square, were full of people hanging out to see what went on. None of it had any effect on the targets, and there was some danger from ricochets.

"Look!" said Phyllis suddenly. "This one's bulging."

She was pointing at the nearest. The previously smooth fore-and-aft sweep of its top was now disfigured at the highest point by a small, domelike excrescence. It was lighter colored than the metal beneath; a kind of off-white, semiopaque substance which glittered viscously under the floods. It grow as one watched it.

"They're all doing it," she added.

There was a single shot. The excrescence quivered, but went on swelling. It was growing faster now. It was no longer dome-shaped, but spherical, attached to the metal by a neck, inflating like a balloon, and swaying slightly as it distended.

"It's going to pop. I'm sure it is," Phyllis said, apprehensively.

"There's another coming up further down its back," I said. "Two more, look."

The first excrescence did not pop. It was already some two foot six in diameter and still swelling fast.

"It *must* pop soon," she muttered.

But still it did not. It kept on expanding until it must have been all of five feet in diameter. Then it stopped growing. It looked like a huge, repulsive bladder. A tremor and a shake passed through it. It shuddered jellywise, became detached, and wobbled into the air with the uncertainty of an overblown bubble.

In a lurching, amoebic way it ascended for ten feet or so. There it vacillated, steadying into a more stable sphere. Then, suddenly, something happened to it. It did not explode. Nor was there any sound. Rather, it seemed to slit open, as if it had been burst into instantaneous bloom by a vast number of white cilia which rayed out in all directions.

The instinctive reaction was to jump back from the window away from it. We did.

Four or five of the cilia, like long white whiplashes, flicked in through the window, and dropped to the floor. Almost as they touched it they began to contract and withdraw. Phyllis gave a sharp cry. I looked round at her. Not all of the long cilia had fallen on the floor. One of them had flipped the last six inches of its length on to her right forearm. It was already contracting, pulling her arm towards the window. She pulled back. With her other hand she tried to pick the thing off, but her fingers stuck to it as soon as they touched it. "Mike!" she cried. "Mike!"

The thing was tugging hard, looking tight as a bowstring. She had already been dragged a couple of steps towards the window before I could get after her in a kind of diving tackle. The force of my jump carried her across to the other side of the room. It did not break the thing's hold, but it did move it over so that it no longer had a direct pull through the window, and was forced to drag round a sharp corner. And drag it did. Lying on the floor now, I got the crook of my knee round a bed leg for better purchase, and hung on for all I was worth. To move Phyllis then it would have had to drag me and the bedstead, too. For a moment I thought it might. Then Phyllis screamed, and suddenly there was no more tension.

I rolled her to one side, out of line of anything else that might come in through the window. She was in a faint. A patch of skin six inches long had been torn clean away from her right forearm, and more had gone from the fingers on her left hand. The exposed flesh was just beginning to bleed.

Outside in the Square there was a pandemonium of shouting and screaming. I risked putting my head round the side of the window. The thing that had burst was no longer in the air. It was now a round body no more than a couple of feet in diameter surrounded by a radiation of cilia. It was drawing these back into itself with whatever they had caught, and the tension was keeping it a little off the ground. Some of the people it was pulling in were shouting and struggling, others were like inert bundles of clothes.

I saw poor Muriel Flynn among them. She was lying on her back, dragged across the cobbles by a tentacle caught in her red hair. She had been badly hurt by the fall when she was pulled out of her window, and was crying out with terror, too. Leslie dragged almost alongside her, but it looked as if the fall had mercifully broken his neck.

Over on the far side I saw a man rush forward and try to pull a screaming woman away, but when he touched the cilium that held her his hand became fastened to it, too, and they were dragged along together. As I watched I thanked God I had grabbed Phyllis's arm, and not the cilium itself in trying to free her.

As the circle contracted, the white cilia came closer to one another. The struggling people inevitably touched more of them and became more helplessly enmeshed than before. They struggled like flies on a flypaper. There was a relentless deliberation about it which made it seem horribly as though one watched through the eye of a slow-motion camera.

Then I noticed that another of the misshapen bubbles had wobbled into the air, and drew back hurriedly before it should burst.

Three more cilia whipped in through the window, lay for a moment like white cords on the floor, and then began to draw back.

When they had vanished across the sill I leaned over to look out of the window again. In several places about the Square there were converging knots of people struggling helplessly. The first and nearest had contracted until its victims were bound together into a tight ball out of which a few arms and legs still flailed wildly. Then, as I watched, the whole compact mass tilted over and began to roll away across the Square towards the street by which the sea-tanks had come.

The machines, or whatever the things were, still lay where they had stopped, looking like huge gray slugs, each engaged in producing several of its disgusting bubbles at different stages.

I dodged back as another was cast off, but this time nothing happened to find our window. I risked leaning out for a moment to pull the casement windows shut, and got them closed just in time. Three or four more lashes smacked against the glass with such force that one of the panes was cracked.

Then I was able to attend to Phyllis. I lifted her on to the bed, and tore a strip off the sheet to bind up her arm.

Outside, the screaming and shouting and uproar was still going on, and among it the sound of a few shots.

When I had bandaged the arm I looked out again. Half a dozen objects, looking now like tight round bales were rolling over and over on their way to the street that led to the waterfront. I turned back again and tore another strip off the sheet to put round Phyllis's left hand.

While I was doing it I heard a different sound above the hubbub outside. I dropped the cotton strip, and ran back to the window in time to get a glimpse of a plane coming in low. The cannon in the wings started to twinkle, and I threw myself back, out of harm's way. There was a dull woomph! of an explosion. Simultaneously the windows blew in, the light went out, bits of something whizzed past and something else splattered all over the room.

I picked myself up. The outdoor lights down our end of the Square had gone out, too, so that it was difficult to make out much there, but up the other end I could see that one of the sea-tanks had begun to move. It was sliding back by the way it had come. Then I heard the sound of the aircraft returning, and went down on the floor again.

There was another woomph! but this time we did not catch the force of it, though there was a clatter of things falling outside.

"Mike?" said a voice, from the bed, a frightened voice.

"It's all right, darling. I'm here," I told her.

The moon was still bright, and I was able to see better now.

"What's happened?" she asked.

"They've gone. Johnny got them with the plane—at least, I suppose it was Johnny," I said. "It's all right now."

"Mike, my arms do hurt."

"I'll get a doctor as soon as I can, darling."

"What was it? It had got me, Mike. If you hadn't held on—"

"It's all over now, darling."

"I—" She broke off at the sound of the plane coming back once more. We listened. The cannon were firing again, but this time there was no explosion.

"Mike, there's something sticky—is it blood? You're not hurt?"

"No, darling. I don't know what it is, it's all over everything."

"You're shaking, Mike."

"Sorry. I can't help it. Oh, Phyl, darling Phyl— So nearly— If you'd seen them—Muriel and the rest—it might have been —"

"There, there," she said, as if I were aged about six. "Don't cry, Micky. It's over now." She moved. "Oh, Mike, my arm does hurt."

"Lie still, darling. I'll get the doctor," I told her.

I went for the locked door with a chair, and relieved my feelings on it quite a lot.

It was a subdued remnant of the expedition that foregathered the following morning—Bocker, Ted Jarvey, and ourselves. Johnny had taken off earlier with the film and recordings, including an eyewitness account I had added later, and was on his way to Kingston with them.

Phyllis's right arm and left hand were swathed in bandages. She looked pale, but had resisted all persuasions to stay in bed. Bocker's eyes had entirely lost their customary twinkle. His wayward lock of gray hair hung forward over a face which looked more lined and older than it had on the previous evening. He limped a little, and put some of his weight on a stick. Ted and I were unscathed. He looked questioningly at Bocker. "If you can manage it, sir," he said, "I think our first move ought to be to get out of this stink."

"By all means," Bocker agreed. "A few twinges are nothing compared with this. The sooner, the better," he added, and got up to lead the way to windward.

The cobbles of the Square, the litter of metal fragments that lay about it, the houses all round, the church, everything in sight glistened with a coating of slime, and there was more of it that one did not see, splashed into almost every room that fronted on the Square. The previous night it had been simply a strong fishy, salty smell, but with the warmth of the sun at work upon it it had begun to give off an odor that was already fetid and rapidly becoming miasmic. Even a hundred yards made a great deal of difference, another hundred, and we were clear of it, among the palms which fringed the beach on the opposite side of the town from the harbor. Seldom had I known the freshness of a light breeze to smell so good.

Bocker sat down, and leaned his back against a tree. The rest of us disposed ourselves and waited for him to speak first. For a long time he did not. He sat motionless, looking blindly out to sea. Then he sighed. "Alfred," he said, "Bill, Muriel, Leslie. I brought you all here. I have shown very little imagination and consideration for your safety, I'm afraid."

Phyllis leaned forward. "You mustn't think like that, Dr. Bocker. None of us *had* to come, you know. You offered us the *chance* to come, and we took it. If—if the same thing had happened to me I don't think Michael would have felt that you were to blame, would you, Mike?"

"No," I said. I knew perfectly well whom I should have blamed —forever, and without reprieve.

"And I shouldn't, and I'm sure the others would feel the same way," she added, putting her uninjured right hand on his sleeve.

He looked down at it, blinking a little. He closed his eyes for a

moment. Then he opened them, and laid his hands on hers. His gaze
strayed beyond her wrist to the bandages above. "You're very good
to me, my dear," he said.

He patted the hand, and then sat straight, pulling himself together.
Presently, in a different tone: "We have some results," he said. "Not,
perhaps, as conclusive as we had hoped, but some tangible evidence
at least. Thanks to Ted the people at home will now be able to see
what we are up against, and thanks to him, too, we have the first
specimen."

"Specimen?" repeated Phyllis. "What of?"

"A bit of one of those tentacle things," Ted told her.

"How on earth?"

"Luck, really. You see, when the first one burst nothing came in
at my particular window, but I could see what was happening in
other places, so I opened my knife and put it handy on the sill, just
in case. When one did come in with the next shower it fell across
my shoulder, and I caught up the knife and slashed it just as it began
to pull. There was about eighteen inches of it left behind. It just
dropped off on the floor, wriggled a couple of times, and then curled
up. We posted it off with Johnny."

"Ugh!" said Phyllis.

"In future," I said, "we, too, will carry knives."

"Make sure they're sharp. It's mighty tough stuff," Ted advised.

"If you can find another bit of one I'd like to have it for examination," said Bocker. "We decided that one had better go off to the experts. There's something very peculiar indeed about those things.
The fundamental is obvious enough, it goes back to some type of
sea anemone—but whether the things have been bred, or whether
they have in some way been built up on the basic pattern—?" He
shrugged without finishing the question. "I find several points extremely disturbing. For instance, how are they made to clutch the
animate even when it is clothed, and not attach themselves to the
inanimate? Also, how is it possible that they can be directed on the
route back to the water instead of simply trying to reach it the
nearest way?

"The first of those questions is the more significant. It implies specialized purpose. The things are *used,* you see, but not like weapons in the ordinary sense, not just to destroy, that is. They're more like snares."

We sat thinking that over for a bit.

"But—why—?" said Phyllis.

Bocker frowned. "*Why!*" he repeated. "Everybody is always asking 'why?' Why did the things come to the Deeps? Why didn't they stay at home? Why do they now come out of the Deeps on to the land? And now, why do they attack us this way and not that? How can we possibly hope to know the answers until we can find out more about the sort of creatures they are? The human view would suggest one of two motives—but that isn't to say that they don't have entirely different motives of their own."

"Two motives?" said Phyllis, meekly.

"Yes. They may be trying to exterminate us. For all we can tell they may be under the impression that we *have to* live on coastlines, and that they can gradually wipe us out in this way. You see, it is so difficult: we don't know how much they know about us, either. But I shouldn't think that is the purpose—it doesn't account for the tactics of rolling the victims back to the water—at least, not fully. The coelenterates could as easily crush them and leave them. So it looks as if the other motive might fit—simply that they find us—and perhaps other land creatures, if you recall the disappearance of goats and sheep on Saphira—good to eat. —Or even both: plenty of tribes have an old established custom of eating their enemies."

"You mean that they may have come sort of—well, sort of shrimping for us?" Phyllis asked, uneasily.

"Well, we land creatures let down trawls into the sea, and eat what they catch there. Why not a reverse process for intelligent sea creatures? But, of course, there again I am giving them a human outlook. That's what we all keep trying to do with our 'whys.' The trouble is we have all of us read too many stories where the invaders turn up behaving and thinking just like human beings, whatever their shape happens to be, and we can't shake loose from the idea that their behavior must be comprehensible to us. In fact, there is no reason why it should be, and plenty of reasons why it shouldn't."

"Shrimping," repeated Phyllis, thoughtfully. "How disgusting! But it could be."

Bocker said firmly: "We will now drop this 'why': we may, or may not, learn more about it later. The important thing now is *how: how* to stop the things, and *how* to attack them."

He paused. I must confess that I went on thinking about the "why"—and feeling that even if the purport were right, Phyllis might have chosen some pleasanter and more dignified analogy than "shrimping." Presently Bocker went on: "Ordinary rifle fire doesn't appear to trouble either the sea-tanks or these millebrachiate things —unless there are vulnerable spots that were not found. Explosive cannon shells can, however, fracture the covering. The manner in which it then disintegrates suggests that it is already under very strong stress, and not very far from breaking point. We may deduce from that that in the April Island affair there was either a lucky shot, or a grenade was used. What we saw last night certainly explains the natives' talk of whales and jellyfish. These sea-tanks might easily, at a distance, be taken for whales. And regarding the 'jellyfish' they weren't so far out—the things must almost without doubt be closely related to the coelenterates.

"As to the sea-tanks the contents seem to have been simply gelatinuous masses confined under immense pressure—but it is hard to credit that this can really be so. Apart from any other consideration it would seem that there must be a mechanism of some kind to propel those immensely heavy hulls. I went to look at their trails this morning. Some of the cobblestones have been ground down and some cracked into flakes by the weight, but I couldn't find any trackmarks, or anything to show that the things dragged themselves along by grabs as I thought might be the case. I think we are stumped there for the present.

"Intelligence of a kind there undoubtedly is, though it appears not to be very high, or else not very well co-ordinated. All the same, it was good enough to lead them from the waterfront to the Square which was the best place for them to operate."

"I've seen army tanks carry away house corners in much the same way as they did," I observed.

"That is one possible indication of poor co-ordination," Bocker replied, somewhat crushingly. "Now have we any observations to add to those I have made?" He looked round inquiringly. "Anything else? Did anyone notice whether the shots appeared to have any effect at all on those tentacular forms?" he added.

"As far as I could see, either the shooting was lousy, or the bullets went through without bothering them," Ted told him.

"H'm," said Bocker, and lapsed into reflection for a while.

Presently I became aware of Phyllis muttering. "What?" I inquired.

"I was just saying 'millebrachiate tentacular Coelenterates,' " she explained.

"Oh," I said.

Nobody made any further comment. The four of us continued to sit on, looking out across a blandly innocent azure sea.

Among the other papers I bought at London Airport was the current number of *The Beholder*. Though it is, I am aware, not without its merits and even well thought of in some circles, it leaves me with an abiding sense that it is more given to expressing its first prejudices than its second thoughts. Perhaps if it were to go to press a day later. However, the discovery in this issue of a leader entitled: DOCTOR BOCKER RIDES AGAIN did nothing to alter my impression. The text ran something after this fashion:

"Neither the courage of Dr. Alastair Bocker in going forth to meet a submarine dragon, nor his perspicacity in correctly deducing where the monster might be met, can be questioned. The gruesome and fantastically repulsive scenes to which the E.B.C. treated us in our homes last Tuesday evening make it more to be wondered at that any of the party should have survived than that four of its members should have lost their lives. Dr. Bocker himself is to be congratulated on his escape at the cost merely of a sprained ankle when his sock and shoe were wrenched off, and another member of the party on her even narrower escape.

"Nevertheless, horrible though this affair was, and valuable as some of the Doctor's observations may prove in suggesting countermeasures, it would be a mistake for him to assume that he has now been granted an unlimited license to readopt his former role as the world's premier scaremonger.

"It is our inclination to attribute his suggestion that we should proceed forthwith to embattle virtually the entire wesern coastline of the United Kingdom, to the effect of recent unnerving experiences upon a temperament which has never shunned the sensational, rather than to the conclusions of mature consideration.

"Let us consider the cause of this panic-stricken recommendation. It is this: a number of small islands, all but one of them lying within the tropics, have been raided by some marine agency of which we, as yet, know little. In the course of these raids some hundreds of people —to an estimated total no larger than that of the number of persons injured on the roads in a few days—have lost their lives. This is unfortunate and regrettable, but scarcely grounds for the suggestion that we, thousands of miles from the nearest incident of the kind, should, at the taxpayers' expense, proceed to beset our whole shoreline with weapons and guards. This is a line of argument which would have us erect shockproof buildings in London on account of an earthquake in Tokyo . . ."

And so on. There wasn't a lot left of poor Bocker by the time they had finished with him. I did not show it to him. He would find out soon enough, for *The Beholder's* readership had no use for the unique approach: it liked the popular view, custom tailored.

Presently the helicopter set us down at the terminus, and Phyllis and I slipped away while pressmen converged on Bocker.

Dr. Bocker out of sight, however, was by no means Dr. Bocker out of mind. The major part of the Press had divided into pro and anti camps, and, within a few minutes of our getting back to the flat, representatives of both sides began ringing us up to put leading questions to their own advantage. After about five of these I seized on an interval to ring the E.B.C. and tell them that as we were about to remove our receiver for a while they would probably suffer, and would they please keep a record of callers. They did. Next morning there was quite a list. Among those anxious to talk to us I noticed the name of Captain Winters, with the Admiralty number against it.

Phyllis talked to him. He had called to get from us confirmation of eyewitness reports, and to give us the latest on Bocker. It seems he had firmly put forth the theory which we had heard before, that the sea-tanks themselves didn't have intelligence, that this intelligence was in actuality somewhere in the Deeps, and directed them by some remote means of communication at present unknown. But the most trouble had been caused, apparently, by his use of the word pseudo-coelenterate. As Winters put it, "he says they are not coelenterates, not animals, and probably not in the accepted sense, living creatures at all, but that they may well be artificial organic constructions *built* for a specialized purpose. He read Bocker's statement on the subject to Phyllis over the phone.

" 'It is far from inconceivable that organic tissues might be constructed in a manner analogous to that used by chemists to produce plastics of a required molecular structure. If this were done and the resulting artifact rendered sensitive to stimuli administered chemically or physically, it could, temporarily at least, produce a behavior which would, to an unprepared observer, be scarcely distinguishable from that of a living organism.

" 'My observations lead me to suggest that this is what has been done, the coelenterate form being chosen, out of many others that might have served the purpose, for its simplicity of construction. It seems probable that the sea-tanks may be a variant of the same device. In other words, we were being attacked by organic mechanisms under remote, or predetermined, control. When this is considered in the light of the control which we ourselves are able to exercise over *in*organic materials, remotely, as with guided missiles, or predeterminedly, as with torpedoes, it should be less startling than it at first appears. Indeed, it may well be that once the technique of building up a natural form synthetically has been discovered, control of it would present less complex problems than many we have had to solve in our control of the inorganic.' "

"Oh—oh—oh!" said Phyllis painedly, to Captain Winters. "I've a good mind to go straight round and shake Dr. Bocker. He *promised* me he wouldn't say anything yet about that 'pseudo' business. He's just a kind of natural-born *enfant terrible,* it'd do him *good* to be shaken. Just wait till I get him alone."

"It does weaken his whole case," Captain Winters agreed.

"Weaken it! Somebody is going to hand this to the newspapers. They play it up hard as another Bockerism, the whole thing will become just a stunt—and that will put all the sensible people against whatever he says. —And just as he was beginning to live some of the other things down, too!"

A bad week followed. Those papers that had already adopted *The Beholder's* scornful attitude to coastal preparations pounced upon the pseudobiotic suggestions with glee. Writers of editorials filled their pens with sarcasm, a squad of scientists which had trounced Bocker before was marched out again, to grind him still smaller. Almost every cartoonist discovered simultaneously why his favorite political butts had somehow never seemed quite human.

The other part of the Press already advocating effective coastal defenses, let its imagination go on the subject of pseudo-living structures that might yet be created, and demanded still better defense against the horrific possibilities thought up by its staffs.

Then the sponsor informed E.B.C. that his fellow directors considered that their product's reputation would suffer by being associated with this new wave of notoriety and controversy that had arisen around Dr. Bocker, and proposed to cancel arrangements. Departmental Heads in E.B.C. began to tear their hair. Time-salesmen put up the old line about any kind of publicity being good publicity. The sponsor talked about dignity, and also the risk that the purchase of the product might be disregarded as tacit endorsement of the Bocker theory which, he feared, might have the effect of promoting sales resistance in the upper income brackets. E.B.C. parried with the observation that build-up publicity had already tied the names of Bocker and the product together in the public mind. Nothing would be gained from reining-in in midstream, so the firm ought to go ahead and get the best of its money's worth.

The sponsor said that his firm had attempted to make a serious contribution to knowledge and public safety by promoting a scientific expedition, not a vulgar stunt. Just the night before, for instance, one of E.B.C.'s own comedians had suggested that pseudo life might explain a long-standing mystery concerning his mother-in-law, and if this kind of thing was going to be allowed, etc., etc. E.B.C. promised that it would not contaminate their air in future, and pointed out that if the series on the expedition were dropped after the promises that had been made, a great many consumers in all income brackets were likely to feel that the sponsor's firm was unreliable . . .

Members of the B.B.C. displayed an infuriatingly courteous sympathy to any members of our staff whom they chanced to meet.

But there was still the telephone bringing suggestions and swift changes of policy. We did our best. We wrote and rewrote, trying to satisfy all parties. Two or three hurried conferences with Bocker himself were explosive. He spent most of the time threatening to throw the whole thing up because E.B.C. too obviously would not trust him near a live microphone, and was insisting on recordings.

At last, however, the scripts were finished. We were too tired of them to argue any more. We packed hurriedly and departed blasphemously for the peace and seclusion of Cornwall.

The first noticeable thing as we approached Rose Cottage, 268.6 miles this time, was an innovation.

"Good heavens!" I said. "We've got a perfectly good one indoors. If I am expected to come and sit out in a draught there just because of lot of your compostminded friends—"

"That," Phyllis told me, coldly, "is an arbor."

I looked at it more carefully. The architecture was unusual. One wall gave an impression of leaning a little.

"Why do we want an arbor?" I inquired.

"Well, one of us might like to work there on a warm day. It keeps the wind off, and stops papers blowing about."

"Oh," I said.

With a defensive note, she added. "After all, when one is bricklaying one has to build *something*."

It was a relief to be back. Hard to believe that such a place as Escondida existed at all. Still harder to believe in sea-tanks and giant coelenterates, pseudo or not. Yet, somehow, I did not find myself able to relax as I had hoped.

On the first morning Phyllis dug out the fragments of the frequently neglected novel and took them off, with a faintly defiant air, to the arbor. I pottered about wondering why the sense of peace wasn't flowing over me quite as I had hoped. The Cornish sea still lapped immemorially at the rocks. It was hard indeed to imagine our home sea spawning such morbid novelties as had slid up the Caribbean beaches of Escondida. Bocker seemed, in recollection, like an impish sprite who had had a power of hallucination. Out of his range, the world was a more sober, better ordered place. At least, so it appeared for the moment, though the extent to which it was not was increasingly borne in upon me during the next few days as I emerged from our particular concern to take a more general look at it.

The national airlift was working now, though on a severe schedule of primary necessities. It had been discovered that two large airfreighters working on a rapid shuttle service could bring in only a little less than the average cargo boat could carry in the same length of time, but the cost was high, and in spite of the rationing system the cost of living had already risen by about two hundred per cent.

With trade restricted to essentials, half a dozen financial conferences were in almost permanent session. Ill feeling and tempers were rising here and there where a disposition to make the delivery of necessities conditional on the acceptance of a proportion of luxuries was perceptible. There was undoubtedly some hard bargaining going on.

A few ships could still be found in which crews, at fortune-making wages, would dare the deep water, but the insurance rate pushed the cargo prices up to a level at which only the direst need would pay.

Somebody somewhere had perceived in an enlightened moment that every vessel lost had been power driven, and there was a worldwide boom in sailing craft of every size and type. There was also a proposal to mass-produce clipper ships, but little disposition to believe that the emergency would last long enough to warrant the investment.

In the backrooms of all maritime countries the boys were still hard at work. Every week saw new devices being tried out, some with enough success for them to be put into production—though only to be taken out of it again when it was shown that they had been rendered unreliable in some way, if not actually countered. Nevertheless, that the scientists would come through with the complete answer one day was not to be doubted—and always, it might be tomorrow.

From what I had been hearing, the general faith in scientists was now somewhat greater than the scientists' faith in themselves. Their shortcomings as saviors were beginning to oppress them. Their chief difficulty was not so much infertility of invention as lack of information. They badly needed more data, and could not get it. One of them had remarked to me: "If you were going to make a ghost-trap, how would you set about it? —Particularly if you had not even a small ghost to practice on." They had become ready to grasp at any straw—which may have been the reason why it was only among a desperate section of the scientists that Bocker's theory of pseudo-biotic forms received any serious consideration.

As for the sea-tanks, the more lively papers were having a great time with them, so were the newsreels. Selected parts of the Escondida films were included in our scripted accounts on E.B.C. A small footage was courteously presented to the B.B.C. for use in its newsreel, with appropriate acknowledgement. In fact the tendency to play the things up to an extent which was creating alarm puzzled me until I discovered that in certain quarters almost anything which diverted attention from the troubles at home was considered worthy of encouragement, and sea-tanks were particularly suitable for this purpose.

Their depredations, however, were becoming increasingly serious. In the short time since we had left Escondida raids had been reported from ten or eleven more places in the Carribbean area, including a township on Puerto Rico. A little further afield, only rapid action by Bermuda-based American aircraft had scotched an attack there. But this was small scale stuff compared with what was happening on the other side of the world. Accounts, apparently reliable, spoke of a series of attacks on the east coast of Japan. Raids by a dozen or more sea-tanks had taken place on Hokkaido and Honshu. Reports from further south, in the Banda Sea area, were more confused, but obviously related to a considerable number of raids upon various scales. Mindanao capped the lot by announcing that four or five of its eastern coastal towns had been raided simultaneously, an operation which must have employed at least sixty sea-tanks.

From the inhabitants of Indonesia and the Philippines, scattered upon innumerable islands set in deep seas, the outlook was very different from that which faced the British, sitting high on their continental shelf with a shallow North Sea, showing no signs of abnormality, at their backs. Among the Islands, reports and rumors skipped like a running fire until each day there were more thousands of people forsaking the coasts and fleeing inland in panic. A similar trend, though not yet on the panic scale was apparent in the West Indies.

I started to see a far larger pattern than I had ever imagined. The reports argued the existence of hundreds, perhaps thousands of these sea-tanks—numbers that indicated not simply a few raids, but a campaign.

"They must provide defenses, or else give the people the means to defend themselves," I said. "You can't preserve your economy in a place where everybody is scared stiff to go near the seaboard. You *must* somehow make it possible for people to work and live there."

"Nobody knows where they will come next, and you have to act quickly when they do," said Phyllis. "That would mean letting people have arms."

"Well, then, they should give them arms. Damn it, it isn't a function of the State to deprive its people of the means of self-protection."

"Isn't it?" said Phyllis, reflectively.

"What do you mean?"

"Doesn't it sometimes strike you as odd that all our governments who loudly claim to rule by the will of the people are willing to run almost any risk rather than let their people have arms? Isn't it almost a principle that a people should not be allowed to defend itself, but should be forced to defend its Government? The only people I know who are trusted by their Government are the Swiss, and, being landlocked, they don't come into this."

I was puzzled. The response was off her usual key. She was looking tired, too. "What's wrong, Phyl?"

She shrugged. "Nothing, except that at times I get sick of putting up with all the shams and the humbug, and pretending that the lies aren't lies, and the propaganda isn't propaganda. I'll get over it again. Don't you sometimes wish that you had been born into the Age of Reason, instead of the Age of the Ostensible Reason? I think that they are going to let thousands of people be killed by these horrible things rather than risk giving them powerful enough weapons to defend themselves. And they'll have rows of arguments why it is best so. What do a few thousands, or a few millions of people matter? Women will just go on making the loss good. But Governments are important—one mustn't risk them."

"Darling—"

"There'll be token arrangements, of course. Small garrisons in important places, perhaps. Aircraft standing-by on call—and they will come along after the worst of it has happened—when men and women have been tied into bundles and rolled away by those horrible things, and girls have been dragged over the ground by their hair, like poor Muriel, and people have been pulled apart, like that man who was caught by two of them at once—*then* the airplanes will come, and the authorities will say they were sorry to be a bit late, but there are technical difficulties in making adequate arrangements. That's the regular kind of brush-off, isn't it?"

"But, Phyl, darling—"

"I know what you are going to say, Mike, but I *am* scared. Nobody's really *doing* anything. There's no realization, no genuine attempt to change the pattern to meet it. The ships are driven off the deep seas; goodness knows how many of these sea-tank things are ready to come and snatch people away. They say: 'Dear, dear! Such a loss of trade,' and they talk and talk and talk as if it'll all come right in the end if only they can keep on talking long enough. When anybody like Bocker suggests *doing* something he's just howled down and called a sensationalist, or an alarmist. How many people do they regard as the proper wastage before they *must* do something?"

"But they are trying, you know, Phyl—"

"Are they? I think they're balancing things all the time. What is the minimum cost at which the political setup can be preserved in present conditions? How much loss of life will the people put up with before they become dangerous about it? Would it be wise or unwise

to declare martial law, and at what stage? On and on, instead of admitting the size of the danger and getting to work. Oh, I could—"
She stopped suddenly. Her expression changed. "Sorry, Mike. I shouldn't have gone off the handle like that. I must be tired, or something." And she took herself off with a decisive air of not wanting to be followed.

The outburst disturbed me badly. I hadn't seen her in a state anything like that for years. Not since the baby died.

The next morning didn't do anything to reassure me. I came round the corner of the cottage and found her sitting in that ridiculous arbor. Her arms lay on the table in front of her, her head rested on them, with her hair straying over the littered pages of the novel. She was weeping forlornly, steadily.

I raised her chin, and kissed her. "Darling—darling, what is it—?"
She looked back at me with the tears still running down her cheeks. She said, miserably: "I can't do it, Mike. It won't work."

She looked mournfully at the written pages. I sat down beside her, and put an arm round her.

"Never mind, Sweet, it'll come—"
"It won't, Mike. Every time I try, other thoughts come instead. I'm frightened."

I tightened my arm. "There's nothing to be frightened about, darling."

She kept on looking at me. "You're not frightened?" she said.
"We're stale," I said. "We stewed too much over those scripts. Let's go over to the north coast, it ought to be good for surfboards today."

She dabbed at her eyes. "All right," she said, with unusual meekness.

We really needed to relax, to relieve the dreadful concentration. And so for the next six weeks we rested completely; not going near a script, cutting off the telephone and the radio, not approaching the novel.

Certainly, in six weeks I had become addicted to this life and might have continued longer had a twenty-mile thirst not happened to take me into a small pub close upon six o'clock one evening.

While I was standing at the bar with the second pint the landlord turned on the radio, the archrival's news-bulletin. The very first item shattered the ivory tower that I had been gradually building. The voice said: "The roll of those missing in the Oviedo-Santander district is still incomplete, and it is thought by the Spanish authorities that it may never be completely definitive. Official spokesmen admit that the estimate of 3,200 casualties, including men, women, and children, is conservative, and may be as much as fifteen or twenty per cent below the actual figure.

"In the House today, the Leader of the Opposition, in giving his party's support for the feelings of sympathy with the Spanish people, expressed by the Prime Minister, pointed out that the casualties in the third of this series of raids, that upon Gijon, would have been considerably more severe had the people not taken their defense into their own hands. The people, he said, were entitled to defense. It was a part of the business of government to provide them with it. If a government neglected that duty, no one could blame a people for taking steps for its self-protection. It would be much better, however, to be prepared with an organized force.

"The Prime Minister replied that the nature of the steps that would, if necessary, be taken would have to be dictated by the emergency, if one should arise. These, he said, were deep waters: there was much consolation to be found in the reflection that the British Isles lay in shallow waters."

The landlord reached over, and switched off the set.

"Cor!" he remarked, with disgust. "Makes yer sick. Always the bloody same. Treat you like a lot of bloody kids. Same during the bloody war. Bloody Home Guards all over the place waiting for bloody parachutists, and all the bloody ammunition all bloody well locked up. Like the Old Man his bloody self said one time: 'What kind of a bloody people do they think we are?' "

I offered him a drink, told him I had been away from any news for days, and asked what had been going on. Stripped of its adjectival monotony, and filled out by information I gathered later, it amounted to this: In the past weeks the scope of the raids had widened well beyond the tropics. At Bunbury, a hundred miles or so south of Fremantle in Western Australia, a contigent of fifty or more sea-tanks had come ashore and into the town before any alarm was given. A few nights later La Serena, in Chile, was taken similarly by surprise. At the same time in the Central American area the raids had ceased to be confined to islands, and there had been a number of incursions, large and small, upon both the Pacific and Gulf coasts. In the Atlantic, the Cape Verde Islands had been repeatedly raided, and the trouble spread northward to the Canaries and Madeira. There had been a few small-scale assaults, too, on the bulge of the African coast.

Europe remained an interested spectator. In the opinion of its inhabitants, it is the customary seat of stability. Hurricanes, tidal waves, serious earthquakes, et cetera, are extravagances divinely directed to occur in the more exotic and less sensible parts of the earth, all important European damage being done traditionally by man himself in periodic frenzies. It was not, therefore, to be seriously expected that the danger would come any closer than Madeira—or, possibly, Rabat or Casablanca.

Consequently when, five nights before, the sea-tanks had come crawling through the mud, across the shore, and up the slipways at Santander they had entered a city that was not only unprepared, but also largely uninformed about them.

Someone telephoned the garrison at the *cuartel* with the news that foreign submarines were invading the harbor in force; someone else followed up with the information that the submarines were landing tanks; yet another somebody contradicted that the submarines themselves were amphibious. Since something was certainly, if obscurely, amiss, the soldiery turned out to investigate.

The sea-tanks had continued their slow advance. The military, on their arrival had to force their way through throngs of praying townspeople. In each of several streets patrols came to a similar decision: if this were foreign invasion, it was their duty to repel it; if it were diabolical, the same action, even though ineffective, would put them on the side of Right. They opened fire.

In the *comisaría* of police a belated and garbled alarm gave the impression that the trouble was due to a revolt by the troops. With this endorsed by the sound of firing in several places, the police went forth to teach the military a lesson.

After that, the whole thing had become a chaos of sniping, counter-sniping, partisanship, incomprehension, and exorcism, in the middle of which the sea-tanks had settled down to exude their revolting coelenterates. Only when daylight came and the sea-tanks had withdrawn had it been possible to sort out the confusion, by which time over two thousand persons were missing.

"How did there come to be so many? Did they all stay out praying in the streets?" I asked.

The innkeeper reckoned from the newspaper accounts that the people had not realized what was happening. They were not highly literate nor greatly interested in the outer world, and until the first coelenterate sent out its cilia they had no idea what was going to happen. Then there was panic, the luckier ones ran right away, the others bolted for cover into the nearest houses.

"They ought to have been all right there," I said.

But I was, it seemed, out of date. Since we had seen them in Escondida the sea-tanks had learned a thing or two; among them, that if the bottom story of a house is pushed away the rest will come down, and once the coelenterates had cleared up those trampled in the panic, demolition had started. The people inside had had to choose between having the house come down with them, or making a bolt for safety.

The following night, watchers at several small towns and villages to the west of Santander spotted the half-egg shapes crawling ashore at mid-tide. There was time to arouse most of the inhabitants and get them away. A unit of the Spanish air force was standing-by, and went into action with flares and cannon. At San Vicente they blew up half a dozen sea-tanks with their first onslaught, and the rest stopped. Several more were destroyed on the second run; the rest started back to the sea. The fighters got the last of them when it was already a few inches submerged. At the other four places where they landed the defenses did almost as well. Not more than three or four coelenterates were released in all, and only a dozen or so villagers caught by them. It was estimated that out of fifty or so sea-tanks engaged, not more than four or five could have got safely back to deep water. It was a famous victory, and the wine flowed freely to celebrate it.

The night after there were watchers all along the coast ready to give the alarm when the first dark hump should break the water. But all night long the waves rolled steadily on to the beaches, with never an alien shape to break them. By morning it was clear that the sea-tanks, or those who sent them, had learned a painful lesson. The few that had survived were reckoned to be making for parts less alert.

During the day the wind dropped. In the afternoon a fog came up, by the evening it was thick, and visibility down to no more than a few yards. Somewhere about ten-thirty in the evening the sea-tanks came sliding up from the quietly lapping waters at Gijon, with not a sound to betray them until their metal bellies started to crunch up the stone ramps. The few small boats that were already drawn up there they pushed aside or crushed as they came. It was the cracking of the timbers that brought men out from the waterside *posadas* to investigate.

They could make out little in the fog. The first sea-tanks must have sent coelenterate bubbles wobbling into the air before the men realized what was happening, for presently all was cries, screams and confusion. The sea-tanks pressed slowly forward through the fog, crunching and scraping into the narrow streets while, behind them, still more climbed out of the water. On the waterfront there was panic. People running from one tank were as likely to run into another. Without any warning a whip-like cilium would slash out of the fog, find its victim, and begin to contract. A little later there would be a heavy splash as it rolled with its load over the quayside, back into the water.

Alarm, running back up the town, reached the *comisaría*. The officer in charge put through the emergency call. He listened, then hung up slowly. "Grounded," he said, "and wouldn't be much use in this, even if they could take off."

He gave orders to issue rifles and turn out every available man. "Not that they'll be much good, but we might be lucky. Aim carefully, and if you do find a vital spot, report at once."

He sent the men off with little hope that they could do more than offer a token resistance. Presently he heard sounds of firing. Suddenly there was a boom that rattled the windows, then another. The telephone rang. An excited voice explained that a party of dockworkers was throwing fused sticks of dynamite and gelignite under the advancing sea-tanks. Another boom rattled the windows. The officer thought quickly. "Very well. Find the leader. Authorize him from me. Put your men on to getting the people clear," he directed.

The sea-tanks were not easily discouraged this time, and it was difficult to sort out claims and reports. Estimates of the number destroyed varied between thirty and seventy; of the numbers engaged, between fifty and a hundred and fifty. Whatever the true figures, the force must have been considerable, and the pressure eased only a couple of hours before dawn.

When the sun rose to clear the last of the fog it shone upon a town battered in parts, and widely covered with slime, but also upon a citizenry which, in spite of some hundreds of casualties, felt that it had earned battle honors.

The account, as I had it first from the innkeeper, was brief, but it included the main points, and he concluded it with the observation: "They reckons as there was well over a bloody 'undred of the damn things done-in them two nights. And then there's all those that come up in other places, too—there must be bloody thousands of the bastards a-crawlin' all over the bloody sea bottom. Time something was bloody done about 'em, I say. Bu' no. 'No cause for alarm,' says the bloody Government. Huh! It'll go on being no bloody cause for bloody alarm until a few hundred poor devils somewhere 'as got their bloody selves lassooed by flying jellyfish. *Then* it'll be all emergency orders and bloody panic. You watch."

"The Bay of Biscay's pretty deep," I pointed out. " A lot deeper than anything we've got around here."

"So what?" said the innkeeper.

And when I came to think of it, it was a perfectly good question. The real sources of trouble were without doubt way down in the greater Deeps, and the first surface invasions had all taken place close to the big Deeps. But there were no grounds for assuming that sea-tanks *must* operate close to a Deep. Indeed, from a purely mechanical point of view a slowly shelving climb should be easier for them than a steep one—or should it? There was also the point that the deeper they were the less energy they had to expend in shifting their weight. Again the whole thing boiled down to the fact that we still knew too little about them to make any worthwhile prophecies at all. The innkeeper was as likely to be right as anyone else.

I told him so, and we drank to the hope that he was not. When I left, the spell had been rudely broken. I stopped in the village to send a telegram to Phyllis, who had gone up to London for a few days, and then went back to pack my things. I left for London the following day.

To occupy the journey by catching up on the world I bought a selection of daily and weekly newspapers. The urgent topic in most of the dailies was "coast preparedness"—the Left demanding wholesale embattlement of the Atlantic seaboard, the Right rejecting panic-spending on a probable chimera. Beyond that, the outlook had not changed a great deal. The scientists had not yet produced a panacea (though the usual new device was to be tested), the merchantships still choked the harbors, the aircraft factories were working three shifts and threatening to strike, the Communist Party was pushing a line of Every Plane is a Vote for War.

Mr. Malenkov, interviewed by telegram, had said that although the intensified program of aircraft construction in the West was no more than a part of a bourgeois-fascist plan by warmongers that could deceive no one, yet so great was the opposition of the Russian people to any thought of war that the production of aircraft within the Soviet Union for the Defense of Peace had been tripled. Indeed, so resolutely were the Peoples of the Free Democracies determined to preserve Peace in spite of the new Imperialist threat, that war was not inevitable—though there was a possibility that under prolonged provocation the patience of the Soviet Peoples might become exhausted.

The first thing I noticed when I let myself into the flat was a number of envelopes on the mat, a telegram, presumably my own, among them. The place immediately felt forlorn.

In the bedroom were signs of hurried packing, in the kitchen sink some unwashed crockery. I looked in the desk-diary, but the last entry was three days old, and said simply: "Lamb chops."

I picked up the telephone. It was nice of Freddy Whittier to sound genuinely pleased that I was in circulation again.

After the greetings: "Look," I said, "I've been so strictly incommunicado that I seem to have lost my wife. Can you elucidate?"

"Lost your what?" said Freddy, in a startled tone.

"Wife—Phyllis," I explained.

"Oh, I thought you said 'life.' Oh, she's all right. She went off with Bocker a couple of days ago," he announced cheerfully.

"That," I told him, "is not the way to break the news. Just what do you mean by 'went off with Bocker'?"

"Spain," he said, succinctly. "They're laying bathytraps there, or something. Matter of fact, we're expecting a dispatch from her any moment."

"So she's pinching my job?"

"Keeping it warm for you—it's other people that'd like to pinch it. Good thing you're back."

The flat was depressing, so I went round to the Club and spent the evening there.

The telephone jangling by the bedside woke me up. I switched on the light. Five A.M. "Hullo," I said to the telephone, in a five A.M. voice. It was Freddy. My heart gave a nasty knock inside as I recognized him at that hour.

"Mike?" he said. "Good. Grab your hat and a recorder. There's a car on the way for you now."

My needle was still swinging a bit. "Car?" I repeated. "It's not Phyl—?"

"Phyl—? O, Lord no. She's okay. Her call came through about nine o'clock. Transcription gave her your love, on my instructions. Now get cracking, old man. That car'll be outside your place any minute."

"But look here— Anyway, there's no recorder here. She must have taken it."

"Hell. I'll try to get one to the plane in time."

"Plane—?" I said, but the line had gone dead.

I rolled out of bed, and started to dress. A ring came at the door before I had finished. It was one of E.B.C.'s regular drivers. I asked him what the hell, but all he knew was that there was a special charter job waiting at Northolt. I found my passport, and we left.

It turned out that I didn't need the passport. I discovered that when I joined a small, blear-eyed section of Fleet Street that was gathered in the waiting room drinking coffee. Bob Humbleby was there, too.

"Ah, the Other Spoken Word," said somebody. "I thought I knew my Watson."

"What," I inquired, "is all this about? Here am I routed out of a warm though solitary bed, whisked through the night—yes, thanks, a drop of that would liven it up."

The Samaritan stared at me. "Do you mean to say you've not heard?" he asked.

"Heard what?"

"Bathies. Place called Buncarragh, Donegal," he explained, telegraphically. "And very suitable, too, in my opinion. Ought to feel themselves really at home among the leprechauns and banshees. But I have no doubt that the natives will be after telling us that it's another injustice that the first place in England to have a visit from them should be Ireland, so they will."

It was queer indeed to encounter that same decaying, fishy smell in a little Irish village. Escondida had in itself been exotic and slightly improbable; but that the same thing should strike among these soft greens and misty blues, that the sea-tanks should come crawling up on this cluster of little gray cottages, and burst their sprays of tentacles here, seemed utterly preposterous .

Yet, there were the ground-down stones of the slipway in the little harbor, the grooves on the beach beside the harbor wall, four cottages demolished, distraught women who had seen their men caught in the nets of the cilia, and over all the same plastering of slime, and the same smell.

There had been six sea-tanks, they said. A prompt telephone call had brought a couple of fighters at top speed. They had wiped out three, and the rest had gone sliding back into the water—but not before half the population of the village, wrapped in tight cocoons of tentacles, had preceded them.

The next night there was a raid further south, in Galway Bay.

By the time I got back to London the campaign had begun. This is no place for a detailed survey of it. Many copies of the official report must still exist, and their accuracy will be more useful than my jumbled recollections.

Phyllis and Bocker were back from Spain, too, and she and I settled down to work. A somewhat different line of work, for day-to-day news of sea-tank raids was now Agency and local correspondent stuff. We seemed to be holding a kind of E.B.C. relations job with the Forces, and also with Bocker—at least, that was what we made of it. Telling the listening public what we could about what was being done for them.

And a lot was. The Republic of Ireland had suspended the past for the moment to borrow large numbers of mines, bazookas, and mortars, and then agreed to accept the loan of a number of men trained in the use of them, too. All along the west and south coasts of Ireland squads of men were laying mine fields above the tidelines wherever there were no protecting cliffs. In coastal towns pickets armed with bomb-firing weapons kept all-night watch. Elsewhere planes, jeeps, and armored cars waited on call.

In the southwest of England, and up the more difficult west coast of Scotland similar preparations were going on.

They did not seem greatly to deter the sea-tanks. Night after night, down the Irish coast, on the Brittany coast, up out of the Bay of Biscay, along the Portuguese seaboard they came crawling in large or small raids. But they had lost their most potent weapon, surprise. The leaders usually gave their own alarm by blowing themselves up in the mine fields; by the time a gap had been created the defenses were in action and the townspeople had fled. The sea-tanks that did get through did some damage, but found little prey, and their losses were not infrequently one hundred per cent.

Across the Atlantic serious trouble was almost confined to the Gulf of Mexico. Raids on the east coast were so effectively discouraged that few took place at all north of Charlestown; on the Pacific side there were few higher than San Diego. In general it was the two Indies, the Philippines, and Japan that continued to suffer most, but they, too, were learning ways of inflicting enormous damage for very small returns.

Bocker spent a great deal of time dashing hither and thither trying to persuade various authorities to include traps among their defenses. He had little success. Scarcely any place was willing to contemplate the prospect of a sea-tank trapped on its foreshore, but still capable of throwing out coelenterates for an unknown length of time, nor did even Bocker have any theories on the location of traps beyond the construction of enormous numbers of them on a hit-or-miss basis. A few of the pitfall type were dug, but none ever made a catch. Nor did the more hopeful-sounding project of preserving any stalled or disabled sea-tank for examination turn out any better. In a few places the defenders were persuaded to cage them with wire netting instead of blowing them to pieces, but that was the easy part of the problem. The question what to do next was not solved. Any attempt at broaching invariably caused them to explode in geysers of slime. Very often they did so before the attempt was made—the effect, Bocker maintained, of exposure to bright sunlight. And it still could not be said that anyone knew any more about their nature than when we first encountered them on Escondida.

It was the Irish who took almost the whole weight of the north-European attack which was conducted, according to Bocker, from a base somewhere in the minor Deep, south of Rockall. They rapidly developed a skill in dealing with the things that made it a point of dishonor that even one should get away. Scotland suffered only a few minor visitations in the Outer Isles, with scarcely a casualty. England's only raids occurred in Cornwall, and they, too, were small affairs for the most part—the one exception was an incursion in Falmouth harbor where a few did succeed in advancing a little beyond hightide mark before they were destroyed, though much larger numbers, it was claimed, were smashed by depth charges before they could even reach the shore.

Then, only a few days after the Falmouth attacks, the raids ceased. They stopped quite suddenly, and, as far as the larger land masses were concerned, completely.

A week later there was no longer any doubt that what someone had nicknamed the Low Command had called the campaign off. The continental coasts had proved too tough a nut, and the attempt had flopped. The sea-tanks withdrew to less dangerous parts, but even there their percentage of losses mounted, and their returns diminished.

A fortnight after the last raid came a proclamation ending the state of emergency. A day or two later Bocker made his comments on the situation over the air: "Some of us," he said, "some of us, though not the more sensible of us, have recently been celebrating a victory. To them I suggest that when the cannibal's fire is not quite hot enough to boil the pot, the intended meal may feel some relief, but he has *not,* in the generally accepted sense of the phrase, scored a victory. In fact, if he does not do something before the cannibal has time to build a better and bigger fire, he is not going to be any better off.

"Let us, therefore, look at this 'victory.' We, a maritime people who rose to power upon shipping which plied to the furthest corners of the earth, have lost the freedom of the seas. We have been kicked out of an element that we had made our own. Our ships are only safe in coastal waters and shallow seas—and who can say how long they are going to be tolerated even there? We have been forced by a blockade, more effective than any experience in war, to depend on air transport for the very food by which we live. Even the scientists who are trying to study the sources of our troubles must put to sea in *sailing ships* to do their work! Is *this* victory?

"What the eventual purpose of these coastal raids may have been, no one can say for certain. They *may* have been trawling for us as we trawl for fish, though that is difficult to understand; there is more to be caught more cheaply in the sea than on the land. Or it may even have been part of an attempt to conquer the land—an ineffectual and ill-informed attempt, but, for all that, rather more successful than our attempts to reach the Deeps. If it was, then its instigators are now better informed about us, and therefore potentially more dangerous. They are not likely to try again in the same way with the same weapons, but I see nothing in what we have been able to do to discourage them from trying in a different way with different weapons.

"The need for us to find some way in which we can strike back at them is therefore not relaxed, but intensified.

"It may be recalled by some that when we were first made aware of activity in the Deeps I advocated that every effort should be made to establish understanding with them. That was not tried, and very likely it was never a possibility, but there can be no doubt that the situation which I had hoped we could avoid now exists—and is in the process of being resolved. Two intelligent forms of life are finding one another's existence intolerable. I have now come to believe that no attempt at *rapprochement* could have succeeded. Life in all its forms is strife; the better matched the opponents, the harder the struggle. The most powerful of all weapons is intelligence; any intelligent form dominates by, and therefore survives by, its intelligence: a rival form of intelligence must, by its very existence, threaten to dominate, and therefore threaten extinction.

"Observation has convinced me that my former view was lamentably anthropomorphic; I say now that we must attack as swiftly as we can find the means, and with the full intention of complete extermination. These things, whatever they may be, have not only succeeded in throwing us out of their element with ease, but already they have advanced to do battle with us in ours. For the moment we have pushed them back, but they will return, for the same urge drives them as drives us—the necessity to exterminate, or be exterminated. And when they come again, if we let them, they will come better equipped . . .

"Such a state of affairs, I repeat, is *not* victory . . ."

I ran across Pendell of Audio-Assessment the next morning. He gave me a gloomy look.

"We tried," I said, defensively. "We tried hard, but the Elijah mood was on him."

"Next time you see him just tell him what I think of him, will you?" Pendell suggested. "It's not that I mind his being right—it's just that I never did know a man with such a gift for being right at the wrong time, and in the wrong manner. When his name comes on our program again, if it ever does, they'll switch off in their thousands. As a bit of friendly advice, tell him to start cultivating the B.B.C."

As it happened, Phyllis and I were meeting Bocker for lunch that same day. Inevitably he wanted to hear reactions to his broadcast. I gave the first reports gently. He nodded:

"Most of the papers take that line," he said. "Why was I condemned to live in a democracy where every fool's vote is equal to a sensible man's? If all the energy that is put into getting votes could be turned to useful work, what a nation we could be! As it is, at least three national papers are agitating for a cut in 'the millions squandered on research' so that the taxpayer can buy himself another packet of cigarettes a week, which means more cargo space wasted on tobacco, which means more revenue from tax, which the government then spends on something other than research—and the ships go on rusting in the harbors. There's no sense in it. This is the biggest emergency we have ever had."

"But those things down there have taken a beating," Phyllis pointed out.

"We ourselves have a tradition of taking beatings, and then winning wars," said Bocker.

"Exactly," said Phyllis. "We have taken a beating at sea, but in the end we shall get back."

Bocker groaned, and rolled his eyes. "Logic—" he began, but I put in: "You spoke as if you thought they might actually be more intelligent than we are. Do you?"

He frowned. "I don't see how one could answer that. My impression, as I have said before, is that they think in a quite different way —along other lines from ours. If they do, no comparison would be possible, and any attempt at it misleading."

"You were quite serious about their trying again? I mean, it wasn't just propaganda to stop interest in the protection of shipping from falling off?" Phyllis asked.

"Did it sound like that?"

"No, but—"

"I meant it, all right," he said. "Consider their alternatives. Either they sit down there waiting for us to find a means to destroy them, or they come after us. Oh, yes, unless we find it very soon, they'll be here again—somehow—"

Phase 3

Even though Bocker had been unaware of it when he gave his warning, the new method of attack had already begun, but it took six months more before it became apparent.

Had the ocean vessels been keeping their usual courses, it would have aroused general comment earlier, but with transatlantic crossings taking place only by air, the pilots' reports of unusually dense and widespread fog in the west Atlantic were simply noted. With the increased range of aircraft, too, Gander had declined in importance so that its frequently fogbound state caused little inconvenience.

Checking reports of that time in the light of later knowledge I discovered that there were reports about the same time of unusually widespread fogs in the northwestern Pacific, too. Conditions were bad off the northern Japanese island of Hokkaido, and said to be still worse off the Kurils, further north. But since it was now some time since ships had dared to cross the Deeps in those parts information was scanty, and few were interested. Nor did the abnormally foggy conditions on the South American coast, northward from Montevideo attract public attention.

The chilly mistiness of the summer in England was, indeed, frequently remarked, though more with resignation than surprise.

Fog, in fact, was scarcely noticed by the wider world-consciousness until the Russians mentioned it. A note from Moscow proclaimed the existence of an area of dense fog having its center on the meridian 130° East of Greenwich, at or about, the 85th Parallel. Soviet scientists, after research, had declared that nothing of the kind was on previous record, nor was it possible to see how the known conditions in those parts could generate such a state, let alone maintain it virtually unchanged for three months after its existence had first been observed. The Soviet Government had on several former occasions pointed out that the Arctic activities of the hirelings of capitalist warmongers might well be a menace to Peace.

The territorial rights of the U.S.S.R. in that area of the Arctic lying between the meridians 32° East, and 168° West of Greenwich were recognized by International Law. Any unauthorized incursion into that area constituted an aggression. The Soviet Government, therefore, considered itself at liberty to take any action necessary for the preservation of Peace in that region.

The note, delivered simultaneously to several countries, received its most rapid and downright reply from Washington.

The Peoples of the West, the State Department observed, would be interested by the Soviet Note. As, however, they had now had considerable experience of that technique of propaganda which had been called the prenatal *tu quoque,* they were able to recognize its implications. The Government of the United States was well aware of the territorial divisions in the Arctic—it would, indeed, remind the Soviet Government, in the interests of accuracy, that the segment mentioned in the Note was only approximate, the true figures being: 32° 04′ 35″ East of Greenwich, and 168° 49′ 30″ West of Greenwich, giving a slightly smaller segment than that claimed, but since the center of the phenomenon mentioned was well within this area the United States Government had, naturally, no cognizance of its existence until informed of it in the Note.

Recent observations had, curiously, recorded the existence of just such a feature as that described in the Note at a center also close to the 85th Parallel, but at a point 79° West of Greenwich. By coincidence this was just the target area jointly selected by the United States and Canadian Governments for tests of their latest types of long-range guided missiles. Preparations for these tests had already been completed, and the first experimental launchings would take place in a few days.

The Russians commented on the quaintness of choosing a target area where observation was not possible; the Americans, upon the Slavonic zeal for pacification of uninhabited regions. Whether both parties then proceeded to attack their respective fogs is not on public record, but the wider effect was that fogs became news, and were discovered to have been unusually dense in a surprising number of places.

Had weather ships still been at work in the Atlantic it is likely that useful data would have been gathered sooner, but they had been "temporarily" withdrawn from service, following the sinking of two of them some time before. Consequently the first report which did anything to tidy up the idle speculation came from Godthaab, in Greenland. It spoke of an increased flow of water through the Davis Strait from Baffin Bay, with a content of broken ice quite unusual for the time of year. A few days later Nome, Alaska, reported a similar condition in the Bering Strait. Then from Spitzbergen, too, came reports of increased flow and lower temperature.

That, straightforwardly explained the fogs off Newfoundland and certain other parts. Elsewhere they could be convincingly ascribed to deep-running cold currents forced upwards into the warmer waters above by encounters with submarine mountain ranges. Everything, in fact, could be either simply or abstrusely explained, except the unusual increase in the cold flow.

Then, from Godhavn, north of Godthaab on the west Greenland coast, a message told of icebergs in unprecedented numbers and often of unusual size. Investigating expeditions were flown from American arctic bases, and confirmed the report. The sea in the north of Baffin Bay, they announced was crammed with icebergs.

"At about Latitude 77, 60 degrees West," one of the fliers wrote, "we found the most awesome sight in the world. The glaciers which run down from the high Greenland icecap were calving. I have seen icebergs formed before, but never on anything like the scale it is taking place there. In the great ice cliffs, hundreds of feet high, cracks appear suddenly. An enormous section tilts out, falling and turning slowly. When it smashes into the water the spray rises up and up in great fountains, spreading far out all around. The displaced water comes rushing back in breakers which clash together in tremendous spray while a berg as big as a small island slowly rolls and wallows and finds its balance. For a hundred miles up and down the coast we saw splashes starting up where the same thing was happening. Very often a berg had no time to float away before a new one had crashed down on top of it. The scale was so big that it was hard to realize. Only by the apparent slowness of the falls and the way the huge splashes seemed to hang in the air—the majestic pace of it all—were we able to tell the vastness of what we were seeing."

Just so did other expeditions describe the scene on the east coast of Devon Island, and on the southern tip of Ellesmere Island. In Baffin Bay the innumerable great bergs jostled slowly, grinding the flanks and shoulders from one another as they herded on the long drift southward, through the Davis Strait, and out into the Atlantic.

Away over on the other side of the Arctic Circle Nome announced that the southward flow of broken pack ice had further increased.

The public received the information in a cushionly style. People were impressed by the first magnificent photographs of icebergs in the process of creation, but, although no iceberg is quite like any other iceberg, the generic similarity is pronounced. A rather brief period of awe was succeeded by the thought that while it was really very clever of science to know all about icebergs and climate and so on, it did not seem to be much good knowing if it could not, resultantly, do something about it.

The dreary summer passed into a drearier autumn. There seemed to be nothing anybody could do about it but accept it with a grumbling philosophy.

At the other end of the world spring came. Then summer, and the whaling season started—in so far as it could be called a season at all when the owners who would risk ships were so few, and the crews ready to risk their lives fewer still. Nevertheless, some could be found ready to damn the bathies, along with all other perils of the deep, and set out. And the end of the Antarctic summer came news, via New Zealand, of glaciers in Victoria Land shedding huge quantities of bergs into the Ross Sea, and suggestions that the great Ross Ice-Barrier itself might be beginning to break up. Within a week came similar news from the Weddell Sea. The Filchner Barrier there, and the Larsen Ice-Shelf were both said to be calving bergs in fantastic numbers. A series of reconnaissance flights brought in reports which read almost exactly like those from Baffin Bay, and photographs which might have come from the same region.

The Sunday Tidings, which had for some years been pursuing a line of intellectual sensationalism, had never found it easy to maintain its supply of material. The policy was subject to lamentable gaps during which it could find nothing topical on its chosen level to disclose. It must, one fancies, have been a council of desperation over a prolonged hiatus of the kind which induced it to open its columns to Bocker.

That the Editor felt some apprehension over the result was discernible from his italicized note preceding the article in which he disclaimed, on grounds of fair-mindedness, any responsibility for what he was now printing in his own paper.

With this auspicious beginning, and under the heading: *The Devil and the Deeps,* Bocker led off: "Never, since the days when Noah was building his Ark, has there been such a well-regimented turning of blind eyes as during the last year. It cannot go on. Soon, now, the long Arctic night will be over. Observation will again be possible. Then, the eyes that should never have been shut *must* open...."

That beginning I remember, but without references I can only give the gist and a few recollected phrases of the rest. "This," Bocker continued, "is the latest chapter in a long tale of futility and failure stretching back to the sinkings of the *Yatsushiro*, and the *Keweenaw*, and beyond. Failure which has already driven us from the seas, and now threatens us on the land. I repeat, *failure*.

"That is a word so little to our taste that many think it a virtue to claim that they never admit it. All about us are unrest, inflating prices, whole economic structures changing—and, therefore, a way of life that is changing. All about us, too, are people who talk about our exclusion from the high seas as though it were some temporary inconvenience, soon to be corrected. To this smugness there is a reply; it is this:

"For over five years now the best, the most agile, the most inventive brains in the world have wrestled with the problem of coming to grips with our enemy—and there is, on their present findings, nothing at all to indicate that we shall ever be able to sail the seas in peace again.

"With the word 'failure' so wry in our mouths it has apparently been policy to discourage any expression of the connection between our maritime troubles and the recent developments in the Arctic and Antarctic. It is time for this attitude of 'not before the children' to cease.

"I do not suggest that the root problem is being neglected; far from it. There have been, and are, men wearing themselves out to find some means by which we can locate and destroy the enemy in our Deeps. What I do say is that with them still unable to find a way, we now face the most serious assault yet.

"It is an assault against which we have no defenses. It is not susceptible of direct attack.

"What is this weapon to which we can oppose no counter?

"It is the melting of the Arctic ice—and a great part of the Antarctic ice, too.

"You think that fantastic? Too colossal? It is not. It is a task which we could have undertaken ourselves, had we so wished, at any time since we released the power of the atom.

"Because of the winter darkness little has been heard lately of the patches of Arctic fog. It is not generally known that though two of them existed in the Arctic spring; by the end of the Arctic summer there were eight, in widely separated areas. Now, fog is caused, as you know, by the meeting of hot and cold currents of either air or water. How does it happen that eight novel, independent warm currents can suddenly occur in the Arctic?

"And the results? Unprecedented flows of broken ice into the Bering Sea, and into the Greenland Sea. In these two areas particularly the pack ice is hundreds of miles north of its usual spring maximum. In other places, the north of Norway, for instance, it is further south. And we ourselves have had an unusually cold, wet winter.

"And the icebergs? Obviously there are a great many more icebergs than usual, but *why* should there be more icebergs?

"Everyone knows where they are coming from. Greenland is a large island—greater than nine times the size of the British Isles. But it is more than that. It is also the last great bastion of the retreating ice age.

"Several times the ice has come south, grinding and scouring, smoothing the mountains, scooping the valleys on its way until it stood in huge ramparts, dizzy cliffs of glass-green ice, vast slow-crawling glaciers, across half Europe. Then it went back, gradually, over centuries, back and back. The huge cliffs and mountains of ice dwindled away, melted, and were known no more—except in one place. Only in Greenland does that immemorial ice still tower nine thousand feet high, unconquered yet. And down its sides slide the glaciers which spawn the icebergs. They have been scattering their icebergs into the sea, season after season, since before there were men to know of it, and why, in this year, should they suddenly spawn ten, twenty times as many? There must be a reason for this. There is.

"If some means, or some several means, of melting the Arctic ice were put into operation, a little time would have to pass before its effect namely the rise of the sea level became measurable. Moreover, the effects would be progressive; first a trickle, then a gush, then a torrent.

"In this connection I draw attention to the fact that in January of this year the mean sea level at Newlyn, where it is customarily measured, was reported to have risen by two-and-one-half inches."

"Oh, dear!" said Phyllis, when she had read this. "Of all the pertinacious stickers-out-of-necks! We'd better go and see him."

It did not entirely surprise us when we telephoned the next morning to find that his number was not available. When we called, however, we were admitted. Bocker got up from a desk littered with mail, to greet us.

"No earthly good your coming here," he told us. "There isn't a sponsor that'd touch me with a forty-foot pole."

"Oh, I'd not say that, A.B." Phyllis told him. "You will very likely find yourself immensely popular with the sellers of sandbags and makers of earth-shifting machinery before long."

He took no notice of that. "You'll probably be contaminated if you associate with me. In most countries I'd be under arrest by now."

"Terribly disappointing for you. This has always been discouraging territory for ambitious martyrs. But you do try, don't you?" she responded. "Now, look, A.B." she went on, "do you really *like* to have people throwing things at you, or what is it?"

"I get impatient," explained Bocker.

"So do other people. But nobody I know has quite your gift for going just beyond what people are willing to take at any given moment. One day you'll get hurt. Not this time because, luckily you've messed it up, but one time certainly."

"If not this time, then probably not at all," he said. He bent a thoughtful, disapproving look on her. "Just what do you mean, young woman, by coming here and telling me I 'messed it up'?"

"The anticlimax. First you sounded as if you were on the point of great revelations, but then that was followed by a rather vague suggestion that somebody or something must be causing the Arctic changes—and without any specific explanation of how it could be done. And then your grand finale was that the tide is two-and-a-half inches higher."

Bocker continued to regard her. "Well, so it is. I don't see what's wrong with that. Two-and-a-half inches is a colossal amount of water when it's spread over a hundred and forty-one million square miles. If you reckon it up in tons—"

"I never do reckon water in tons—and that's part of the point. To ordinary people two-and-a-half inches just means a very slightly higher mark on a post. After your build-up it sounded like such a let-down that everyone feels annoyed with you for alarming them— those that don't just laugh, and say: 'Ha! ha! These professors!' "

Bocker waved his hand at the desk with its load of mail. "Quite a lot of people have been alarmed—or at least indignant," he said. He lit a cigarette. "That was what I wanted. You know that at every stage the great majority, and particularly the authorities have resisted the evidence as long as they could. This is a scientific age—in the more educated strata. It will therefore almost fall over backwards in disregarding the abnormal, and it has developed a deep suspicion of its own senses. Very reluctantly the existence of something in the Deeps was belatedly conceded. There has been equal reluctance to admit all the succeeding manifestations until they couldn't be dodged. And now here we are again, balking at the newest hurdle.

"We've not been altogether idle, though. The Arctic Ocean is deep, and even more difficult to get at than the others, so there was some bombing where the fog patches occurred, but the devil of it is there's no way of telling results.

"In the middle of it the Muscovite, who seems to be constitution-ally incapable of understanding anything to do with the sea, started making trouble. The sea, he appeared to be arguing, was causing a great deal of inconvenience to the West; therefore it must be acting on good dialectically materialistic principles, and I have no doubt that if he could contact the Deeps he would like to make a pact with their inhabitants for a brief period of dialectical opportunism. Any-way, he led off, as you know, with accusations of aggression, and then in the back-and-forth that followed began to show such truculence that the attention of our Services became diverted from the really serious threat to the antics of this oriental clown who thinks the sea was only created to embarrass capitalists.

"Thus, we have now arrived at a situation where the 'bathies,' as they call them, far from falling down on the job as we had hoped, are going ahead fast, and all the brains and organizations that should be working full speed at planning to meet the emergency are congenially fooling around with those ills they have, and ignoring others that they would rather know not of."

"So you decided that the time had come to force their hands by —er—blowing the gaff?" I asked.

"Yes—but not alone. This time I have the company of a number of eminent and very worried men. Mine was only the opening shot at the wider public on this side of the Atlantic. My weighty companions who have not already lost their reputations over this business are working more subtly. As for the American end, well, just take a look at *Life* and *Collier's* this next week. Oh, yes, something is going to be done."

"What?" asked Phyllis.

He looked at her thoughtfully for a moment, then shook his head slightly. "That, thank God, is someone else's department—at least, it will be when the public forces them to admit the situation.

"It's going to be a very bloody business," he said seriously.

"What I want to know—" Phyllis and I began, simultaneously.

"Your turn, Mike," she offered.

"Well, mine is: how do you think the thing's being done? Melting the Arctic seems a pretty formidable proposition."

"There've been a number of guesses. They range from an incredible operation like piping warm water up from the tropics, to tapping the Earth's central heat—which I find just about as unlikely."

"But you have your own idea?" I suggested. It seemed improbable that he had not.

"Well, I think it *might* be done this way. We know that they have some kind of device that will project a jet of water with considerable force—the bottom sediment that was washed up into surface currents in a continuous flow pretty well proved that. Well, then, a contraption of that kind, used in conjunction with a heater, say an atomic reaction pile, ought to be capable of generating a quite considerable warm current. The obvious snag there is that we don't know whether they have atomic fission or not. So far, there's been no indication that they have—unless you count our presenting them with at least one atomic bomb that didn't go off. But if they *do* have it, I think that might be an answer."

"They could get the necessary uranium?"

"Why not? After all, they have forcibly established their rights, mineral and otherwise, over more than two-thirds of the world's surface. Oh, yes, they could get it, all right, if they know about it."

"And the iceberg angle?"

"That's less difficult. In fact, there is pretty general agreement that if one has a vibratory type of weapon which their attacks on ships led us to believe they had, there ought to be no great difficulty in causing a lump of ice—even a considerable sized lump of ice—to crack."

"Suppose we can't find a way of hindering the process, how long do you think it'll take before we are in real trouble?" I asked him.

He shrugged. "I've absolutely no idea. As far as the glaciers and the icecap are concerned, it presumably depends on how hard they work at it. But directing warm currents on pack ice would presumably show only small results to begin with and then increase rapidly, very likely by a geometrical progression. Worse than useless to guess, with no data at all."

"Once this gets into people's heads, they're going to want to know the best thing to do," Phyllis said. "What would you advise?"

"Isn't that the Government's job? It's because it's high time they thought about doing some advising that we have blown the gaff, as Mike put it. My own personal advice is too impracticable to be worth much."

"What is it?" Phyllis asked.

"Find a nice, self-sufficient hilltop, and fortify it," said Bocker, simply.

The campaign did not get off to the resounding start that Bocker had hoped. In England, it had the misfortune to be adopted by the

Nethermore Press, and was consequently regarded as stunt territory wherein it would be unethical for other journalistic feet to trespass. In America it did not stand out greatly among the other excitements of the week. In both countries there were interests which preferred that it should seem to be no more than a stunt. France and Italy took it more seriously, but their governments' political weight in world councils was lighter. Russia ignored the content, but explained the purpose; it was yet another move by cosmopolitan-fascist warmongers to extend their influence in the Arctic.

Nevertheless, official indifference was slightly breached, Bocker assured us. A Committee on which the Services were represented had been set up to inquire and make recommendations. A similar Committee in Washington also inquired in a leisurely fashion until it was brought up sharply by the State of California.

The average Californian was not greatly worried by a rise of a couple of inches in the tide level; he had been much more delicately stricken. Something was happening to his climate. The average of his seaboard temperature had gone way down, and he was having cold, wet fogs. He disapproved of that, and a large number of Californians disapproving makes quite a noise. Oregon, and Washington, too, rallied to support their neighbor. Never within the compass of their statistical records had there been so cold and unpleasant a winter.

It was clear to all parties that the increased flow of ice and cold water pouring out of the Bering Sea was being swept eastward by the Kuroshio Current from Japan, and obvious to at least one of the parties that the amenities of the most important State in the Union were suffering gravely. Something *must* be done.

In England the spur was applied when the April spring tides overflowed the Embankment wall at Westminster. Assurances that this had happened a number of times before and was devoid of particular significance were swept aside by the triumphant we-told-you-so of the *Nethermore Press.* A hysterical Bomb-the-Bathies demand sprang up on both sides of the Atlantic, and spread round the world. (Except for the intransigent sixth.)

Foremost, as well as first, in the Bomb-the-Bathies movement, the *Nethermore Press* inquired, morning and evening: "WHAT IS THE BOMB FOR?"

"Billions have been spent upon this Bomb which appears to have no other destiny but to be held up and shaken threateningly, or, from time to time, to provide pictures for our illustrated papers. The people of the world, having evolved and paid for this weapon are now forbidden to use it against a menace that has sunk our ships, closed our oceans, snatched men and women from our very shores, and now threatens to drown us. Procrastination and ineptitude has from the beginning marked the attitude of the Authorities in this affair. . . ." and so on, with the earlier bombings of the Deeps apparently forgotten by writers and readers alike.

"Working up nicely now," said Bocker when we saw him next.

"It seems pretty silly to me," Phyllis told him, bluntly. "All the same old arguments against the indiscriminate bombing of Deeps still apply."

"Oh, not that part," Bocker said. "They'll probably drop a few bombs here and there with plenty of publicity and no results. No, I mean the urge towards planning. We're now in the first stage of stupid suggestions like building immense levees of sandbags, of course; but it is getting across that something has got to be done."

It got across still more strongly after the next spring tides. There had been strengthening of the sea defenses everywhere. In London the riverside walls had been reinforced and topped for their whole length with sandbags. As a precaution, traffic had been diverted from the Embankment, but the crowd turned out to throng it and the bridges, on foot. The police did their best to keep them moving, but they dawdled from one point to another, watching the slow rise of the water, waving to the crews of passing tugs and barges which presently were riding above the road-level. They seemed equally ready to be indignant if the water should break through, or disappointed if there were an anticlimax.

They were not disappointed. The water lapped slowly above the parapet and against the sandbags. Here and there it began to trickle through on to the pavements. Firemen, Civil Defense, and Police watched their sections anxiously, rushing bags to reinforce wherever a trickle enlarged, shoring up weak-looking spots with timber struts. The pace gradually became hotter. The bystanders began to help, dashing from one point to another as new jets started up. Presently there could be little doubt what was going to happen. Some of the watching crowd withdrew, but many of them remained, in a wavering fascination. When the breakthrough came, it occurred in a dozen places on the north bank almost simultaneously. Among the spurting jets a bag or two would begin to shift, then, suddenly, came a collapse, and a gap several yards wide through which the water poured as if over a dam.

From where we stood on top of an E.B.C. van parked on Vauxhall Bridge we were able to see three separate rivers of muddy water pouring into the streets of Westminster, filling basements and cellars as they went, and presently merging into one flood. Our commentator handed over to another, perched on a Pimlico roof. For a minute or two we switched over to the B.B.C. to find out how their crew on Westminster Bridge was faring. We got on to them just in time to hear Bob Humbleby describing the flooded Victoria Embankment with the water now rising against New Scotland Yard's own second line of defenses. The television boys didn't seem to be doing too well; there must have been a lot of bets lost on where the breaksthrough would occur, but they were putting up a struggle with the help of telephoto lenses and portable cameras.

From that point on, the thing got thick and fast. On the south bank water was breaking into the streets of Lambeth, Southwark, and Bermondsey in a number of places. Up river it was seriously flooding Chiswick, down river Limehouse was getting it badly, and more places kept on reporting breaks until we lost track of them. There was little to be done but stand by for the tide to drop, and then rush the repairs against its next rise.

The House outquestioned any quiz. The replies were more assured than assuring.

The relevant Ministries and Departments were actively taking all the steps necessary, claims should be submitted through Local Councils, priorities of men and material had already been arranged. Yes, warnings had been given, but unforseen factors had intruded upon the hydrographers' original calculations. An Order in Council would be made for the requisition of all earth-moving machinery. The public could have full confidence that there would be no repetition of the calamity; the measures already put in hand would insure against any further extension. Little could be done beyond rescue work in the Eastern Counties at present, that would of course continue, but the most urgent matter at the moment was to ensure that the water could make no further inroads at the next high tides.

The requisition of materials, machines and manpower was one thing; their apportionment, with every seaboard community and low-lying area clamoring for them simultaneously, quite another. Clerks in half a dozen Ministries grew pale and heavy-eyed in a welter of demands, allocations, adjustments, redirections, misdirections, subornments, and downright thefts. But somehow, and in some places, things began to get done. Already, there was great bitterness between those who were chosen, and those who looked like being thrown to the wolves.

Phyllis went down one afternoon to look at progress of work on the riverside. Amid great activity on both banks a superstructure of concrete blocks was arising on the existing walls. The sidewalk supervisors were out in their thousands to watch. Among them she chanced upon Bocker. Together they ascended to Waterloo Bridge, and watched the termitelike activity with a celestial eye for a while.

"Alph, the sacred river—and more than twice five miles of walls and towers," Phyllis observed.

"And there are going to be some deep but not very romantic chasms on either side, too," said Bocker. "I wonder how high they'll go before the futility comes home to them."

"It's difficult to believe that anything on such a scale as this can be really futile, but I suppose you are right," said Phyllis.

They continued to regard the medley of men and machinery down below for a time.

"Well," Bocker remarked, at length, "there must be at least one figure among the shades who is getting a hell of a good laugh out of this."

"Nice to think there's even one," Phyllis said. "Who?"

"King Canute," said Bocker.

We were having so much news of our own at that time that the effects in America found little room in newspapers already straitened by a paper shortage. Newscasts, however, told that they were having their own troubles over there. California's climate was no longer Problem Number One. In addition to the difficulties that were facing ports and seaboard cities all over the world, there was bad coastline trouble in the south of the United States. It ran almost all the way around the Gulf from Key West to the Mexican border. In Florida, owners of real estate began to suffer once again as the Everglades and the swamps spilled across more and more country. Across in Texas a large tract of land north of Brownsville was gradually disappearing beneath the water. Still worse hit were Louisiana, and the Delta. The enterprise of Tin Pan Alley considered it an appropriate time to revive the plea: "River, Stay 'Way from My Door," but the river did not—nor, over on the Atlantic coast, did other rivers, in Georgia and the Carolinas.

But it is idle to particularize. All over the world the threat was the same. The chief difference was that in the more developed countries all available earth-shifting machinery worked day and night, while in the more backward it was sweating thousands of men and women who toiled to raise great levees and walls.

But for both the task was too great. The more the level rose, the further the defenses had to be extended to prevent outflanking. When the rivers were backed up by the incoming tides there was nowhere for the water to go but over the surrounding countryside. All the time, too, the problems of preventing flooding from the rear by water backed up in sewers and conduits become more difficult to handle. Even before the first serious inundation which followed the breaking of the Embankment wall near Blackfriars, in October, the man in the street had suspected that the battle could not be won, and the exodus of those with wisdom and the means had already started. Many of them, moreover, were finding themselves forestalled by refugees from the eastern counties and the more vulnerable coastal towns elsewhere.

Some little time before the Blackfriars breakthrough a confidential note had circulated among selected staff, and contracted personnel such as ourselves, at E.B.C. It had been decided, as a matter of policy in the interests of public morale, we learned, that, should certain emergency measures become necessary, etc., etc., and so on, for two foolscap pages, with most of the information between the lines. It would have been a lot simpler to say: "Look. The word is that this thing's going to get serious. The B.B.C. has orders to stay put, so for prestige reasons we'll have to do the same. We want volunteers to man a station here, and if you care to be one of them, we'll be glad to have you. Suitable arrangements will be made. There'll be a bonus, and you can trust us to look after you okay if anything does happen. How about it?"

Phyllis and I talked it over. If we had had any family, we decided, the necessity would have been to do the best we could by them— in so far as anyone could know what might turn out to be best. As we had not, we could please ourselves. Phyllis summed up for staying on the job.

"Apart from conscience and loyalty and all the proper things," she said, "Goodness knows what is going to happen in other places if it does get really bad. Somehow, running away seldom seems to work out well unless you have a pretty good idea of what you're running to. My vote is for sticking, and seeing what happens."

So we sent our names in, and were pleased to find that Freddy Whittier and his wife had done the same.

After that, some clever departmentalism made it seem as if nothing were happening for a while. Several weeks passed before we got wind of the fact that E.B.C. had leased the top two floors of a large department store near Marble Arch, and were working full speed to have them converted into as near a self-supporting station as was possible.

"I should have thought," said Phyllis, when we acquired this information, "that somewhere higher, like Hampstead or Highgate would have been better."

"Neither of them is quite London," I pointed out. "Besides, E.B.C. probably gets it for a nominal rent for announcing each time: 'This is the E.B.C. calling the world from Selvedge's.' Goodwill advertising during the interlude of emergency."

"Just as if the water would just go away one day," she said.

"Even if they don't think so, they lose nothing by letting E.B.C. have it," I pointed out.

By that time we were becoming highly level-conscious, and I looked the place up on the map. The seventy-five foot contour line ran down the street on the building's western side.

"How does that compare with the archrival?" wondered Phyllis, running her finger across the map.

Broadcasting House appeared to be very slightly better off. About eighty-five feet above mean sea level, we judged.

"H'm," she said. "Well, if there is any calculation behind our being on the top floors, they'll be having to do a lot of moving upstairs, too. Gosh," she added, glancing over to the left of the map. "Look at their television studios! Right down on the twenty-five foot level."

In the weeks just before the breakthrough London seemed to be living a double life. Organizations and institutions were making their preparations with as little ostentation as possible. Officials spoke in public with an affected casualness of the need to make plans "just in case," and then went back to their offices to work feverishly on the arrangements. Announcements continued to be reassuring in tone. The men employed on the jobs were for the most part cynical about their work, glad of the overtime pay, and curiously disbelieving. They seemed to regard it as a stunt which was working nicely to their benefit; imagination apparently refused to credit the threat with any reality outside working hours. Even after the first breakthrough, alarm was oddly localized with those who had suffered. The wall was hurriedly repaired, and the exodus was still not much more than a trickle of people. Real trouble came with the next spring tides.

There was plenty of warning this time in the parts likely to be most affected. The people took it stubbornly and phlegmatically. They had already had experience to learn by. The main response was to move possessions to upper stories, and grumble loudly at the inefficiency of authorities who were incapable of saving them the trouble involved. Notices were posted giving the times of high water for three days, but the suggested precautions were couched with such a fear of promoting panic that they were little heeded.

The first day passed safely. On the evening of the highest water a large part of London settled down to wait for midnight and the crisis to pass, in a sullenly bad-tempered mood. The buses were all off the streets, and the underground had ceased to run at eight in the evening. But plenty of people stayed out, and walked down to the river to see what there was to be seen from the bridges. They had their show.

The smooth, oily surface crawled slowly up the piers of the bridges and against the retaining walls. The muddy water flowed upstream with scarcely a sound, and the crowds, too, were almost silent, looking down on it apprehensively. There was no fear of it topping the walls; the estimated rise was twenty-three feet, four inches, which would leave a safety margin of four feet to the top of the new parapet. It was pressure that was the source of anxiety.

From the north end of Waterloo Bridge where we were stationed this time, one was able to look along the top of the wall, with the water running high on one side of it, and, to the other, the roadway of the Embankment, with the street lamps still burning there, but not a vehicle or a human figure to be seen upon it. Away to the west the hands on the Parliament clock tower crawled round the illuminated dial. The water rose as the big hand moved with insufferable sloth up to eleven o'clock. Over the quiet crowds the note of Big Ben striking the hour came clearly down wind.

The sound caused people to murmur to one another; then they fell silent again. The hand began to crawl down, ten-past, a quarter, twenty, twenty-five, then, just before the half-hour there was a rumble somewhere upstream; a composite, crowd-voice sound came to us on the wind. The people about us craned their necks, and murmured again. A moment later we saw the water coming. It poured along the Embankment towards us in a wide, muddy flood, sweeping rubbish and bushes with it, rushing past beneath us. A groan went up from the crowd. Suddenly there was a loud crack and a rumble of falling masonry behind us as a section of the wall, close by where the *Discovery* had formerly been moored, collapsed. The water poured through the gap, wrenching away concrete blocks so that the wall crumbled before our eyes and the water poured in a great muddy cascade on to the roadway.

Before the next tide came the Government had removed the velvet glove. Following the announcement of a State of Emergency came a Standstill Order, and the proclamation of an orderly scheme of evacuation. There is no need for me to write here of the delays and muddles in which the scheme broke down. It is difficult to believe that it can have been taken seriously even by those who launched it. An unconvincing air seemed to hang over the whole affair from the beginning. The task was impossible. Something, perhaps, might have been done had only a single city been concerned, but with more than two-thirds of the country's population anxious to move on to higher ground, only the crudest methods had any success in checking the pressure, and then not for long.

But, though it was bad here, it was still worse elsewhere. The Dutch had withdrawn in time from the danger areas, realizing that they had lost their centuries-long battle with the sea. The Rhine and the Maas had backed up in flood over square miles of country. A whole population was trekking southward into Belgium or southeast into Germany. The North German Plain itself was little better off. The Ems and the Weser had widened out, too, driving people southward from their towns and farms in an increasing horde. In Denmark every kind of boat was in use ferrying families to Sweden and the higher ground there.

For a little time we managed to follow in a general way what was happening, but when the inhabitants of the Ardennes and Westphalia turned in dismay to save themselves by fighting off the hungry, desperate invaders from the north, hard news disappeared in a morass of rumor and chaos. All over the world the same kind of thing must have been going on, differing only in its scale. At home, the flooding of the Eastern Counties had already driven people back on the Midlands. Loss of life was small, for there had been plenty of warning. Real trouble started on the Chiltern Hills where those already in possession organized themselves to prevent being swamped by the two converging streams of refugees from the east and from London.

Over the untouched parts of Central London a mood of Sunday-like indecision hung for several days. Many people, not knowing what else to do, still tried to carry-on as nearly as usual. The police continued to patrol. Though the underground was flooded plenty of people continued to turn up at their places of work, and some kinds of work did continue, seemingly through habit or momentum, then gradually lawlessness seeped inwards from the suburbs and the sense of breakdown became inescapable. Failure of the emergency electric supply one afternoon, followed by a night of darkness gave a kind of *coup de grâce* to order. The looting of shops, particularly food-shops, began, and spread on a scale which defeated both the police and the military.

We decided it was time to leave the flat and take up our residence in the new E.B.C. fortress.

From what the short waves were telling us there was little to distinguish the course of events in the low-lying cities anywhere— except that in some the law died more quickly. It is outside my scope to dwell on the details; I have no doubt that they will be described later in innumerable official histories.

E.B.C.'s part during those days consisted largely in duplicating the B.B.C. in the reading out of government instructions hopefully intended to restore a degree of order: a monotonous business of tell-ing those whose homes were not immediately threatened to stay where they were, and directing the flooded-out to certain higher areas and away from others that were said to be already overcrowded. We may have been heard, but we could see no evidence that we were heeded. In the north there may have been some effect, but in the south the hugely disproportionate concentration of London, and the flooding of so many rails and roads, ruined all attempts at orderly dispersal. The numbers of people in motion spread alarm among those who could have waited. The feeling that unless one reached a refuge ahead of the main crowd there might be no place at all to go was catching—as also was the feeling that anyone trying to do so by car was in possession of an unfair advantage. It quickly became safer to walk wherever one was going—though not outstandingly safe at all. It was best to go out as little as possible.

The existence of numerous hotels and a reassuring elevation of some seven hundred feet above normal sea level were undoubtedly factors which influenced Parliament in choosing the town of Harrogate, in Yorkshire, as its seat. The speed with which it assembled there was very likely due to the same force as was motivating many private persons—the fear that someone else might get in first. To an outsider it seemed that a bare few hours after Westminster was flooded, the ancient institution was performing with all its usual fluency in its new home.

As for ourselves, we began to shake down into a routine. Our living quarters were on the top floor. Offices, studios, technical equipment, generators, stores, etc., on the floor beneath. A great reserve of diesel oil and petrol filled large tanks in the basement, whence it was pumped as necessary. Our aerial systems were on roofs two blocks away, reached by bridges slung high over the intervening streets. Our own roof was largely cleared to provide a helicopter landing, and to act as a rainwater catchment. As we gradually developed a technique for living there we decided it was pretty secure.

Even so, my recollection is that nearly all spare time in the first few days was spent by everyone in transferring the contents of the provision department to our own quarters before it should disappear elsewhere.

There seems to have been a basic misconception of the role we should play. As I understood it, the idea was that we were to preserve, as far as possible, the impression of business as usual, and then, as things grew more difficult, the center of E.B.C. would follow the administration by gradual stages to Yorkshire. This appears to have been founded upon the assumption that London was so cellularly constructed that as the water flowed into each cell it would be abandoned while the rest carried on much as usual. As far as we were concerned bands, speakers, and artists would all roll up to do their stuff in the ordinary way until the water lapped our doorsteps —if it should ever reach as far—by which time they would presumably have changed to the habit of rolling up to the Yorkshire station instead. The only provision on the program side that anyone had made for things not happening in this naïve fashion was the transfer of our recorded library before it became actually necessary to save it. A dwindling, rather than a breakdown, was envisaged. Curiously, quite a number of conscientious broadcasters did somehow manage to put in their appearances for a few days. After that, however, we were thrown back almost entirely upon ourselves and the records. And, presently, we began to live in a state of siege.

I don't propose to deal in detail with the year that followed. It was a drawn out story of decay. A long, cold winter during which the water lapped into the streets faster than we had expected. A time when armed bands roved the streets in search of untouched foodstores, when, at any hour of the day or night, one was apt to hear a rattle of shots as two gangs met. We ourselves had little trouble; it was as if, after a few attempts to raid us, word had gone round that we were ready to defend, and with so many other stores raidable at little or no risk we might as well be left until later.

When the warmer weather came there were noticeably fewer people to be seen. Most of them, rather than face another winter in a city by now largely plundered of food and beginning to suffer epidemics from lack of fresh water and drainage, were filtering out into the country, and the shooting that we heard was usually distant.

Our own numbers had been depleted, too. Out of the original sixty-five we were now reduced to twenty-five, the rest having gone off in parties by helicopter as the national focus became more settled in Yorkshire. From having been a center we had declined to the state of an outpost maintained for prestige.

Phyllis and I discussed whether we would apply to go, too, but from the description of conditions that we pried out of the helicopter pilot and his crew the E.B.C. headquarters sounded congested and unattractive, so we decided to stay for a while longer, at any rate. We were by no means uncomfortable where we were, and the fewer of us that were left in our London aerie, the more space and supplies each of us had.

In late spring we learned that a decree had merged us with the archrival, putting all radio communication under direct Government control. It was the Broadcasting House lot that were moved out by a swift airlift since their premises were vulnerable while ours were already in a prepared state, and the one or two B.B.C. men who stayed came over to join us.

News reached us mainly by two channels: the private link with E.B.C., which was usually moderately honest, though discreet; and broadcasts which, no matter where they came from, were puffed with patently dishonest optimism. We became very tired and cynical about them, as, I imagine, did everyone else, but they still kept on. Every country, it seemed, was meeting and rising above the disaster with a resolution which did honor to the traditions of its people.

By midsummer, and a cold midsummer it was, the town had become very quiet. The gangs had gone; only the obstinate individuals remained. They were, without doubt, quite numerous, but in twenty-thousand streets they seemed sparse, and they were not yet desperate. It was possible to go about in relative safety again, though wise to carry a gun.

The water had risen further in the time than any of the estimates had supposed. The highest tides now reached the fifty-foot level. The floodline was north of Hammersmith and included most of Kensington. It lay along the south side of Hyde Park, then to the south of Piccadilly, across Trafalgar Square, along the Strand and Fleet Street, and then ran northeast up the west side of the Lea Valley; of the city, only the high ground about St. Paul's was still untouched. In the south it had pushed across Barnes, Battersea, Southwark, most of Deptford, and the lower part of Greenwich.

One day we walked down to Trafalgar Square. The tide was in, and the water reached nearly to the top of the wall on the northern side, below the National Gallery. We leaned on the balustrade looking at the water washing around Landseer's lions, wondering what Nelson would think of the view his statue was getting now.

Close to our feet, the edge of the flood was fringed with scum and a fascinatingly varied collection of flotsam. Further away, fountains, lampposts, traffic lights and statues thrust up here and there. On the far side, and down as much as we could see of Whitehall, the surface was as smooth as a canal. A few trees still stood, and in them sparrows chattered. Starlings had not yet deserted St. Martin's church, but the pigeons were all gone, and on many of their customary perches gulls stood, instead. We surveyed the scene and listened to the slipslop of the water in the silence for some minutes. Then I asked: "Didn't somebody or other once say: 'This is the way the world ends, not with a bang but a whimper?' "

Phyllis looked shocked. " '*Somebody or other!*' " she exclaimed. "That was Mr. Eliot!"

"Well, it certainly looks as if he had the idea that time," I said.

Presently Phyllis remarked: "I thought I was through a phase now, Mike. For such a long time it kept on seeming that something could be done to save the world we're used to—if we could only find out what. But soon I think I'll be able to feel; 'Well, that's gone. How can we make the best of what's left?'—All the same, I wouldn't say that coming to places like this does me any good."

"There aren't places like this. This is—was—one of the uniques. That's the trouble. And it's a bit more than dead, but not yet ready for a museum. Soon, perhaps, we may be able to feel, 'Lo! All our pomp of yesterday is one with Nineveh and Tyre'—soon, but not quite yet."

There was a pause. It lengthened.

"Mike," she said, suddenly. "Let's go away from here—now."

I nodded. "It might be better. We'll have to get a little tougher yet, darling, I'm afraid."

She took my arm, and we started to walk westward. Halfway to the corner of the square we paused at the sound of a motor. It seemed, improbably, to come from the south side. We waited while it drew closer. Presently, out from the Admiralty Arch swept a speedboat. It turned in a sharp arc and sped away down Whitehall, leaving the ripples of its wake slopping through the windows of august Governmental offices.

"Very pretty," I said. "There can't be many of us who have accomplished that in one of our waking moments."

Phyllis gazed along the widening ripples, and abruptly became practical again. "I think we'd better see if we can't find one of those," she said. "It might come in useful later on."

The rate of rise continued to increase. By the end of the summer the level was up another eight or nine feet. The weather was vile and even colder than it had been at the same time the previous year. More of us had applied for transfer, and by mid-September we were down to sixteen.

Even Freddy Whittier had announced that he was sick and tired of wasting his time like a shipwrecked sailor, and was going to see whether he could not find some useful work to do. When the helicopter whisked him and his wife away, they left us reconsidering our own position once more.

Our task of composing never-say-die material on the theme that we spoke from, and for, the heart of an empire bloody but still unbowed was supposed, we knew, to have a stabilizing value even now, but we doubted it. Too many people were whistling the same tune in the same dark. A night or two before the Whittiers left we had had a late party where someone, in the small hours, had tuned in a New York transmitter. A man and a woman on the Empire State Building were describing the scene. The picture they evoked of the towers of Manhattan standing like frozen sentinels in the moonlight while the glittering water lapped at their lower walls was masterly, almost lyrically beautiful—nevertheless, it failed in its purpose. In our minds we could see those shining towers—they were not sentinels, they were tombstones. It made us feel that we were even less accomplished at disguising our own tombstones; that it was time to pull out of our refuge, and find more useful work. Our last words to Freddy were that we would very likely be following him before long.

We had still, however, not reached the point of making definite application when he called us up on the link a couple of weeks later. After the greetings he said: "This isn't purely social, Mike. It is disinterested advice to those contemplating a leap from the frying pan —don't!"

"Oh," I said, "what's the trouble?"

"I'll tell you this. I'd have an application in for getting back to you right now—if only I had not made my reasons for getting out so damned convincing. I mean that. Hang on there, both of you."

"But—" I began.

"Wait a minute," he told me.

Presently his voice came again. "Okay. No monitor on this, I think. Listen, Mike, we're overcrowded, underfed, and in one hell of a mess. Supplies of all kinds are way down, so's morale. The atmosphere's like a lot of piano strings. We're living virtually in a state of siege here, and if it doesn't turn into active civil war in a few weeks it'll be a miracle. The people outside *are* worse off than we are, but seemingly nothing will convince them that we aren't living on the fat of the land. For God's sake keep this under your hat, but stay where you are, for Phyl's sake if not for your own."

I thought quickly. "If it's as bad as that, Freddy, and you're doing no good, why not get back here on the next helicopter. Either smuggle aboard—or maybe we could offer the pilot a few things he'd like?"

"All right. There certainly isn't any use for us here. I don't know why they let us come along. I'll work on that. Look for us next flight. Meanwhile good luck to you both."

"Good luck to you, Freddy, and love to Lynn—and our respects to Bocker, if he's there and nobody's slaughtered him yet."

"Oh, Bocker's here. He's now got a theory that it won't go much over a hundred and twenty-five feet, and seems to think that's good news."

"Well, considering he's Bocker, it might be a lot worse. 'Bye. We'll be looking forward to seeing you."

We were discreet. We said no more than that we had heard the Yorkshire place was already crowded, so we were staying. A couple who had decided to leave on the next flight changed their minds, too. We waited for the helicopter to bring Freddy back. The day after it was due we were still waiting. We got through on the link. They had no news except that it had left on schedule. I asked about Freddy and Lynn. Nobody seemed to know where they were.

There never was any news of that helicopter. They said they hadn't another that they could send.

The cold summer drew into a colder autumn. A rumor reached us that the sea-tanks were appearing again for the first time since the waters had begun to rise. As the only people present who had had personal contact with them we assumed the status of experts—though almost the only advice we could give was always to wear a sharp knife, and in such a position that it could be reached for a quick slash by either hand. But the sea-tanks must have found the hunting poor in the almost deserted streets of London, for presently we heard no more of them. From the radio, however, we learned that it was not so in some other parts. There were reports soon of their reappearance in many places where not only the new shore lines, but the collapse of organization made it difficult to destroy them in effectively discouraging numbers.

Meanwhile, there was worse trouble. Overnight the combined E.B.C. and B.B.C. transmitters abandoned all pretense of calm confidence. When we looked at the message transmitted to us for radiation simultaneously with all other stations we knew that Freddy had been right. It was a call to all loyal citizens to support their legally elected Government against any attempts that might be made to overthrow it by force, and the way in which it was put left no doubt that such an attempt was already being made. The thing was a sorry mixture of exhortation, threats, and pleas, which wound up with just the wrong note of confidence—the note that had sounded in Spain and then in France when the words must be said though speaker and listener alike knew that the end was near. The best reader in the service could not have given it the ring of conviction.

The link could not, or would not, clarify the situation for us. Firing was going on, they said. Some armed bands were attempting to break into the Administration Area. The military had the situation in hand, and would clear up the trouble shortly. The broadcast was simply to discourage exaggerated rumors and restore confidence in the government. We said that neither what they were telling us, nor the message itself inspired us personally with any confidence whatever, and we should like to know what was really going on. They went all official, curt and cold.

Twenty-four hours later, in the middle of dictating for our radiation another expression of confidence, the link broke off, abruptly. It never worked again.

Until one gets used to it, the situation of being able to hear voices from all over the world, but none which tells what is happening in one's own country, is odd. We picked up inquiries about our silence from America, Canada, Australia, Kenya. We radiated at the full power of our transmitter what little we knew, and could later hear it being relayed by foreign stations. But we ourselves were far from understanding what had happened. Even if the headquarters of both systems, in Yorkshire, had been overrun, as it would appear, there should have been stations still on the air independently in Scotland and Northern Ireland at least, even if they were no better informed than ourselves. Yet, a week went by, and still there was no sound from them. The rest of the world appeared to be too busy keeping a mask on its own troubles to bother about us any more—though one time we did hear a voice speaking with historical dispassion of 'l'écroulement de l'Angleterre.' The word écroulement was not very familiar to me, but it had a horribly final sound.

The winter closed in. One noticed how few people there were to be seen in the streets now, compared with a year ago. Often it was possible to walk a mile without seeing anyone at all. How those who did remain were living we could not say. Presumably they all had caches of looted stores that supported them and their families; and obviously it was no matter for close inquiry. One noticed also how many of those one did see had taken to carrying weapons as a matter of course. We ourselves adopted the habit of carrying them—guns, not rifles—slung over our shoulders, though less with any expectation of needing them than to discourage the occasion for their need from arising. There was a kind of wary preparedness which was still some distance from instinctive hostility. Chance-met men still passed on gossip and rumors, and sometimes hard news of a local kind. It was by such means that we learned of a quite definitely hostile ring now in existence around London; how the surrounding district had somehow formed themselves into miniature independent states and forbidden entry after driving out many who had come there as refugees; how those who did try to cross the border into one of these communities were fired upon without question.

In the new year the sense of things pressing in upon us grew stronger. The high-tide mark was now close to the seventy-five foot level. The weather was abominable, and icy cold. There seemed to be scarcely a night when there was not a gale blowing from the southwest. It became rarer than ever to see anyone in the streets, though when the wind did drop for a time the view from the roof showed a surprising number of chimneys smoking. Mostly it was wood smoke, furniture and fitments burning, one supposed; for the coal stores in power stations and railway yards had all disappeared the previous winter.

From a purely practical point of view I doubt whether anyone in the country was more favored or as secure as our group. The food originally supplied, together with that acquired later, made a store which should last sixteen people for some years. There was an immense reserve of diesel oil, and petrol, too. Materially we were better off than we had been a year ago when there were more of us. But we had learned, as had many before us, about the bread-alone factor, one needed more than adequate food. The sense of desolation began to weigh more heavily still when, at the end of February, the water lapped over our doorsteps for the first time, and the building was filled with the sound of it cascading into the basements.

Some of the party grew more worried. "It *can't* come very much higher, surely. A hundred feet *is* the limit, isn't it?" they were saying.

It wasn't much good being falsely reassuring. We could do little more than to repeat what Bocker had said; that it was a guess. No one had known, within a wide limit, how much ice there was in the Antarctic. No one was quite sure how much of the northern areas that appeared to be solid land, tundra, was in fact simply a deposit on a foundation of ancient ice; we just had not known enough about it. The only consolation was that Bocker now seemed to think for some reason that it would not rise above one hundred and twenty-five feet—which should leave our aerie still intact. Nevertheless, it required fortitude to find reassurance in that thought as one lay in bed at night, listening to the echoing splash of the wavelets that the wind was driving along Oxford Street.

One bright morning in May, a sunny, though not a warm morning, I missed Phyllis. Inquiries eventually led me on to the roof in search of her. I found her in the southwest corner gazing towards the trees that dotted the lake which had been Hyde Park, and crying. I leaned on the parapet beside her, and put an arm around her. Presently she stopped crying. She dabbed her eyes and nose, and said: "I haven't been able to get tough, after all. I don't think I can stand this much longer, Mike. Take me away, please."

"Where is there to go?—if we could go," I said.

"The cottage, Mike. It wouldn't be so bad there, in the country. There'd be things growing—not everywhere dying, like this. There isn't any hope here—we might as well jump over the wall here if there is to be no hope at all."

I thought about it for some moments. "But even if we could get there, we'd have to live," I pointed out, "we'd need food and fuel and things."

"There's—" she began, and then hesitated and changed her mind. "We could find enough to keep us going for a time until we could grow things. And there'd be fish, and plenty of wreckage for fuel. We could make out somehow. It'd be hard—but, Mike, I can't stay in this cemetery any longer—I can't.

"Look at it, Mike! Look at it! We never did anything to deserve all this. Most of us weren't very good, but we weren't bad enough for this, surely. And not to have a chance! If it had only been something we could fight—But just to be drowned and starved and forced into destroying one another to live—and by things nobody has ever seen, living in the one place we can't get at them!

"Some of us are going to get through this stage, of course—the tough ones. But what are the things down there going to do then? Sometimes I dream of them lying down in those deep dark valleys, and sometimes they look like monstrous squids or huge slugs, other times as if they were great clouds of luminous cells hanging there in rocky chasms. I don't suppose that we'll ever know what they really look like, but whatever it is, there they are all the time, thinking and plotting what they can do to finish us right off so that everything will be theirs.

"Sometimes, in spite of Bocker, I think perhaps it is the things themselves that are inside the sea-tanks, and if only we could capture one and examine it we should know how to fight them, at last. Several times I have dreamed that we have found one and managed to discover what makes it work, and nobody's believed us but Bocker, but what we have told him has given him an idea for a wonderful new weapon which has finished them all off.

"I know it all sounds very silly, but it's wonderful in the dream, and I wake up feeling as if we had saved the whole world from a nightmare—and then I hear the sound of the water slopping against the walls in the street, and I know it isn't finished; it's just going on and on and on.

"I can't stand it here any more, Mike. I shall go mad if I have to sit here doing nothing any longer while a great city dies by inches all round me. It'd be different in Cornwall, anywhere in the country. I'd rather have to work night and day to keep alive than just go on like this. I think I'd rather die trying to get away than face another winter like last."

I had not realized it was as bad as that. It wasn't a thing to be argued about. "All right, darling," I said. "We'll go."

Everything we could hear warned us against attempting to get away by normal means. We were told of belts where everything had been razed to give clear fields of fire, and there were booby traps and alarms, as well as guards. Everything beyond those belts was said to be based upon a cold calculation of the number each autonomous district could support. The natives of the districts had banded together and turned out the refugees and the useless on to lower ground where they had to shift for themselves. In each of the areas there was acute awareness that another mouth to feed would increase the shortage for all. Any stranger who did manage to sneak in could not hope to remain unnoticed for long, and his treatment was ruthless when he was discovered—survival demanded it. So it looked as though our own survival demanded that we should try some other way.

The chance by water, along inlets that must be constantly widening and reaching further, looked better, and but for the luck of our finding that sturdy little motorboat, the *Midge,* I don't know what would have happened to us. It came to us through the rather ghastly accident of the owner's being shot trying to escape from London. Ted Jarvey found it and brought it to us, knowing we had been searching futilely for weeks for just such a boat.

An uneasy feeling that some of the others might wish to get away, too, and press to come with us turned out to be baseless. Without exception they considered us crazy. Most of them contrived to take one of us aside at some time or another to point out the willful improvidence of giving up warm, comfortable quarters to make a certainly cold and probably dangerous journey to certainly worse and probably intolerable conditions. They helped to fuel and store the *Midge* until she was inches lower in the water, but not one of them could have been bribed to set out with us.

Our progress down the river was cautious and slow, for we had no intention of letting the journey be more dangerous than was necessary. Our main recurrent problem was where to lay up for the night. We were sharply conscious of our probable fate as trespassers, and also of the fact that the *Midge* with her contents was tempting booty. Our usual anchorages were in the sheltered streets of some flooded town. Several times when it was blowing hard we lay up in such places for several days. Fresh water, which we had expected to be the main problem turned out not to be difficult; one could almost always find some still in the tanks in the roof spaces of a partly submerged house. Overall, the trip which used to clock at 268.8 (or .9) by road took us slightly over a month to make.

Round the corner and into the channel the white cliffs looked so normal from the water that the flooding was hard to believe—until we looked more closely at the gaps where the towns should have been. A little later, we were right out of the normal, for we began to see our first icebergs.

We approached the end of the journey with caution. From what we had been able to observe of the coast as we came along there were often encampments of shacks on the higher ground. Where the land rose steeply there were often towns and villages where the higher houses were still occupied though the lower were submerged. What kind of conditions we might find at Penllyn in general and Rose Cottage in particular we had no idea.

I took the *Midge* carefully into the Helford River, with shotguns lying to hand. Here and there a few people on the hillsides stopped to look down at us, but they neither shot nor waved. It was only later that we found they had taken her to be one of the few local boats that still had the fuel to run.

We turned north from the main river. With the water now close on the hundred-foot level the multiplication of waterways was confusing. We lost our way half a dozen times before we rounded a corner on an entirely new inlet and found ourselves looking up a familiar steep hillside at the cottage above us.

People had been there, several lots of them, I should think, but though the disorder was considerable the damage was not great. It was evidently the consumables they had been after chiefly. The stand-bys had vanished from the larder to the last bottle of sauce and packet of pepper. The drum of oil, the candles, and the small store of coal were gone, too.

Phyllis gave a quick look over the debris, and disappeared down the cellar steps. She re-emerged in a moment and ran out to the arbor she had built in the garden. Through the window I saw her examining the floor of it carefully. Presently she came back. "That's all right, thank goodness," she said.

It did not seem a moment for great concern about arbors.

"What's all right?" I inquired.

"The food," she said. "I didn't want to tell you about it until I knew. It would have been too bitterly disappointing if it had gone."

"What food?" I asked, bewilderedly.

"You've not much intuition, have you, Mike? Did you really think that someone like me would be doing all that bricklaying just for fun? I walled-off half the cellar full of stuff, and there's a lot under the arbor, too."

I stared at her. "Do you mean to say—? But that was ages ago! Before the flooding even began."

"But not before they began sinking ships so fast. It seemed to me it would be a good thing to lay in stores before things got difficult, because it quite obviously was going to get difficult later. I thought it would be sensible to have a reserve here, just in case. Only it was no good telling you, because I knew you'd just get stuffy about it."

I sat down, and regarded her. "Stuffy?" I inquired.

"Well, there are some people who seem to think it is more ethical to pay black-market prices than to take sensible precautions."

"Oh," I said. "So you bricked it in yourself?"

"Well, I didn't want anybody local to know, so the only way was to do it myself. As it happened, the food airlift was much better organized than one could have expected, so we didn't need it, but it will come in useful now."

"How much?" I asked.

She considered. "I'm not quite sure, but there is a whole big truckload here, and then there's all the stuff we've got in the *Midge,* too."

I could see, and do see, several angles to the thing, but it would have been churlishly ungrateful to mention them just then, so I let it rest, and we busied ourselves with tidying up and moving in.

It did not take us long to understand why the cottage had been abandoned. One had only to climb to its crest to see that our hill was destined to become an island, and within a few weeks two crawling inlets joined together behind us, and made it one.

The pattern of events, we found, had been much the same here as in other parts—except that there had been no influx: the movement had been away. First there was the cautious retreat as the water began to rise, later the panicky rush to stake a claim on the higher ground while there was still the chance. Those who remain, and still remain, are a mixture of the obstinate, the tardy, and the ever-hopeful who have been saying since the beginning that tomorrow, or, maybe, the next day the water will cease to rise.

A state of feud between those who stayed and those who shifted is well established. The uplanders will allow no newcomers into their strictly-rationed territory: the lowlanders carry guns and set traps to discourage raids on their fields. It is said, though I do not know with how much truth, that conditions here are good compared with Devon and places further east, for, once the inhabitants of the lower ground had been driven out of their homes and set on the move, very many of them decided to keep on going until they should reach the lush country beyond the moors. There are fearsome tales about the defensive warfare against starving gangs that goes on in Devon, Somerset, and Dorset, but here one hears shooting only occasionally, and then on a small scale.

The completeness of our isolation has been one of the difficult things to bear. The radio set, which might have told us something of how the rest of the world, if not our own country, was faring, failed a few days after we arrived, and we have neither the means of testing it, nor of replacing parts.

Our island offers little temptation, so we have not been molested. The people about here grew enough food last summer to keep themselves going, with the help of fish, which are plentiful. Our status is not entirely that of strangers, and we have been careful to make no demands or requests. I imagine we are thought to be existing on fish and what stores we had aboard the *Midge*—and that what can be left of it now is not worth the trouble of a raid on us. It might have been different had the crops been poorer last summer.

I started this account at the beginning of November. It is now the end of January. The water continued to rise slightly, but since about Christmas there seems to have been no increase that we can measure. We are hoping that it has reached its limit. There are still icebergs out in the channel, but they are fewer now.

There are still not infrequent raids by sea-tanks, sometimes single, but more usually in fours or fives, but as a rule they are more of a nuisance than a danger. The people living close to the sea keep a rota of watchers who give the alarm. The sea-tanks apparently don't like climbing, they seldom venture more than a quarter of a mile from the water's edge, and when they find no victims they soon go away again.

By far the worst thing to face has been the cold of the winter. Even making allowance for the difference in our circumstances it has seemed a great deal colder than the last. The inlet below us has been frozen over for many weeks, and in calm weather the sea itself is frozen well out from the shore. But mostly it has not been calm weather; for days on end there have been gales when everything is covered with ice from the spray carried inland. We are lucky in being sheltered from the full force of the southwest, but it is bad enough. Heaven knows what life must be like in the encampments up on the moors when these blizzards blow.

We have decided that when the summer comes we shall try to get away. We shall aim south, in search of somewhere warmer. We could probably last out here another winter, but it would leave us less provisioned and less fit to face the journey that we shall have to make sometime. It is possible, we think, that in what is left of Plymouth or Devonport we may still be able to find some fuel for the engine, but, in any case, we shall rig a mast, and if we are warned-off, or if there is no fuel to be found, then we shall try to make it under sail.

Where to? We don't know yet. Somewhere warmer. Perhaps we shall find only bullets where we try to land, but even that will be better than slow starvation in bitter cold.

And Phyllis agrees. "We'll be taking 'a long shot, Watson; a very long shot!' " she says. "But, after all, what is the good of having been given so much luck if you don't go on using it?"

4th May.

We shall *not* be going south.

This ms. will *not* be left here in a tin box on the chance of some-one finding it some day. It will go with us.

And here is why: Two days ago we sighted the first aircraft that we have seen since we came here—or for some time before that. A helicopter that came trundling along the coast, and then turned in-land to pass along our own inlet.

We were down by the water, working to get the *Midge* ready for her trip. There was a distant buzzing, then this craft came bumbling along right towards us. We looked up at it, shading our eyes. It was against the sun, but I could make out the R.A.F. circle on its side, and I thought I could see someone waving from the cabin. I waved my hand. Phyllis waved her paintbrush.

We watched it plough along to our left, and then turn north. It disappeared behind our hill. We looked at one another as the sound of the engine dwindled. We did not speak. I don't know how it took Phyllis, but it made me feel a bit queer. I had never thought to find myself in a situation where the throb of an airplane engine would be a kind of nostalgic music in my ears.

Then I realized that the sound was not getting any further away. The craft reappeared, round the other side of the hill. Apparently it had been giving our island a looking over. We watched it steady up and then begin to lower towards the curve of the hill that sheltered us. I dropped my screw driver, and Phyllis her paintbrush, and we started to run up the hill towards it.

It came down lower, but obviously it was not going to take the risk of landing among the stones and the heather. While it hung there, a door in the side opened. A bundle dropped out, and bounced on the heather, then came a rope ladder, unrolling as it fell. A figure began to climb down the ladder, negotiating it carefully. The helicopter was drifting slowly across the top of the hill, and presently the man dangling on the ladder was hidden from our sight as we panted upwards. We were still some little way from the top when the machine rose and sheered off over our heads, with the ladder being pulled up by someone inside.

We kept on struggling up the slope. Presently we reached a point from which we were able to see a darkly clad figure sitting in the heather apparently exploring itself for breakages.

"It's—" Phyllis began. "It *is*! It's *Bocker!*" she cried, and sped recklessly over the rough ground.

By the time I got there she was on her knees beside him, with both her arms twined round his neck, and crying hard. He was patting her shoulder avuncularly. He held out his other hand to me as I came up. I took it in both of mine, and felt not far from weeping, myself. He was Bocker, all right, and looking scarcely changed from the last time I had seen him. There didn't seem to be much to say for the moment except: "Are you all right? Have you hurt yourself?"

"Only a bit shaken up. Nothing broken. But there seems to be more skill in it than I'd thought," he said.

Phyllis raised her head to tell him: "You never ought to have tried it, A.B.! You might have killed yourself." Then put it back, and went on crying comfortably.

Bocker looked at the tousel of hair on his shoulder for some thoughtful seconds, and then up at me, inquiringly.

I shook my head. "Others have had to face a lot worse—but it has been lonely; and very depressing," I told him.

He nodded, and patted Phyllis's shoulder again. Presently she began to get more control of herself. Bocker waited a little longer, then he remarked: "If you, sir, would care to remove your wife just for a moment, I'd like to find out if I am still able to stand."

He could. "Nothing but a bump and a bruise or two," he announced.

"A lot luckier than you deserve," Phyllis told him severely. "It was a perfectly ridiculous thing to do at your age, A.B."

"Just what I was thinking when I was about halfway down," he agreed.

Phyllis's lips were still trembling as she looked at him. "Oh, A.B.," she said. "It's wonderful to see you again. I still can't believe it."

He put one arm round her shoulders, and linked his other into mine. "I'm hungry," he announced, practically. "Somewhere round here there's a parcel of food that we dropped."

We went down to the cottage, Phyllis chattering like mad all the way except for the pauses in which she stopped to look at Bocker and convince herself that he was really there. When we arrived, she disappeared into the kitchen. Bocker sat down, cautiously.

"There should be drinks now—but they were finished some time ago," I told him sadly.

He pulled out a large flask. He regarded a severe dent in it for a moment. "H'm," he said. "Well, let's hope it's more comfortable going up than coming down." He poured whisky into three glasses, and summoned Phyllis. "Here's to recovery," he said. We drank.

"And now," I said, "since nothing in our experience has been more unlikely than you descending from the skies on a trapeze, we'd like an explanation."

"That wasn't in the plan," he admitted. "When I found out from the London people that you had set out for Cornwall, I guessed that this was where you would be, if you had made it. So, when I was able to, I came to take a look. But the pilot didn't like your bit of terrain at all, and wouldn't risk landing his machine. So I said I'd go down, and they could buzz off to somewhere where they could land, and come back to pick me up in three hours' time."

"Oh," I said, rather flatly. Phyllis just stared at him.

"It's all very well your looking like that, but I'd have been with you before this if you'd stayed where you were. Why didn't you?"

"It got us down, A.B. We thought you'd died when the Harrogate place was overrun. The Whittiers never came back. The link went dead. The helicopter stopped coming. There wasn't a British station to be heard on the air. After a bit it looked as if things really had come to a finish. So we came away. Even rats prefer to die in the open."

Phyllis got up and started to lay the table. "I don't think you would just have quietly stayed there waiting for an inevitable end, either, A.B.," she said.

Bocker shook his head. " 'Oh ye of little faith!' This isn't Noah's world, you know. The twentieth century isn't a thing to be pushed over quite as easily as all that. The patient is still in a grave condition, he's been very, very sick indeed, and he has lost a tragic lot of blood —but he's going to recover. Oh, yes, he's going to recover all right, you'll see."

I looked out of the window at the water spread over former fields, at the new arms of the sea running back into the land, at the houses that had been homes, and now were washed through by every tide. "How?" I asked.

"It isn't going to be easy, but it's going to be done. We lost a great deal of our best land, but the water hasn't risen any more in the last six months, and we reckon that we ought to be able to grow more than enough to feed five million people, once we get organized."

"Five million?" I repeated.

"That's the rough estimate of the present population—not much more than a guess really, of course."

"But it was something like forty-six millions!" I exclaimed.

That was a side that Phyllis and I had avoided talking about, or thinking about more than we could help. In our more depressed moments I had had, I fancy, a vague idea that in the course of time there would be a few survivors living in barbarism, but I had never considered it in figures.

"How did it happen? We knew there was fighting, of course, but this—!"

"Some were killed in the fighting, and of course there were places where a lot were cut off and drowned, but that doesn't really account for more than a small percentage. No, it has been pneumonia mostly that has done the damage. Undernourishment and exposure through three bitter winters; with every dose of flu, every cold, leading to pneumonia. No medical services, no drugs, no communications; nothing to be done about it." He shrugged.

"But, A.B.," Phyllis reminded him, "we just drank to 'Recovery.' Recovery?—With nine out of ten gone?"

He looked steadily at her, and nodded. "Certainly," he said, with confidence. "Five million can still be a nation. Why, damn it, there were no more of us than that in the time of the first Elizabeth. We made ourselves count then, and, by God, we can do it again. But it'll mean working—that's why I'm here. There's a job for you two."

"Job?" said Phyllis, blankly.

"Yes, and it won't be putting across soaps and cheeses this time, it'll be selling morale. So the sooner you both start to brush up your own morale, the better."

"Just wait a minute. I can see this is going to need some explanation," said Phyllis.

She fetched the meal, and we drew our chairs up to the table. "All right, A.B.," she said. "I know you never allow mere eating to interfere with talking. Let's have it."

"Very well," said Bocker. "Now, imagine a country which is nothing but small groups and independent communities scattered all over the place. All communications gone, nearly all of them barricaded off for defense, scarcely anyone with any idea of what may be going on even a mile or two outside his area. Well now, what have you got to do to get a condition like that into working order again? First, I think, you've got to find a way into these tight, isolated pockets so that you can break them up. To do that you have first to establish some kind of central authority, and then to let the people know that there *is* a central authority—and give them confidence in it. You want to start parties and groups who will be the local representatives of the central authority. And how do you reach them? Why, you just start talking to them and telling them—by radio.

"You find a factory, and start it working on turning out small radio receivers and batteries that you can drop from the air. When you can, you begin to follow that up with receiver-transmitter sets to give you two-way communication with the larger groups first, and then the smaller ones. You break down the isolation, and the sense of it. One group begins to hear what other groups are doing. Self-confidence begins to revive. There's a feeling of a hand at the helm again to give them hope. They begin to feel there's something to work *for*. Then one lot begins to co-operate with, and trade with, the lot next door. And then you have started something indeed. It's a job our ancestors had to do with generations of men on horseback—by radio we ought to be able to make a thundering good start on it in a couple of years. But there will have to be staff—there'll have to be people who know how to put across what might be put across. So, what do you say?"

Phyllis went on staring at her plate for some moments, then she looked, shiny-eyed, at Bocker, and put her hand on his. "A.B.," she said shakily, "have you ever thought that you were nearly dead, and then had a sudden shot of adrenalin?" She leaned across the corner of the table, and kissed him on the cheek.

"Adrenalin," I said, "doesn't take me quite the same way, but I support Phyllis. I very heartily subscribe."

"It makes me feel more drunk than alcohol ever did," said Phyllis.

"Fine," said Bocker. "Then you'd better get busy with the packing up. We'll send a bigger helicopter to take you and your baggage off in three days' time. —And don't leave any food behind; it's going to be a long time yet before we can afford to waste any of that."

He went on explaining and giving instructions, but I doubt whether either of us heard much of them. Then, somehow, he was telling us how he and a few others had escaped after the attack on Harrogate, but there was little room in our minds for that, either, just then. For myself, at any rate, quite an hour must have passed before

I came out of the daze which the sudden change of prospects inspired. Then, however, I did get round to realizing that we were being a bit parochial. The operation of unfreezing the masses of locked water might have been carried to a point where it menaced us no further, but that did not mean that it would not be followed by some new, and perhaps equally devastating, form of attack. As far as we knew, the true source of all our troubles was still lurking safely out of reach in its Deeps. I put the point to Bocker.

He smiled. "I don't think I've ever been called an unbridled optimist—"

"I shouldn't think so," agreed Phyllis.

"So," Bocker went on, "I am hoping it will carry some weight when I say that to me the outlook is distinctly hopeful. There have been plenty of disappointments, of course, and there may be more, but it does look as if, for the present at any rate, we have got hold of something which is too much for our xenobathetic friends."

"What, without these cautious qualifications, would it be?" I asked.

"Ultrasonics," he proclaimed.

I stared at him. "But they've *tried* ultrasonics, half a dozen times at least. I can distinctly remember—"

"Mike, darling, just shut up; there's a love," said my devoted wife. She turned to Bocker. "How have they done, A.B.?" she asked him.

"Well, it's well enough known that certain ultrasonic waves in water will kill fish and other creatures, so there were a lot of people who said all along that it would very likely be the right answer to the Bathies—but obviously not with the wave-initiator working on the surface, at a range of five miles or so. The problem was to get the ultrasonic emitter down there, close enough for it to do damage. You couldn't just let it down, because its cable would be electrified or cut—and, judging by precedent, that would happen long before it got anywhere like deep enough to be useful.

"But now the Japs seem to have found the answer. A very ingenious people, the Japs; and, in their more sociable moments, a credit to science. So far, we have only had a general description by radio of their device, but it seems to be a type of self-propelled sphere which cruises slowly along, emitting ultrasonic waves of great intensity. But the really clever thing about it is this: it not only produces lethal waves, but it makes use of them itself, on the principle of an echo sounder, and steers by them. That is to say, you can fix it to sheer off from any obstacle when it receives an echo from it at a given distance.

"You see the idea? Set a flock of these things for a clearance of, say, two hundred feet, and start 'em going at the end of a narrow Deep. Then they'll cruise along, keeping two hundred feet from the bottom, two hundred feet from the sides of the Deep, two hundred feet from any obstructions, two hundred feet clear of one another, and turning out a lethal ultrasonic wave as they go. That's just the simple principle of the things—the Japs' real triumph has been not only in being able to build them, but to have built them tough enough to stand the pressure."

"None of it sounds in the least simple to me," Phyllis told him. "The important point is, the things really do work?"

"Well, the Japs claim they do, and there'd not be much object in lying about it. They say they've cleared a couple of small Deeps already. Large masses of organic jelly came up, but they've not been able to make much of that because the pressure change had broken it up and it decomposed quickly in sunlight, but afterwards they tested with cables right down to the bottom, and nothing happened. They're working on other small Deeps now until they've got enough gear to tackle bigger ones. They've flown plans of the things over to the States, and the Americans—who've not been hit nearly as badly as we have in this small island—are going to put them into production, so that's a testimonial.

"It's bound to take some time before they can get busy on a really large scale. However, that isn't our affair for the moment—we haven't any important Deeps near us, and, anyway, it is going to be some time before we can produce anything more than immediate necessities. We were very badly overcrowded on this island, and we've paid for it heavily. We shall have to take steps to see that that doesn't happen again."

Phyllis frowned. "A.B.," she said. "I've had to tell you before about your habit of going just one step further than people are willing to follow you," she told him, severely.

Bocker grinned. "Perhaps it's lucky this one is not going to come up in my time," he admitted.

The three of us sat in Phyllis's arbor, looking out at the view that had changed so greatly in so short a time. For a while, none of us spoke. I stole a sidelong glance at Phyllis; she was looking as though she had just had a beauty treatment.

"I'm coming to life again, Mike," she said. "There's something to live for."

I felt like that, too, but as I looked out over the blue sea still set with a few glistening bergs, I added: "All the same, it isn't going to be any picnic. There's this ghastly climate; and when I think of the winters . . !"

"Oh," A.B. said, "research is being done on that now, and the reports indicate that the water will warm up gradually. As a matter of fact," he said, chuckling, "now the ice has gone we may have an even better climate than before, in three or four years' time."

We went on sitting there, and finally Phyllis spoke again. "I was just thinking—Nothing is really new, is it? Once upon a time there was a great plain, covered with forests and full of wild animals. I expect some of our ancestors used to live there, and hunt there, and make love there. Then, one day, the water came up and drowned it all—and there was the North Sea.

"I think we have been here before. And we got through that time."

We were silent for a while. Then Bocker looked at his watch, and said: "That machine will be coming back soon. I'd better make ready for my death-defying act."

"I wish you wouldn't, A.B.," Phyllis told him. "Can't you just let them take a message, and stay here with us until the big helicopter comes?"

He shook his head. "Can't spare the time, I'm really playing truant as it is—only I thought I'd like to be the one to give you two the news. Don't you worry, my dear. The old man's not too doddery to climb a rope ladder yet."

He was as good as his word. When the machine descended over

the crest of the hill, he caught the trailing ladder adroitly, clung to it a moment, and then began to climb. Presently arms reached down to help him aboard. He turned in the doorway to wave to us. The machine speeded up, and started to climb. Quite soon it was only a speck that vanished in the distance.